the indoor boy

the indoor boy

antony sher

viking

VIKING
Published by the Penguin Group
Viking Penguin, a division of Penguin Books USA Inc.,
375 Hudson Street, New York, New York 10014, U.S.A.
Penguin Books Ltd, 27 Wrights Lane,
London W8 5TZ, England
Penguin Books Australia Ltd, Ringwood,
Victoria, Australia
Penguin Books Canada Ltd, 10 Alcorn Avenue, Suite 300,
Toronto, Ontario, Canada M4V 3B2
Penguin Books (N.Z.) Ltd, 182–190 Wairau Road,
Auckland 10, New Zealand

Penguin Books Ltd, Registered Offices:
Harmondsworth, Middlesex, England

First American Edition
Published in 1992 by Viking Penguin,
a division of Penguin Books USA Inc.

1   3   5   7   9   10   8   6   4   2

PUBLISHER'S NOTE
This is a work of fiction. Names, characters, places, and incidents
either are the product of the author's imagination or are used
fictitiously, and any resemblance to actual persons, living or
dead, events, or locales is entirely coincidental.

LIBRARY OF CONGRESS CATALOGING IN PUBLICATION DATA
Sher, Antony, 1949–
The indoor boy / Antony Sher.
p.   cm.
ISBN 0-670-84456-X
I. Title.
PR6069.H4556I54   1992
823'.914 — dc20   91–39949

Printed in the United States of America

For Richard Wilson

PART I

JEWS-ASYLUM

ONE

L isten, I've only got a sec. Only a sec left. I know it for absolute sure as I wake today, panting. Which dream was it this time? Maybe the one about the fat man who stops running. Wow, things are getting a bit desperate, when you've already seen all your dreams. It must mean that time is running out and like fast. The thought is scary, but at least clear. My other waking thoughts are still a mess. Soft crippled things, they shuffle round the brainbox, slowly forming a queue, each wanting some attention, some explanation.

I squint at the nearest digital: 7.02. So this is early morning. Lying back, I listen to the London traffic – a distant wash, it could almost be the beachfront back home.

Ja . . .

I knew there had to be something else, something more than an old dream, to wake me so early. The *Decision* – I've made the *Decision*. Must've been sometime in the small hours, roaming the dark house, trailing some vodka juice. Now how to tell Angela?

I paddle across the bed – it's quite a way – and mould myself to her back, fitting my head onto her shoulder, and nuzzling through her great frizz of chestnut-and-silver hair. 'What's it like to be loved?' I ask. No reply. I up the stakes: 'What's it like to be adored?' Nothing. I try one last time: 'What's it like to be worshipped?' This has some effect. 'Bubs, no . . .' she mutters, and klups my hand out of her crotch.

3

I suppose she thinks I'm trying to soft-talk my way into a quick sesh, but actually just some comfort would do. Christ, today's hangover! – this one could show up on the Richter Scale.

7.20 exactly, and Angela heaves herself to the side of the bed, and she's up, up and away.

(Hell, remember those Superman comics?)

By the time I stumble down to the kitchen, she's fully dressed, slurping a quick decaff, and eyeballing the *Guardian*. Today it's kvetshing on about a mass freedom demonstration somewhere. China, Europe or home, who wants to know? OK, so there's still a state of emergency at home; so it's the fiftieth anniversary of World War II starting; so scientists haven't yet found an antidote for poisonous penises. That's the scene at this sec. But, *moenie* worry, it'll all change.

Meanwhile my good wife whispers to herself, 'What incredible times we're living through,' then adds a dramatic 'Crikey!'

When Angela was a kid, she wanted to be an actress, but never really stood much chance. Her beauty is too offbeat. Some might call her overweight, though she prefers the word 'Rubensesque', and she'll say it with a self-mocking giggle which I really dig. So she settled for teaching instead. Drama and English. These days at Hadsworth House, one of those swanky, arty schools for rich brats. Which is ironic, when you think of her own background.

When we met, I remember being helluva shocked to discover that her folks were labourers, as simple and poor as our natives back home. I couldn't believe it. I mean, Angela's voice is more pukka than the Queen's. It's only occasionally, when pissed, tearful or randy, that this other voice slips out. She calls it 'a bit of Dudley' slipping out. She means her hometown – Dudley in the grimy old Midlands – but I think of 'Dudley' as a person. And I get really fired up by his brief appearances: this rough, male-ish thing trapped inside my utterly soft, mothery mound of a woman.

With the front of my dressing-gown now rising and parting, I move round the kitchen table and go in for a hug. Angela yawns and stretches, then rests her chin on my head. (Oh *ja*, she's also quite tall.)

'Who's an early worm!' she purrs, giving my lust a tickle, before hurrying into the hallway.

I follow. 'By the way,' I say, 'I've decided.'

That stops her dead.

She looks at me steadily, half-excited, half-suspicious, the contact lenses glazing over. Then she says, 'Well, if you've decided, you've decided,' clicks her briefcase shut and is gone.

I expected more of a fight. 'If you've decided, you've decided' – that sounds like she's given in. She's coming along!

Now that feeling again – the empty house, me in the hallway, a funny draught under the door. Funny because it's another baking morning out there. This weather's incredible. Mind you, English summers, good or bad, only make me nervous. You never know when the damn thing might suddenly end.

I catch a glimpse of myself in the hall mirror and whisper 'Eek!' Overnight, my flesh has turned bright red, as red as my hair, and it's nothing to do with a suntan. Such a morning must come to all the friends of Smirnoff.

Scooping up the mail, I flee back to the kitchen.

Angela's laid out breakfast for me. She's a fab cook, yet all she's offering here is one Ryvita and a thin slice of pawpaw. We're both on a slimming kick, but today I ain't in the mood. Hangovers always affect me in two ways: I get hungry and I get horny. In a while I'll sprawl out with the baby oil and a porn video, but for now I drag a chair over to the fridge. Opening the door, there's a whiff of guava. That's the second time today I could've been back home. I chew on last Sunday's shoulder of lamb, two cold roast potatoes, and a bar of fruit-and-nut. I leave the guava, so I can open the fridge again later.

Lots of letters for old Angela, mostly bills. I add them to her pile on the mantelpiece – she'll have to do one of her blitzes soon. No letters for me of course, but some nice junk mail. Like this new food delivery service, where you can order a whole range of international dishes, Greek, Indian, Chinese, all from this one set-up in Camden Town. No South African graze, of course. With all of us living in the UK now, somebody could make a fortune. Somebody, but not me. Tried it a few years ago. Poured money into this butcher shop that was planning to specialise in *boerewors*, *biltong*, and so on. Complete flop. Someone mounted a campaign – 'Nazi nosh', that kind of kak.

5

Anyway, the future holds *boerewors* and *biltong* aplenty. The Decision is made!

A swim in our pool, a dip in our jacuzzi, a wire-pull to a porn video, two lime-flavoured Vit Cs, a massive Bloody Mary, and my hangover is successfully tamed. I give our mini-cab people a bell, and a car zips round pronto. The driver's wearing shorts and isn't entirely repulsive, so I sit in the front and varder his crotch.

And so the journey from Hampstead to the West End passes in a sec.

Getting out of the cab at the other end, someone touches my side. A pickpocket? Swing round – nobody there. Must've just been a new roll of fat unpopping. Keeps happening. Bits are starting to touch other bits. I'm folding, I'm slipping; I'll end up on ground level, just a thick puddle.

Air South Africa turns out to be a weird place. To get in, you have to bash your nose on the door. It's their security system. Suspecting nothing, you head in through the glass door, only to stagger back with your nose on fire. Then there's a little click and the doors open.

Wiping away a tear from the blow, I look round. The walls are hung with pictures of all the different South African animals (safer, I suppose, than pictures of all the different South African peoples), and then one aerial shot of Table Bay. Bloody beautiful, except it's a bit bleached, like an old postcard.

The office is busy; there's only one free place along the counter. I sit. The guy doesn't look up. Maybe he's busy with his computer or something. I wait. But so does he. We're both equally still.

'Hi ... howzit?' I say after about a minute of this strange silence. 'Listen, can I please book two first-class returns to Cape Town?'

Now he looks up and almost smiles, as though pleased to hear my accent. He's young, quite cute. A real little Boer farmboy, with all the works – the blond hair Brylcreemed to a standstill, the broken nose from some sweaty-balled rugby triumph.

'*Verskoon tog, meneer?*' he says.

(Afrikaans! Who remembers Afrikaans?)

'... *Waarheen wil u gaan?*'

I clear my throat. 'To Cape Town please.'

'*Na Kaapstad, meneer?*'

'Yes. How regular are the flights?'

'*Meneer, ekskuus?*'

As if speaking Afrikaans isn't bad enough, he also keeps one forefinger crooked in front of his mouth. Like he has bad teeth – except he hasn't. They're very white, very delicious. Showing against vivid blushes on his cheeks; so permanent they could be birthmarks. Now he's started sweating too. Maybe this is his first day here, he doesn't seem to have a clue. I have to give him our dates two, three times, and then he can't get them into the computer. And meanwhile – *ai!* – he's been taught to engage the customer in polite chat.

'*Gaan meneer* . . . on holiday, sir?'

'Sort of. It's my parents' wedding anniversary. Their golden wedding.'

'*'Skuus?*'

'My parents uhh . . . *moeder en vader, ja? Dis hulle se . . .*' I stop. He's giving me a shy half-smile, like a kid who's playing a practical joke, yet can't keep a straight face. (He must be fluent in English. This is the London office of ASA – he must be!)

'Anyway,' I mumble, 'it's their fiftieth anniversary.'

'So, a visit . . . *huis toe, meneer?*' he says.

'Yes, a visit home, yes.'

'That is very, very nice, meneer. And when did meneer last go home to the Republic?'

'I haven't actually been recen – I don't live there anymore.'

Now I've also started blushing and sweating. I mean, what must I tell him? Just because I was born in the old RSA, it doesn't mean I'm going to die there. It's your country, you Afrikaners are always saying – so OK, you sort it out, you die for it.

'Look,' I say, 'how are we doing? Are there any seats on that flight?'

'*Ag, meneer, verskoon tog meneer – as u net 'n rukkie kan wag . . .*' and he practically disappears into the computer screen, tapping away at all the buttons he hasn't yet tried.

I frown. Is he pulling my leg? Or is it actually possible that Air South Africa has appointed this schmo, this farmboy, this walking van-der-Merwe joke, to work in their *London* office?

Eventually, don't ask me how, but he makes the booking. Or at least he says he does. Or I think that's what he says.

Paying for the tickets is the next prob. He can't even work the credit-card machine! It takes a full five minutes before he hands back my card, along with a rather scrunched receipt. Desperate to get out of here, I forget about the security doors and *SPLAT!* Dazed, I stumble onto the pavement – only to realise that I forgot to tell the cab to wait. That means hailing a black cab, which isn't easy. Most prefer travelling around London with their FOR HIRE signs off, on mysterious missions that never involve passengers.

By the time I get home to Wynn Chase, I'm exhausted I wanna tell you, but now really *exhaaaausted*! I make a dive for my latest drink: vodka and Aqua Libra. Calms the nerves and restores the alkaline balance all in one. Must think about marketing it. *Vod-qua*.

I'm a bit slammed by the time Angela comes home, her arms full. Along with her briefcase, there's her petition for some East End teachers who've had to resign, and a genuine Tiffany lamp which she spotted somewhere recently, but resisted buying – until today. I take all the gear out of her arms, and wrap myself in there. 'Hi, La.'

'Hello, Bubs,' she says, yawning.

'My sludsiwudsi.'

'Noopi-pomsills.'

'Wanna fuck?' I ask while the going's good.

'Hn-hh, too tired.'

'That's fine. Just lie back and –'

'No, don't make me,' she says, doing a slow thrash-round à la Fay Wray. 'Don't, don't!' she cries, running her fingers over my flab, 'oh, don't lay this monstrous burden on me!' She suddenly stops. 'Leon! Your tits are bigger than mine.'

'Impossible!' I ease hers out. On and on they come, more and more. To finally hold one in each hand is to feel good. To gather them together like an incredible pair of balls – this is to blow your mind. Her cleavage is always moist. I put my nose in there, inhaling the sweetness, as I collect her silver crucifix between my teeth. And now we go into one of our routines. 'Wha' will happen to me?' I ask out the side of my mouth. 'Is this a sin?'

'Can't remember,' says Angela, who's starting to enjoy my fiddling fingers.

'If you can't remember, why d'you still wear it?'

'Uhm . . . can't remember either.'

I funnel my tongue and gobble the little Christ.

'Oh lawks a' mercy,' says Angela, her breath starting to quaver, 'well, you must do your worst. After all, whether the gods exist or not, we can be ruddy sure that – *oh!* – they don't bother themselves with us.'

I haven't heard that one before, so I know what she wants me to ask next. I make her wait a mo, meanwhile unzipping her skirt; then – 'That's a groovy concept. Whose is it?'

'Oh now,' she murmurs, as I trace one finger down the soft skin between her hip and tum, 'it was Epicurus . . . I think.'

I groan with satisfaction. Whenever she pretends not to be sure of her facts, it really fires me up. She doesn't want to show me up as the barbarian of the family – she lets me do that myself. It's very kind, and very sexy. Bringing herself down to my level, and gently placing me on top. And yet, take a look at the upbringing we each had, and ask – who's actually the second-class citizen here? Masters and servants hey, teachers and pupils, men and women – is there anything sexier than when you start buggering around with those double-acts?

'By the by,' I whisper now, as she unbuttons my slacks and starts to forage, 'I met someone today who was even dumber than me.'

'Never!' she giggles, and then, dropping her voice an octave and – yes! – letting *Dudley* slip out, adds, 'Oo duck, you're joshin' me.'

'No, no,' I pant, licking the apple blusher from her cheek, 'I kid you not. When I – *aa!* – when I booked our tickets at Air South Africa this morning, I got served by this class idiot who –'

I feel her freeze in my arms. She leans back to look at me. 'When you booked us on *which* airline?'

(Oh shit. I've crashed into another door.)

9

I suppose I should've stopped to think. Angela spends hours reading the labels in supermarkets, in case we buy South African produce. Meanwhile, she's happy to live off my bucks, which are of course South African bucks. I glance at the Tiffany lamp. How much did that cost? Certainly more than a schoolteacher can afford. She's maybe thinking the same thing as she stares at me now, plump brow bunching. Then she picks up the lamp and wanders into the lounge, to find a space among her other antiques.

So that was today. The vodka bottle's low, the Aqua Libra's long gone. I'm sitting up here in my attic den, listening to Love Themes from the Movies. The room is dark except for a tiny ruby-coloured eye on the tape deck, fluttering in time to the music.

Angela's downstairs, hoovering. She always hoovers when she's depressed. Hoovers and dusts and cleans. I mean, we could easily afford a full-time cook, maid, chauffeur and gardener, but no – something in Angela's conscience says no. She prefers to do it all herself, saving it for special occasions like tonight, as a kind'f self-punishment. Don't ask me to explain. You'd need to be Catholic to understand, or working-class, or maybe both.

Meanwhile I've got to schlep back to Air South Africa tomorrow and cancel our tickets, so I can re-book them with British Airways. Just imagine the problems that boy's going to have *cancelling* a pair of tickets!

The thing I keep remembering is his forefinger on his lips, hiding his perfect teeth – bent there like a question mark.

Hey, did I just see the little ruby eye slowly wink at me? Did I? Or does Lara's Theme pause in the middle like that?

TWO

This is unreal – this could be yesterday. I'm facing the boy across the counter, he's talking Afrikaans, I'm talking English and we're getting like nowhere fast. And my nose is stinging again; courtesy of Air South Africa's security system.

Glancing round, I notice that the rest of the staff are staring. I reckon I'm not the first to suffer at the hands of this brain-damaged farmboy. One of the girls slips away and returns with a man in an airline uniform.

When the boy sees him, he goes white. Even his permanent blushes go white. Although they talk in Afrikaans, the boy still can't string two sentences together. The man sighs and interrupts a lot. His grey hair is neat but wavy like airline pilots in Hollywood flicks, and he's got the little moustache too. The sight of a uniformed Afrikaner can empty my bowels on the spot, but this particular specimen is all smiles and charm, with that sing-song formality they use when speaking English, which sounds like when kids recite poetry.

'Mr Lipschitz,' he says, 'is it now correct that you wish hereby to terminate your prior, but as yet unticketed First Class reservations on ASA Flight 154 departing Saturday the 22nd of July?'

'That is indeed correct,' say I, catching his tone.

'Very well, sir,' he says, still courteous, but with a strange sigh. It's as though I'm letting him down somehow. Does he suspect that I'm cancelling for political reasons? I go cold.

11

'Sir will be pleased to know,' he continues, 'that a First Class reservation entitles sir to a fully refundable termination.' He holds out his hand for my booking receipt and gives a synthetic chuckle. 'In fact, we should thank you, sir. Only this morning we had to open a waiting list, inclusive of First, Business and Economy Classes, for the aforementioned flight.'

'No, really?' say I, keeping hold of the receipt.

'*Ja*, sir. Just one of those rather very busy weekends.'

I think fast. Angela's term doesn't finish till the Friday, and Mom and Dad's anniversary is on the Monday. So we *have* to fly out that weekend. If the ASA flights are all full, what about the other airlines? Do I want to risk it?

Meanwhile the man has muttered an order to the boy, who scoots off, half-tripping. Two of the other staff roll their eyes.

The man leans forward now, tapping into the computer. 'Mr Lipschitz,' he whispers, 'I must please apologise if our service here has been less than one hundred percent efficient. As such.'

I'm thrown by this new intimacy. 'Well, I . . .'

'The young man attending to you has only just joined us, and unfortunately has also and in addition been a little unwell since he arrived.'

'That a fact?' Glancing over, I see the boy fumbling in the filing cabinet. He's got a scrum-half's bod. Sweat has drenched his clothes, showing nervous muscles underneath, and just outlining the top of his bum, which is actually a bit fabulous.

The older man is tapping away at the computer.

'Excuse me, what are you doing?' I ask.

'I'm terminating your reservations, sir. Is that not what sir requested?'

We blink at one another for a moment, while I run one finger along the edge of my booking receipt. How valuable is this piece of paper? '*Ai!*' I whimper as it almost slices my skin.

'Sir?'

'No, don't terminate them,' I say, and then hear myself add, 'Who asked you to terminate them? Not me. I came in this afternoon to check they'd actually been booked.' I nod towards the boy. 'He was so incompetent yesterday, I didn't know where the hell I was. I mean, I'm sorry if there's been a mix-up, but . . . well, blame him.'

The man gives another of his strange sighs, this time of relief, as if he'd been hoping I'd name names.

The boy is heading back towards us, the overhead neon catching his wet, red face. He looks brutish now. Like only Afrikaners can look, or hairybacks as we call them, or rock-spiders, or crunchies.

I remember a pressing appointment, and rise. The older man promises to handle the rest of my booking personally, and to personally send the tickets, and to blah, blah, blah.

'*Ja*, OK, that's cool, thanks,' I say, giving a little wave before turning to the door.

SPLAT!

And damn me yes, dazed again, I stumble out of that tiny South African enclave, back into the UK.

The UK at a standstill. There's a full rail and bus strike today. But at least I remembered to hold onto my cab. I pull down both windows. It's a boiling day. Getting here took almost two hours. Getting home looks like it'll be even worse.

Oh Jesus, how'm I going to tell Angela we're flying Air South Africa after all?

We've already had another row over it. This morning's *Guardian* headline was about South Africa, and she wanted me to look. I said, No thank you, but as we used to say in the bioscope queue, swapping comics, 'Seen, seen, seen.' She said, You may have lived in South Africa, but you've *seen* sod-all. I said, Talk to you again when you've seen for yourself. She said, I'm not sure I'm coming along. I said, What? She said, I can't discuss it now, I'm late for work. I said, *WHAT?* She said, Work – remember work? It's what the rest of the world does every day.

What a cunt. I said it, knowing how the word hurts. I told her to go wash her cuntface – it was grubby with the morning's news – her fingertips were spreading that *Guardian* grey everywhere. So then she calls me light-in-the-brain, and digs her grey fingers right into the guava she'd been slicing for my breakfast, that lovely sweet guava smelling of home (actually, the label said Brazil), and out she flounces.

How dare she! How dare she bring up that taboo of taboos –

13

work! She wants to try being me. She thinks it was easy being born rich. She must try it first. It's terrible. You lose your sense of purpose. There's so much plenty, what's the point in making more? A person can suffocate in plenty.

I picture it like that day Dad took me down to the docks because a lot of his cargo ships were in and he wanted me to see them together. Or maybe he wanted to see *us* together – his only child and his fleet. I was just a little *outjie* of seven or eight. While we were there, a gang of his native boys were carting some bales into a warehouse, when this one guy suddenly went berserk, don't ask me why, and started to hack at the bales with a panga. They were full of ostrich feathers. It was a windy day, the south-easter really giving it big stick, so the great wooden hall filled, floor to ceiling, with feathers: looking like clouds, grey, white and black clouds that had blown indoors and got trapped there. In the kerfuffle I was separated from Dad and found myself inside this crazy storm. It should've been wonderful, these soft and precious things destined for the fashion houses of Europe, but the wind was too strong, the feathers fell on you, now like blankets, now like needles. There was red on some. Maybe bits of gunge from the birds, or maybe from the mad native boy who was cutting himself in his frenzy, or maybe from me. And there was a stink, an odd sort'f animal, birdy stink. I tried to run, but the floor was too soft, rolling and falling; like falling through mid-air, falling through more dirty white clouds stinking of blood and birds.

I was still running when someone whisked me away to safety. My little legs were still running through the air as I was carried back to Daddy. And I've never stopped running. Even now, in this slow taxi getting nowhere, even now I'm running. Feel my heart.

So after that day who could blame me for not following Dad into the business? And what else was there? I've tried backing various schemes and products, I've tried setting up restaurants, I've tried thinking about dentistry, I've tried this and that. So OK, so none of it's worked out yet, so what? I've kept busy. Running.

Like those Roadrunner cartoons, with twirling fireworks for legs, the Lipschitzes have spent most of this century running, specialising in the cross-country. Some leaving Russia, some

14

leaving Poland, now some leaving SA, off to the trouble-free climes of Canada, Australia, the UK. And then Angela has the gall to mention that I'm a little light in the brain. Of course I am. It's travel sickness.

(Agh, but how'm I going to tell her we're flying ASA? How'm I, hey?)

'Summer in the city,' goes a passing ghetto-blaster, 'Summer in the city...'

London turns metallic when the weather's this good. The sunlight flares on the tarmac and shop windows, throwing up a haze which you can taste, a rusty city taste, not unpleasant, kind'f sexy in fact, mixing with the smell of meat frying in basement kitchens, and of sun oil and sodden perfume coming from all us bodies jam-packed in these narrow streets, abandoned by London Transport, walking or cycling or inching along in our cars, with time to look around, time to scratch and pull at our sticky clothes.

Those who are wearing clothes. There's a dolly there who's maybe only wearing paper. The sun beams through her little frock, showing the lot. Men gaze at her; I gaze at them. Oh, what I wouldn't do for some dick right now. For an item that's so common, why is it so difficult laying your hands on one?

If that blond cyclist draws alongside my window I swear I'll grab him. Whoever designed these new tight cycling shorts, they should be ashamed. Looks like this boy's loins are covered only in a layer of black oil. Oh my God – he's pulling his T-shirt off. Glimpse the hair under his arms and imagine his other secrets! And now the traffic's stopping and he's sliding alongside. One leg drops to the tarmac, while the other bends up, an inch away from my hand on the window. If I yawned now and stretched my fingers, I could brush the fur of his thigh and he'd think it was just a warm city draught. And people *complain* about these transport strikes?

And now, even as my lust is up, the cab window slowly offers me a telephone box. It's redder than normal in the bright light, demanding you look at it and think about who you might phone. And, just to help, the traffic stops again, very definitely.

'Don't go without me,' I say to the driver, as I leap from the cab and into the phone box. I dial, stab in my coins, then hesitate, grimacing, as I hear:

'Awfully sorry I'm not able to take your call at the moment, but do please leave – '

I slam down the phone. For God's sake, I've never understood why Charlotte can't keep a secretary! She must earn enough. Instead she expects her customers to leave their names on a tape which can then be grabbed by the drugs squad, and next thing we're talking persecution again and probably deportation. They want to get me running again, hey?

The traffic'll move off in a sec. What to do? Agh, risk it! I dial again.

'Hi, Charlotte,' I say to her machine, 'Leon Lipschitz here, hope you remember me. I was just wondering if you can fix me up with some uh ... *ballet tickets*. So please give me a bell. My number, if you don't still have it, is 794 2412. OK, ciao.'

The rest of the journey home is a total nightmare! Crawling up towards Hampstead, inch by bloody inch, as the afternoon slowly passes.

'She's not going to phone,' I tell myself out loud when I'm finally back in the house, mixing a half pint of iced Vodqua. 'She's not going to phone. Or else she's already phoned, or else she's been busted, or God knows what, but she's not going to phone.'

She phones just as Angela gets home.

'Oh hi, Charlotte, howzit?' I say as softly as I can. 'Nice to hear from you again. So listen, can you fix me up with some ballet tickets?'

(Angela's squeezing past with some books. Please God, make her not listen.)

Meanwhile I'm listening open-mouthed as Charlotte describes the quality of tickets currently on the market. '*Front* stalls!' I say. 'Jesus, I'd better take three.' But now she says she hasn't actually got any in, and she'll have to ring back.

So again she's got me sitting here waiting. See what I mean – is this any way to run a business?

At least, thank God, Angela didn't hear. Her reaction I can live without. 'The ballet? *You're* going to the ballet?'

She comes by, carrying another stack of books, and collapses in the chair by the phone.

'The traffic!' she puffs. 'The traffic and the heat! A lady of quality should not be required to venture abroad in such conditions.' She mimes throwing open a fan, and modestly drops her gaze.

I laugh politely, glancing at the phone, checking that her elbow hasn't knocked the receiver.

'Incredible development at school this morning,' she says. 'I was summoned by the Great Beatrice – to discuss the *weather* of all things! It's inspired an outbreak of that forbidden fabric, denim. Anyway, after we'd drawn up a list of culprits, I happened to mention I was going to South Africa for the hols, and next thing, Beatrice starts wondering if it wouldn't be a good subject for our end-of-term show? South Africa. Bring in the History and Geography Departments, make it a cross-curricular initiative. She got more and more excited, said it was the perfect topic for our multi-racial establishment. *Multi-racial*! There isn't a black kid in sight. You try telling Prince Aziz ibn Rashid al Khalifa that he represents our black brothers, and you'll find yourself hauled away by his bodyguards, never to be seen again. However, the Great Beatrice had spoken and I wasn't going to argue. Never mind the kids – it's a chance to educate *myself* before our trip.'

'So – you are coming with?' I slip in quickly.

'On British Airways,' she says, even quicker.

'All done!' I say, like a flash.

'Good. Anyway, I fought through the traffic to Waterstone's. Grabbed everything they had on South Africa.'

'Ah-huh, and . . .' I nod towards the stack of books, then check myself. I was going to ask how much they cost, but now's not the time for a fight. She watches me staring at the books. We go quiet.

(Please God, don't let Charlotte ring now.)

'What are you drinking?' Angela asks.

'A new speciality. Wanna try?'

'But only teensy. Whatever the alcohol is, don't give me more than a threat. I *must* do some work.'

I'm heading for the kitchen when the phone rings. I lunge for it, but Angela's already there.

(Oh grief.)

'A South African,' she whispers, passing it over.

'What?'

'Meneer Lipschitz?' says the voice at the other end. 'This is Gerhardus van der Bijl, Air South Africa.'

That weird boy! I wait. He waits. A funny noise, like he's crying.

'*Meneer, hulle het my afgedank.*'

'What?'

'*Ek is nou afgedank.*'

'Look, I'm sorry, but I've told you – I don't remember much Afrikaans. Is my booking all right?'

'Fire ... fire...'

'Fire? My booking? What?'

'Fire ... *d.*'

'You've been fired?'

'*Dis korrek, meneer,*' he confirms with a sob.

I stare at the phone, before shouting into it, 'Are you blaming me?'

'*Nee meneer, ek vra net om verskoning!*'

'What? What are you saying?'

'Pardon, sir. Your pardon.'

His sobs are so loud now, I have to hold the phone away. Angela's watching, wide-eyed. *Ai gevalt!* And Charlotte – is Charlotte trying to get through? But this poor kid. I mean, it *is* sort of my fault.

'Listen, I'm busy,' I say to him. 'What's your number? I'll bell you later.'

The number he gives isn't Air South Africa's. I know theirs by heart because I spent an hour dialling it earlier this afternoon before driving over; they operate one of those switchboards where they only pick up the phone after your first nervous breakdown. Like railway stations and West End theatres.

So if this number isn't the Airways, it means he took mine home. A weird, weird guy.

'Don't even ask,' I say to Angela as I bolt for the kitchen. 'It's because we're cancelling the tickets. All sorts of complications.'

The phone goes again. I grab the kitchen extension, just as Angela lifts the one in the hall.

(OK God, give me a break now.)

'Leon?' I hear Charlotte say.

(Please God, *please*.)

And lo and behold, Angela puts down her extension, and I hear her hauling her new books upstairs, into her beloved study, her Room Of My Own.

'Leon,' says Charlotte, 'you're going to the ballet!'

THREE

An hour or two later I've fought my way through the traffic jams again, and I'm steering the Jag into one of the streets of Islington. A long row of house fronts. In England they're not that keen on a whole house, just the front. These are 'Georgian' they tell me; named after a king who must've fancied straight lines. The roofs, windows, railings, all in straight lines, even on the houses which are abandoned and decaying: all very neat, very English.

Charlotte takes a long time answering her door. I glance round nervously. Could the drugs squad have a camera planted in that parked van, or in a house across the road?

Now there's lots of unbolting from behind Charlotte's door and finally she appears, shading her eyes against the setting sun. Charlotte's a night bird really, thin and nervy in vest and tracksuit bottoms.

Upstairs, her lounge is exactly as I remember it, with the blinds constantly drawn, which makes the room very yellow. The air is thick and there's a faint smell of gas. My foot slips and I find a sleeping bag squiggled along the floor like a giant old johnnie.

'Do excuse the mess,' she says, 'it was my birthday on Mon – no, Sunday. Well, both actually. I'm afraid it went on rather.'

'Hey, it's mine in a few weeks. How old were you?'

'Twenty-three. No. Yes. Twenty-three.'

'Hell – you don't look it.'

She doesn't – she looks forty. Partly because she's so thin and partly because she's so posh. She's got that upper-class knack of talking without moving her lips. As if she's been dubbed.

'It's been a long time,' she says, suddenly realising I'm not one of her regulars.

I laugh. '*Ja*, I've been behaving myself. It must be almost two years.'

'So you're having one for each.'

'Sorry?'

'Two tickets.'

'Three.'

'Three,' she tells herself, going out.

I swallow hard to pop my ears. I feel sick with the thrill of it all. What am I doing here? In someone else's house. Someone else's country. Where am I?

'You did say four?' asks Charlotte, returning with a handful of tiny improvised envelopes.

'Three.' I undo one envelope. She opens a drawer and lifts out a large hand-mirror with blade and McDonald's straw.

'This stuff looks good,' I say, trying to sound knowledgeable, as I chop us a couple of biggies.

'Oh, astonishingly good,' she says, finding a tissue tucked down the sofa, and clearing her nose. 'Front, *front* stalls. Which isn't easy these days.'

'Indeed not,' I say, wondering what she's referring to. 'I always meant to ask you,' I say, offering her first go, 'why you call them ballet tickets?'

'It's what I most wanted when I was little,' she says, lifting the mirror and aiming the straw, 'most wanted to be a – *oogh!* – a ballerina.'

'Ah.'

'Yaah, but – *oogh!* – too tall.'

'Agh, shame.'

She passes me the mirror. I'm not very good at juggling it all, mirror and straw, so I put it on the floor and bow like a Muslim. As I take the first snort I get that smell. My God, I'd forgotten. It's sharp, a bit like piss, but piss you wouldn't mind dabbing behind the ear – Monroe's or James Dean's.

21

I sit back on my haunches, smiling at her like a dog, going sniff-sniff. My nose is stinging slightly. Maybe still tender from Air South Africa.

But now, oh that tingle, that numbness. So subtle. And oh, the feeling now, as the first gorgeous glob slips down the throat. 'Perhaps I will take all four,' I say, counting out four times seventy quid, then hurrying to her lav.

I'm in there, leaking with excitement, when I hear it – a police siren!

I flatten myself against the door, reaching for the lock. There isn't one. I glance at the window. Just one size too small. If only I'd taken our diet more seriously! What to do, what to do?

Using a low, ducking run, I return to the lounge. 'It's happening,' I say, in a kind'f whispered scream. 'I knew it – oh Jesus, oh God, it's happening!'

'Nothing's happening,' she says tensely, peering round the blind. Down in the street, some kids are fighting with a tall man. It's all so wild, in and out among the parked cars, you can't tell who's attacking who. Now the cops get stuck in too. The kids continue to fight like cats, with a kind of high-speed madness, even as they're arrested. Maybe they're high. I glance at Charlotte, wondering if she's responsible, but she's tutting and sighing.

'Oh, this area,' she says, letting the blind close, and drifting into the middle of the room. 'I'm simply on the wrong side of the borough.' She finds a bottle of rum on the floor. 'Will you have a drink?'

'Can't – I'm driving.'

I'm not staying, no thank you. I've heard all her stories: her father the judge, her mother the piss-cat, her brother, the love of her life, a dashing officer in Ulster. She keeps her eyes on me, hoping I'll change my mind. Her sleepless eyes. Now she brushes a strand of hair off her forehead and tucks it into the tight black bun she wears. The thought of her as a ballerina makes a person want to laugh.

Leaving her house, I find the street calm and empty again – except for the tall man who was in the fray. He's still wandering around dazed. Now I realise he's a tramp – not worth arresting, I guess. I'm a keen tramp-watcher (imagine life with no rules at all!), but now isn't the time. I leap into the Jag and make for the leafy heights of Hampstead and – *oo-la-la!* – the night ahead.

Peering round Angela's study door, I can just see a pool of light on the desk, a decanter of malt whisky, and her hands among skyscrapers of books. She lifts a sheet of foolscap. It carries the light to her face, making her look so damn tranquil. Knowledge is her drug. I go in and hug her.

'Love you,' I say.

She smiles. 'What're you after?'

'Nothing. Just want you to know that you're loved.'

She snuggles into my arms, her big eyes warm with booze. 'Want some dinner? I've made some scrummy fresh pasta in a sauce of –'

'No thanks, not hungry.'

She looks at me in surprise. I quickly stop working my tingling gums, then say, 'Someone's got to remember the diet.' She laughs. 'Tired?' I ask, rocking her.

'Hmm.' She strokes the stack of South African books. 'These are very interesting, y'know. You should –'

'Naa,' I say quickly, 'be wasted on me. Be wasted on your barbarian.' I give another hug, and rock her as hard as I dare. '*Aren't* you tired?'

'I am.' She yawns and stretches. 'I'll just watch the news.'

So now I've got to wait another fucking half-hour while she watches the fucking world going nuts. I pace in the hallway, listening to it coming through the wall – BUZZ, BUZZ goes the newscaster, POW! ZAP! goes the world.

At last it's over and Angela's climbing the stairs with sleepy sighs.

After snorting up some courage, I dig out a porn mag, turn to the classified ads, and dial one of the numbers.

'Yes . . . ?' The voice is tired, but cautious.

'Can you send someone round, please?'

'Have you used our agency before, sir?'

'I have. The name's McTavish. I'd like someone young and slimmish . . .'

'Young and slimmish, mn.'

'Blond if possible, but not essential . . .'

'Preferably blond, mm-hh.'

'No Asians or Orientals . . .'

It's like ordering a pizza, except again you're dealing with people who need a course in business management. Their game is to make you wait while they ring round to see who's available. Why can't they have the info at their fingertips? Anyway, *Got tsu dank!*, tonight they phone back quickly, to say that a very nice, young, slim, white-but-alas-not-blond boy will be with me in half an hour. Called Phil. I remind them he's to come to the garden door.

No turning back now. Right; two rules for the evening. One – keep it safe. Two – save some ballet tickets. I'm already halfway through the first, so I keep one more, put the others in the Jag, and drive it out of reach, parking a few streets away in Bishop's Avenue, and hurry back to the garden.

The evening is warm and dark. The bedroom lights are off, Angela's fast asleep already. I suddenly feel scared. What if he's a *skollie* boy, this Phil: what if he tries robbing me, or worse?

I dash into the house and scribble a note.

'Dear La – if I'm murdered, it's a whore from the escort agency circled in my porn mag (bottom drawer in den). Guy called Phil. May be a false name. Mine too – I'm McTavish for the evening. Don't mind being murdered, but I'd like the culprit to suffer. Sorry about all this. Love you – Bubs.'

And so to the garden door. *Where is he?* Enough with the waiting! Today's been nothing but waiting. People who think decadence is the easy way out must please try it first.

Footsteps. And yes.

With one hand behind my back, fingers crossed, I open the door.

'Mr McTavish?' a voice asks from the shadows, 'I'm Phil.' And he steps forward.

I don't think this one's going to murder me. Looks a bit of a dumbo. Cute though, in a slightly forlorn way. Certainly better than some of the rubbish they've previously sent round.

'This is a brill place you've got here,' he says as we descend the long black lawn to the pool.

'Where're you from?' I ask. 'What's that accent?'

'Sandfields, Port Talbot. Welsh.'

'Ah-huh. Been in London long?'

He gives a small, shy laugh. 'Two months.'

My God, he's new to the game. Couldn't ask for no more.

'Oh hell – this is posh now!' he says in the changing room, gawping at the sauna, jacuzzi and huge gilt mirror.

'*Ja, ja*, pour yourself some champers.'

'Champagne – brill!'

'I'll just take a leak.'

I've got the gear in the lav. Snort, sniff. Melt, you little white crystals, melt, and send me down the glistening slopes – a ballerina on skis!

I get him to strip slowly, pausing for my favourite bits. The first naked foot. I study the toes, measuring his extremities. As he pulls off his T-shirt, I freeze-frame again, contemplating the hair under his arms and down his belly. So I piece him together. The male body's like that. All these clues and trails leading to the centre. And now we're almost there – he's standing just in his boxers, a little embarrassed, but grinning. (Reminds me of the boy at Air South Africa.) The boxers come off, finally revealing bush and shlonger. He gives it a quick shake, to loosen the length.

'Splendid,' I say. 'Now you stay there and I'll sit here. Help yourself to baby oil.'

So, with a room's distance for safety, and me really whizzing now, we proceed.

'Tell me about your first sexual experiences,' I suggest.

It starts well. Fumblings under school desks and on the Port Talbot beach. But then suddenly we're in Phil's poky little house and his dad's unemployed because the steelworks has closed, and his mother's working five shifts a day at the cigar factory, and his –

'Hang on, hang on,' I say. 'If this was my idea of a turn-on, I could be watching the late night discussion on Channel 4.'

'Ey?'

'Never mind. Let's go back again to the first time you saw pubic hair . . .'

Up and down with the fist, in and out of the lav, and – what gives? – he's suddenly wiping himself down and getting dressed.

'You've had like over an hour,' he says firmly. Maybe he's not so inexperienced after all. Reminds me of one of my ex-shrinks. She also had this built-in clock, and no matter how well you were flying, she'd also just call a halt, no arguments, finished and *klaar!* And y'know something else that fascinates me about them – whores, not shrinks – it's the way they have a good time, they cum, yet they still expect to be paid. The chutzpah, hey?

Still, I hand over the fifty quid (plus travel expenses) with nary a twinge, see him to the garden door, good night and good riddance.

Right, hang onto your horses, let's get this night up to speed. I'm naked in the garden, in the pool, in front of the giant gilt mirror, in love at last, and bowing to Allah in the small mirror, meeting his gaze, *no fear*, nose to nose, courtesy of McDonald's. Mirror, mirror, on the wall, on the floor. That shrink, the one with the built-in clock, she was always recommending a good hard stare at yourself naked in the mirror, so I'm only doing what I was told. And my oh my, the second gram's gone already, so off to the car, jawling along the three a.m. pavements of Bishop's Avenue, keeping to the walls and hedges, but fairly bold all the same, not like the daytime Leon who'd worry about being naked in Bishop's Avenue. *Jeeesus* – I'm naked in Bishop's Avenue! '*Kaalgat*', as the Boers say – which loosely translated means nude hole – and who's to stop a nude hole going anywhere? And my oh my, here I am back in the changing room with another whole little envelope to spill across the mirror like spray-can snow. It's gonna be a white, white Chanukah this year with white clouds, white feathers, white storms for white boys to get lost in. Even the air in the garden – that's whitish, or at any rate no longer black.

Funny.

Really quite pink now. Yellow. That's very fast. The sun's a ballerina . . .

A noise near the pool.

Oh . . .

Angela stands in the doorway. Flicks on the light – SQUINK! – the room twinkling with baby oil, the mirrors streaked with it, me slippery as soap. Angela looks a bit cross.

'What time is it?' I ask.

'Seven thirty.'

'Oh dear.'

'What's this?' – she holds out a piece of paper. It's the note I left her, in case I was murdered. 'Well?' – her voice is horribly quiet – 'Speak.'

'Pardon me, madam. Pardon your poor barbarian.'

FOUR

The last summer this good was the summer of '76. The summer I met La and my life changed.

I was in the UK on holiday when South Africa exploded. It's incredible, y'know: you turn your back for five minutes and what happens? – the schoolkids in Soweto go bananas, the cops go bananas, and hey presto, paradise is lost.

It was a boiling Tuesday afternoon, I remember. I was in Trafalgar Square, doing a bit of conventional sight-seeing in between touring some local lavs, when I suddenly found myself surrounded by this demonstration outside South Africa House. People think the English are nice, reserved folk. Well, they want to see these nice reserved folk when they're klomped together in a mob, and it's hot weather, and their English sunburns are raw.

I took one look and, following an old Lipschitz tradition, ran. CRUNCH! – into one of the demonstrators. She was carrying a placard. My skull crashed against the pole, and that was me finished for the next ten minutes. I came to in a pub with her shoving a brandy in my hand.

'I'm Angela Greensill,' she said. 'Now come along, duck, you drink it all down.'

It was only a single, but I was touched by the gesture. And touched by her appearance. Tall, plump, badly cut hair, big specs – yet pretty.

The moment she discovered I was a real, live, *white* South African, she tucked away her placard – BRITISH TEACHER BACKS SOWETO PUPILS – and asked to hear the white point of view. Well, I wasn't sure if this was a trap, so I said I was a dissident living here, and shouldn't we get back to the demonstration? But a few rounds later (on doubles, with me paying), it became clear she was perfectly happy staying in the pub, just having a good old camp-around.

From then on we became friends. We were both foreigners to London; she'd just fled Dudley, and her background (she hoped), and had begun teaching at a direct grant school in Croydon. So now we explored the big city together – mostly via its watering-holes – and shared our terror of it. Like the London *A–Z*: all this was just *one* city?

I picked up the bills along the way. I was thunderstruck by how little she earned – for a white person. And for someone so clever. When we went to the opera or ballet, she could tell me all the stories beforehand, all the ins-and-outs.

Although these shows were often mega-boring, seeing them made me feel sort'f . . . British. Cultured. New feelings. Up until then, I was a moffie purely because I liked dick, rather than Maria Callas.

(Angela was fascinated by this word: *moffie*. 'What language is it?' she asked. Afrikaans. It's actually their word for mitten. 'How bizarre,' she said. 'So what's the word in Zulu, or Xhosa?' As if I'd have a clue! Do they even do it?)

Angela's only other friend in London, a teacher at her school, was also a moffie, and now he started taking us round the clubs and bars. Angela quickly became popular on the scene. 'La', the boys called her, transforming her name to something grand, musical and French – 'La!'

The boys weren't always that friendly. Not when you were hunting them. Although my bod then had a certain stubby oomph ('satyr-like,' La said), there was no way I could compete as a beauty. So I used other hunting weapons. Humour and cash. Others might have Grecian profiles or twelve-inch shlongers to flash. I flashed my cash, and it always drew admirers.

And then, with that night's stranger perched alongside me, I'd drop La off at her bedsit. She'd give both of us a hug, and, in Dudley's deep tones, say, 'Have one on me, lads!' before tottering, well pissed, into the darkness.

At that time, she herself was still a virgin. Incredible, I know. She must've been – what? – in her late twenties. 'Oh, but *doing it* seems so much bother,' she'd say, 'and anyway, look at the great virgins of history – everyone from Mother Mary to Jane Austen. Like them, I'm happy to be sent back unopened.'

And then one night we went to see this *Doctor Faustus* show at the Shakespearian Company. Angela was strangely turned-on afterwards – she was shivering from the excitement of it! Drank more than ever; we got through four bottles of champers at supper later. She kept talking about hell, and 'the attraction of evil', while tracing her finger through the mist on the ice bucket.

As I was preparing to pay the bill, she suddenly said, 'What are you after? What is it? My soul? Is that what you're hoping I'll sell?' – then she lifted my Standard Bank credit card, and rattled it between her teeth.

That night I felt the first prickle of sex between us.

It was scary, but sort of welcome (I'd always thought of my moffieness as a passing phase, albeit a bit prolonged), yet I couldn't figure out what she meant by 'the attraction of evil'. Or what the connection was. Who – us – white South Africans?

The next day, as we settled into a pub with our first lunchtime drink, she said:

'Of course you lot aren't evil. You're just *horrendously human*! Grabbing the whole country for yourselves. But y'know, would I behave differently? Offered all that sunshine and wealth. Probably not. Oh, I dream of setting the world to rights. But most of the time I just inch along from moment to moment, snatching what comfort I can. And it's easy to make excuses – because of my background. Easy to say: it's my turn. I try not to. I read the decent papers, go on the marches, give what pennies I can to good causes, pick up litter in the street. If I lived in the country, I'd probably put up bat-boxes, and stand at hedgerows, booing the hunt. It's all a little disappointing, a little unheroic, but there we are. Oh my flower, shall we have another drink?'

The more we talked, the more Angela convinced me that

the writing was on the wall back in SA, and the writing said
AMANDLA – black power. Since I didn't fancy getting butchered
in my bed, I slipped on my running shoes. I popped back, packed
up, and pissed off. Getting cash out wasn't a prob, since Dad
already had a huge stockpile in Guernsey through his shipping
firm. He called it our nest-egg for a rainy day.

It was, in fact, snowing the morning I finally flew back into
Heathrow for good, and I'd never seen snow before. Man,
England that morning was so bloody beautiful and strange.

Angela was at the airport to meet me. We hugged and hugged.
There was a special link between us now: we'd both left our
families far behind.

Apart from Dad's British accountant, a guy called Pallister,
Angela was my only contact in the UK. The rest of the crowd
were strangers – in the streets, in the pubs, in my bed. But I was
relatively happy, and was just jawling along like that, when word
suddenly came that my life was threatened again. The word came
from America, and it was a new word, a new four-letter word.
AIDS. Not a British word yet, but I smelt danger. Call it instinct.
Call it the Lipschitz sixth sense. Call it our knack for beating the
starter's pistol.

Hell! I'd only just finished my cross-country race, and here I
was, on my marks again, poised and trembling.

But as well as the Lipschitz sixth sense, there's also Lipschitz
luck.

Every summer, me and La held a little celebration – the anniversary of our meeting in Trafalgar Square. In summer '82, we partied
at my place in Hampstead, just the two of us. A fabulous
evening. Late sunlight slouched into the house, pulling the rooms
wonderfully out of shape, and staying there in the corners, long
after it should. Then we lit candles and stayed up, boozing and
talking. It was just before dawn when we made an amazing
discovery – something we hadn't confessed to one another before,
maybe because it was a peculiar confession for a moffie and a
virgin to make. But there was something we both wanted more
than anything in the world. Kids.

Long, *long* ago, I decided the Lipschitzes had survived so much,
I wouldn't let the side down; I wouldn't let my moffie leanings

stop us from making it all the way to eternity and back. I'd been biding my time, but now time was running out – boy oh boy, was it ever!

So, as the sun slouched into the house again, but now from the other side, me and La collapsed into bed, and that bed happened to be the same one.

My God, it was good! She was like a field, an English field in summer, warm, wide and safe, safe, safe – and there on top was a Lipschitz, a kosher male Lipschitz, digging himself in!

When we woke, our hangovers were so gross there was nothing for it but to hit the Bloody Marys. Two hours later, giggling like *domkops*, and with Angela's moffie teacher friend plus an old tramp (who we yanked off the street) as our witnesses, we went to a Register Office and got married.

It was Angela's idea. When all's said and done, she's quite old-fashioned (like the way she *smaaks* booze but not drugs), so she wanted everything 'legitimate'. I didn't protest. In that single stroke, by marrying her, I'd not only saved my skin, but gained two passports: a British passport, and a passport to eternity.

Over the next few days, we stayed at home, in bed, 'rooting' as we now called it. Then we sat back and waited for the results. When none came, we shrugged our shoulders, and started rooting some more.

And we've been doing that for seven years now.

Agh, sure, we've had all the tests – with every super deluxe Harley Street bigshot – and they say there's nothing wrong. With either of us.

I'm not convinced.

Angela's thirty-seven. Pushing it already. She's got maybe a couple of years left. And then I'll have to do some serious thinking.

But whatever I decide, I'll always be grateful to her. During the first few years of our marriage, while she was my only rooting partner, that new four-letter word crossed the Atlantic, and caught on here – with a vengeance.

The three A's are at my heels, hey, but I'm still one step ahead. The three A's – Apartheid, Anti-semitism and AIDS – like something from the Book of Revelation in Angela's half of the

Bible – and *ja*, people say that God's signature is on all three, on Apartheid, Anti-semitism, and AIDS. Well, maybe that's the reason why I keep escaping. Because me, I'm an African, a savage, a barbarian, and God hasn't even been invented yet.

'. . . Say that again,' whispers Angela, still standing at the changing-room door, as I crawl towards her, dripping with baby oil.

'I'm a barbarian,' I mumble, dazed by the light, 'I'm innocent, blameless.'

FIVE

S he can be surprisingly humourless at times, Angela. She walks across the changing room, and punches me. Then she throws what's left of ticket no. 3 into the swimming pool, and then runs amok for a bit, smashing all the blooms on a nearby rose-bush. Talk about 'barbarian' – we both loved that bush. Antique Roses, I think they're called.

It's the drugs that are giving her grief, more than the sex (I am allowed the odd fling) – though she does want to know was I compos mentis enough last night to keep things 'safe'? So at least I'm able to assure her on that score. Jesus, I didn't even shake the boy's *hand*!

'All right – why?' she asks next. 'You haven't had a lapse like this for yonks. What's happened?'

'What's happened is that I wanna go home,' I reply, surprised at how sober my voice sounds. 'We're not booked on British Airways. The British Airways flights are full. Actually all the other airlines are full. Yet you won't fly ASA. And meanwhile all I want is to get home and see my folks. I haven't seen them in thirteen years. You've *never* seen them. My wife has never seen my folks! And now it's their golden wedding! And yet she's worried about flying on ... on ...'

Well, I'm howling by now so she finally holds me in her arms, saying 'Shh, all right Bubsies, shh now, all right, we'll fly with the sodding fascists. Oh, what difference does it make? Who am I to talk anyway . . . ?' – and she starts howling too.

Now I feel even worse. Because I never checked British Airways, or any of the other airlines. I hate lying to Angela. If I could find another way of making her see my point of view, I'd go for it.

She tilts back her head, to stop her make-up running, and pulls some faces, to get the contact lenses back into place. 'Crikey!' she says, peering at her watch as she mops up. 'Must whiz.'

'Don't,' I mumble, 'don't go. Please. Don't leave me on my ace.'

'Well, sorry, chum,' she says, 'but you should've thought of that last night. I can't miss school. Not today. We start rehearsing my South African show today.'

After she leaves, I don't have that great a morning. I spend most of it sneezing and rinsing blood out of handkerchiefs. Giant sneezes, they hurl you across the room – TSCHAAAA! Hangovers are easy compared to coke-overs. You haven't slept and you can't now. Oh, my skin. It's juddering, like when you cut yourself underwater – you're trailing a flap, no pain yet, no red cloud, but any moment . . .

TSCHAAAA! And another handkerchief fills with blood.

The sneeze has thrown me onto the lav seat. From my belly, distant noises like whale song. Reminds me of a huge journey long ago, can't say where or when. From the airing cupboard, the hot-water boiler joins in, doing train impressions. Better than when it does cicadas. That always makes me ache. Now it switches to castanets, then sewing machines. And finally a noise of such bloody rage and pain, I swear there's a living thing in there.

Then silence. Utter silence.

I go from room to room (my walk is like Dad's, heavy and groaning), and switch on a TV, a CD player, a radio, until the place is meshuggeh with Tom and Jerry, Mozart and Gardeners' Question Time.

Get out of here, quick!

But in the streets, the traffic is weird: loud and angry, coming stupidly close to the kerb. And my balance isn't terrific today. And when you cross the road, which way do you look?

I rush back indoors.

Now the shadowy rooms are buzzing with strangers. In one,

all these people are discussing the Holocaust. I flip channels. Pictures of soldiers fighting. Black or Arab, can't tell through the dust. Now they're dead. Why do the corpses of soldiers always have their flies undone? Who is it that dashes over when they're gunned down, for a quick rummage? We're in Namibia, the newscaster tells me. I flip channels. A condom advert. At – what? – ten in the morning? Flip. Some footage on Auschwitz. Hold on, this isn't normal morning viewing. The three A's – *the three A's* – they've come to roost in my telly! I lunge for the remote thingy and the screen sizzles to black.

I *must* talk to someone. Easier said than done. It's either Angela's family in Dudley (and believe me, loneliness is more fun), or ... or who? Friends don't feature much in our lives. I sometimes wonder if it's because Angela's ashamed of me? In the early years, when we had people round, I suppose I did screw-up a bit – serving South African wines, or saying that Apartheid had its good points. Agh, but anyway, friends are hard work. Letters, phone calls. Friends want to collect bits of you.

I dial our number in Sea Point. Good old Lizzie answers the phone. Our Coloured cook.

'*Haai*, Master Leon!' she yells.

'Hi, Lizzie, and howzit by you?'

'No, it's good, Master Leon, and by Master?'

'Fine, fine. Listen, is Mom ...?'

'Agh, Master, the Madam was now up already, but she wasn't feeling so hot...'

'As per usual.'

'*Ja, foeitog*, hey, Master? So she's gone back to bed, and she says to me she's not to be disturbed, not even if I get word they're dropping the bladdy bomb!'

'Never mind. So. And how're you?'

'No, OK thanks, Master.' She goes quiet. Maybe embarrassed by the cost of the call.

'And tell me, how's your weather there?' I ask.

'No, it's also OK thanks, Master.'

'Isn't it a bit windy and wet?'

'Yes, Master.'

'Here it's very hot.'

'Is it so, Master?'

Ja. OK, well, nice to chat. Tell the folks I rang.'

'No, for sure, Master. Is there a . . . ?'

'Nothing urgent. Just my love to them.'

'OK Master, I'll tell them Master, bye-bye Master.'

Stupid sad old Coloured tit.

What's this number scribbled here? Oh Jesus – that schmo from Air South Africa. Mind you, better than nothing.

The phone is answered, but no one speaks.

'Hullo?' I call into the receiver. 'Hu-llo?'

'Yes, hullo. Who is it you want please?' The voice is South African, white, quite cultured.

'Uhh . . . I dunno his name, but is there a guy there who works for – or *worked* for – Air South Africa?'

'Meneer Lipschitz,' the voice exclaims.

'You! But . . .'

Ja, dis ek, meneer – hoe gaan dit, meneer?'

(Why is he suddenly speaking Afrikaans? He was speaking English a moment ago – wasn't he?)

Anyway I bowl him this story about how bad I'm feeling over his dismissal, and would he like to come round for a drink? He accepts instantly.

Now that I know someone is coming, I feel calmer. I flop onto the couch in the conservatory, burrowing into the bleached cushions, and straightaway there's that lovely feeling as the brain starts to melt.

Funny. I thought I'd switched off the TV, yet I can still hear that programme on World War II.

'There'll be bluebirds over the white cliffs of Dover . . .'

But they're not white, the cliffs. They're dust-coloured. I'm walking with a man – Dad? – along the top. We stop to look back over our route and realise that we've been practically walking on thin air. Just a lip of earth with everything eroded away underneath. If the path's like that behind us, what about where we're standing? We look down. The ground seems so solid, so reliable, with grass and litter. What should we do? If we run, we might break the ledge. If we don't, it might break anyway. Then I realise there's no choice. The other man's too fat to run.

37

A coastguard rings an alarm.

I open one eye and stare at the bleached cushion. I can still hear ringing. It's the doorbell.

I don't want to answer it. What do I look like? Is my skin still juddering? I won't answer it.

TSCHAAAAA!

But the sneeze blows me thataways. And as I reach for the latch, I feel that odd, icy draught from under the door, even though it's another baking day out there.

Away from the neon glare of Air South Africa, his face really is stunning. Something to do with how flat it is, almost like a black's. Except it's very pale – and then these permanent blushes on his cheeks. Almost bruises. *Ja*, it's as if he's been in a fight; the broken nose and puffy eyes. Yet it isn't brutal, the damage – it's delicate.

He's turned up with a chick, which is a surprise. She's called Alphonsia, and she's short, voluptuous and black (so our little Boer *boytjie* is doing a little sinning while he's overseas); one of those black Cockneys whose voices don't fit their faces.

'I'm well impressed here, well impressed,' Alphonsia says as they go into the lounge, reminding me of the Welsh whore gawping at everything last night. What's the matter with kids in this country – have they all grown up in slums?

Alphonsia raves on about the room, while the boy – I've forgotten his name – sits quietly on the couch. He's dressed in a short-sleeved khaki shirt (that's got to be from home) and jeans. He's more relaxed than at Air SA, though he still can't meet your gaze, and still keeps one finger crooked over his white, white teeth.

'Drinks?' I say.

'Sure you should?' asks Alphonsia, with a wink. 'Wild night, am I right? You look well gutted.'

I'm about to protest, when she cuddles me. Now she flops next to the boy and pulls him into her tits, where he disappears. Just one eye resurfaces, making him look like a baby in the arms of a maid.

'OK,' he says, that one eye suddenly fixed on me.

'Sorry?' I say.

'A drink, Meneer Lipschitz, please.'

'Don't call me meneer – it's ridiculous. I'm Leon.'

'Le-on,' he repeats, making it sound the clumsiest little word, 'and me – Gerhardus. But you must please call me by Gertjie.'

'Gertjie,' I say.

'Fuck me,' exclaims Alphonsia, 'you can get your gob round it. When I try, it comes out as *Gerty*!'

Gertjie laughs. '*Gerty* – this is the name of a woman, isn't it?'

'I'm afraid so, pal,' I say, then, turn to Alphonsia. 'You've got to make the sound in your throat. Like when a Scotchman says lo*ch*. That *ch* sound. *Ch*-err-kie. Gertjie.'

'Right,' says Alphonsia, '– Gerty.'

They laugh and start cuddling again. Feeling a bit of a spare prick, I wander over to the liquor cabinet and contemplate the forest of bottles.

'Fancy a Hurricane?' asks Alphonsia, bouncing over, 'an Antigua Hurricane? My old man, right? – it's his speciality. I'll make us all some, yeah?'

Two Hurricanes later and Alphonsia is growing on me. Her laugh is infectious, starting high and dropping fast, like a cartoon of someone falling from a great height.

Who would've thought this *farkackteh* day would turn out so well? A few more Hurricanes and we're tumbling down the long lawn to the pool. Gertjie says he doesn't feel like a swim, so I say me neither. I'm not going to have him scrutinising every pink and ginger kilo of me. But Alphonsia, stripped down to bra and undies, flops straight into the water. She goes for the whole Esther Williams bit, flipping and twisting her fleshy black body in the turquoise pool, laughing her crazy laugh – 'Wheeeyoooo!' – while we dodge her splashes and yell like kids. Her great tits gleam through the bra, with great nutty nipples, and when she drags herself out, her undies are like cling-film. Mmm. I could get stuck into a bit of sinning too. Doing it with blacks could be even naughtier than doing it with blokes. And doing it with them both …. Of course they'd never consent. Unless I could get them pissed enough.

'TSCHAAAA!' – the sneeze blows me backwards.

(Hey, there's still the fourth ballet ticket locked in the Jag!)

'Listen,' I say, voice shivering a bit, 'I'll be right back, make yourselves at home, there's drinks in the changing room.'

Walking to the car, I remember making this journey naked last night and feel sick with shame. And excitement. I can't believe it – back to the ballet so soon! A quick pas-de-threesome with the strange little Boer *boytjie* and the fabulous black shiksa – my word, talk about dismantling Apartheid!

Now with the fourth little envelope tucked into my pocket, I let myself back into the garden quiet as poss, then cross the lawn with a leopard-crawl – till I can just peek over the brow. Sure enough they're both on the sun-lounger now, smooching like maniacs, hands deep in one another's laps. And yet, it's funny, he still looks like a kid; a kid being ravished by the maid.

'Hi,' I call, charging over, hoping to catch a close-up of something I shouldn't.

'Wheeeyooo!' she laughs, adjusting her undies, forgetting they're transparent.

He's zipped himself up like a shot. My eyes skim down his front. Her wet body has printed the shirt across his tight pecs and tum, but nothing shows through the thick denim below.

When I produce the little envelope, Alphonsia claps her hands and whispers, '*Charlie!* What a superb idea! Leon, you're a king. A serious fucking king. Gerty, look – it's Charlie!'

Gertjie, of course, doesn't have a clue who or what Charlie is. So now we introduce him. Alphonsia snorts a demonstration line, and I talk him through it. As I lean in to correct his fingers on the straw, I catch my first whiff of him – even through my wrecked nostrils I catch it – a subtle cocktail of sweat and aftershave. It's like a tiny shock. My fingers twitch, nudging his. He splutters, turns away, and coughs – right into the opened envelope. The stuff shoots up Alphonsia's wet chest. Even against her black skin, the powder hardly shows before dissolving. I glance into the envelope. Maybe enough left for two lines each.

'That was like the Woody Allen movie,' laughs Alphonsia, 'y'know the one – where he sneezes into a tinful of Charlie. Ever so comic!'

I glare at her. Gertjie goes still.

'Tons left,' chirps Alphonsia.

'Tons? Maybe for you kids. Daddy here likes bigger portions.'

Gertjie starts crying – instantly, without preparation, like a baby.

''ere, Leon,' says Alphonsia, 'it was an accident, all right? Much regretted, mucho sorry, but let's not make it a hanging offence, yeah? Gerty didn't mean –'

'It's *Gertjie*!' I shout, stopping her dead and making him jump. I've even startled myself, saying his name like that. As though I know him better than her.

'Listen, it doesn't matter,' I say quickly, with a smile. 'Why don't you take what's left home? I didn't really want any more. I had a whole load last night. Take it, I want you to.'

She can't believe her ears. I wait till she reaches for the open envelope, before I take aim . . .

'TSCHAAAA!'

Fumbling for my handkerchief, I say, 'Oh *ja*, I remember that Woody Allen flick now. *Ja*, it was comic, hey?'

The moment the door closes behind them, I sigh with joy. I've been saved from another bout of craziness. All is well, the house feels safe again and I'll finally be able to sleep.

And hell's bells, it turns into one of the longest, loveliest sleeps of my life. Best of all is the sense that sometime in the middle of it, Angela creeps alongside and holds me. I know for sure because when I finally wake at about noon, her scent is on my pillow; her Body Shop mixtures. Angela has come and gone. I follow her spoor round the house: her towel, still damp, in the bathroom; and a square of kitchen roll on the breakfast table with her fingerprints in *Guardian* grey.

Wise, good Angela; Angela who loves me despite everything; Angela who has become my family – lover and sister; Angela who will give me a child and a passport to the future; sweet, warm Angela who helps keep craziness at bay.

I will *never* visit the ballet again. I want to hang on to this

41

morning's feeling for the rest of my life, the feeling of being rested and clean.

I go out into the sunny garden, and I make me a little *braai*, char-grilling a couple of Marks 'n Sparks burgers, while a smoky-voiced *outjie* on Radio 2 plays me some numbers from the fifties: Crosby, Mario Lanza and someone's Big Band Bonanza. Oh, the innocent sleaze and ease of it, of sax and harps and Hollywood choirs! Man, it sends me quick-stepping round the patio and straight down memory lane. There was this one comic-book when I was a kid – Little Lulu, Dagwood? – anyway, they go to the beach for the day, and there was this picture, a whole page high, of a beach full of Yankees clapped out in the sun, with cooldrinks and hot-dogs. That was my life too. One page high of sea and sand and happy holiday people, breaking into dots of colour as I pressed my eight-year-old nose right up close till I couldn't see nothing but light.

I scoff the hamburgers, and I'm just thinking about treating myself to some more, when the doorbell goes.

Alphonsia and Gertjie are standing there grinning. She gives him a nudge. He hesitates, and then, in English (which means she rehearsed him), he asks:

'Well, Leon, are we going to be mates?'

SIX

'So tell me, why are you away from South Africa?'
Gertjie looks fazed. We've spent a week together without me
asking. He thinks for a long time, before answering:
'I . . . how must I say? . . . looking at overseas.'
'You're seeing Europe.'
'*Ja.*'
'So it's just a holiday?' He nods and shrugs at the same time.
'But if you hadn't lost your job at ASA, wouldn't it be a damn
long holiday?'
'Air South Africa? *Nou ja*, it was not so good a plan. *Oom
Hendrik het dit vir my moontlik gemaak*. My ma's brother, Oom
Hendrik, he . . . fixed it up. He's now a top boss by the Airways.'
'Ah-huhn. So – not just a holiday?'
'*'Skuus?*'
'You being here – it isn't just a holiday.'
He goes silent and stares at the Thames.
We're sitting on the wall of a riverside pub in Hammersmith.
There's another transport strike today. We've been to the flicks
nearby, and now we're stranded, waiting for the traffic to die
down. Meanwhile, this has got to be one of the most beautiful
evenings I've ever seen. Half past eight and the light hasn't even
started to go. The river's low (they're talking about a drought if
this weather continues) and as still as a mirror. People stroll along
the shore below us, each footstep clear, like potato crisps being

munched. The dogs don't romp and bark; they trot. And the seagulls overhead – nothing as strenuous as flying; they glide. And the people along this wall, they're quite drunk already, but summer drunk; no noise, just lazy nuzzling.

So why do I feel uneasy?

Gertjie hasn't moved since my question. His eyes are in shadow, one finger fixed on his lips. It looks like he might cry again.

'Are you in some kind'f shit?' I ask. He shakes his head immediately. 'What then? I'm only curious why you're here. It's an innocent ques—'

'Ja, ja, ons sal later daaroor praat.'

I sigh. 'Why d'you do that? You can speak English, I know you can. You understand everything I say – don't you?'

He doesn't look at me, but meets the challenge all the same. 'When I know you, then we talk.'

'But unless we talk, we won't get to know one another.'

He thinks again, then says, 'Why's *you* here?'

'No future for my grandchildren back home,' I say, glancing at him.

(Has it ever occurred to him I could be a moffie?)

'So,' he says slowly, 'nothing political?'

I laugh. '*Me?* Naa, it's very simple. Whatever's going to happen back home, it'll never be as nice as it was. And that's looking on the bright side. So I packed my bags. Joined the white exodus, the Chicken Run. Hey, is it true they call it the Owl Run now? – now that it's a wiser move.'

He says nothing. (Could *he* be political?)

'Anyhow, most people we know have left. But not my folks. Well, my Dad fled Poland just before the war, so he's already done his exodus. *Ja.* But y'know what always makes me laugh? – half the people we know are making their exodus to Israel. *Israel* – for a safer future? Anyway, I was able to afford the UK. We run this shipping line you see, so getting our bread out wasn't as difficult as it is for –' I stop. Maybe it's better not to go into detail. 'Your turn,' I say.

A long pause. 'OK – *dis my pa se skuld. Ons het 'n ... uitval gehad.'*

'A fight with your father, ah-huh. Why?'

He turns to stare at me. I know this is all too soon, too intimate. Yet I get the feeling he wants to talk. If I just keep pushing.

But now Alphons turns up with the drinks.

'We thought you were never coming back,' I say, and then, in case it sounded wishful, laugh loudly.

'Three deep at the fuckin' bar, 'int they?' she grumbles, 'and they didn't have no Aqua Libra for your vodka so I shoved in some tonic, hope that's all right, and here's your change.'

'Keep it for the next round.'

She hesitates, then pockets the money.

I'd've thought the pattern was clear by now. I do the paying and they do the legwork. But I know she's misreading it. Typical of blacks, isn't it? They want equality, yet don't like fetching the drinks.

She takes a big swig of her lager, and then does a disgusting ritual – she kisses Gertjie, passing over her mouthful. Some of it dribbles down his chin. I laugh good-naturedly and reach for my drink. She's forgotten to put ice in it.

'Say, guys,' she says, in the Yankee accent we've started using, 'isn't it a swell fucking evening?'

'Shucks, sure is,' I throw in.

'Honest injun – fine and fokken dandy,' grins Gertjie. He loves this game.

(Funny – when we talk like this, his English suddenly improves a hundred percent.)

Gertjie lives for the movies. Morning, noon and night – if me and Alphons allowed it. Old silent slapstick comedies are his best, followed by all the Disney full-length features. But nothing with explicit violence. Or actually any violence. I saw him looking away the other day when the rat was given a hammering in *Lady and the Tramp*.

Angela's met Gertjie a couple of times and, natch, wanted to know if I fancy him. It was nice to be able to say no and mean it. Absolutely not. No ways! No, no, no. No, as I told her, I'm just taking a fatherly interest in a compatriot stranded in London.

(It was a mistake using the word 'fatherly'. That started another whole discussion about her latest bright idea: why don't we *adopt* a kid? She doesn't seem to understand that it's a Lipschitz I'm planning to propel into the future, not a bloody stranger. I have to bite my teeth in these discussions. I mean, it's another wife I'll *adopt* before some anonymous kid.)

But it's interesting watching Angela also fall under Gertjie's spell. It's his extraordinary looks, plus the puppy dog thing. He's helpless one moment, happy the next. And when he shines that white smile on you – man, you feel good! You're suddenly the kindest, strongest person in the world. You're suddenly the perfect parent.

I glance from Gertjie to Alphons now, on this beautiful summer evening, and suddenly feel sorry for her. Dunno why. It's like I know her thing with Gertjie is doomed.

'OK, you guys,' I say, draining my glass, 'so where's the action now?'

'Well, shucks,' says Gertjie, chewing imaginary gum. 'Gee, why don't we mosey on down to the picture palace and catch us a picture show?'

'Knock it on the head, Gerts,' says Alphons, dropping the accent. 'Another movie? Can't we shoot off to the Hippodrome or someplace?'

I ease myself off the wall. 'Well, you guys sort it out. Me – I'm goin' for a little ol' leak.'

'Me also,' says Gertjie, immediately falling alongside; like a kid who'd been dying to go, just waiting for Daddy to take him.

In the lav, there are only two stalls on the weeing wall. Our shoulders are practically touching as we unzip. I stare straight ahead, unable to pee, trying to think of something to say. Near my nose, the graffiti reads: *Condom man seeks arse. Make date.*

Gertjie finishes and shakes off vigorously. His elbow brushes mine.

'Sorry, buddy,' he says.

'Hh? 's OK.'

Now he's behind me at the basin. He's got a bit of a hand-washing phobia. And actually not just hands. Several times this week, when they've been at the house, he's asked to shower. Disappears upstairs. It's a funny feeling – chatting on to Alphonsia, while you hear the whoosh of the shower. I think he leaves the door open. Yet he'll never get into the swimming pool. No matter how hot it gets, he never undoes one button in public. So he pours with sweat, and despite all this washing, never loses his smell. It's not like B O. Much subtler. He douses himself in Woolworths aftershave, a weak scent that just boosts his own.

I've finally started to pee, when I hear him cry, *'Jou doos – jou moer!'*

Glancing over my shoulder, I see him trying to rip the basin from the wall.

'Gertjie, what's the matter?'

'Water, water!' he grunts. *'Dis 'n wasbak, né? Die fokken ding moet mos vir mens water kan gee! Dis 'n fokken stuk kak!'*

'Gertjie, Gertjie!' I say, pointing to a sign scribbled next to the basin: OUT OF USE – BLAME THE WATER SHORTAGE.

'Jou moer!' he screams. His grip slides along the porcelain and onto a chipped corner. Gasping, he flicks his hand wildly, and blood darts across the tiles and between my legs. I pee all over the damn show.

' *'skuustog* – sorry,' he mutters.

I finish and turn. His face is incredible. Purple. Swollen. Teeth bared.

(I've just remembered – Angela thought he might be having a minor breakdown.)

'Sorry,' he says, then suddenly comes into my arms, and hugs me. Or rather hugs *us*. We stay like this for a sec, rocking together, me watching in the mirror above the basin. The worst thing about being red-haired is how you blush.

47

SEVEN

'Bubs,' says Angela gently, 'don't have another.'
'It's OK.'

'But you're already had half a dozen. And the champers. And there's wine on the way.'

'Sure, sure, it's OK.' I grab the arm of a passing waitress. 'Another large vodka tonic, my dear.' The waitress nods grimly and goes. I don't think the staff here like being grabbed, but it's the only way to get served. The owner of the joint, Mrs Worsfield, has trained everyone to copy her walk – so stuck up, her nose can test for dust on the ceiling.

Mrs Worsfield was a housekeeper at Buckingham Palace before opening this swanky country-house hotel. In the hall there are framed letters from the Royal Family, or their secretaries. Tassels hang from anything that'll let them. Bowls of dried petals everywhere. I thought one was Bombay Mix and – *ja*, I'm afraid so.

It's Saturday night and it's my birthday (forty-six by God), and this little stay-over is Angela's surprise treat. I was planning to invite Gertjie over for a birthday *braai* today (with Alphons, of course), so it certainly was a surprise to find myself at Euston Station first thing this morning. In fact, the word surprise doesn't quite say it all – maybe only people who've been through a hijack know what I'm talking about. There was nothing for it but to hit the buffet car, and I don't remember much after that: a couple of hours swaying to and fro with armfuls of dinky vodkas, then a big

48

station, then a cab, then suburbs, then countryside, then here. What's the odds? They're all the same, these Egon doodah hotels: 'the former country seat of Lord blah-blah, nestling in its own lovely blah-blah', while meanwhile you feel like you've been committed to a bloody nursing home. I reckon this one is somewhere in the Midlands, because the staff speak in Angela's old accent.

My good wife is picking up all the bills this weekend (she specially saved her wages), so I've got to muster some enthusiasm.

She smiles at me now. I blink, suddenly realising how long we've been sitting here without talking. Mind you, the atmosphere in the dining room doesn't help. It's like an art gallery. A hushed silence, broken by little gasps and whispers as people view the next masterpiece.

'What the fuck's this?' I ask Angela as a dish lands in front of me, covered in a glass bell. In the middle is a tiny greenish puddle with a nut on it. The menu was in French, so Angela's done all the ordering. The waitress meanwhile looks a little thunderstruck, but that's her prob. I don't believe in talking clean just because the servants are around. I hated it at home, when everyone went silent each time old Lizzie brought in the next course.

Now the waitress lifts the glass bell and announces, '*Petites bouchées aux épinards.*'

'Are you sure?' I ask, 'I thought maybe the chef had some problem and wanted us to see a specimen.'

I wink at her, but she sweeps off, shnozz akimbo. Angela's giggling though, or trying to. She's been letting me call the tune all day: constantly smiling, squeezing my hand, sending little signals – are you all right?, are you happy?

(So why do I feel so bloody lonely?)

Things perk up as the drinks arrive. I knock back the vodka neat, Commie-style, then sit back, burping, as the table is rearranged to accommodate the wine, Perrier, and so on. I let Angela taste the wine; it makes her feel grand. She sniffs and swirls it, holds it up to the candle – but the wine waiter hardly waits for her 'Yes, fine' before pouring.

He's slim and bleached-blond, dishy in a cold way, and might do as a fantasy later, when me and La get rooting. Agh, so long as the booze keeps flowing, the graze is good, and there's sex at the end of the day, my birthday needn't be a total write-off.

'You're quiet,' Angela says when we're alone again. 'Are you having a good time?'

'Very.' I kiss her plump knuckles. 'I'm very grateful. And when I get you upstairs later, I'm gonna show you just how grateful.'

She tickles my palm. 'I only wish you loved these weekends in the country as much as I do.'

'No, I do too, 'strue as God I do – I always have. It's a terrific way of seeing Britain. Great Britain.' I dive into my glass again, so that she can't see the lie in my eyes. It's funny, but my British passport suddenly doesn't seem that big a deal anymore. It's happened since meeting Gertjie, don't ask me why. But since then I've found myself taking out my old South African passport, coloured a military green, and gazing at the snipped corners, or the pages with CANCELLED stamped on them.

'My barbarian,' Angela whispers, smiling.

'Look who's talking – Miss Dudley herself!'

'Oo-ar,' she says, 'but nah, folk weren't barbarian in Doodlay – nah, nothin' so racy as that. In those small rooms wi' the blokes snorin' in front a' the telly, an' the missus jus' gerrin' a bit wild on the umpteenth pot a' tea.'

'And where were you in all this?'

'Oo duck – I were like a fresh flower in a field a' dung.'

We laugh and toast one another, me emptying my glass in one. (Oh yes, this is more like it – everything is starting to blur nicely.)

'But then,' I prompt her, 'then you discovered a certain book at school.'

She sighs nostalgically. 'Then, yes, a certain book came on the syllabus. My copy was from the school library. Wasn't much to look at – no dust jacket, all thumbed, the main themes underlined in dark pencil – but the moment I opened it, it was like opening a window. *Pride and Prejudice . . .*'

As she goes into a familiar spiel about how this book changed her life, I cut off the sound, and just feast my eyes on her. Eat your heart out Peter Paul Rubens – your paints never achieved what hers have tonight. And she's wearing this fab green silk number that she bought at *Sotheby's*! (She tried to resist going to the auction, but failed.) It's designed by Poiret apparently, and she's adorned it with favourite jewellery I've given her over the years – some rocks and serious gold. I feel a groiny prickle and a tightening of cloth.

'. . . and of course *Northanger Abbey*, reading them all in my bedroom, with the door closed, as though they were obscene. Which they were somehow – in a council flat.' Angela gives her self-mocking giggle. 'But I suppose . . . well, that year I was being reborn – into the middle classes. D'you think?'

'Dunno. But I can recommend a good shrink.'

She stares at me. 'What?'

'A joke,' I say quickly, wondering why that's kept happening today – why my wisecracks have kept misfiring? And why they've kept coming out a bit cruel? (I hear myself doing it, yet can't stop – and don't want to somehow.) Angela's gone quiet now. I shrug and refill our glasses. From across the room, the wine waiter glares. *He's* supposed to do that. God, the British, hey? Who pours this, who reads that. Who cares? There's masters and servants – that's the only fact of life, the beating heart, the nub, the core. Masters and servants – that's the thing you've got to watch.

Knowing what'll get Angela turned-on again, I say 'OK – teach me. Teach me about this Jane Austen woman. What's the big attraction?'

'I don't want to *teach* you about her,' she replies sharply, 'when you *teach* her, you kill her. I've just explained how they almost killed her for me in Dudley High – weren't you listening?'

'Yes,' I mutter, 'sorry.'

She checks herself, and forces a smile. 'No, all I can say is that I'd like to have met her. I think she must've been a bit of a laugh, Auntie Jane.'

'Would I have liked her?' I ask.

'*Adored* her. She saw the world rather like you.'

I chuckle. 'How so?'

'In miniature.'

I chuckle again.

'All indoors,' adds Angela.

'Indoors?'

'Mh-hh. The outside world is hardly visible.'

'But man,' I laugh, 'we South Africans love the big outdoors!
All that rugby, all that sunshine.'

Angela smiles. An odd, private smile. Vaguely hostile.

(Where *is* all this aggro coming from?)

As I sit back, my right foot peeps out under the tablecloth.
There's a drop of blood on my shoe, dried blood. Hey, that's right
– I was wearing these when Gertjie freaked out in Hammersmith.
I rub my head, to change its wavelength. Why does everything
keep drifting back to Gertjie these days? Yanking my foot out of
view, I blow my cheeks. Hadn't noticed before, but it's really hot
tonight. I can hear my sweat sizzling. My socks are wet with the
stuff. I picture it bubbling up, through my shoe, freshening
Gertjie's blood. It feels dangerous, but also –

'*Salade de rognons de veau tiedes au chou croquet.*'

Mrs Worsfield is at my side, the candlelight catching on her
pearl necklace and blondish hair, lacquered like a crash helmet.
Why is she serving us? Are the others running scared? Bugger
them. I pick my nose and peer at the new dish: rawish kidneys,
cabbage, carrot threads and a sort'f red jelly.

'Hell – tiny main courses you people serve here!' I grin at Mrs
Worsfield. 'Have to order me a big sweet, hey?'

She gives an icy smile and goes.

'This isn't the main course,' says Angela, catching Worsfield's
expression, 'this is the fish course.'

'You ordered me *fish kidneys?*'

She sighs. 'You don't like fish, do you? So Mummy ordered you
another starter. All right? Savvy?'

We stare at one another. We could stop now.

'I mean – really!' mutters Angela.

''Rahli!' I echo, 'oh, 'rahli! Speak in your own bloody voice,
man! That other voice belongs to an England that's more foreign
to you than me.'

'Oh no!' laughs Angela, 'This *is* my turf, mate! And don't worry
– I know my way round.' She shakes her head. 'But poor you –
you still think of England as some cosy old place, mother of the
free! Thank goodness, thinks the wandering Lipschitz, I've found
somewhere safe at last! But, my lovely, you haven't. There's no

safe place – not unless we make it safe. The fascism in current Tory policies is as ...'

'And now suddenly she's gone *political*!' I cry, leaning my forehead into the cold kidney mess on my plate. 'How, how in the name of all that's fuckable, how did that happen?'

She flares. 'What d'you mean? I've always been political! Fairly political.'

'Oh yeah?' I call from among the flattened food.

'Yeah! Certainly a lot, *lot* more than you'd ever realised.'

I jerk up, kidneys sliding down my face.

She blushes. 'It's just this show I'm doing. The more I read about South Africa, the more I think I was wrong before. The whites aren't just being *human*, ordinary. It's ... something else, something more.'

'Hey!' I say, grabbing the wine waiter as he passes. (I think he's *very* dishy, but it's difficult to focus.) 'Can I have a large vodka, doll? Or, hang on, make it a triple. No, a fourple.'

'Leon,' says Angela, 'there's wine!'

'Oh ja – and more wine,' I tell the waiter, emptying the current bottle into my row of glasses.

He goes.

Angela says quietly 'That's Corton Charlemagne. It's very dear.'

' 's all right, I'll pay.'

'But this is my treat. For your –'

'Fuck your treat. Fuck my birthday.' I go from glass to glass, throwing back each. She watches, round chin trembling.

'If you could see yourself,' she says eventually, 'if you could see the way you drink.'

'*Ja*, well, 's up to me.'

'Oh not the amount – Crikey no, I'm in no position to talk. No, no, the *way*. The way in which you drink and eat and perform what you think of as love-making. What's the rush?, I've always meant to ask. Because it's tremendously disgusting. I'm sorry, I probably should've mentioned this before, but it really is disgusting being near you. It really is a problem for me – holding back the vomit.'

The wine waiter returns with my massive vodka, and another bottle of wine. He shows it to Angela, who says 'Oh just pour it!'

As he leans in, his crotch bulges over the edge of the table. Quick as a flash, I stretch over and tickle it. The guy springs back, confused – did that happen or didn't it? He flees.

Angela sighs. 'Oh, and that's the other thing. My other problem. Being married to a moffie. It isn't easy, y'know.'

'It can't be,' I say, reaching for my vodka. 'Bit like being married to one of those ladies who hang round moffies. In South Africa we call them fruit-flies.'

Now the head waiter approaches, leading a procession with our main courses, veggies and sauces. Raising her voice, Angela says, 'Take that away, and bring us the bill!' With hardly a pause, the head waiter goes on tiptoe like a dancer, then twirls round and ushers his minions back to the kitchen.

We wait, neither moving.

Mrs Worsfield brings the bill. 'Is something the matter?' she asks.

'Nothing at all thank you,' says Angela, snatching the bill from her. Mrs Worsfield gives her icy smile, then offers a pen, expecting Angela to sign it onto our room.

But Angela has gone grey. She says, 'Can I have the wine list please – I'd like to check something.'

Mrs Worsfield smiles again, and sweeps off.

I lean forward. Even reading the bill upside down, I can spot three-figure numbers each time the word WINE appears. I reckon that Angela's careful budget for this weekend has been well buggered-up.

Now the wine waiter delivers the wine list – keeping his hips out of reach.

'There's been a mistake,' Angela says after studying the list. 'I didn't order *that* Corton Charlemagne. I ordered the other one.'

'Did I not show you the bottle, madam?' asks the wine waiter. 'On both occasions? Before uncorking?'

'Yes,' gulps Angela. 'But I assumed it was the one I ordered.'

'It *was* the one you ordered, madam.'

'It wasn't, I would never order *that* one. So I didn't think it necessary, y'know, to double-check . . .' She's spluttering now. 'Y'know, in a place like this!'

'I'm sorry madam,' he says, 'but it is what you ordered.' And he withdraws.

Angela slumps, staring at the bill.

With one hand I reach for it, with the other I produce my credit card, and bring the two together.

'I was wondering,' I say slowly, 'if we should split up?'

She gives a shudder. Small, almost involuntary. Something similar goes through me. I can't believe I said what I just did, and yet I carry on:

'What d'you reckon? We've never had much more than fuck-all in common. So why don't we just do it, hey? Just get it over with.'

I watch her – so sexy tonight in the dress, jewellery and contact lenses that I've paid for. So sexy, yet so impotent, her great brain useless, her blabbing jaw struck into silence. *Wragh!* – it's firing me up so much, my arse is starting to pulse.

'What d'you think?' I say, 'It can't be nice for you – living off all this South African loot. Hell, it must eat you up! When you think of all those kaffirs working their balls off for the Lipschitzes – making us those big bucks, and then us just *sommer* squandering it all. Doesn't that – ?'

'Not squandering all of it,' she says suddenly. 'Not all of it.'

I laugh. 'No?'

'No,' she says, finally meeting my gaze. 'We give a lot of it away. To good causes.'

I laugh louder. 'Like for instance?'

'Like for instance the ANC, Anti-Apartheid, BDAF, SATIS, and others. Monthly donations – big monthly donations, really big. The name of Lipschitz is quite famous among the dissident community. We're among the biggest benefactors in town, we ...'

'We?' I ask, my laughter going sticky.

'We – that's right. We. Not that it matters with the joint account, but I've signed some of the standing orders, you've signed some of the others. Over the years. Some of these go back yonks.'

I narrow my eyes, hiding my expression, giving myself time to think.

All those times she does her blitzes on our paperwork – she brings me sheaves of things to sign. It's usually at night; I'm usually well-gone. It's never occurred to me I should *read* anything!

'So y'see,' says Angela, 'I don't feel too bad about South Africa. I feel I'm doing my bit. Being fairly political. For a Lipschitz.' Smiling glumly, she pours herself a huge glassful of the Corton Charlemagne, pausing to study the bottle. 'Well, I've certainly learned a lesson tonight. Always to double-check anything that's put in front of me.'

With a gasp, I release the grip on my credit card. Mrs Worsfield's hand swoops down, like those eagles that divebomb fish, and whisks it away.

People are glancing over from other tables. I grin, lift the bottle of Corton Charlemagne, and drink from the neck. Meanwhile Angela's news comes at me again and again, like someone slapping my face. To think all that's been going on without me knowing. Like she's been having an affair.

When my card is returned, I hurry up to our room. Angela follows. We say nothing. We undress; me kicking my shoe with Gertjie's blood well out of sight; she climbing carefully out of the Poiret dress, and zipping it into a Gucci garment bag. We brush teeth, have a leak. All in silence. We climb into bed, switch off the lights and lie in silence.

It's hard to tell who makes the first move. Tomorrow we'll both say it was the other one. But within seconds we're rooting like maniacs; it's more like mutual rape than love-making, with gob, dead skin and loose hairs flying. Snarling and puffing, hauling one another's big bods round and round in a whirlpool of sheets, and – FOOMF! – onto the floor, and across it, twisting along like a massive eight-legged crab, here, there and everywhere, and up onto Mrs Worsfield's chintzy overweight couch, and overturning it with a WHONK!, and writhing onwards, into the bathroom – icy tiles suddenly against the knees! – and now, still not unfastening (talk about *wedlock*), it's heave-ho, up and over, into the bath-tub, where one of our limbs bangs a tap and the shower comes on, and we throw back our heads under the mad spray, calling out, swearing and crying, and cumming like that – GOOSH! – both of us, I'm almost sure!

And then cleaning up, mopping the bathroom floor, tidying the bedroom furniture, and untangling the sheets. And climbing into bed, far apart, and lying there, waiting for sleep. Everything silent again.

If we strike lucky tonight, what kind of kid will he be? Quite angry I think. Quite a survivor.

Sunday. Churchbells. No longer my birthday. I feel like *drek*. Hardly slept, or just dipped in and out. Had my clifftop dream somewhere in it, and another where I'm being interrogated; 'Why?' they kept asking, 'Why?' It hangs over me for hours, that 'Why?' – in a cartoon bubble, with the question mark very hooked. I feel uneasy passing under anything.

Me and Angela don't speak all day. She goes on country walks, while I stay at base, drinking and dozing. Somewhere in this haze we have Sunday lunch, and sometime afterwards we climb into a cab, heading for the station.

As the countryside changes from green to grey, from fields to factories, I notice a roadsign pointing to the left, saying DUDLEY, 8 MILES. I almost shout out, 'Hey, look!' – but that would be too friendly, too normal for today. Angela's seen it anyway, and twists round to look as we shoot past the turn-off. She's never been back to Dudley, never in fifteen years (instead, *oich*, her folks or sister and brood sometimes invade Hampstead) – but how weird to think we were so near the place all weekend. Isn't she curious to see it again? Doesn't she miss it at all? I glance at her, at her neck and the side of her face, as she gazes out of the window. She's wearing sunglasses, so nothing shows of her eyes. And if anything's boiling around inside her – pain or longing – it's silent as hell.

Why? How? How is it possible, when you've spent a lifetime fleeing your people, your class, your territory, how is it possible to stay so *calm*? It pisses me off! It's so fucking Christian, her calmness, so Christian and so British!

What is it about this little island that keeps the populace so calm? Governments come and go, bombs explode in the street, suburbs are invaded by dark-skinned aliens, the weather grows ever stranger, and yet the locals carry on as though they'd seen it all before. Incredible, It costs me a lot of energy to keep calm –

avoiding the papers, switching off the news – but the British, they get calmness for free.

Mind you, I wonder if they're not the losers? A life without worries is like food without salt and pepper.

C'mon, I want to yell at Angela as we speed past the Dudley turn-off, c'mon have a howl. You've just spent a weekend near your old home and you were too scared to go look – scared of it shaking your precious calm! Have a howl over that.

(Wow, will it be a different story when I get within sniffing distance of Cape Town!)

Still not a word as we reach Birmingham New Street, and climb into a first-class compartment, Euston-bound. Angela takes a file from her briefcase, puts on her Walkman, and settles down to work, hair flopping forward.

Watching from the corner of my eye, I notice her rewinding the tape again and again, while she studies a music sheet titled, 'The National Anthem: *Nkosi Sikelel' iAfrika*'.

'Difficult words, hey?' I say, after a while.

She pretends not to hear.

'Is it Xhosa?' No response. 'I think it is – or Zulu. For your school concert?' Now she gives a vague nod. 'Want any help?'

She thinks for a long time, then sighs, and pulls out her earplugs. 'How?' she mumbles.

'Give us your Walkman.'

I listen to the song. A lone voice. Soaring, but sad. Not like the anthem we learned at school: '*Die Stem*'. Man, that one lifted the hairs on your neck.

'*Ja*, it's difficult,' I say; 'Maybe if we could find English words that sound similar.'

'How do you mean?'

'Well . . .' I replay the beginning. *Nkosi sikelel' iAfrika*. 'A cosy sick . . . old lady . . . in Africa.'

Angela stares at me, wide-eyed. For a moment I think she's going to lunge across and give me a klup. But then she bursts out laughing. 'Leon, you are without shame.'

I listen to the next line. *Maluphakanyisw' uphondo lwayo'*. 'Mails a . . . fucking nit . . . to a pond along you.'

Angela puts her head in her hands.

'Well?' I ask, 'are you going to tell me it isn't easier to learn?'

She looks at me steadily, then says, 'I hate you.'

'So I've gathered.'

'I don't regret . . . what I told you about last night.'

'Fair enough.'

'So. What are you going to do?'

I shrug. I'm still just numb from it all. Maybe she is too. Grateful for today's mind-blowing hangover – which not even booze can shift. But tomorrow I've got some hard thinking to do.

Meanwhile, I move across and kiss her hair.

'D'you remember our weekend at that fancy hotel near Chichester?' I ask, 'and how you also taught me an anthem on the train coming back? And how I also changed the words?' I sing softly:

'Bring me a boy with burning bum

Bring me my arrow of desire . . .'

Angela looks out of the window, whispering to herself, then slowly joins in:

'We will not cease from Marital Fight,

Nor shall my Sword slip in your Puss,

Till we have built Jews-asylum

In England's greedy peasant land.'

EIGHT

The house, without lights on, looks dazed; as though it wasn't expecting us back so soon. The glow from another fab summer evening slouches in here and there, but the body of the house is dim. Coming back after a weekend away, I can smell the house like a visitor would; the smell they'd think of as ours. Furniture polish, Brasso and tropical plants – the heady fragrance of Victoriana, as Angela might say.

I'm sitting in the hall and she's upstairs, unpacking – you can hear her klomping back and forth across the ceiling. It's a safe sound. Reminds me of when I was a kid, the family schlepping home after a long Sunday picnicking at Stellenbosch or swimming at Muizenberg, listening to the folks moving around in other rooms, organising what's left of the evening. And there I'd be sitting in the middle of the house, still drowsy from the car, waiting to be fed and bathed.

'Hungry?' asks Angela, coming downstairs.

'Mm.'

'Shall I warm up some bagels?'

'Mmmm.'

(Angela has learned to make the most divine bagels; we got the recipe off old Lizzie back home.)

'With boiled eggs mashed in mayonnaise and onion?'

'Mmmmmm.'

Noticing there are two messages on the answer-machine, Angela flicks it to PLAY. It springs into its crazy little routine – whirr, click, whirr. *Ai!* – such energy for a Sunday evening.

'*Veels geluk liewe Leon*
Omdat jy verjaar . . .'

It takes a moment to realise that the voice is singing Happy Birthday in Afrikaans. A strange thrill creeps through me. I quickly yawn, stretch and say, 'Oh, 's Gertjie.'

'*Mag die Here jou seën*
En nog baie jare spaar.'

'Sweet,' says Angela.

'Silly kid,' I say – meanwhile blushing so badly, I have to yawn again, stretching my arms over my face. I freeze as I hear the next message.

'Leon? Charlotte here.'

'Who?' asks Angela.

I shrug wildly and lean towards the machine.

'I'm organising a little do for this chap, Pope – you must've heard of him – well, he's won an award from one of the alternative magazines, and I thought some mates should go along and cheer. D'you want to join the party? It's on the 24th . . . or is it the 25th? Anyhow, do let me know if you want to come – and how many tickets you'll need. Cheerio.'

(*Tickets?* Is this message a code for something?)

'Sounds interesting,' says Angela. 'But who's Charlotte?'

'Oh, someone I met through uhh . . .' I yawn again, hinting that the name's so obvious it's hardly worth saying, 'uhhh-aaaaaa-uhmm . . .' I stretch and stretch until Angela starts yawning too, and strolls away.

'I'd love to meet Pope,' she says, lingering at the kitchen door.

'Who?'

'This incredible new director-stroke-designer. Theatre, opera, pop videos, whatever he can lay his hands on. And he's just brought out his autobiography, though he can't be more than twenty-five. Someone had a copy in the staff room the other day, and we were all falling about. It's done as a cartoon-strip, very raunchy, very *street*. Oh we should go. Upon

61

my word, to parade among such fashionable quality! Oh yes, let's go.'

First thing Monday morning, I visit our bank. It's in the West End; one of the fancy ones. A monstrous goldfish floats in the foyer, while all around men in frock coats glide to and fro, playing out some mysterious British fantasy.

I'm shown into a private room, narrow, tall and windowless, and then one of the banker-butlers brings me our files, with records of the regular allowance from Dad's Guernsey account, and all our statements over the years.

Angela wasn't bullshitting. There are standing orders with at least half a dozen South African organisations. And also with others she didn't mention: women's groups, gay groups, Friends of the Earth, the Mouth and Foot Painters Association. Some of the orders go back to 1982. Signed by Angela, and, yup, in some cases, me.

Angela talks about South Africans wallowing in comfort. But what's all this about – all these lunatic donations? Nobody's going to tell me they don't give her *comfort*. Listen, I know about handing out cash, and it's just another way of getting a fix. Ballet tickets or charities, what's the difference? If it feels good, I can't be that cunt I see in the mirror.

What am I going to do? Stop the standing orders, and have it out with Angela? Get her to finally face up to the life she's chosen – her every whim, even her guilt, financed with South African bucks. But then I might have to face up to her leaving me. And, funny thing, I couldn't live without her. I just couldn't. So what to do? Ring Pallister, Dad's British accountant? Does he know about the standing orders? Probably not. And if I tell him, and he tells Dad, what then? What happens when Dad finds out that we, Angela *and* me, have been funding various groups that want him dead?

As I shuffled, dazed, from the bank and into the nearest pub, another alternative presents itself.

I could do nothing.

It's a course of action which has often served me well.

Ja – just do nothing. See what happens. Blue murder or poverty, at least it'll get the old blood racing.

Even as I reach the decision, a weird exhilaration takes over. It's like being high. High on a clifftop. There's still ground under my feet, but only inches thick.

Then fresh air, plenty of it.

NINE

'**B**ut . . .' says Angela, 'I still don't know who this Charlotte person is.'

I decide to come clean. I mean, she's not going to turn back now, not all ritzed up to the nines – this *fantastic* black thirties number by Worth – and after she's looked forward to it all week.

'Charlotte? Oh, she deals in coke.'

The Jag swerves slightly. (Angela's driving – I've already had a few.) When she speaks, her voice is horribly calm.

'We're spending this evening with a coke dealer?'

'Yup – your idea.'

'I'm sorry?'

'I don't give a stuff about this do tonight. Listen, I'm supposed to get excited about someone called *Pope* already? You're the one crazy to go.'

She's thinking hard and fast, but still heading for Islington, where we're picking up Charlotte.

'So . . .' she sighs, 'you *are* still doing drugs?'

'*I am not!* I don't even know if Charlotte is bringing any for herself. Or for this Pope character, or for who-all are coming tonight. And I don't care. If I'm offered any, I'll just say . . .'

'Oh yeah?'

'All right – I'll bet you.'

'You'll – bet – me?' Angela repeats each word slowly, suddenly coming the schoolmarm with me.

'Yes,' I cry. 'I'll *bet* you that I don't touch so much as a crystal tonight. I'll bet you our wealth!'

I look at her. No reaction. Since my birthday weekend, we've made no mention of her crazy donations. Yet she must be wondering why I haven't stopped the standing orders, and what I'm planning to do. She must be feeling pretty damn jumpy at the moment.

She gives a small laugh. 'Our wealth? But that's already mine. Or in what sense are you using the word "our"?'

'Look, you have my promise,' I say, with quiet dignity, 'and if that's not enough, turn back.'

She smiles to herself, but drives on.

As before, Charlotte takes forever to answer the door, but when she appears – wow! She's just returned from a trip to South America, and her tan glows from inside the white hood of her silk sweatshirt. Hanging from long shoulder straps is a small Chanel bag (I wonder what's in there?). Charlotte greets Angela so warmly that all antagonism is knocked for a loop. Good old Charlotte. Despite her shot brain, her sleepless eyes and raw nose, she can still queen it when she wants to, and with such bloody style, man. Humility's the great trick, isn't it? – that's what the British aristocracy have down to a T. They know how to make *you* feel important.

'Where on earth are we going?' asks Charlotte, as we overshoot the movie palace at King's Cross, where the alternative awards do is to be held.

'The rest of our group are over by the East End,' I explain.

'The East End – how thrilling! So like Calcutta these days.'

As we drive on, I'm getting this funny feeling deep in my belly. Half-nice, half-scary.

I haven't seen Gertjie since we got back from our weekend in the country. On the phone, both he and Alphons have been a bit distant. Something's going on, don't ask me what. Actually, Gertjie may even have told me – but in Afrikaans. Fire him a tricky question, and he retreats straight into the laager.

He's standing on the pavement, waiting for us. God, my heart! Can the others hear? He's wearing a suit that I swear was sewn in Bloemfontein in the fifties. Brown-striped, miles too short in the arms and legs. His hair is Brylcreemed senseless, making him look almost bald, and his cute ears look slightly stranded. A beautiful monkey in a tiny suit.

'Where's Alphons?' I ask, rolling down the window.

He shrugs, glancing nervously at Charlotte – a stranger.

'Is she on her way down?' I ask, peering up at the battered block of flats behind him, its walls scribbled with threats, slogans, and sex organs.

Gertjie's never invited me into his bedsit, so it's still a fantasy place, a place I only visit in my thoughts; usually just before and after sleep, when my brain is soft and my lust is up. These are such hazy visits, I don't have to worry too much about them. Sometimes I picture all four of us together: me and Angela, Gertjie and Alphons, and sometimes it's other combinations.

Now Gertjie climbs into the back seat, next to Charlotte. He still hasn't said anything, or even greeted us. We all twist round to view him. I catch a powerful whiff of his scent – his body and the Woolworths stuff. It's a smell of Saturday nights from long ago.

'You OK?' I ask.

He nods briskly.

'Where's Alphons?'

'*Sy kan nie kom nie.*'

'She's not coming with,' I translate for the others.

As the Jag pulls off, I keep fixed on Gertjie. Something's wrong. I wish I could use our Yankee-talk – 'Say buddy, wanna chew some cud?' – but Angela would think I'd gone nuts.

'*Ons is nie meer saam nie,*' Gertjie says suddenly, privately, touching my sleeve.

'Sorry?'

'*Alphons is weg.*'

Weg means gone. She's gone.

'Why?'

Gertjie is silent.

'Just had enough, hey?' I suggest.

He glares at me – I've insulted him, questioned his manhood – then shrugs and leans his forehead on the window. Suddenly there's a real Boer in the car, a real rock-spider, watching London slip past his nose with an expression of lazy anger.

'What is he saying?' asks Charlotte, with a patient smile; very much the memsahib.

'Nothing,' I answer, 'all is well,' and turn round to face the front.

(Alphons is gone!)

The alternative awards do is more casj than we expected. I should never've worn a tie, Gertjie certainly shouldn't've worn that suit, and Angela suddenly looks ridiculous in the thirties number, with her Rubensesque back exposed. The audience milling round the foyer are mostly kids, dressed just anyhow, and the few folk in our age-group are wearing gear which looks a bit 1960s . . . I think.

If I'm a bit vague when it comes to the sixties, it's because they were banned in South Africa. We went straight from our prosperous fifties to our troublesome seventies without any licentious interlude. Oh for sure, some things happened in the sixties – Sharpeville, Mandela's trial, Verwoerd's spectacular assassination, Roman-style, in Parliament – but nothing to really rock the boat. Nothing to cause that kind of life-changing experience that sixties folk tell me they had here.

'Pope!' Charlotte suddenly cries and rushes across to some bloke. There's another man with them too, but before I can get a proper look, they go into a little scrum with Charlotte, doing prolonged handshakes. Then the other man shoots off to the lav – so Charlotte *is* carrying! – while she brings Pope over to meet us.

He's all in black – except for his signature, in white, embroidered on one lapel. He's signed himself like a work of art, and one can see his point of view. He has long lashes, blue shadows round his eyes, rippling cheekbones, apricot lips. You stare hard, unable to believe this isn't make-up. It's so arresting, it takes a moment longer to notice the nicotine on his teeth, and tiny layer of scum on his black pigtail. And now you're even more impressed. Beauty and dirt: a delicious mixture.

His smile is modest, his accent mid-Atlantic-Cockney. He holds each handshake longer than normal, treasuring it. 'Hi, Leon,' he says, 'hi, Angela', even 'hi, *Gertjie*' – getting the pronunciation right! He smiles warmly at Gertjie, then says, 'Great suit. Very witty. And Brylcreem too. Gel's had its day, let's bring back Brylcreem *again*, yeah?' and he sniffs Gertjie's head long and hard.

(Who is this guy?)

To my surprise, Gertjie blushes only moderately.

Now, having conquered us all, Pope excuses himself and gives a quick interview to a Channel 4 film crew waiting nearby.

'Beware,' Charlotte whispers to our group. 'He was my lover for five weeks, so I know what I'm talking about. Oh, I shouldn't have come tonight!' She starts talking faster. 'Lover? I wasn't his lover, I was just another "sponsor". He has this addiction for sponsorship. Needs it more and more as his fucking work gets more and more high-tech! Bit of a linguist too, so he hunts his sponsors abroad.' Now she points into the crowd. 'And here's his latest victim. This one's from Istanbul apparently. Oh, just look at the poor man! Isn't it just so sad?'

I can't say there's anything remotely sad about the Turkish man now returning from the lav. Wearing a purple satin suit that starts tight and sweeps down to flares over lamé platform boots, he comes through the crowd with a hip-rolling shimmy and raised arms, as though receiving an ovation. He squeezes Pope's hand, palming something, and then, as Pope shoots off to the lav, approaches us.

He is Delican. Like Pope there is no other name offered, just Delican (which he pronounces *Delijan*); but while Pope's aura comes from God, Delican's is straight out of the paint-box. Underneath, there's a surprisingly hefty man, like an ex-boxer.

As he stubs out one ciggie and lights another, I notice that he wears transparent nail polish.

'My sweethearts,' he says, greeting me and Angela at the same time, one in each hand, 'I greet you with pleasure, and the pleasure is maddening. My dear . . .' he says, coolly, to Charlotte, then grasps Gertjie. 'And as for you! What a *kurabiye*, what a biscuit! Ha? Aren't you?'

Gertjie freezes. Delican does the same, and they stay poised like this, reared like animals.

It's funny, but there's a similarity. Both have broken noses and puffy eyes.

'Hug to hug
Brain to brain
Heart to heart'
– says Delican, or rather, sings it; his voice is high, but smoky. Noticing our astonished expressions, he adds:
'It's OK, we've met once before, your friend and I – in the year of black luck.'

He is absolutely serious. But then, as Pope arrives back from the lav, going sniff-sniff, Delican relaxes again.

'Alas, it is my fate – the black luck. I can't move without sinning. If I step on a stone I leave a mark. Is that not so, my darlo, *canim?*' He kisses Pope's hand and tells us, 'Ohhh, I'm so in love with this man, I'm jealous of myself. When his hair touches his neck, I'm jealous of his hair. When he pins a rose to his chest, I'm jealous of the rose.'

Now, as the audience start ambling towards the auditorium, Delican takes my arm. I lunge for Angela, and end up escorting both.

'And what do you do, darlo?' Delican asks me.

I clear my throat. 'Agh, this and that. It's complicated to explain. Shipping, the stock market –'

'It sounds beautiful.'

'What about yourself?'

'A humble Palace singer.'

'Sorry?'

'You know the Palace, yes?'

'Which particular pala—?'

'Yes, of course we do,' says Angela quickly, then whispers to me, 'It's another name for the Ottoman Empire.'

'Our lost empire,' sighs Delican, overhearing. 'But I still sing her songs – the Palace songs.'

'So,' I say, 'and is there a decent living to be made from this kind of singing?'

'No. Only billions.' Delican winks. 'It is very, *very* popular. In Istanbul, Bodrum, Ankara, also Turkish communities in Hamburg and Melbourne, I could not walk like this. There, people must, they *must* tear souvenirs from me.'

He stops abruptly, and points to the no-smoking sign at the

auditorium entrance. 'Oh,' he gasps; 'take my life, oh God, rather than inflict this torture!' Grimacing, he stubs out his ciggie and sweeps in. 'Oh, you barbaric Britishers!'

'*Ja*,' I say, laughing butchly. 'By the by, I'm not British. I'm South African.'

'South Africa?' he says, in a different, softer voice. He glances to Gertjie. 'That is where he is from also?'

'*Ja.*'

He nods and goes silent. When the smile vanishes, his face looks ugly and heavy. The make-up seems to slide like the colours on bad meat.

I'm so absorbed by this creature, this bird, this clapped-out peacock, that I fail to notice the others taking their seats. Gertjie ends up several places away, next to Pope, who seems *very* attentive.

The awards ceremony sort of starts. It's difficult to be sure, since everyone's determined not to take it seriously. Alternative comedians sort of tell jokes, and then they sort of present an award. And the audience sort of jeer rather than cheer. It's all very modern.

But anyhow, apart from the brief moment when Pope gets his award, our party isn't really focused on the stage. An ivory phial is being passed around, accompanied by much folding and shaping of handkerchiefs. Someone watching might think this was an outing of magicians. I watch Pope showing Gertjie how to do it.

When the phial reaches our end, I refuse. Angela gives my arm a squeeze. I feel proud and depressed.

In the same way as it started, the show now sort of ends.

'You are all my guests for dinner,' Delican tells us, after we've dashed to the exit so he can light a ciggie. 'I know this gorgeous Greek restaurant off the Tottenham Court Road.'

'A *Greek* restaurant? Surely not,' says Angela, testing him. She hasn't made up her mind about him yet. She likes his humour, but not his drugs.

'Oh, but certainly!' replies Delican, 'I adore Greek restaurants. They are Allah's curse on the Greek people for daring to war with the Turks. Now these Greeks are destined for all eternity to run

late-night eateries across the globe, from Tottenham Court Road
to downtown Melbourne. And darlo, you cannot grasp the full
horror of this curse until you've *played* downtown Melbourne.'
Holding his ciggie high, he cries, 'My sweethearts – summon your
coiffeurs and follow me!'

He's got a chauffeur-driven Rolls, which he hires 'when in
town'. Gertjie begs to ride in it. I suppose my disappointment
shows, because Delican suddenly asks if he may travel with us.

Then, as we drive to the restaurant, he charms the pants off
Angela – they start talking Jane Austen, would you believe! – while
I huddle in a corner, trying to work out the set-up here. Are
Delican and Pope a couple? Why has Pope never left Gertjie's side
all evening?

It's happening again – everyone wants to cuddle the puppy.

And the eternal question – is Gertjie as straight as he
seems?

But by the time we reach the restaurant, there's a new development: Charlotte is going all-out for a reunion with Pope. The two
of them have retreated to the furthermost corner of our table, a
shadowy corner, and, in between sniffs at the ivory phial, they're
whispering at top speed.

Delican beats me to the seat next to Gertjie, orders champers
and food, then turns back to Angela.

'People don't know this too much, but your Miss Austen – she
was writing about Palace society. It's true,' he says, slapping
Angela's wrist when she laughs. 'She's a Palace author. In *Sense
and Sensibility* when Marianne is visited by ... what's that gorgeous gringo called? ... Mr Darcy –'

'No,' says Angela firmly, 'Darcy's from –'

'Oh, who cares, darlo – it's all the same story. Young women
so, so bored with *aaaaalll* this spare time and oh my God,
everyone's dying with love and their hearts are burnt to a cinder,
but all they can do is talk, look, signal and tease. And the Ameri-
cans think they've only just invented safe sex? No, no, it was Jane
Austen who invented safe sex.'

Angela hoots with mirth. Delican stubs out his ciggie and lights
two more, handing one to Pope in the shadows.

'In the Palace, my darlo,' continues Delican, 'the people are

71

addicted to suffering. In those times they use the moon calendar, you know? And on full moon, the master will put his guests into boats, and he will pay for music boats, and they will all row to a part of the Bosporus where the river joins. And here on the moonlit bay, with all the stars in the heavens, the greatest star of them all, the Palace singer, now gives voice to everyone's suffering . . .'

As Delican starts to sing, one hand springs to his temple – half-protective, half-defiant – like good old Judy Garland. His face, that painted boxer's face, contorts with exquisite pain, his throat opens, and a Muslimy warble comes out, cutting across the Greek muzak, and silencing every table. Even Pope and Charlotte come out of the shadows to listen.

As soon as he has everyone's attention, Delican stretches out his arms, and whispers:

'And suddenly the singer stops, and the music stops, and now there is silence in the boats, and now everyone listens to . . . to what? Ah, to the nightingales.'

'Ah,' cries Angela, and raises her glass, 'bravo!'

Delican takes her hand. 'Oh darlo, I should have lived then. Because where did it go – this addiction of suffering? Where did it make these tortured men and women go? To their own sex, where else.'

Angela laughs.

'It's true, darlo, it's true. The women rush to their women friends for weeping, and the men rush to their men friends for wrestling. To fight-fight-fight with the frustration.' He grabs Gertjie's arms to demonstrate, flailing them around. 'It's true. It's all in your Miss Austen – just read it.'

'D. H. Lawrence more like,' laughs Angela.

'Tch! It's all the same story, darlo,' says Delican, keeping hold of Gertjie. 'The world turns around the same story. When you are overflowing, you visit your same sex.'

I watch Gertjie. He's not following much of the spiel, but he doesn't like Delican holding his hand.

'The Palace understood this,' continues Delican, 'this need for your same sex. The *Ichoglan* . . .' He turns to Pope. 'How would you say this?'

Pope pauses, taking the limelight for a sec, then, giving one of those quick modest smiles, says, 'Well, you could say interior boy, indoor boy. Tribute boy. I guess it's like a page-boy.'

'OK, these things. So – a boy, non-Muslim, he is kept for the sake of the master inside one of the big houses. Later the boy will go away and get married himself. But for now he must learn the Koran, music, falconry, shampooing, turban-dressing. And, from the master, the older man, he must learn wisdom and he must ... *koli kesmek*?' he asks Pope.

'Cut parcel' – is Pope's translation. He directs it to Gertjie, so it is Gertjie who speaks for us all:

'What?'

'He must be fucked.'

Gertjie drops his gaze and fixes it on the tablecloth. I've never seen him look so red. Like in the car earlier, there's suddenly a real Afrikaner among us, burning with Afrikaner piety.

My God, he's as straight as they come!

All these weeks of thinking about him, and always pretending I wasn't. All that energy.

The table's gone silent. Have people heard my thoughts? I laugh, then say to Pope, 'So you speak Turkish?'

'Naa, not much. Just enough to get by in – just some of the swearing.' He smiles. Over the evening these smiles have become more like shivers. He's at a different party, and returns to it now. In the shadowy corner, Charlotte is refilling the ivory phial from supplies in her handbag. The phial just catches the light as Pope slips it under his napkin.

What I wouldn't do for one little sniff.

I turn to Angela. I need either her blessing or her strength. Her strength? She's hitting the champers like crazy. She'd never notice if I – No! I cannot, *cannot* go through another coke-over day.

'So, this is fascinating,' Angela says to Delican. 'You're saying that it was all right to be gay in Ottoman – sorry, Palace times?'

'My life, my love, *canim*,' he says, 'when has it ever been all right? Which society? When? The Ottomans were no different from modern-day Turks. On the one hand, our boys are cutting parcel all over the show. On the other, there is punishment.' He chuckles. 'And my dear, our jails are not as glamorous as these movies you see. Yeah,' he drawls, suddenly staring at Gertjie again in that strange, leaden way.

'How long were you in for?' asks Angela quietly.

Delican smiles, kisses her shoulder, then says, 'Where is our food? In Istanbul, my arse could not hit a chair without twenty dishes hitting the table first. But ah! – I still don't get to eat. People come up, one following the other: "Sing for us, Delican, please sing for my wife, for my mother – she's worshipped you for thirty years – for my daughter, lighten her soul with song."'

Delican blows a smoke-ring, before continuing. 'And then there is another line of pilgrims to my table. Young men, all with the same frightened look, all with the same question, though most don't get up the courage to ask it. "How did you do it, Delican? How did you find a way of living openly, freely – as what you are – in our society?"'

'Everyone knows about you then?' asks Angela.

'Knows or decides not to know. And the blind and deaf – maybe they don't know. Back home I write in the newspapers, talk about it on TV.'

'So it is permitted?'

'Permitted? No, no. These pilgrims are young and don't remember. It is true I have always lived openly, but not always freely. You asked how long I was *in* for. Who knows? In and out over the years. It's difficult to avoid, when many of your lovers are policemen. They get cross when you ditch them.'

'And in jail . . . you were mistreated?'

'Oh certainly,' says Delican, amazed by such a stupid question. He turns to Gertjie, who has looked up. 'Hmn?' purrs Delican.

'He doesn't speak much English,' I volunteer.

'But of course he does,' says Delican, again amazed by our stupidity. 'But he too has been...' he smiles at Angela, '"mistreated". And sometimes after you have been mistreated, silence is easier.'

Angela and I look at Gertjie. His expression is as surprising as Delican's news. He seems relieved.

I stare and stare.

'You get to know the face,' Delican explains. 'It can be from another jail. It can be for another crime. It can be from another country. But you know him.'

'Why the word "crime"?' asks Angela. 'Why not "crusade"?'

'I love her,' Delican cries, turning to me. 'I love your wife. Can I have her? I must have her! I love her pretty British words.' He turns to Gertjie. 'Were you *in* for a *crusade*, cicim? And was it your *crusade* they *mistreated* you for?'

His piss-take is done gently, but Angela goes quiet. Delican reaches over to the dark corner of the table and plucks the ivory phial from between the rowing, jabbering pair – they're up to such speed, they could be on fast-forward – and, without bothering with the napkin, he takes two massive snorts, both up the same nostril.

'They *mistreated* this half more,' he explains, tapping the other nostril, then offers the phial.

'And is that the reason?' Angela asks, gently pushing away his hand – *ai!* – 'Is that your reason for taking this stuff?'

'Certainly, yes,' laughs Delican. 'Why not? Once or twice a year. But boy – what a once or twice! As, if God permits, you will see tonight. Do you know what the name Delican means?' He drops his voice an octave – 'Mad heart.'

Angela gives in suddenly, giggling. (She's pissed.) 'Oo duck,' she says in deepest Dudley, 'I don't half love a heart wi' madness pulsin' through it.'

'Try then,' says Delican, offering the phial again.

She shakes her head. 'Too scared,' she whispers. 'Too scared of the madness in me own.'

They grin and kiss, and the phial is passed to Gertjie. Now Delican cries, 'At last – our feast!' and we turn to see some waiters approaching the table.

A trip to the ballet makes two things impossible: sleeping and grazing. So me and Angela are the only hungry ones. Delican watches us start *fressing* like pigs, then he nudges Gertjie and they shift their chairs into the dark corner, joining Pope's party.

Half an hour later, when me and Angela finally flop back, our very veins thick with hummus, the other group are very, very speedy. Delican wipes some grease from the corner of Angela's mouth and says, 'You need a wash, darlo. So, all my loved ones

– summon your coiffeurs please and follow Delican back to the hotel, for one of his famous, famous SHOWER PARTIES!'

This time everyone else rides in the Rolls, while me and Angela stagger to the Jag. Angela really shouldn't drive, but does. I huddle against the window, squinting at my reflection. All I can see is my squat forehead, with cartoon bubbles escaping:

So Gertjie's straight.

He's been in jail.

What for?

He was mistreated there.

How exactly?

(We should go home. This evening is up to no good.)

By the time we reach Delican's suite in Thingamajig on the Strand, the others are well settled in. Gertjie's even speedier; grinning a lot, licking his itching gums, and his Brylcreemed hairdo has split into strands. (Someone ruffled it, maybe?) Charlotte's very uptight. She reaches into her Chanel bag. There's another bag within, a plastic bag like for fruit at the supermarket, but full of powder. She plonks this white balloon on the glass coffee-table. Pope is pacing round the walls, cat-like with his black suit and sleek black hair, running one hand over the faux-marbled and mirrored surfaces. Delican relaxes on the sofa.

'Welcome,' he says. 'We waited for you.'

Waited? What for? He can't have been serious about the shower. I glance at Angela. She looks excited.

'Come, please,' says Delican and leads into the bathroom. The shower is giant. We *could* all fit in. At a squeeze. But Delican walks past it to the sink. He wets a tissue, wipes Angela's greasy mouth, then leads, thank God, back to the lounge.

I'm very sorry, but if he'd been serious about the shower, I'd've been forced to get my nose into that white balloon, and I don't think anyone could blame me. The thought – *oich*! – of my pink and ginger kilos exposed to them all. And Angela's big bod – *oich*!

'My darlos,' says Delican, 'please feel yourselves at home.' I head straight for the mini-bar, grabbing a mini-Smirnoff, and handing Angela a mini-Moët.

'Got any decent porn?' asks Pope, noticing that a video machine has been installed under the TV.

'Only of chaps,' says Delican, eyes a-flutter.

'That'll do,' says Pope, then turns to us all. 'Any objections?'

'Huh!,' mutters Charlotte, who's teasing out eight-inch lines across the table.

Gertjie has dropped his gaze, cheeks burning.

I laugh nervously. 'Actually *I'm* not that keen. Y'know. To watch a bunch of consenting adults catching AIDS. Y'know, who needs it?'

Pope fixes his dark gaze on me. 'That remark is, with respect, bollock-bendingly dumb.'

'Leon's only joking,' says Angela quickly. 'Go on, put on what you want. We don't mind. 'll be fun.'

Pope mumbles something, then switches on the TV. While he searches for a tape, we find ourselves watching a late night discussion. It's on South African sanctions! I bury my nose in my glass, and arrange my fingers so I can spy on Gertjie.

He's sitting forward, alert.

'We are tired,' a black man is saying, 'tired of hearing how sanctions will hurt us . . .'

I glance at the screen. A heavy face with red eyes.

'What we say is: Are we not hurting already? So OK, let us be hurt one more time, and then be cured.'

'You know him?' Gertjie asks quietly.

I shake my head.

'The poet, Mafeje. In exile here.'

Although Gertjie's voice is calm, his expression is terrible. Dazed and raw.

'A hero of the people . . .' Gertjie adds vaguely.

I mustn't keep staring. I turn back to the screen, and gasp. Before my eyes, the black face turns into a white dick. An erect white dick pointing at us; the camera descending like a mouth.

Angela giggles. 'Could be a wildlife programme,' she says, 'you know, when they suddenly surprise an earthworm in close-up.'

'Nothing like our Islington earthworms,' says Charlotte, aiming a McDonald's straw at the table. 'In fact – *oogh!* – I've never seen an earthworm – *oogh!* – as huge.'

77

'No?' says Pope, standing. 'You've got a short memory then,' and he reaches for his flies.

'Oh!' me and Angela squeal.

'Dear me, *yours*,' yawns Charlotte. 'Now, remind me – did I ever see that upright?'

'I dunno, darling,' he replies, 'would you remember if you'd seen it painted green?'

'OK kids, kids!' says Delican, clapping his hands.

Pope walks to the bathroom, says, 'Right, who's for a shower?', and goes in, leaving the door open.

'Me . . .' says Angela, with a little sigh, and rises.

'Don't be crazy,' I whisper, pulling her back.

But I'm powerless to stop the next volunteer. Gertjie bolts into the bathroom, closing the door.

I look at the others. Angela and Delican chuckle indulgently, while Charlotte hides her face and doodles in a spread of powder. I look at the TV. On a sunny, snowy mountain-top, a Canadian Mountie and a Red Indian are smooching.

'Uhm . . .' I whisper to Delican, 'I think you'd better warn Pope – Gertjie's straight.'

'Even when he's indoors?' asks Delican.

'What?'

'*Ichoglan*, yes? An indoor boy.'

'Is he?'

'In your home.'

'What?'

'Where he is educated and cuts some parcel.'

'*What?* No! Absolutely not! He's straight.'

Delican smiles and crosses to the bathroom door. A cloud of steam escapes as he opens it. He waves, then returns to the sofa. Angela goes over for a look. She does the same thing – chuckles and waves. Charlotte is next. She neither chuckles nor waves.

Trembling, I go to the door. Within a fog of steam, the first thing is Pope's black suit on the white floor, then Gertjie's clothes nearby. The boys are in the shower. Not touching. Pope looks half-erect, though it's difficult to tell – he's got such a hosepipe. Gertjie's back is to me. It's a beautiful back, the spine pointing like an arrow – WHOOMF! – to that hard, jutting *toches*, and the fur on his legs, darker than I expected, running with water.

'Come and join us,' Pope calls.

I chuckle, wave and return to my seat.

'Well, sweetheart,' asks Delican, 'does our little biscuit look straight to you?'

'Yes he does, actually. He's having a wash. He often washes.'

Delican whoops and turns to Angela. 'I love your husband. This husband I must have.'

'Be my guest,' giggles Angela. 'You two can wash next.'

They shriek with laughter. Angela opens another quarter Moët, which explodes, bubbling, over her dress, while Delican bends over a huge line on the table. I don't warm to him so much anymore. In fact, I wouldn't mind jumping on that bowed head, with its lacquered hair, and smashing it through the glass.

There are no more Smirnoffs in the fridge. I open a Kentucky bourbon.

Still giggling, Angela goes for another look in the bathroom. A good long look. 'Yes indeed, washing away,' she says, falling back onto the sofa.

'Lay-lay-lum,' sings Delican, visiting the door. 'Oh my God!' he says, hand to forehead, 'certainly, yes – this is *washing*!' He pops into the bathroom and re-emerges with one hand covered in foam. Touching a dollop to my nose as he passes, he flops in front of the TV. A lumberjack has joined the Mountie and the Indian.

'Your turn,' says Delican, without turning to me. Angela giggles.

'Oh, please,' I mutter, and rise. I stroll round the room, examining its splendour, a *tsatske* here, a *tsatske* there, dwelling at the window, gazing at the moonlit Thames. Finally I reach the bathroom door.

My God, they *are* washing! Separate, not touching; each observing the other soap himself. Pope's shlonger looks even longer, though it's still aiming down. Actually, it could do with a good wash. One of those discoloured ones, y'know. Maybe a tar brush once passed his way.

Gertjie still has his back to the door. He glances over his shoulder at me, and smiles almost teasingly.

I stagger back to my seat. Things have gone very still. Charlotte sits huddled in anger, while Angela and Delican are glued to the Canadian gang-bang. I put back my head, staring at the chandelier. I hear the lumberjack grunting, the Indian moaning, and the Mountie muttering things like, 'Yeah, do it, just do it, that's right, yeaahh!'; and, all the time, a disco beat, *doef-doef-doef*. Angela reaches out and takes my hand. Nice. Until I realise her finger is scratching my palm. I shake my head and withdraw. She sighs and reaches into the mini-bar – bringing out a lager for God's sake! I hate seeing her drunk. Her skin unravels, and she grows extra elbows and knees. I grab another bourbon.

Now Delican picks up the remote control and slowly presses the sound button. The Canadian gang-bang slowly quietens, the *doef-doef-doef* slowly fades, and the noise of the shower slowly takes over: *shhhhhhh* . . .

Angela is first to snigger.

'OK,' Delican whispers, 'whose turn?'

Charlotte springs up and darts to the door. This time the view makes her gasp. She turns, tries to head back, but is trampled in our stampede. The boys are on the shower floor, Pope lying on top of Gertjie, about to kiss him.

Leaving Delican and Angela ogling, I lurch to the table. 'Can I?' I ask Charlotte, nodding to the white balloon. She shrugs, indicating it's Delican's. 'Agh, won't mind,' I mutter. The ivory phial is lying abandoned. I plough it into the balloon, then clip it shut, and put it in my pocket.

'Your friend should feel flattered,' says Charlotte. 'Normally Pope doesn't do it with anyone but future sponsors.'

'Ah-huhn.'

'In fact, *you* should've been this evening's victim.'

'Oh well, there you go.' I march back to the bathroom door, and, without looking in, grab Angela's arm. 'Right, are we ready to roll?'

'But –'

'But what?' I ask, steering her across the room. 'Haven't you got school tomorrow?'

'Ohh!'

'OK, people,' I say to anyone who's listening, 'thanks very much, *dankie en tot siens*, great evening, ciao' – and we're out of that suite at last! Into the silent, normal corridor, the graceful lift, the deserted foyer, the early morning Strand.

I shouldn't drive, I know I shouldn't, but what the fuck hey?, and my Jag cartwheels home.

Inside, Angela climbs the stairs on hands and knees, and vanishes.

I search my wine cellar and open the oldest claret we've got: Chateau Latour 1937. '37 was the year my dad fled Poland. I think the bottle was one of La's special presents for something or other. I pour, listening to the stuff go *lap-lap-lap*....

To snort or not to snort? That is the question.

I roam the dark house, trailing bottle and glass, doing Dad's walk, heave-ho, heave-ho. Remember hearing him as a kid, hey? The way he'd roam the house every night, heave-ho.

There's a photograph somewhere on the mantelpiece, somewhere among all Angela's Victoriana crap; a photograph of Dad's parents getting married in Poland. Nothing special. A couple of old-fashioned Jews, staring out with very serious faces. Pissed off, actually. Because they can't see. They can stare out, yet they can't see. So they're wondering what we look like: the descendants they're about to go fuck into being; the great Lipschitz trail they're determined to leave, snail-like, across history. And they can't even see us!

Well, dear old *zaideh* and *bobbeh*, I share your feelings about history, so let me tell you how yours turned out. Here we are, in England and South Africa; some have fled onwards to Canada, Australia, Israel. Who would've thought you could cast your seed so wide, hey? Here we are in our big houses at night. Big rich rooms lit by little rich lights, ruby and turquoise, from the digital clocks on our videos, microwaves and radio alarms. They're good for night duty, these lights; they keep you asleep and awake at the same time, but they're cold – colder than moonlight. Even the moonlight over the Bosporus. Did you ever travel to the Bosporus, my dear old *zaideh* and *bobbeh* – did you, darlos? You tell me, while I just put this ivory phial to my nose and breathe in till I can breathe no more. Nothing for you to worry about; you know the Lipschitzes suffer from sinus trouble.

Wragh! – and OK, let's jawl!

I phone the cops and report a wild coke party in a famous hotel. I give all details, except my name.

Back into the Jag. Ah, summer nights in London. Digital moons and grubby orange skies. Warm, bright, still hours; the perfect time for some. A lady tramp, the fattest you've ever seen, with a puppy on a rope. She uses these warm, bright hours to move her collection of bags. She adds one load to a pile already on the traffic island, then goes back for more. I hope no one steals any while she's away.

I park on the crest of the Heath, next to Jack Straw's Castle, and walk to the top of a path which plunges, black and deep, into the undergrowth.

(And here he is again: the fat man standing on a clifftop.)

I step forward.

The path's so steep, and the Heath so dark, I keep missing my footing; it's like stepping on feathers; I half-run, half-fall into the forest below.

Haven't been here for years, but I can still remember the magic route. The coven's just ahead, in that clump of trees. Haven't seen anyone yet. Probably won't be a soul these days – these safety-first days.

But heavens, the coven is swarming with glow-worms! Dozens of travelling ciggies. The hot weather has brought them from the moffie-houses and bars, everyone too itchy to sleep.

A blast up each nostril, then I unzip and plunge in. The scrum reeks of amyl, booze and spunk. OK, guys, I'm here – do with me what you will! But each shadow just takes one look and moves on. *How does he know?* I can't see him, so how can he see me? How does he know I'm this pink and ginger blob? I dart into some bushes and sniff the phial. Someone's nearby, at waist level. Either a midget, or on his knees. He starts sucking me. It's very nice, but somebody's got to remember their safety first. 'Why are you always doing that?' he splutters as I withdraw. I peer into the dark and whisper, 'I'm sorry, do I know you?' But he's gone. I stagger back into the main scrum and fondle someone's leg. It's the root of a tree. So who's fussy? I stay there, snorting my ivory and pulling my wire. People pass. The darkness makes everyone look negroid. Gertjie should come here; it'd be interesting for a

Boer. I wonder how a British jail will compare with his experiences in SA? Be interesting for him anyway.

It's his fault I'm on the Heath again. It's his fault I'm snorting again. It's *all* his fault, so he deserves whatever shit lands on his head, the little cunt-sucking bum-boy!

And *whoopsadaisy*, here I am alone in the dawn light, hanging onto a tree, my chin dripping with snot or tears, trousers round my ankles – giving an early jogger one helluva bloody fright.

TEN

So – another coke-over day. Another dead day, another day when only fingernails and stubble grow.

Despite my feelings about newspapers, I make a lunge for the *Standard* when Angela brings it home. She doesn't notice. Still grey from last night, she goes into the conservatory for a zizz. I unfold the paper. Nothing on the front, so I straightaway start jumping with joy. Listen, I was so drunk I could easily have imagined that call to the cops. But on page four, there's a tiny item.

> POPE IN DRUGS BUST
>
> The theatre and video whiz-kid, Pope, was last night arrested on a charge of possessing cocaine. Earlier this year, Pope, twenty-six, whose real name is John Paul Dicks, published a comic-strip autobiography, *Pope's Progress*, which although portraying a racy lifestyle, specifically condemns drug-taking. Arrested with him was a Turkish entertainer, Cihangir Delican, fifty-seven.

Why is there no mention of Gertjie and Charlotte?

I'm sitting there trembling, when the phone rings. 'Leon?' says a familiar voice.

'*Charlotte!*'

'Have you heard?' she asks.

'*Ja*. But who could've . . . ?'

84

'Perhaps the people in the next suite. After you left, things got a little rowdy. Delican tried to join them in the shower, but Pope locked the door. So Delican broke it down. Then Hirkie threw –'

'Who? *Gertjie?*'

'Mm. He threw up. So I offered to take him home. Just in time, as it happens. We actually passed the fuzz in the foyer.'

'Hell, poor kid must be shocked shitless. I'd better give him a bell.'

'No, he's still here. Let me see if I can stir ... Hirkie? Hirkie? It's Leon.'

I listen, horrified. He's there – he's lying next to her!

'Nope,' she says, returning to the receiver. 'I'm afraid we stayed up rather. He's completely hopeless as a stud. Just wants to cuddle. Which actually suits me tickety. Especially the way he cuddles – my word, he can make one feel rather special! Oh, but I mustn't go and fall in love again, must I?'

'What?'

'Well, you saw the previous miscarriage.'

'I'm sorry?'

'Pope.'

'Oh, *ja.*'

'Serves the turd right though, don't you think?'

'Falling in love with you?'

'The bust.'

'Ah-huhn. Oh – the doorbell!' I suddenly yell, staring down the silent hallway.

I ring off, but keep hold of the receiver. Why don't I bell the cops again? Why don't I give them an address in Islington?

No. Enough, as they say.

The weather gets hotter. You wake with a feeling of hopelessness; the air in the bedroom is stale, the sheets half their former size. You go into the bathroom and the cold tap runs hot. Down in the kitchen, you have to keep turning up the fridge. And all round the house, curtains and blinds must be constantly drawn to stop the bleaching of La's books, and the roasting of her plants.

These sunny-dark rooms are so unEnglish.

Likewise the streets – with the stink of trash leaking from tilting dustbin lids, and fat insects humming. The cars are dusty, or tacky with sap that's fallen like sweat from the trees. The lawns, squares and parks are going bald under crowds of panting office workers; tinny music coming from ice cream vans and a hundred rusting wirelesses. On building sites, the young labourers strip down to running shorts, and the red brick dust coats them like tribal warriors.

I spend hours flopped out by our pool, leafing through my collection of comics: I've got originals from the forties and fifties – Dells, Marvels, Superman DC's, a 3-D Mighty Mouse, and the very first *Mad Magazine*. Although I stay under a parasol, the sunrays still manage to seek me out. They love a red-head. At night, if I sit near a lightbulb, it burns. During the day, the heat from traffic burns.

As well as the comics, I'm reading Angela's diary. I got into the habit after her confession on my birthday weekend.

It's mostly very boring; she hardly mentions me. All just stuff about her show at school. She met up with some anti-Apartheid and ANC people for her research. They already knew of her, because of the huge monthly donations. She promptly made another, paying for repairs to one of their offices; they'd had a fire, maybe arson. Now they're so crazy with gratitude, they're helping on her show.

My wife, the great liberal champ. Or chump.

But mind you, she's been very supportive about the Gertjie business. I came clean, admitted that my brain got jammed on Gertjie. Angela reckons it's been jammed on him all my life. She was wondering if maybe the South African Jew isn't obsessed by the Afrikaner, because of his vague, and sometimes not so vague, resemblance to a certain German type in recent history. Well, I'm sure that's all very interesting, but I still see it as good old-fashioned infatuation. My brain just jammed on him.

Anyhow, who needs an immature, dumb, bisexual, Afrikaans-speaking ex-convict who's busy having a nervous breakdown? Or worse than a nervous breakdown? I reckon the boy hasn't actually got both oars in the water; he isn't actually a full box of chocolates.

So he's not for me, no thank you. I've cut him out of my life one hundred and one percent. He phones quite a lot, but never gets past the answer-machine. He's written as well. I threw away the letters without a glance, which I'm damn proud of.

If I'm ever tempted to weaken, I just have to remember one incident.

We were fooling around on the long lawn one hot arvie, me, him and Alphonsia (who was still around then), when I fetched out my Polaroid. Gertjie said he hated having his photo taken. C'mon, said Alphons, I haven't got a single snap of you. No, he said. Yes, she said, aiming the camera. He went bananas – started hitting his own face. Really hard. Again and again. Like he was seriously trying to blatt himself. When we forced his hands down, that beautiful face was a mess of blood.

So – best way to remember him, hey?

ELEVEN

G ertjie is staring at me. Nearby, something is ticking, or tapping. What is it? I dare not shift my eyes off him. Now he takes a deep breath.

'I was born in the Eastern Cape. Right over by the Ciskei border. The dorp where I'm from is in a very dry area. You know what this word means – *dorp*?'

'Of course. Little town.'

'Called Suurvlei. O K and translate this – *Suurvlei*.'

I shrug. 'Sour something? A lake?'

'A sort of shallow lake. Sour shallow lake. Suurvlei. Your Afrikaans is better than you pretend.'

'So is your English.'

He smiles. 'Yes.'

(*Excuse me, but is this happening?*)

It's Sunday morning. Angela's away rehearsing her show. *Ja*, on a Sunday – apparently the kids have gone nuts for the township music, and voted (it's a democratic school) to rehearse today. I only woke up just now. Unbelievable hangover, completely *unreal*, so I knocked back a Bloody Mary and staggered down to the pool with the Sunday papers; I *smaak* the mags and comics. I'd just finished coating myself in every sunscreen known to man (ending up like a sculpture in cream cheese), when the doorbell went.

Gertjie standing there. A new, articulate Gertjie. 'I owe you an explanation,' he says; 'please can I come in?'

So we're sitting by the pool. The day is hot and still – except for this mysterious ticking, tapping noise. Gertjie's refused a drink and asked me not to either. He has a story to tell and wants me to listen carefully.

'I haven't been in jail,' he says now. 'Delican made a mistake there. What he smelt on me was my father's scent. A policeman. Ran the station at Suurvlei single-handed. Which wasn't helluva hard. Suurvlei is like those one-horse towns you can see in the cowboy movies. I grew up a real *plaasjapie* . . .'

'Country-bumpkin,' I say, before he can ask.

'*Ja*. But I wasn't a very good country bumpkin. Wasn't very good at the outdoor life. Playing rugby or hunting dassies. So, as you can imagine, Leon, I was a bit of a disappointment to my Pa. He's a real old-style Boer. Down to earth. That kind of hard strength, you know? And there I was, his only child, but nothing in common. Like you and your father, isn't it?'

Surprised that he knows, I gesture vaguely.

'I take after my Ma more. She was the schoolteacher at Suurvlei, with a great love of language and learning. Every month, when the travelling library came through, she'd *sommer* borrow everything and anything. Reading, reading. I'd always see her with her head down, reading . . .'

'Angela,' I murmur.

'Very like Angela. That same need, almost desperation, to keep learning. But if Angela was frustrated in her hometown . . . Derek?'

'Dudley.'

'*Ja-nee*, she must first come and spend a week or two in Suurvlei. Farmers talking about sheep, their wives talking about church. And the policeman's home full of books! *O' yirra*, he was so ashamed of it all – Ma's books, and me.' Gertjie grins – that fabulous white grin.

I shift on the sun-lounger, and rearrange my Harrods beach wrap-around.

'When I was ten, Pa was transferred to Joburg. *Joeys* – the big city! I was happier there. More books and less rugby. More disappointment for Pa. Our first big showdown came when I left school. He was still hoping I'd follow him into the force. He was by now *Major* van der Bijl. But I was set on varsity. Anyhow, after my two years in the army, up on the Angola border, a bad time which . . . agh, never mind, I went to Wits, reading Aeronautical Engineering.'

'Jesus!'

'This was the mid-eighties. The state of emergency had just come in. Mind-blowing times. Among my people, I'd never heard anyone slate the government. Now suddenly I'm hearing nothing else. Loads of unrest on the campus . . .' He stops and thinks. 'It's funny that Delican smelt jail on me. And "mistreatment". Because actually I was always treated with kid gloves when I was arrested. Major van der Bijl's son. But then, one time – this must be about two years ago – a group of us were arrested during a demo, and taken to police headquarters, the Blue Hotel. As soon as we come there, I'm separated from the others, taken into this lift, along a corridor, on and on, finally into this office. Panelled in yellow-wood. A polite secretary gets me coffee. She notices my forehead was cut during the arrest, so she sends for a nurse. A kind old *tannie* comes, and she cleans the cut. Then I'm asked to wait. Here I am – in the notorious Blue Hotel, sipping a cup of coffee and nibbling a Marie biscuit.'

(I can't stop gawping. Can this be Gertjie? He looks like Gertjie, smells like Gertjie, but doesn't sound like Gertjie. His voice has caught that cool tune from all the Yankee soap operas on South African TV. The only thing that still sounds like the *plaasjapie* Gertjie, is the way he says 'wif' for 'with').

'The guy who now comes into the office, looks a bit familiar. Maybe he's been with Pa round by our house a few times. A very courteous, soft-spoken man. Introduces himself as Colonel Fourie, but asks me please to call him *Oom*. I reply no thank you sir, but you're not my uncle, so I'll call you Colonel Fourie. He doesn't take offence. He starts talking. I interrupt, saying I refuse to conduct the conversation in Afrikaans. He doesn't take offence. Switching to English, he now asks me to please stop all my political activities. He says it is breaking my father's heart. I tell him that's not his business. He says no, with the greatest respect, I'm wrong here. Unfortunately, it is very much his business. And the business of all my father's colleagues. They're all finding it very hard to keep protecting me. Protecting me? *Ja*, he says, my father's work is sensitive. The whole situation is more sensitive than I realise. I laugh. "Sensitive" – this is now a word from spy movies, hey? OK, I say, so tell me what you mean by "sensitive"? So he tells me.'

As Gertjie pauses now, the ticking, tapping noise starts up again. He twists round to look. On the step to the diving board, a bird has a snail in its beak, smashing the shell against the marble edge. Gertjie gives a dry laugh, then turns back.

'*Ja*, so he told me. I was surprised by my reaction. Sick there and then. Almost before I'd absorbed the news. Sick on his yellow-wood floor. I was so unprepared. Him being so nice hadn't helped. The word "sensitive" hadn't helped. D'you see?'

I nod, without quite following, though a chill travels through me. *Tuk-tuk* goes the snail shell against the marble, *tuk-tuk*.

'Colonel Fourie summoned his secretary and she summoned the kind old nurse. One cleaned my vomit, the other cleaned me. When we were alone again, Fourie said he understood how I felt. Explained that nobody finds Pa's work pleasant, and that he was one of the few men brave enough to do it. Now I was scared of his words. *Brave*? Oh yes, he said, very brave. There is a war going on here in this land, God's land – a holy war. And in times of war, prisoners have to be questioned. And to question a fellow human being, to force him into areas he's resisting – this is going to take a sacrifice on both sides. Obviously from the man refusing to answer the questions, but also from the man doing the asking. Nobody who witnesses human suffering at close quarters gets to walk away in peace. But the difference is that the man asking the questions, he has *volunteered* to enter this hell. For his country, he has volunteered. This takes bravery.'

My mouth is hanging open. Gertjie takes my hand. 'Maybe,' he says, 'this is what Delican smelt on me.'

'Maybe,' I mumble. I feel no sexual charge holding his hand (his skin is rougher than I expected); I just wish I could fetch a drink. This heat is terrible. The Sunday papers have already turned yellow, which makes their news look old. In the garden, every leaf and flower is dying. There's a hosepipe ban these days.

91

Angela's been sneaking out under cover of darkness, to water the more precious stuff.

'So what happened?' I asked Gertjie.

'Huh?'

'After you found out about your dad.'

'It's hard to explain. Suddenly ordinary things look different – routine things. Pa coming home in the evening. He showers straightaway; changes his clothes. A lot of people do that after work, but it suddenly seems different. The thought, y'know? Watching him touch Ma. So gentle, y'know?' Gertjie scratches a piece of dead skin from his palm. 'I started washing my hands a lot, like he does. Then it got worse. Then I couldn't go for longer than an hour or so without washing all over. Sometimes I still can't.'

I blink, picturing him and Pope in Delican's shower.

'I dropped out of varsity. Dropped out of everything. Started wandering round the city. It felt like when I first arrived from Suurvlei. A ten-year-old *boerklong* in the big city. I went back to speaking Afrikaans only – a childish, *plaasjapie* Afrikaans. It felt safe. It still does; when I'm frightened.'

'Yes,' I say.

He smiles. 'You've noticed?'

'I've noticed.'

We grin at one another. This time a sexual charge does go through me. I'd do anything for a drink!

'But agh, thereafter . . .' sighs Gertjie, 'things really went *holdersebolder*. So I entered this nursing home. Signed my-self in. Stayed there for a long time. Ma and Pa visited every weekend.'

'Does she know about him?' I ask.

'I don't know. Probably. Anyhow, she loves him.'

Gertjie says this casually. It's a fact of life; to be regretted maybe, but not questioned.

'I couldn't go back to living with them,' he says, 'when I left the nursing home. I was supposedly cured, except now I had veld fever – just longing for all that fresh air and clean earth! So I went back to Suurvlei.' He smiles. 'Shame. Poor old Suurvlei, the one-horse town of my childhood: even the one horse had left.

Now it was like a ghost town from the cowboy movies.' He winces. '*Eina!* Everything gone. Except the police station. A big new police station. Just in case the holy war ever reached that far. Hoo boy no, I couldn't stay in Suurvlei either.'

'So you came here?' I say.

'*Ja*, well, everybody agreed a few years overseas would be a good idea. See the world, as they say, the *outside* world. And my ma's brother is a bigshot with Air South Africa. And after all, I had been studying Aeronautical Engineering!' He laughs. 'ASA did their best to train me, but . . . you saw the results.'

We both laugh.

I look at him. 'It's funny, y'know, to think that the weirdo I met there was you.'

'No, well, *ja* . . .' He rubs his face, his cheeks – as if trying to rub away those permanent blushes. 'I've still not completely come right. Agh, it sounds too pathetic to say, but I can still sort of go in and out of myself. Like those boys in the army who go bush-mad – the thousand-yard stare. You see it happening and you think why don't they just stop it? Same with me. I see it happening, so why don't I just stop it? *Toemaar, alles sal regkom, né*? It'll just take time.'

Suddenly he points to the pool. 'Funny to see English sunlight in a swimming pool. If you close your eyes half-half, you can imagine you're back home.'

I try it. 'Mmn.'

'Do you miss it?' he asks.

'South Africa? More and more.'

'*Ja*? I was drawn to you from that first morning in the Airways. Drawn to you. That's why I took your phone number when they fired me.'

I swallow hard. 'Drawn? How d'you mean?'

'Your eyes. First and foremost.'

I shift on the sun-lounger. My eyes are, by the way, my best feature. Green. They have been described as dreamy. At the moment they're pointing straight out front. My heart's going nuts. *Tuk-tuk* goes the bird with another snail, *tuk-tuk*.

'Your eyes,' Gertjie says again.

'Mmm?'

'The eyes of someone who's really, *really* looked into the future.'

'Someone who's what?'

'I'm not talking about heroes, freedom fighters. I'm talking about ordinary people. You and me.'

'You and me?'

'People who've maybe run away. People who can't bear the thought of what's going to happen next.'

'Happen next?'

'In the Republic.'

I sit back, fazed.

'You see,' he says, 'whether it's a black revolution, or a white police coup – with Pa leading the troops – or a peaceful hand-over of power ... doesn't matter, man, the one certainty is that we're going to vanish. White South Africans will become extinct. Legendary, notorious, but extinct. Like French royalty or White Russians. This is now our destiny also. What were they like, future generations will ask – what were white South Africans like? People who pushed out the frontiers of evil, while trumpeting the name of the Lord – did it make them all go crazy? Or is evil banal and invisible? What were they like, oh tell us, where were they *like*?'

Gertjie leans forward and takes my hand again. 'So you see – that's why we can't make sense of our lives, you and me. History is going to swallow us up. And History knows this. In the great scheme of things, we're already ghosts. A lonely feeling, hey?' Although tears are flowing, his face remains calm and his voice steady. 'And *that* is why we were drawn to one another.'

'Well, not quite.' Blushing, I quickly laugh. 'Ghosts! Did I ever tell you that my mom's into spiritualism?'

He stares at me blankly.

I sigh. 'Maybe we should have a talk.'

'I don't think we need to talk anymore.' He strokes my hand. 'We both know.'

My heart starts up again. 'Know?'

'Yes.'

'You're saying ... ?'

'Yes.'

'What, that ... ?'

'Yes.'

'Maybe we're not talking about the same thing.'

'I think we are.'

I'm giddy. I can't see – my eyes are stinging from a sudden flood of sweat and sunscreen. Am I hearing Gertjie right? Don't ask – just kiss. Or does he need a fatherly hug first? *Fatherly*! I'm about to squeak and faint.

Holding my hand, he leads me to the changing room. The timber walls give off a stuffy smell, a good smell, a smell that Dad must've known in Poland during the summer months.

'One promise?' Gertjie asks.

'Anything.'

'If we become boyfriends now ...'

'Yup?'

'It must only be for a short time. Just till your trip back home. By the time you get back I won't even be in London anymore. Understood?'

'Understood.'

'You mustn't – *mustn't* – rely on me,' he says with such urgency I go cold.

Until he hugs me. Or rather, hugs *us*; rocking us, like he did in the lav of that Hammersmith pub. When was that? Not long ago. Not much more than a sec.

TWELVE

Charlotte was right – Gertjie ain't the hottest of lovers. No hard-ons or anything like that. But she was also right about the way he hugs you. It's like he's trying to find shelter. And no one else will do; no one else exists. Man, it's just the best feeling. It could put hard-ons out of business for good.

So I feel a bit dirty somehow, in a glorious kind'f way. I mean, there he is, responding to me with such purity; and there's me – I take one look at his perfect, tense, scrum-half's body, and immediately it's SPROING, YOO-HOO! We're entwined, but in different embraces. I'm the father whose kid crawls into bed while he's asleep, and who wakes with the kid in his arms, and a length of lust throbbing away below. Shame, horror and strength.

I cum like shaken champagne.

Now we're lying peacefully, just licking the sweat off one another.

(Screwing was not on the agenda. Just because a person's meshuggeh with desire, he doesn't have to forget his safety-first. Being Jewish has its advantages: paranoia's not a bad suit of armour. I mean, right now I'm lying here wondering if disease can be carried in sweat?)

Then, from across the lawn, we hear the doorbell.

'Ohh, who?' I groan. 'At one o'clock on a Sunday arvie – who?'

For the second time today, I open my front door to a surprise.

96

'Sorry,' says Angela, her arms full of rehearsal props – assegais, sjamboks and solar topees – 'Can't reach my keys.'

She pushes past, followed by a stranger. Very tall and very black. 'Johnnie Lunguza,' says Angela, 'this is Leon, my husband.'

'OK, hi there, *broe',*' this blue-black character says, giving me a wet hand to shake. Half his jacket is wet too, and there's a fierce smell of whisky. He follows Angela into the kitchen, bumping into the door frame.

'Incredible developments,' Angela cries, unloading her props and rushing into my arms. How different her shape feels to Gertjie; so much taller and fuller. Can she smell him on me? Probably not, thanks to the whisky fumes coming off Johnnie Lunguza.

He's discovered that a half-jack of Teacher's has smashed in his breast pocket. 'Bloody bad thing,' he mutters, then starts emptying the debris and lazily checking for injuries.

'Darling, give Johnnie a drink,' says Angela, digging out her filofax and lifting the phone.

'What's going on?' I ask.

She dials urgently. 'Oh please, let him be in!'

'That man moves about, sister,' says Johnnie, flopping into a chair, 'so many damn meetings – *heh!*'

'We're phoning Moses,' Angela tells me, drumming her fingers on the wall.

'You're phoning Moses?'

'Yes. He'll help.'

'Moses will help?'

'We think so.'

'Which Moses is this?'

'Darling, get us some drinks, please, I'll explain all in a – *Moses!*' she cries into the phone, 'thank goodness you're there. This is Angela Lipschitz – you remember I came to see you about the show I'm doing at my school?'

I go into the lounge, with Johnnie lurching after. We stop at the liquor cabinet. 'What would you – ?' I ask, but he's already reached past.

'Whisky's fine, *broe',*' he says, returning to the kitchen with a twenty-five-year-old Glenmorangie.

I grab a Bell's and give chase.

But before I can do the exchange, Angela hands Johnnie the phone and leads me out onto the patio. I sit at the table, dazed, listening to Johnnie hakking away in some native lingo. And now here comes Gertjie over the lawn; fully dressed, hair neatly combed.

'Ah – Gertjie's here,' says Angela.

'Ah,' say I.

She goes very still. Does she suspect? No – how can she? – Gertjie's blushes are no worse than normal. Then I see her glance to the kitchen door. Ah. Politics, not sex. She's worried about her black South African friend meeting my little Afrikaner one. I smile to myself. Angela still thinks of Gertjie as a little rock-spider farmboy. She's going to be pleased to hear his story.

As Gertjie reaches the patio, Johnnie tumbles out of the kitchen, and says, 'Sister, he's coming round.'

'Moses is coming round,' she repeats breathlessly, and swigs from the bottle of Bell's.

I turn to Gerjie. 'Moses is coming round.'

'Moses?' he says.

'Apparently.'

'Mafeje?' he asks Angela.

'Yes,' she cries, 'coming to our house!' Now she hesitates – she didn't expect Gertjie to know this Moses character. With a puzzled smile, she passes the bottle to him. Johnnie meanwhile carries my Glenmorangie off across the long lawn.

'Hey, *broe'*,' he calls over his shoulder. 'Smart joint!'

(Funny how they use that word, hey? – *broer* is Afrikaans for 'brother'.)

'Angela,' I say, 'that bloke is very drunk.'

'Yes,' she agrees solemnly.

'That's Johnnie Lunguza?' says Gertjie, amazed.

'Yes,' says Angela, 'in *our* house.'

'He'll be in our swimming pool soon,' I say, watching him stroll onto the diving board. 'Angela, please, what is going on?'

Well, the story goes, she and her kids were rehearsing today with Johnnie Lunguza (who's apparently quite a bigshot jazz musician), when the father of one of her cast burst in. A Mr Paul Chagbury, he's a Tory MP; only a backbencher, not well-known – except in the business world, where he's got big South African investments. As well as removing his son from rehearsals, he's threatening to take up the matter with the Board of Governors. South Africa is not, he says, a fitting theme for a school show.

I listen, chin resting on my hands, smelling Gertjie on my fingers. He sits opposite, alert, sweating in the boiling afternoon sun. I reach over and take the bottle of Bell's from his hands, careful not to touch. Not that Angela would notice. Doing this show is changing her – it's not just charitable donations anymore; she's starting to put her mouth where her money is.

'Well, I'm sorry,' I say when she's finished her spiel, 'but I can see this Mr Chagbury's point of view.'

'Why? We've done shows on Saudi Arabia and Japan in the past. What's the difference?'

'Look, I dunno what's in this show of yours – '

'It's the history of South Africa.'

'And that's political.'

'It's *history*!' she cries, bright-eyed. 'The Chagburys of this world want history to be innocent. As innocent as it was during their schooldays. Actually, they'd probably prefer if we didn't teach history at all – just passed round coffee-table books on the English country house. They – '

'*OK*, Angela,' I say, 'we don't need a whole lecture on – '

'Yes, it's boring, I'm sorry.' She thinks, then adds, 'I'm only a teacher of Drama and English, but I don't know how to teach these things without teaching history. I don't know how to teach *Shrew* without mentioning the Pankhursts, *Othello* without mentioning...' She gestures towards Johnnie Lugunza. He's clapped out on my sun-lounger, where, an hour ago, I sat listening to Gertjie's story.

'So all right, what are you organising?' I ask.

'We'll bring things out into the open. Encourage a public debate. A show on South African history, 1652 to present day – should it be allowed to proceed? Discuss.'

'When you say "public", what do you – ?'

'That'll be up to the media.'

'The media,' I groan, putting my head in my hands. 'Angela, Angela, shouldn't you phone Beatrice first?'

'Who's Beatrice?' asks Gertjie.

'Beatrice is our principal,' says Angela, 'principal of Hadsworth House, which offers, as our prospectus puts it, a broad mix of academic, social and artistic activities. Which means that right-wing pricks like Chagbury end up sending his little Sebastian, who happens to be good at drawing, to our leafy portals. Oh, it's all so daft – the school itself is a converted country house.' She closes her eyes. 'Crikey, I am *such* a hypocrite.'

'Angela,' I say, 'phone her. Please. Phone Beatrice before you take another step.'

'I have. And she was very supportive. So long as she doesn't have to be involved.' Angela laughs harshly.

I glance over to Johnnie. 'So, you're going to the media via . . .' I drop my voice, 'the ANC?'

'Well yes, I'll seek the aid of one or two exiles.'

'Exiles!' I scoff, as I watch Johnnie's head nod forward, and the Glenmorangie dribbling into a parched flower-bed.

'Yes, exiles,' she says. 'Exiles get pissed. It is one of the things exiles do. You and Gertjie get pissed. For your different reasons, you all get pissed. I'd better go to him.'

Gertjie intercepts her. 'You're a good woman, Angela. I must just say that, hey? You're not a hypocrite. At least you're trying to do something.'

She puts her head to one side and looks at him; perhaps noticing that he's different, more articulate, or perhaps noticing the rawness round his mouth, where it has chafed against my unshaven jaws. She strokes his hair and round his ear, like you would a puppy – and then she sweeps down the lawn to join our glamorous, pissed exile by the pool.

So *ja*, a funny Sunday, all in all.

When Moses arrives I can't believe my eyes. I'm sorry if this sounds prejudiced, but I honestly *do* find black faces difficult to distinguish from one another. Yet, boy oh boy, not his! Lugubrious

100

and red-eyed. I'm not easily going to forget this face talking about sanctions on the TV, before suddenly turning into a Canadian Mountie's dick.

Don't Angela and Gertjie remember too?

Apparently not. They greet Moses like his namesake. 'Sir,' says Gertjie, almost crying with excitement, 'I'm from *home* also. If there's any way I can help . . . ?'

Flabbergasted, I sink into a corner chair, and watch the war council assemble in my kitchen.

Following Moses, there's a black and white English couple, Robert and Elizabeth, both teachers at Angela's school (geography and history); and then the bloke around whom media attention will apparently be centred: the opera-singer, Nathaniel Roshney. 'In our home,' Angela whispers, though bugger me if I've ever heard of him. Anyhow, it seems he's got a lot of qualifications for this event. Firstly, he's a parent at the school, secondly he's a South African Jew famous for his anti-Apartheid stance, and thirdly he's currently a big hit in some opera at the Coliseum.

Nathaniel, or *Nat*, as he insists we call him, looks like my dentist back in Cape Town. Short, chunky, with neat beard and tinted specs. As we shake hands, we say 'Hi, howzit?' in unison, and I feel an instant kinship. And yet. There's something behind the specs, a particular brand of intelligence. Why is he in exile? Just for career reasons, or do I smell a Commie in my kitchen?

He embraces Moses and Johnnie, calling them 'brothers' and, sure enough, '*comrades*'.

I retreat to the lounge and have a snuffle around my liquor cabinet. Exiles will be exiles, so La said, and exiles will be piss-cats. Armed with assorted spirits, I return to the kitchen and play barman for the rest of the arvie. As I get quickly woozy, I smile to myself. Here I am waiting upon commies and kaffirs. I think back to the cooks, maids, gardeners and chauffeurs when I was a kid – how they smelled; how I would wipe anything they touched, especially cutlery.

I wonder what these famous, big-brained exiles make of my London home? Do they wonder where the money comes from?

Well, I've got news for you, Messrs Mafeje, Lunguza and Roshney

– the Lipschitzes have nothing to be ashamed of. You should see my dad arriving at the docks each morning, stopping his Rolls half a dozen times for a chat with his labourers. They love him, man. '*Die oubaas*', as they say – the senior boss. You wanna watch them smile at him first before you start inciting them to murder.

I slump in the corner again, my eyes flicking from Angela to Gertjie. She's amazed, enchanted by him, this new Gertjie, eloquent and committed, arguing and plotting with the rest.

How can you? – I want to ask him – *why are you bothering?* What you said to me earlier, about white South Africans, that's explained things to me for the first time – so why are you bothering with these people? Leave them be, leave history to make ghosts of them, and come here. Let me pull the khaki shirt out of your jeans, and let me have another look at your belly. The trail of hair from your navel was so beautifully dark. Coarse, criss-crossed. Reminded me of stitches. And my cum reminded me of candlewax; candlewax falling on the stitches, and that reminded me of time passing, plip, plup.

Suddenly Johnnie Lunguza brings out a penny whistle and starts to play.

(Hell, when did I last hear a penny whistle?)

He plays '*Nkosi sikelel*'' as a sort of township *kwela*, with his hands wrapped round the penny whistle like it's a prayer. Pissed and homesick now, Moses and Nat get to their feet, hold up their fists, and sing along; Nat really giving it big stick, the full Coliseum version. The two teachers from Angela's school, Robert and Elizabeth, they don't know the words, so they just mumble through it, but with fists held high. It's not a pretty sight, hey? – the black power salute. It's not a polite V-sign for victory. It's not a raised palm swearing allegiance. It's a thick, ugly fist going to war, going for broke. It's the real thing.

(Who invited it into my kitchen?)

Hauling myself out of my corner chair, I throw one arm into the air, half black power, half sieg heil, and, barely controlling the giggles, I add my voice to the din:

'A cosy sick old lady in Africa
Mails a fucking nit to a pond along you!'

THIRTEEN

M y problem with politics is very simple – *it doesn't last.*
After the Lipschitzes' travels this century: brief stop-overs
in Tsarist Russia, pre-war Poland, and white South Africa, I've
developed a taste for things that last.

Like my marriage. Angela will last. Good old British labouring
stock. She dreamed of being an actress, but ended up a teacher.
Why? Because it's more sensible; it'll last.

When she goes to work in the morning and comes home in
the evening, and when I look through the study door and watch
her at the desk, head bowed, reading, learning, I get such a good
feeling, man. She's like an anchor. Even in her dizzy moments,
getting sloshed or squandering our cash, you know she'll pull
through, make ends meet. You know she'll be sitting at some
desk somewhere in twenty years' time, head bowed, reading,
learning. Lasting.

I need that near me. Even if it doesn't set my blood racing to
its limit. My blood was brewed in a nomad's pot, so it wants a
few shakes and bumps to get it really going. Drugs, sex and so
on. But *politics*? Forget it. It's water in the hands, pal – boring,
transparent, and hey presto, gone!

Take the meeting in our kitchen a couple of Sundays ago. That
brave little band of comrades were going to change the world.
They were going to expose British hypocrisy over Apartheid –
from classroom to House of Commons. Then what happens? The

'right-wing prick', Paul Chagbury MP, suddenly backs out of the fight. Maybe because he didn't fancy getting involved in one of Nat Roshney's famous publicity campaigns, or maybe because he's just accepted that his son's at the wrong school, and he's making other plans. Anyhow, he's keeping little Sebastian out of the show, and one or two other parents are doing likewise, but the show itself goes on.

Now, was it worth the fuss?

Of course it was, says Angela – if they *hadn't* met that Sunday, the show would've been cancelled.

She's missing my point. Who cares if the show is cancelled? Who cares about the history of South Africa? It's all going to change now. Any sec. We're at the dawn of a new era. Isn't that what they want, the brave comrades? The history of South Africa will become, you might say, a thing of the past. As Gertjie explained so clearly.

Mind you, I don't trust him. Whatever he might say, he still *cares*. I don't. I mean, if it was rotten somehow, our history, a *mistake* perhaps, how can a person care? All these politicians, intellectuals, lawyers and theologians, they all get together and cook up Apartheid. It's for the good of all, they say, and it's founded in the Bible. So my generation, whites and blacks, we're taught this is how the world is. We're taught this along with our alphabet and our two times table. But now, just a few decades later, people are suddenly saying, Oh hang on, sorry – two and two makes five, and the alphabet goes ZYX...

And other people are screaming 'Fascists, torturers, murderers!'

'What – *us*?'

Listen, if terrible things have been going on, and if I was part of it without even noticing, then stuff it, hey – who can care?

When me and Gertjie get up this morning, we find Angela in the kitchen with a summer cold.

'It's so frustrating,' she calls from inside a man-sized tissue, 'when there's still so much to do on the show.'

'Shame, my poor *engeltjie*,' says Gertjie, hugging her. This is his name for her – *engeltjie*, little angel. Me he sometimes calls *Pa*. He's wearing my long white Harrods dressing-gown, and she's wearing hers. It makes them look, for a moment, like family.

'Let me cook you some breakfast,' says Angela, mopping her nose. 'At least I can do something.'

Angela does us a good old South African breakfast, steak and eggs, and serves it with orange juice, down by the pool. I crack open a bottle of champers to add the final touch.

'Ah, the morning sunlight in Buck's Fizz,' I say. 'Cheers, folks!'

'*Op ons!*' chirps Gertjie.

'Uhhh . . .' groans Angela, clutching a Lemsip and a box of tissues.

'This is damn good,' says Gertjie, chewing on his steak.

'I find it a bit tough actually,' I say. 'Not like Transvaal beef.'

'Agh well, no,' says Gertjie.

'But this is like home,' I say, adding some orange juice to our second Buck's Fizz. 'The British have finally discovered real orange juice. We never had anything else. First thing in the morning, as soon as Lizzie started work, she'd squeeze a whole load for breakfast. Did your girl do that in Joburg?'

'Oh, sure.'

Angela's shaking with laughter.

'Whatzit?' I ask.

'If you two could hear yourselves,' she says. 'Oh, the beef that was! The orange juice that was! The orchard that was! The Moscow that was! Oh, we must go back! You should hear yourselves.'

I frown – *Moscow?* – then clear my throat. 'We're going to swim now.'

'Oh, right,' she says, with a small sigh. 'I must get out of this sun anyway.' She collects our plates and heads off across the lawn.

I said 'swim', but Angela knows that nobody swims straight after breakfast. We just like slipping into the water for a while.

The splash makes her stop. Although she doesn't turn round, we pull our nakedness against the side. Strange, hey? – I feel shy in front of my wife.

'Isn't it sad?' she says, touching a cluster of lilies that have collapsed, fatally, in the drought.

'*Ja* . . .' I answer, listening to my voice travelling across the still water. 'I liked those. Nice scent.'

'I'll go round with a watering-can just now,' Gertjie calls, entwining his leg round mine. 'And I'll put the screen over the . . . *dinges* lawn.'

'Camomile lawn,' says Angela. 'Ta.'

She still hasn't turned round, standing there in her long gown, plates in one hand, tissues in the other, the sun beaming through her frizzy hair, making it look whiter than ever.

'Ta,' she says again, and, coughing quietly, drifts into the house.

My wife, the tragedy queen.

No, that's unfair, when she's been such a tresj about Gertjie. She allows him to stay four times a week – which is more than she's allowed before, with other passing fancies. I related Gertjie's story to her, and she was very moved by that. I think she really likes him. Anyway, she's been absolutely terrif about it all. I wish I could show the same grace over Gertjie and Charlotte.

Ja, that's still going on – ever since the Turk's shower party. Islington is where he spends the other three nights a week. Friday to Sunday. So as the countdown starts to our departure date, and time ticks away, ticks and falls, plip, plup, Gertjie keeps coming and going – in every sense. Before each meeting, I never know quite which Gertjie I'm going to find.

'Howzit?' I say, as I pick him up outside Charlotte's on the Monday arvie of our last fortnight. He looks subdued. I stroke his shoulder, restraining myself from a hug. But he doesn't. He takes me in his arms right there – on the street, in front of everyone. Oh, lovely, oh *lekker*!

'By the by,' says Charlotte, 'Pope's out.'

'Sorry?'

'Pope – you remember Pope, yaah? He's out of the clink. One of his former sponsors arranged it. Cancelled the trial too. Pope and I are having dinner on Wednes – no, Tuesday. I'm indebted to him. During the incarceration, he never once mentioned my name to his captors.'

'And what happened to uhh ... what was the Turkish bloke's name?'

We all shrug.

'Delicatessen?' I suggest.

'Oh, Leon,' laughs Charlotte, 'you're so Hebraic!'

'*Ja,*' I say, 'ha-ha!', ushering Gertjie into the Jag and driving off.

I don't like it when people do that. *I* prefer to make the Jewish jokes round here. I mean, with my red hair and chiselled nose, nobody would even guess.

'You O K, Gerks?' I ask.

'O K, Pa,' he murmurs, leaning his head on the window. After a long silence, he suddenly says, 'Can we go by my place? I need to ... uh ...'

I wait. But he's miles away. '*Ja,* of course,' I say, and change course for the East End.

It's my first time in his bedsit. For real. I came here often in my lusty waking thoughts. It's emptier than I imagined, and messier. Big Mac boxes and 7-Up tins. No furniture, no personal mementos, no photos or even reading matter – which surprises me.

But now, next to his bed (a mattress on the floor, with sleeping bag), I notice one small book.

'*Dis my dagboek,*' he says, as I lift it.

'Your diary.' The lock's made of tin: a child could break it. 'So what's in here?'

'My secrets.'

'No, well, those I've heard.'

He smiles. A small, ugly smile somehow. He's slipping away; something's wrong. I sniff the book. An unmistakable scent – Gertjie and Woolworths.

'In English or Afrikaans – your secrets?'

He smiles again. '*Nee, jong – Afrikaans – die moedertaal – natuurlik.*'

'Agh, then I'll get bugger-all joy here,' – and I toss the book onto his bed. He flops on top, and lies there, mummy-like, hands folded over his chest.

I stroll to the window. The sun is dipping, far away from the East End. This street is in shadow, the building cool. Indian music comes shivering up from somewhere below. For the first time in weeks I don't feel warm.

'Why have we come here?' I ask.

'I want to stay here tonight.'

'Alone?'

'I think so . . . I've caught that cold Angela had last week.'

'How can you tell?'

'Huh?'

'How can you tell it's a cold and not all that shit Charlotte bungs up your nose?'

He sits up. 'But I never have any.'

'Oh, please.'

'And she's cutting down too.' He grins, half-shy, half-boastful. 'She says love's better.'

(How dare she use that word!)

'I don't believe you,' I say.

He shrugs, then weeps. Without warning.

'What gives?' I ask.

'You tell me. Why are you the hell-in with me?'

'I'm not . . .' A dull ache goes through me. Tonight without him. Definitely. And there're only twelve nights left. He's not keeping count – I know he's not – and to mention it seems calculating.

He reaches for my hand. 'I just want . . .'

'Some time on your own. Of course you do. Charlotte hassling you from one side, me from the other. Of course you need to –'

'I need to get well.'

'Agh, for shit's sake, it's only a cold!'

'No, no,' he says, frowning, 'I must get *well*. Completely well. You've forgotten. You're relying on me, and you mustn't. Pa, you mustn't.'

Back in Wynn Chase, Angela is ensconced in her Room Of My Own, head bowed, working, with Satie or Chopin or someone playing on the stereo.

'No Gertjie?' she asks without looking up.

'Naa. He's caught that cold you had.'

'You've rowed.'

'Quite the opposite. I just didn't feel like being with him tonight. I'm missing you.' I hug her. Warm, reliable Angela. Oh, the difference. Dull, plump Angela.

'We hardly see one another,' she says, still not looking up.

'You O K?'

'How?'

'About it all.'

'Oh lawks, yes,' she says briskly. 'One gets more cautious about opening doors, but otherwise it's pure Bloomsbury.'

'I still love you, by the way.'

'Good.'

'D'you fancy one of our old pub-crawls tonight?'

'No, no, I'm ... Crikey, in fact, must whiz!' She jumps up, collecting papers. 'Have to check the pronunciation of this township song with Johnnie Lunguza, and if one doesn't catch him relatively early of an evening – my dear, *il est rond!*' She stops at the door. 'My cold, you say?'

'Huhn?'

'Gertjie. Funny not to have him around.'

I stay there, leaning on the desk, listening to her leave. That familiar feeling again, alone in the house. What if something happens to me now? A puncture deep inside, or an explosion, a sudden unravelling, or maybe even spontaneous combustion – though Angela did say this is more likely to happen to Catholics. Anyhow, none of these are propositions I fancy. I want to live long enough to be poor.

I look round Angela's Room Of My Own and smile. This is where she's plotted against the Lipschitzes, slinging away our fortune. What if it runs out? Is it limitless? Not knowing is a funny, nice, frightening feeling.

I sit at her desk, reach under to a wooden button at the back, and open the top left-hand drawer. Her diary is a big dappled Victorian ledger. For the last two weeks there've been no entries, and I'd even stopped looking. But here's a new one, dated last Friday:

No, it isn't overwork, and it isn't imagination. It is what I
dreaded. I actually knew for certain after the report came
back from Lusaka a fortnight ago. Moses M. had insisted on
checking out Gertjie. It's routine apparently; anyone they
work with (G. is helping on the show). I half-hoped G's
story would be a lie: the story of his father, etc. Not sure
why I hoped this. Perhaps so that G. would finally be forced
to leave – to exit from our lives. But Lusaka confirmed his
story. When I heard, I felt ill. Not because of the terrible
facts of his history, but because I knew he'd be staying, and
I finally knew that's what I wanted. He inspires me. He
makes sense of my life: my awful S. African connection. Such
wisdom when he speaks of that country. Wisdom, yet also a
pervading S.A. naivety; that New World radiance. Gertjie's
beauty is unsettling. Broken, imperfect, and therefore imper-
ishable. For L., overflowing with luxuriant negativity, G. is
just another drug. He has said so. For me, G. is a beacon
for white S. Africa. Reformed, redeemed . . . Oh Angela, such
utter bollocks, girl! Isn't the simple truth that you hunger for
him? Yes, yes, all right, yes! I'm starving for him. My baby.
When he stays over, I creep downstairs and sniff his scent
on the basement landing. It's intoxicating – clean sweat and
light, cheap scent. I listen to them through the door. I've
just done it. They're bonking like crazy, or whatever. I stood
there like a teenager, picturing myself in G's arms instead
of that thing he's hugging, that grotesque ginger . . .

I snap shut the diary.

As it tumbles onto my lap, a piece of newspaper slides out. It's
from some anti-Apartheid rag, and shows Angela handing over a
cheque to Moses and crowd, for repairs to their burnt offices. I
peer at it closely. The photographer has caught Angela at a good
angle; the actress who never was, yearning into the camera for
her brief moment of fame. And I always thought politics wasn't
sexy. Yet just look at her: this voluptuous lady in love with my
boyfriend.

*

110

By the time Angela gets home, I'm already in bed, fast asleep and snoring. But actually watching through half-closed lids.

Such panic.

We've been pals, lovers, sisters, you name it. My Angela – setting off for work in the morning and coming home in the evening; everlastingly there. Good old Angela – who's meanwhile betraying me at every opportunity. Funding terrorists with my fortune, fancying my boyfriend, writing me off as grotesque!

I watch her undress. The care she takes slipping off her jewellery and folding her clothes, almost like she's doing some religious ceremony (giving thanks maybe for the silk and silver at her fingertips?); and naked now, a large bluish ghost, she tiptoes round, checking for the edge of furniture with one outstretched hand.

'Aah,' I groan as she climbs into bed.

'Sorry, Bubs,' she whispers, '' tried to be quiet.'

'Ahh, ahh, ahh,' I hear, like it's coming from someone else, as I roll towards her across the expanse of bed.

'Bubs?' she cries.

'Ahh, ahh!' I fall onto her, collecting her head in my hands, and crushing it, smothering it into the heavy flab of my chest.

'You pissed?' she asks, from somewhere in there.

'Ahh!'

'Me too.' With a small laugh, she manages to free her head. I bite her neck, deeply, resting my teeth in her thick flesh, twitching my jaws, feeling their strength, daring myself further.

'Hnnn . . .' she goes, gently pulling away her neck and manoeuvring her face against mine. 'Poor baby,' she murmurs, wiping away my tears and spittle. 'Poor pet.'

'Oh,' I moan, feeling my excitement.

'Was that no?' she whispers.

'Oh, oh, oh,' I cry, through gritted teeth.

'Mm, mm, mm,' she goes.

Her warm boozy mouth could be Gertjie's. I gather her arms and legs round me, forcing her to hug me hard – *harder*! – like he does, like there's no one else in the world, like we've only got a sec left. And as I do, I see him clearly, propped against the headboard in the guest room, reaching for me, nakedness splayed wide. But now, I see another head popping into the picture. Angela! Kissing his navel. Starting down the trail of hair.

'Oh,' I cry.

'Mm,' she squeals.

She's everywhere – here in the bed with me, and in my mind. No fighting it, so relax. Rearrange the pictures. Nudge his head down between her thighs. She arches back – right back – reaching for something. My hand. *Ja*, I'm there too, looking down over her vast moist body to the crown of Gertjie's head. He glances up and smiles at me. Secretly.

'Ga-ga-gaa-gaaaaa,' I bellow.

'My Bubs,' she murmurs as I collapse now. 'Poor baby, I love you.'

I'm back here in the upstairs bedroom. Just with La. 'Wha'?'

'Love you, but . . . must sleep . . . look at the time.'

She loves me! She still loves me, as well as Gertjie. (That's OK – I can identify with that.) She loves me, even though I'm a bit grotesque. (That's OK, too. After seven years of marriage, who isn't?)

In the morning, long after Angela's gone to school, Gertjie rocks up, a knapsack over his shoulder.

The moment the door closes behind him, we go into a deep hug. I use the opportunity to do a quick rummage in the knapsack. A few T-shirts, his aftershave, a pair of slip-slops.

'Going somewhere?' I ask nervously.

'If it's OK by you, Pa, I thought I'd stay here for our last two weeks. So we can have every last minute together.'

'Sure,' I say, casj as poss.

He starts downstairs, heading to the spare room.

'So where shall we bed down?' I ask, staying in the hallway.

'Huh?'

'Down there, or upstairs in the master bedroom?'

'Why – where's Angela going to sleep?'

'Agh, it's a big bed. King sized. Kings, queens, who's fussy?'

His face has gone very stern.

'No,' he says firmly, 'I like Angela, but –'

'Fine. Just thought I'd ask.'

'*No.*'

'Fine. How's your cold?'

'Agh, I think it was what you said – I think it was just all the coke.' He grins and clatters downstairs.

'Hang on, I thought you said –'

But he's already out of earshot. Shrugging, I hurry after.

FOURTEEN

I could kill them. Easily.

I'm sprawled on the dark lawn, and they're in the kitchen, with the light on. It's the only square of light on the back of the house. They're at the table, talking and laughing, all in dumbshow; two happy puppets in a bright frame of light. I can't miss.

I glance at my watch. Ten thirty-six. Wasn't expecting them back so soon.

They're opening a magnum of champagne. Neither knows how to do it. It explodes. The cork strikes the window. It doesn't shatter; the windows round here are built to withstand champagne corks. But no stronger velocities, I bet. The two puppets fall giggling into one another's arms. The two become one. One target. Now – now!

If only this was a rifle, and not my finger.

If only tonight had turned out differently.

We three were setting off for Angela's school concert, when I said I wasn't going, and told Gertjie he must choose – to stay with me or go with her. I hadn't planned this. It just suddenly struck me as so damn dumb – wasting one of our last evenings together seeing a kids' show on South Africa! Angela was shocked shitless, but I didn't care. The affair is making me a little crazy these days. Crazy happy and crazy cross. And aware that Angela's crazy about Gertjie too, yet can't have him. I half-wish she could; so that we could all be crazy together, instead of getting into situations

114

like tonight – where Gertjie had to choose between me and her.

What hurt most is that it didn't take him more than a sec.

And now already they're back – two happy puppets in a bright frame, toasting one another. Growling, I hoist myself up, and rush towards the window. But my foot instantly contacts a round object, my chin hits the grass, and I slide down the long lawn, with the round object travelling in front of my dazed eyes.

It's a bottle of vodka. Looks empty – except for an image of the two bright puppets rolling along inside. Where's all the booze gone? It was full earlier . . .

The slanting lawn abruptly changes into flat marble, and I come to a stop with only my feet splashing into our pool; my feet and the vodka bottle, which bounces in, takes a few deep *sluks*, and drowns, burping.

Unbruised and undeterred, I stand and set off again towards the bright window, squelch-squelch, this time making it all the way, and even further, right indoors. The puppets grow to full-size, seated round the kitchen table.

'Bubsies!' cries Angela. 'We wondered where you were.'

'Watering the lawn,' I mutter.

'You're covered in grass,' says Gertjie.

'Watering it,' I repeat, scowling.

'Your feet are wet,' says Angela, as I squelch past.

'Yes,' I snap. 'When you water grass, it gets wet! And unless you're into levitation, you – '

I stop. They're exchanging a little look, superior and pitying. It's a look which sober people give drunks. OK, we'll soon put an end to that. I fetch a bottle of Davidoff cognac, a handful of brown sugar cubes, and mix two giant champers cocktails for my two loved ones. They're meanwhile beaming at one another across a heap of books, scripts and props.

When I was out on the lawn, I thought the brightness in here was from the electric light, but actually it's from them; from my wife and my boyfriend. They're glowing with a most peculiar energy. It reminds me of Angela's amateur dramatic days, and me going backstage when the shows were over. There she was, on fire – pouring with sweat and paint, melting with different emotions: relief, exhaustion, ecstasy; all these things rising off her like heat off a runway. Athletes look like this too after the event – *we've done it!* And lovers. Yet Gertjie and Angela haven't *done it*. They've just been at a little school concert. And they're dying for me to ask about it.

So I say nothing.

I pour my silence into their energy, my coldness into their heat. It's a fantastic power I possess; a power to rival the Almighty's. Say a big event occurs, a moon landing or a mass murder, a new invention, a hijack or a flood. OK, let it occur, but what if I switch off my TV, chuck my newspaper into the bin? What then? No big deal anymore. I can rewrite history. Kennedy never got shot, Rhodesia never turned into Zambia or Zimbabwe or whichever the fuck it is, and likewise tonight's little school concert just never happened. What I don't see doesn't happen. There's a whole philosophical school based on my view of the world. Angela told me about it once. When you exit from a room, does the room remain behind or does it vanish into thin air?

I exit, squelch-squelch, from the kitchen now, zapping it into a philosophical black hole.

It's Wednesday night. There's Thursday, Friday, then the flight on Saturday.

How will I live, eat or breathe without Gertjie?

The counter on the answer-machine says *1*. Someone must've rung while I was *vrekked* out on the lawn. I wonder what the philosophers make of that? Or have answer-machines buggered up their theory? I flick it onto PLAY, then grit my teeth as it goes into its stupid little routine: whirr, click, whirr.

'Leon, it is Dad here . . .'

(Jesus. He's never rung before – *ever*. When there's a call from home, it's always Mom.)

I lean forward. His thick Polish-Yiddish accent threatens to drag the tape into slow-play.

'. . . Maybe talk later, hahh? I wanted to tell you . . . Hullo? Oh, I thought maybe I hear . . . No. OK. Later.'

And he rings off.

Has he somehow found out about our charitable donations? Is this about money?

No, there isn't that hairy tone in his voice.

No, I know what this is about. The one vaguely human, almost feminine, thing about my father is that he never forgets birthdays or anniversaries, and never lets me forget them either. He's forever dropping notes (usually via his secretary) to remind me about so-and-so's bar mitzvah or wedding. This time he's making sure I don't forget him and Mom — their anniversary on Monday.

Well, if he thinks I've forgotten – then great! They're both in for one helluva bloody surprise.

Picking myself off the carpet (where inexplicably I landed a moment ago), I erase the tape – then sigh. In ten years' time, when the cunt is long dead and buried, this tape with its nothing message could've been quite touching.

I return to the kitchen, and – BLICK! – it exists again.

The giant champers cocktails haven't quite done what I hoped. Angela and Gertjie are glowing even brighter and hotter, hakking on about their show, sticking on some pink and brown clown noses, and speaking in different South African accents. Oh, I get it – the pink nose means white-man, and the brown means black. I suddenly feel empty; empty of the event I missed – like it was me in the black hole, not them.

Gertjie's grinning at Angela, a kid proud of his big sister. Luckily she's a big ugly sister tonight. The excitement has ruined her make-up, leaving her blotched and streaked like a whore. She avoids Gertjie's eyes. Ever since she fell in love, she's so nervous with him; laughing too much, or babbling. It shows a mile off. How he must pity her.

Swaggering over and laying my hand on his shoulder, I say 'Beddybyes.'

I almost expect him to refuse, as a sort of punishment for this evening, but he rises straight into my arms, and nuzzles there.

For a moment, while his head's turned away, me and Angela gaze at one another, half-angry, half-sorry.

Now we drift into the hallway, me clutching Gertjie, and Angela clutching the champers magnum.

'End of term,' she yells muzzily. 'End of term – hoorah, hoorah! Don't you just adore that word – "hoorah"? Does anybody still actually use it?'

'Perhaps Paul Chagbury MP, hey?' says Gertjie.

'Paul Chagbury MP, perhaps. Oh Leon, if only you could've seen Chagbury. He's the parent, y'know, who wanted the show cancelled. If you could've seen him afterwards – when everyone was raving about it. Face like a slapped bottom. Oh, if you could've seen him!'

We've reached the banister, where the stairs turn up and down in one big curve.

'OK, night-night,' I say briskly.

'Night, lads,' she murmurs, smiling vaguely, hardly able to focus. 'Have one on me.'

Gertjie hugs her. 'My *engeltjie*. You did so good tonight, hey?'

'Did I?'

'*Sowaar* – you did bloody good!'

'Hmn . . .' She touches his cheek, then climbs the stairs, quietly singing, 'Cosy sick old lady . . .'

She looks so unlovely, heaving herself up.

I turn away quickly. Gertjie's already gone, clattering downstairs to our bed.

God only knows what time it is when I suddenly wake and find him gone. We don't keep a digital down here.

Without putting on any lights, I search round the basement, then the ground floor. The microwave tells me it's 3.29, the video says 3.31. The answer machine says IP, which I've never figured out.

No Gertjie.

Then I hear a vague noise from upstairs: like panting.

I climb slowly.

In our bedroom, I find Angela propped against the padded headboard, naked and sobbing. The magnum of champers is tucked under one arm, Gertjie under the other. Although fast asleep, he's hugging her tightly; hugging her like he's trying to find shelter, like there's no one else in the world.

I sink onto the side of the bed. (Things *do* happen in my absence.)

118

'You all right?' I ask Angela in a whisper.

'Yes, fine . . .' she replies, catching her breath.'Just everything tonight.'

'*Ja.*'

I stroke her hair, then Gertjie's.

'He climbed in about an hour ago,' she says. 'I thought it was you.'

'It should've been me,' I mumble, 'all through tonight. I should've been there. Sorry.'

'That's what Gertjie said: "Leon should've helped you through tonight – so if he won't, I will." Then he swore in Afrikaans, and then he called you a bastard – in English. I think he may have the measure of you, my flower.'

We smile at one another in the darkness. I think we do.

Then I climb into bed, embracing Angela, one hand reaching round to take hold of Gertjie.

FIFTEEN

For the next two days, Thursday and Friday, we don't move from the house, Gertjie, me and La. She's supposed to attend end-of-term staff meetings, but both days she calls in sick.

For two days we leave the answer-machine on, and ignore the doorbell.

For two whole days we stay naked. With blinds and curtains drawn against the blazing sun, we roam through the shadows: Gertjie, his perfect limbs outlined in sweat; Angela, large and giggling; me the satyr, pronking, ready to rut. In naked combinations of two, three or one, we roam around, discovering each other, and rediscovering. Every naked inch, outside and in, as far as we can reach. Although Angela's equipment doesn't arouse Gertjie any more than mine, he can make screwing seem, as with hard-ons, a very old-fashioned idea. But agh, being a bit old-fashioned, me and La still get stuck in there, while he crawls around and between us; his tongue, fingers, and deep, deep gaze going places no blunt-headed dick can go. Stroking and kissing, he gives you life second by second, which is how I like it. That way it lasts forever, or twists wherever you want. We go backwards now, and give birth to the good family we three never had. It's a crazy family, full of incest and lust, changing roles by the minute, but a good family all the same. (And if me and La strike lucky now, in this great planting-time, what a fantastic spirit we'll set loose on this earth, hey!)

Beyond the drawn curtains, the windows are all thrown open

wide. The back door too. Passing it is like passing a furnace. To step outside is to burn. Which we do happily; later we'll peel one another's skin, gathering the stuff like confetti, and then rub in lotions and coolers. So we step naked into our high-walled London garden, laughing as planes pass overhead – can *they* see? – and we cross the long lawn, where roasting grass crunches underfoot like the veld, so Gertjie says, and we dive into the pool with its hot turquoise water. It never cools – like the air. At night, when we stagger outside again, stuffed with rich graze and vintage wines, the heat is still incredible. Crashing through thick spiderwebs, we flop into the pool, or lie on the lawn, staring up at the humid, discoloured sky, and listening to the noise of parties and sex coming from other gardens.

We're lying on the lawn now, as Friday changes into Saturday. Looking across Gertjie's head, I see an expression on La's face that I've never seen before. Such joy – it's practically shining out of her. It's like all the candles in that church she once took me to in Venice; as if all that light is illuminating the garden, just for a sec. It makes me fear for her, don't know why.

We three stay awake through the night; the same as me and La did long ago, on our first night together; drinking, talking, then falling into bed, and that bed being the same one. Surrounding it is the debris from the last two days. In my toy box, among the array of dildos, fronded condoms and bottles of poppers, I spot a Polaroid camera. I beg Gertjie for just one snap, so that we can take away a picture of him tomorrow.

'No,' he says, crying instantly, in that odd, calm way. '*Nee, ek's jammer, maar* ... no. I hate photos. People think they're capturing memories, but how? On a dead thing? A piece of card? How can it be better than what we've got in our heads? These last days. These pictures – alive – living inside us. Man, *that's* what we must take away tomorrow.'

Before sunrise, there's a breeze; the only breeze of the day – it makes the cherry tree squeak against the gutter. It's starting now. Tomorrow is here. Saturday and no turning back.

Our flight is at 8.10 p.m. We have to check in by six. A cab is coming round at four.

The plan is for Gertjie to trek along to the airport, but by mid-morning we've all had enough. The house is like an asylum; people howling as they make coffee, howling in the shower, howling as they dress. We can't pack. We can't do anything.

And Gertjie has turned into the brain-damaged farmboy I met on that first morning at Air South Africa. Sweating and blushing, speaking Afrikaans only.

Just before eleven, we decide to take him back to the East End.

As I reverse the Jag out of the drive, I notice two men in a blue Ford Escort across the road. Seeing us, one of them lifts something to his face. A camera? They do a quick U-turn, and set off after us.

I hit the accelerator and waste them in a sec.

(Did that happen? Hard to be sure. My brain's pure liquid after the last two days.)

When we reach Gertjie's place, he says goodbye to Angela immediately. They shake hands and peck one another's cheeks. You'd think it was some auntie saying goodbye to her godson. You wouldn't believe they'd been naked together a few hours earlier. But I saw them! Now Gertjie tugs at my shirtsleeve. I'm to come up to his bedsit. I'd prefer not to say goodbye in that dingy room, but I'm not going to argue.

Upstairs, he hands me a sellotaped paper bag.

'Jammer. Dis nie so mooi toegedraai nie.'

I sigh. 'What?'

'Ek wou, maar tyd was min – jy weet mos?'

'Gertjie, don't do this. You can speak English.'

He clamps one finger to his lips and goes very still, staring at the floor.

'Is this a present?' I ask.

He nods.

'Just for me?'

He shakes his head.

'OK, then I'll open it later. With her. Thank you.'

122

We remain on either side of the room. Indian music is shivering up through the floorboards.

'Are we going to meet again?' I ask.

He shakes his head.

'No, that was the deal. Stick to it, hey? Will you you be here when . . . ?'

He shakes his head.

'OK. So what are your plans? Where are you heading for next?'

He shrugs. Although his face is patchy and swollen, the howling is over. He seems angry now. Like I've hurt him; betrayed him somehow. Shown him a good time, then snatched it away.

I move to the door. 'You've said you'll keep an eye on the house while we're away. Water the garden and so on. But if you're buggering-off yourself, how . . . ? Anyway, you've said you'll do that. Are you still going to do that?'

He pauses, then nods.

'All right. I'm leaving this set of keys.' I hold them up, but he keeps staring at the floor. 'Gertjie, look at where I'm putting the keys. Gertjie! Otherwise you won't . . .'

He lifts his head and obediently watches me place the keys on a shelf, then turns his gaze on me, a closed, sulky gaze, asking – anything else?

I go quickly.

Down in the car, Angela looks grey. 'Oh dear,' she says. 'I don't think I can go back. To the house. I'm sorry, but . . . Oh dear. He'll be everywhere. Everywhere.'

'Bullshit,' I say, accelerating fast. A group of Pakistani kids scatter. I've slung Gertjie's present into Angela's lap. She unpicks the sellotape. Inside is a plastic toilet bag, filled with Gertjie's toiletries: aftershave, deodorant, toothpaste.

'Odd gift,' murmurs Angela. She finds a note and reads:

'Dear Engeltjie and Pa – for you to sniff in Africa. A balm for the cosy sick old lady. With my eternal love – Gertjie.'

She turns to me. 'A very odd gift, don't you think? Arrogant somehow. Hmn?' She starts howling again.

123

I shrug.

He put her name first.

I'm not brilliant at packing and unpacking. The nomad in me says no man, no more. So I leave it to Angela, and slope out onto the patio.

The long lawn has finally turned completely yellow.

Incredible to think that this time tomorrow we'll be in winter. I'm not keen on winter, or even autumn, which Angela finds incredible. She puts it down to a certain gloom in my outlook, and maybe she's right. Maybe you've got to be an optimist to like autumn.

By one p.m., we're packed and ready. But since it's much too early to go, we're caught in that horrible departure-day limbo: the cases waiting in the hall, us wandering about, doing one more check-round or having one more drink, rinsing the glass straight afterwards, putting it back on the shelf.

By three p.m., I'm going meshuggeh. So I call our cab firm and ask them to get some wheels round here pronto.

Angela still hasn't stopped howling – and it gets even worse as we load the cab. Luckily the driver is the silent type (he looks Greek or something), and just gives an occasional suspicious glance as I bundle Angela into the back seat.

To my amazement, the blue Ford Escort is there again as we pull out of the drive. This time, the men jump out and rush towards us. One of them *is* carrying a camera.

'Step on the gas,' I hiss to the cab driver. He obeys, but with a frown, as if he's wondering, like I am, what movie we're in.

The photographer manages to shove his camera close to my window as we shoot past, and the flash goes off. A phosphorus circle, like a noose, lodges in my head. I blink and swallow.

'What the fuck was that?' I whisper to Angela.

She shrugs, sniffing. 'Probably ... a story ... on the school concert.'

'*What*? A story on the ... ! Angela, did something happen the other night? Were the newspapers there?' She nods, digging in her bag for a fresh tissue. 'But . . .' I say, 'I thought you promised you weren't going to involve the media.'

'We didn't. But the other side did. Some of the right-wing parents held a little demonstration at the school gates and tipped off the press. Paul Chagbury kept a suspiciously low profile. Anyway, probably just some local paper. Or the *National Front Reveille*.'

I think back to the phone calls and doorbells we've ignored over the last few days, then splutter, 'But . . . but . . . !'

'Oh Leon, it's not important,' Angela says. 'Beatrice wasn't the slightest bit worried. Nor were the school governors. Chagbury's forever causing them trouble. His son's simply at the wrong sodding school.'

'But, I mean . . . reporters camped outside our front door! My God, I mean . . . why didn't you tell me?'

Angela goes very quiet; then leans forward to the cab driver.

'He wants to know why I didn't tell him. The other night was one of the most important nights of my life, and he missed it. My husband missed it. And now he wants to know why I didn't tell him about it. Do you think that's fair?'

The driver glances over his shoulder, bewildered.

'Do you think it's fair?' Angela asks again. 'As an objective observer. Do you?'

Now she starts laughing – or howling. I can't tell. The driver stares straight ahead. We drive on in silence, broken only by Angela's sniffs.

The Saturday afternoon streets are crammed with near-naked people in sunglasses. You can feel them getting ready for the long hot sexy Saturday night ahead. As we travel along, everyone seems to be stripping down even more. Everyone except for a black tramp. He's thickly muffled, and wears a sheepskin coat draped over his head in biblical grandeur. He gestures with one thumb. What is he doing? Hitch-hiking? To *Heathrow*? I follow his gaze. The tarmac stretching before us is a dusty silver. It melts into the horizon, then rises to a vivid, utterly unBritish blue.

Suddenly feeling close to tears myself, I take Angela's hand. 'Did you know that Heathrow is the hottest place in the British Isles today?' I ask.

'No, I didn't,' she sobs, 'I didn't.'

'*Ja*, it was on the weather forecast.'

'My husband listens to the weather forecasts,' she tells the cab driver, 'but never the news.'

The driver looks at us in his mirror. His eyes are quite fearful now. He's picked up some weirdos in his time, but we might be setting a new record.

I laugh weakly. 'Actually I did hear the news this morning,' I say to him, 'and it was all about Heathrow too. Delays because of an air traffic strike somewhere. And an airport terror alert because it's the ... somethingth anniversary in ... Northern Ireland, I think.'

'That's my husband having listened to the news,' sobs Angela. She suddenly lunges forward, trying to hug the man. 'Oh help me, please...'

This is the limit. He starts to brake.

'It's OK,' I say to him, pulling Angela into my arms. 'She's OK. Just drive. Just get us to the airport. I'll pay whatever you want. It's OK, we're not criminals. We're normal people, I promise you. Just drive, please.'

The driver says something in Greek, or whatever it is, but keeps going, thank God. I rock Angela in my arms as she weeps and weeps. Trembling, I lean my head on the window, and close my eyes.

Jesus.

I've just had a weird dream, although I'm wide awake: we were at Heathrow, waiting for our flight to be called, when the cops arrived and pushed everyone to one side. They led a man through, with a jacket covering his head. He was wearing flares and gold lamé boots. It was that Turk, whatsisname, Delicatessen or whatever. They were deporting him. The jacket fell off his face. It wasn't the Turk: it was me.

Oich, I think the affair with Gertjie might've been a mistake. For both me and La. The thing is – it's hacked away the ground from under our feet, and there's nothing below. I mean, *really* nothing.

In these circumstances, boarding a plane isn't the nicest thing. I'm sick all the way home.

PART II

COSY SICK OLD LADY

SIXTEEN

W e're underwater, I swear.

This journey started in a plane, but has ended in a submarine. The cabin's rocking, the portholes are running with water. We've landed, so they tell us, in Afrikaans and English, but I'm not convinced. I peer out, trying to glimpse something familiar, something from that day thirteen years ago when I left; the airport building, or just some tarmac would do. All I see is a churning purple blur. Why is it so dark – at ten o'clock on a Sunday morning?

The tannoy again: '*Dames en here, namens Lug Suid Afrika, maak ons graag verskoning vir . . .*'

It's a freak storm apparently, with the wind reaching gale force, so we're stuck onboard until it's safe to walk the short distance to the terminals.

Muzak is played to calm us down. 'Sarie Marais' and 'Jan Pierewiet' – old Boere tunes: a bit too cute to be trusted. But the other first-class passengers are settling back into their seats, dewy-eyed. I turn to Angela. She didn't sleep so hot. In fact, she had one long howl across the hemispheres.

'OK?' I ask.

'Mm. And the journey began. Neither robbers nor tempests befriended them.'

'Huhn?'

'Austen. *Northanger Abbey.*'

129

Half an hour later, Air SA decide it's safe for us to disembark. But the wind still makes you fight for every foothold on the tarmac. A child is blown away; an old woman falls, bloodying her face.

Inside the building, things are at last familiar. Simple spaces, oldish-modern. You feel you're arriving in a young, little country, not a country of monstrous legend.

Until you get to Customs.

Agh, maybe it's just my prob with Afrikaners in uniform. The one I get is heavy and bearded. He examines my passport like a gorilla with a leaf he's going to eat. Above his head, the thought bubble reads:

'Why is this Lipschitz bloke living in the fokken UK? Looks too *pap* to be political. He's just fokked off. Like all the fokken Jews are doing, fokken *Jode!*, and all the other fokken English-speaking fokken traitors to the blessed Folk.'

He takes a long time choosing a rubber stamp, then grinds it slowly into my passport. It probably says, DON'T LET THIS ONE OUT AGAIN.

There are no cars at the taxi rank – just a queue of passengers, battling to keep upright. The wind is bombing across the Cape Flats, the rain like a whip. In the car park, a limousine has been neatly sliced by a fallen bluegum.

It takes over an hour before we get a cab.

The driver is an old darkish-skinned Coloured. Angela sits alongside him (is that permitted these days?), and here we are again, in another cab, with her chatting to another driver.

'Hello – we're from England. So this is South Africa! Will we see lots of lions and tigers in the streets?' She chuckles warmly. 'I suppose lions and tigers are the least of your problems these days.'

He smiles politely, flicks his de-mister to a noisy high, and leans forward, squinting through the blur of his windscreen wipers. I rub a peep-hole in my window.

Beyond, nothing but water. It's like we've been transferred from the submarine to a diving bell, and we're making our way homewards across the dark sea-bed. I can't spot a single landmark. That colossal corner of Table Mountain, or the outskirts of Nyanga,

Guguletu and Langa. They feature in lots of white nightmares, those townships. If big trouble comes, will the whites make it to the airport? Past Nyanga, Guguletu and Langa.

Groote Schuur Hospital, Woodstock, the Foreshore? Are any of those still out there? But now, as the gale cleans my window in a gust, there's a strange vision above us. A freeway going nowhere, the sweep of concrete abruptly chopped off in mid-air.

'My God,' I say, 'what happened here?'

'Oh *ja*, very bad,' says the driver. 'We ran out of money.' Intrigued by his 'we', I haul myself forward. His headrest is in orangey fur, flattened with oil and sweat. '*Ja*,' he sighs, 'our money's worth nothing these days. Our money's going backwards.'

I nod guiltily. Our pockets are stuffed with rands. We couldn't believe the fortune we got for our sterling.

'And I bet,' says Angela, 'it's you people, you blacks, suffering most.'

(Jesus, all her reading on South Africa, and she still can't tell a Coloured from a black! She still doesn't understand that the Coloureds, with their half-white blood, are, and always will be, one glorious step ahead.)

The driver just smiles, and turns up his de-mister a bit louder.

My window is awash again. Maybe our diving bell will just suddenly surface in Sea Point, and there'll be the blue skies and sunshine of my youth.

'Sea Point,' announces the driver.

Dear God, the storm's even worse here. We're on Main Road. Glimpses of video hire shops and delicatessens. No one about. Left into St John's Road. I *think* it's St John's Road. Right onto High Level Road, and then a bit further, and – oh hell! – we're turning into it now. Avenue des Bois. The line of palm trees along the middle, thrashing in the wind. Up and up, as far as you can go, and then some more. Right onto the slope of Signal Hill, touching the forest. The incline here is *unreal*. As the car pulls up, you feel it'll go into a slow backflip and return, tumbling, to Sea Point.

If it wasn't for the storm, we'd see a palace in front of us now. An apricot-coloured palace, Hollywood-style, complete with turret and sprawling gardens. (It's actually only mansion-sized, but it seemed bigger once.) I step into the rain, and cup my hands over my eyes. Wow, it isn't just the storm obscuring the palace. It's a massive security wall they've built since I was here, with warning signs in English, Afrikaans and a native lingo.

'Help!' laughs Angela, as she gets out of the cab and starts to topple. I lunge for her and we sway, trying to steady one another.

Surprisingly, my key still opens the front gate. Beyond, the wind is like a wall. We push at it, luggage in hand, closing the distance between us and the house. The crazy paving path, with crazy maps for kids' games. The banana tree, the palms.

We reach the stoep and stand panting in its shelter, grateful for a level surface at last. The red tiles, the stone lions.

'Just wait till you see their faces,' I yell above the storm. Angela nods and smiles anxiously. My key turns in the lock, but the door doesn't open. As I fiddle with it, an alarm goes off. Now a light starts flashing on the front gate, sending a yellow beam whirling through the rain, onto the stoep, the stone lions and Angela's popping eyes. Next a huge force hits the door from within. We hear ferocious baying. An intercom flicks on – it's like the animal has leapt out onto us! – then a voice, fighting for control of the microphone.

'Jungle! Jungle, hold it, boy!'

'Lizzie,' I shout, leaping for the button on our side, 'Lizzie!'

'Who's there? Who's messing in the keyhole? The police will –'

'Lizzie, it's Leon!'

'Master Leon?'

'*Ja*!'

'It's never! Master Leon's overseas.'

'Agh man, just peep through the bloody peephole.'

'It *is* Master Leon,' she cries now. 'Hey, sorry, Master! Hang on, Master, I'll just take Jungle . . .'

The intercom goes dead as we hear an almighty struggle inside, with thumps and snarls. Angela takes my hand. I smile reassuringly. The whirling yellow light subsides, and the alarm is switched off. Now just the rush of the storm, an almost peaceful sound.

Bolts are drawn, top and bottom, and the door opens. It's dark inside, Lizzie invisible. We step forward. She closes the door behind us, shutting out all noise. Just our wet clothes dripping onto the marble floor. Plip, plup. Hell, here's memories. The entrance hall on a winter's morning, chilled and shadowy. A smell of furniture polish. Not like in the London house. A richer darker polish – that lustre in the gloom – on African pieces, African wood.

'*Haai*, Master Leon,' says Lizzie, popping into the picture. Our old Coloured cook; a little wrinkly thing, no higher than a kid, nut-coloured skin, black in the creases. She wears a thick blue jersey over her maid's uniform, and woollen bootees. '*Haai*, Master,' she whispers again and again, shaking her head.

I'd like to hug her, but that'd be funny, so I slap her shoulder instead. 'Hi, Lizzie, and howzit by you?'

'No, O K thanks, Master,' she replies, puffing with emotion. 'No, old Lizzie's still on her feet.'

'This is my wife, Lizzie, this is Angela.'

'And – *haai jinnetjietog*! – Master Leon's lovely bride too!'

Laughing, Angela glances round to see who Lizzie means, then takes her hands. 'I've heard so much about you, Lizzie.'

'Thank you, Madam,' mumbles Lizzie, hushed by Angela's bright English accent.

'Oh crikey, don't call me that,' chuckles Angela.

'Sorry, Madam?'

'Please don't call me Madam. I'm Angela.'

'O K,' says Lizzie, 'sorry.'

'Lizzie, we're soaking here,' I say.

'No, well Master, just drop your things on the floor.'

'Like coming back from the beach, hey?'

'That's it, Master, and I'll get you people some towels. 'scuse me, Master, 'scuse me, Madam Angela.'

'No, I'm sorry,' says Angela, stopping Lizzie from leaving, 'I'd really prefer it if you didn't call me Madam –'

'It's all right, Lizzie,' I say quickly, 'go get the towels.' As she scoots off, I turn to Angela. 'Just relax, hey?'

'Yes, sorry,' says Angela, giggling nervously. She adds her coat to the pile I've started, then asks, 'Where're your parents?'

I wipe the rain off my watch. 'Quarter to one. She'll still be in bed. He'll be in his den with a bottle of Polish vodka, listening to Benny Goodman.'

'I'm freezing. Is the heating on?'

'I don't think they have proper heating.' I look round for radiators. 'No. That's right. Nobody here really takes winter seriously.'

'And why's it so dark?'

'Hmn . . .' I gaze at the massive chandelier that used to terrify me, and the carved ebony lamps on the great staircase, with flame-shaped bulbs. *'Ja*, Mom's a big saver. Electricity, envelopes, the change in your pockets, you name it. She used to be poor, y'see. Like you . . .' I stop myself. I meant it as a joke, but Angela's face has gone grim.

Now, as Lizzie returns, loaded with towels, we hear a cop car whooping towards the house.

'Now they turn up,' she grumbles. 'Our new alarm goes straight to the police station, Master, but it still takes them too long, hey? Be a lot of damn use if a person was already chopped to bits by a panga. 'Scuse me, Master, 'scuse me, Madam Angela.'

She pulls her apron over her head and dashes outside. We wrap ourselves in the towels. They're beach towels, still smelling of last summer.

The cop car has started the dog off again. We listen, amazed, to its insane howling.

'Hey, Lizzie, what's with this hound?' I ask when she returns.

'He's special, Master,' she whispers, 'your father got him through his pals there by the police station. One of their alsatians, very, very fierce. I feed him, so I'm the only one who can go near him. So the Master and Madam mustn't please go into the backyard without me there, *hoor*? Agh, I better go shut his trap before he disturbs the Madam upstairs.'

'Is Dad upstairs too? In his den?'

Suddenly upset, Lizzie mumbles something, then zips off again.

'Doesn't Lizzie have any help?' asks Angela. 'She seems to do everything herself.'

'Dunno,' I answer. 'Place used to be knee-deep in staff. Something's funny. C'mon, time for the big surprise.'

'Bubs,' says Angela quietly, 'I'd really rather you went to say hello first.'

'Right,' I say instantly. (My folks never really went that nuts over my marriage. I don't think it's just because Angela's a shiksa – I mean, they don't really observe the faith anymore. Maybe it's just because it happened so far away.)

At the top of the stairs, there's a gate, like for a child. Don't remember that. Must be because of the dog. The landing is dim. I peer down the corridor towards my old room.

'Lizzie?' I hear Mom call, 'what was all that damn racket?'

Her door is half open. Within, there's a sepia light, a heater at work, and Springbok Radio playing softly.

I grab the doorhandle, and enter – 'Ta-daaah!'

Now, I don't know what I expected ... Well, all right, in my wildest dreams, I saw Mom leaping from her bed and showering me with kisses. That's totally unlike her, but after a thirteen-year separation from your only child, who knows what a person could do?

She does nothing.

Nothing. Not a flicker of surprise. Her face is fat and calm as a moon; framed by her great spread of black hair on the pillows. Despite her age – what, seventy-odd? – her hair has stayed dark.

'So,' she says quietly, 'Leon passed on.'

'Sorry?'

'Leon.'

'Hullo?'

'He passed on.'

I hesitate. Her late dad's name was also Leon, and resembled me. Maybe it's because I'm wrapped in white towels. I pat myself and laugh. She stares back glazed.

'Mom,' I say, sitting on the bed and taking her hand, 'I'm home. Home from London.'

'Oh.'

'Were you half-asleep maybe?'

'*Ja* ...' She examines my hand. Hers is like plasticine. A damp, almost greyish colour, blanching slightly as you press it. She's amazingly fat.

Now she lights a Peter Stuyvesant and drags on it slowly. A long, blank silence. Maybe she's in shock.

'How are you?' I ask.

She closes her eyes briefly, then, in a small voice, says, 'Everyone's very puzzled. My physio, my acupuncturist, my reflexologist, nobody knows what the blazes is going on. And just when I was making such progress. Everyone said so. But then the lower back starts up again, and next thing the blood sugar's all over the show, and then the migraines – although they never really took a holiday. Boy oh boy, there's nothing anybody can do about *them*! So there we are, back to square one, with everyone very, very puzzled.'

For as long as I can remember, my mother's been puzzling her medicine men. I used to think she was shamming, but you have only to look into her eyes – her black eyes, swimming in yellow rings – to know that the pain is real and deep.

'I'm home,' I say again, to cheer her up (and in case she still hasn't noticed).

'Yes,' she says gently, 'it's good you're home.'

'Did you . . . know?'

(She's psychic, of course.)

'Well, I knew something was up. Couldn't be a hundred percent.'

'We're back for your golden wedding.'

'Who's the "we"?'

'I've brought Angela.'

'Ah!'

'Mom, give her a chance.'

'Of course I'll give her a chance. A few years back you were bringing home *men* for us to meet, so you think I won't give her a chance?' She puts out her ciggie. 'You didn't bring any Marlboros with?'

'Marlboros?'

'We can't get them anymore. Sanctions.'

'Ah.'

'When Naomi Bloch comes over to visit her mom, she brings hundreds. Duty-free. They make a mint. People will pay anything.'

'I didn't think. I don't smoke anymore.'

'That a fact? But chocs still, hey?'

She keeps a store of Chocolate Logs at her bedside, for blood sugar emergencies.

'Mm!' I squeal, biting through the marshmallow top to the biscuity base. 'Wish they made these in the UK. All right, lemme fetch Angela. Is Dad in his den?'

'Nope.'

'Out?'

'Yup.'

'What time's lunch? What time's he due back?'

'He isn't. We've broken up.'

I carry on walking to the door, munching at my Chocolate Log. I even reach for the handle – before I stop. 'I'm sorry?'

'You heard.'

'What I heard's impossible.'

She shrugs and purses her lips. I go over to the wardrobes. All his are empty. Scrubbed clean. Even his smell has gone.

'But . . . *why*?' I ask.

'Agh, you know what he's like. With his boozing and all the nonsense. With a no-gooder like that, there's only so much a person can take.' She pauses, has a brief coughing spasm, her grey plasticine skin turning a reddish-black, then calms herself, and lights another Peter Stuyvesant. 'My late dad, he always said, Leon . . .'

'*Ja*?'

'No, he was Leon too.'

'I know. I'm saying, *Ja*, carry on.'

'Hmn? No, he never trusted your father. Leon. He'd say – Jewish or not, a *Pole* can't be trusted. And Leon knew what he was talking about, Leon.'

I steady myself against the door. 'But why didn't you let me know?'

She blows out smoke. 'Didn't want to upset you.'

'I . . . I dunno what to say. Mom, it is your *golden wedding* tomorrow!'

'So? Isn't now a good time to admit we made a mistake? Before we go any further.'

'Go any further? Dad's eighty-three! I'd better talk to him. Where's he gone?'

'Haven't a bloody clue. Rotting on the streets.'

'Rotting on the streets? Mom, he's a millionaire.'

'And a lot of good it did him.'

'Listen –'

'Leon, I don't wish to discuss this any further, thank you very much.'

'But we –'

'Thank you, Leon. Fetch your woman now please, and let's get the hullos over and done with. It'll be lunchtime in a mo, and if we make Lizzie late, we'll never hear the end of it. Oi halleluyah, with two extras for lunch, imagine the panic already in that kitchen!'

'Mom, I'm –'

'Leon, fetch your woman!'

'Will you stop calling her *my woman*! Her name is Angela.'

'Right – fetch Angela!'

'Right – I will!'

Downstairs, Angela is alone in the semi-dark, sitting on our cases. She's dug out her tracksuit, and put it on. The storm has battered her make-up, and her hair's still wet, the silver strands clinging to her scalp like a frayed net. I wish she looked prettier for the ordeal ahead.

'How's your mum?' she whispers as we climb the stairs.

'No fine, fine. Listen, I've just had some rather weird news. She and Dad have split up.'

The introductions which follow aren't the most terrific success. Angela does her best, laying on the charm in her fanciest accent, and lots of pillow plumping and sheet tucking. But no go. Mom's black eyes take in Angela's figure (not seen to its best in a tracksuit), and register immediate disapproval. Funny how fat people disapprove of other fat people. They just know this is someone with a problem! And, of course, at Angela's age, Mom was still a great beauty, the raven-haired queen of the Cape Town set.

I endure about five minutes, before suggesting, 'Should we get our luggage upstairs before lunch?'

'Good idea,' says Mom eagerly, pressing a bell above the bed. 'Use your old room. I'll get Lizzie to bring up your things.'

'Where's everyone else?' I ask. 'The rest of your staff?'

'*Shewww!* she groans, 'well, your father took Zakes him with, but that's no real loss. Another drunkard! How he didn't prang the car twice daily I couldn't tell you. But I've also had to get rid of Hester. She started with the boyfriends in the room *again*. And little Sammy, I had to fire him as well – he wasn't just cleaning the silver, he was teaching it to walk. Who else? Fatima, the dressmaker – no, she still comes once a fortnight. Old Khomo in the garden – well, he went and died, of course –'

'Old Khomo died?' I say. 'Shame.'

'*Ja*, a good sort, hey? Specially compared to some that I've had since. But you remember Paula and Joel Singer? Well, they're emigrating to Israel next month, so they're going to leave me their garden boy, who's apparently quite honest. And hygienic. Oh, but they're always going to be a headache, staff. I don't know what the situation is in London, Angela, but as for here – I'm telling you, if I wasn't so bed-bound, I'd rather do the work myself.'

As Angela takes a deep breath, preparing for battle, I clap my hands. 'Right – I need a wash.'

'Yes,' says Mom. 'Well, nice to meet you, Angela.'

(This means she isn't joining us for lunch.)

Back in the corridor, Angela whispers, 'I don't think we're going to get on.'

'Give it a chance,' I say, opening the door to my old room.

'Oh blimey!' says Angela.

My bedroom was done up by an opera designer friend in the early seventies, all in black and gold.

'I expected a child's room,' says Angela, wincing at the sight of my genuine black panther bedspread.

'Hardly,' I say. 'I lived here till I met you.'

'Gosh, yes.' She runs her fingers over the black-mirrored dressing table. 'It's spotless.'

'Still cleaned daily, I suppose.'

'Well, well. We're here . . .'

Her pause stretches and stretches, until we're both thinking the same thing. I'm sure we are, because we avoid one another's eyes. The last few hours have been so chaotic, he hasn't come to mind once. Now this peculiar ache again.

Lizzie knocks and struggles into the room with our luggage. Angela leaps to her aid. They tussle over the cases, getting in one another's way, before Lizzie retreats. ''scuse me, Master, 'scuse me, Madam Angela.'

'I'm going to get depressed if she keeps calling me that,' sighs Angela.

And here we are: *unpacking* again. Outside, the storm is over. Now there's just water gurgling in the gutters and drains.

'*Ai!*' I say, finding my big white Harrods dressing-gown. 'No, this you shouldn't have put in.'

'I thought you'd need it for the cold weather.'

I hold it to her nose.

'Oh,' she says. 'Oh dear.'

'*Ja.*' I bring it to my face. Clear as if he's standing there.

'Again,' whispers Angela.

We pass it back and forth, feasting on his scent. Then Angela digs out his present: the cheap little toilet bag with all his things.

I stop her. 'This is too weird.'

'Shall we phone instead?' she asks.

I stare at her. We agreed not to phone, or write. We agreed to let him make the first move; if he wants to.

'No,' she says, before I can, 'it's Sunday. He'll be at Charlotte's. Stoned out of his head.' She suddenly bends, hugging herself.

'You OK?' I ask.

'No,' she says, 'I'm not. I'm afraid I really am not.'

'C'mon, let me show you my best place when I was a kid.'

I take her down the corridor, and through a small door. Beyond is a narrow wooden staircase, musty-smelling. This isn't cleaned daily. Opening the hatch at the top, there's a blast of icy sea air.

'Oh,' cries Angela, climbing into the turret, rushing to the seaward railing, and lifting her face into the wind. 'Oh yes!'

'You look like Garbo,' I say, hugging her, 'at the end of whatch-amacallit.'

All of Sea Point lies below us, then a huge body of sea, with Robben Island like a bruise in the middle. Everything is still blurred and soggy from the storm. I'd forgotten how bleak this place can be. Blackpool out of season. Maybe that's why Angela likes the view. Now the foghorn starts, way down at Mouille Point. Oh Jesus, all this again; all this nothingness.

Hearing a sudden commotion below, we lean over the other side, and look down into the shadowy yard. You can just make out an animal, hurling itself at the back door. Sensing us, he stops and lifts his snout. A light from the kitchen catches his eyes, turning them into luminous holes.

'I was reading in the *Guardian*,' says Angela, 'how your police here have crossed an alsatian with a Russian grey wolf. It couldn't be that this –?'

'No.'

'Oh, good,' she laughs.

'So the *Guardian*'s spreading stories about Russian wolves in our streets?'

'Mh-hh,' she says. 'Why, were you expecting lions and tigers?'

SEVENTEEN

'I don't know,' says Adam Gool, 'and nobody does.'

'Then it's a mystery,' I say.

'Man, it's a real disappearing trick.'

I shift in my seat. Well, I say mine, but actually it's Dad's. When Adam led me and Angela into Dad's office, we took an awkward stroll round before I perched on his chair. They're magnificent old things, both the chair and desk, in dark stinkwood, with balding black-green upholstery. I remember sitting in this chair as a kid, and how it seemed like a big tub suspended in mid-air, tilting as you flopped round, wandering off in a whole circle if you let it. But I haven't tried it since. It crackles as I shift.

The other noise is a constant shudder from the big windows behind me, as if any sec the rough harbour winds will blast through.

'*Nee, O vader!*' says Adam Gool, as a walkie-talkie on the desk suddenly starts jabbering. 'Excuse me again, please' – and he dashes into the outer office.

Angela's standing at the shuddering windows, gazing at the docks. The black outline of her fab Issey Miyake wrap looks out of place in here. Everything else is dust-coloured. The stacks of files, old sea-traffic maps on the wall, some cardboard boxes in the corner; all covered in dust. Or you think it's dust, until you find it doesn't yield to the touch. It's salt. In the summer months these windows are thrown open to the harbour. Then, along with

142

the salt, you get all sorts of smells drifting in from the warehouses below: hessian, timber, oil and rust.

And once a musty, birdy smell of ostrich feathers. That particular warehouse, scene of the crazy white storm, you can just see the roof from here.

'He owns this little corner of the docks,' I tell Angela. 'Had to wait years to get a lease off SATS. But he was now really determined – because it's where he landed in '37. The boats came in by that pier there. So he wanted his premises *here* and nowhere else. Pulled some strings, did some favours. It's always been his way. It's even how he got into this country in the first place. The authorities weren't that crazy about all the Jews arriving in the thirties. But Dad found a way. Pulled some strings, did some favours.'

'Funny. I expected it to be grander,' she says, scratching at the salt on the window.

'Grander!' I laugh. 'A prime site on the harbour here? The Cape of Good Hope! And you want grander?'

Adam Gool hurries back in. 'Sorry, sorry. *Ja* so, he's just disappeared, as I was saying, uh . . .'

(Note the *uh*, hey? That's where my name should be. He doesn't know what to call me. He's certainly not going to say Master Leon anymore, or even Mister Leon, but he needs permission to say just Leon.)

'You're not just a foreman anymore, are you, Adam?' I ask, appraising the cufflinks, the tinted specs, the manicured beard and moustache.

'No, oh God no. Operations Manager.' Even his accent has been manicured: the Cape Coloured accent which used to zap and twang like elastic. I bet his wife has her hair straightened, and wears one of those skin lighteners. Maybe he does too. Is it my imagination, or was he browner as a kid? That scrappy little *gammatjie* I used to play with when I visited the docks. Our games ranged from Cowboys and Indians to Let's See Yours. His was unbelievably huge, or seemed so then. The bod is still good. Probably goes to a gym, dear God.

'How long is it?' I ask, then quickly add, 'since you've seen him.'

'Last Wednesday.'

'And you're trying to tell me that not even Moshe knows where he is?'

'Moshe?'

'Moshe.'

'Moshe emigrated to California three years ago. Didn't you know?'

I stare at him. *Ja.* Mom must've . . . So, who's helping Dad run the outfit these days?'

A Coloured receptionist looks in. 'Pardon me, Mr Gool, but Tel Aviv are asking again about their August break-bulk delivery.' Like Adam, she's wearing a thick jersey and scarf. (Why is *nowhere* heated properly?)

'Who's Moshe?' asks Angela, when Adam pops out again.

'Moshe? Moshe is my . . . or *was* my dad's partner. A first cousin from Poland. Poor Dad must be running the show on his own. Moshe *gone*! Wow! Shit!'

'Shall we phone him?' she asks suddenly.

'Huhn?'

'It's almost eleven thirty. Nine thirty his time.'

'In California?'

'What? London. He might be back from Charlotte's by now.'

'Oh,' I say, rubbing my face. 'Isn't nine thirty a bit early after a debauched weekend?'

'We don't know he's had a debauched weekend,' she says, criss-crossing her doodle on the window, 'and anyway, we want to catch him before he goes out.'

'Out? Where's he going?'

'How would I know? I'm stranded on the other side of the sodding world! How would I –'

'OK, shh, shh. Phone – phone him if you want.' I push the phone towards her, chewing my lip. (She's really determined to ignore our agreement.)

Adam returns just as Angela dials the number. 'Sorry, Mrs Lipschitz, I'll –'

'No, no,' says Angela, snapping down the receiver.

Adam hesitates, then ushers in the receptionist with coffee and biscuits. I search through the bottom drawers on the desk. Dad keeps his booze somewhere down here. Gifts off the different

boats: sake, bourbon, tequila, and of course, Polish vodka off the
fishing ships that come down from Walvis Bay for repairs. Adam
watches me rummaging with the teeniest scowl.

'We're wondering what we must do about tonight,' he says.

'Ah-huhh,' I say. 'What's happening tonight?'

'The big do for your folks.'

'Oh, of course,' I say, ducking further behind the desk. (Of
course – today's Monday, the big day!)

'We've hired a cruise ship for the evening. Very popular. Dinner
and dance round the harbour. Mind you, the weather yesterday
gave everyone a damn big shock. Thank heavens it's calmer today.'

Adam and the receptionist exchange a glance as I throw a slug
of cognac into my coffee. What's their prob? Dad would be doing
this at eight in the morning. I've waited till practically lunchtime.

'No, well,' I say, 'maybe we'd better cancel the party. Postpone
it, I mean. Until my dad shows up.'

'*Ja*,' says Adam, 'but you see, *uh* . . .'

(Again with the *uh*.)

'. . . trouble is, it's all paid for. The ship, the band, the caterers.
You know your dad's motto: *Ribi-fish, gelt ahfen tish!*'

'They all speak bits of his Yiddish,' I explain, laughing, to
Angela. 'It means "Cash in advance." No, well Adam look, if it's
paid for, let's go ahead. Call it a staff party. Spread the word round
and let's all have ourselves a *lekker* old rave!'

'But the Port Director is invited. And the Controller of Customs.
And –'

'No, no – *them* you'd better cancel.'

'Must I do that, Mr Gool?' asks the receptionist. He nods.
She moves to the door, then stops. 'What must I say has now
happened?'

'Say Mrs Lipschitz is unwell,' Adam replies instantly. (They must
use that one lots.) 'Unwell. Regrettably.' The receptionist nods
sympathetically, then shoots out.

Angela smiles to herself and murmurs, 'Yes, Mrs Lipschitz is
unwell.'

I glance at her. She's in a funny mood again today. 'Excellent,'
I say to Adam. 'We'll have a party just for ourselves.' I heave myself
out of the great chair. 'Call us a cab, hey, Adam.'

'A cab?' he says. 'Oh God no, *uh* ...'

'*Leon*, please,' I say, and then, turning to Angela. 'I've only been gone a few years and already he's forgotten my name.'

'Not at all,' chuckles Adam. 'No, Leon, what I was going to say is that Zakes can drive you back.'

'Zakes is here?'

'He is.'

Adam grimaces discreetly as he says this. He and Zakes aren't the best of pals. Rivals, in fact, for Dad's favour; Zakes is the old man's chauffeur.

'But dammit, Adam,' I say, 'if anyone will know where Dad is, Zakes will.'

'He doesn't,' says Adam, perhaps louder than he intended.

I smile and head for the door. 'Tell me, have you thought about notifying the cop-shop about Dad?'

'Mustn't that be up to your mom?'

'Absolutely.'

In the outer office, more walkie-talkies lying on tables, chattering to one another, while well-groomed, well-wrapped Coloureds scurry to and fro. Speed, speed is the essence – this is Dad's law – speed in moving cargo; a vessel only earns money when it's at sea; speed, speed.

Halfway down the corridor, I notice a brass plate on one door, with Adam's name. I ping it with my fingernails as we pass. 'Hell, Adam, you've really done well,' I say, without a tidge of bitchiness.

'Agh, Leon,' he says bashfully, 'it took years of night classes. There's nothing like education.'

'Nothing like,' says Angela, touching his arm.

'What happened to Freddy whachamacallit?' I ask. 'Dad's old Operations Manager?'

'Freddy Telushkin,' says Adam. 'Australia. '86.'

(I suddenly realise that we've only seen Coloured staff around. The blacks work in the warehouses. But the whites – are they *all* in California or Australia?)

Downstairs in the lobby, the wind finds its way through the revolving doors with a weird shriek. The front of the building is on an exposed corner of the docks. Beyond, nothing but a stretch of wet tarmac and a jumble of concrete blocks serving as breakwater. I remember, as a kid, wishing my dad's job didn't take him to this bleak edge of the world.

We hand in our clip-on security permits, and then Adam pushes through the doors, whupping open an umbrella. He puts his fingers to his lips and whistles. A moment later, Dad's lime-green Rolls drifts round the corner and slides to our feet.

'Zakes,' I cry, jumping into the back seat.

Zakes has no prob with my title. 'Mister Leon,' he chuckles, reaching over his shoulder and grasping my wrist. He grins at me in the mirror above his cap. 'But *kyk nou* who's here – Mister Leon!'

I can't remember seeing Zakes sober. Ever. His eyes loll down his chubby brown cheeks, while a wet lower lip reaches upwards. In between is a moustache, Ronald Colman-thin. Agh, Zakes is a terrible old *skelm*, but with a heart of gold. Zakes *die kat*, they call him round the docks. He's had nine lives all right, and that's just for starters. He began as a stevedore, then worked as a cook on the cargo vessels, travelling the world. A tattoo of the Empire State Building peeks out of one cuff, while on the other hand is a five-dot tattoo, like on dice, which the hoodlums of the old District Six wore as their badge. Zakes has had run-ins with the cops over everything from dagga-dealing to smuggling contraband off the boats. But nowadays he's calmed down. Nowadays the charges are nothing worse than drunken driving – and Dad's always standing by to pay the fine, or to offer the cops free hols in Mauritius.

Dad adores Zakes's spirit: the gypsy, the gambler, the storyteller. Adam he values, but Zakes he adores.

As the car drives off, we turn and wave to Adam. Above his umbrella, a sign says LIPSCHITZ & SON. Dad had that put up the day I was born. But why did he never take it down?

'So Zakesie-babes,' I say, 'howzit, *jou bliksem?*'

'Agh nay-what sir, just taking it easy, just *sommer* hanging cool.'

'Zakes, this is my wife, Angela.'

'Madam,' says Zakes, flipping one palm over his shoulder.

'Oh, please don't call me Madam,' she says, shaking hands.

'No, that's *mos* cool too. What's it now to be – "Lady"? "Sister"?'

'"Angela" will do, ta,' she replies, laughing.

'This a new model, Zakes?' I ask, stroking the dove-grey up-holstery.

'Splinter new, Mister Leon. *Tahkeh gits*, hey?'

'They all speak some of his Yiddish,' I say, giggling, to Angela.

'*Dobrze, dobrze*,' says Zakes.

'And Polish,' I add. I reach up and run my fingers along the soft ceiling. 'A "Royals"-Royce – that's how Dad pronounces it, hey, Zakes?'

'A Royals-Royce sir, a VIP motor for a VIP man, jet set and personality plus. Complete with all the works.' He flicks a switch, and the car fills with music. From every polished, leather-scented fold it comes: Eddie Fisher singing 'Lady of Spain'.

Leaning forward, I gawp at the six-speaker cassette and CD system alive with digital blippers, and, underneath it, Dad's prized collection of music from the forties and fifties. 'The music of freedom' he calls it. Whenever an American ship is in, Zakes is sent onboard to see what his contacts have brought Dad this time: rare recordings of Benny Goodman's early days, Jimmy Durante, and that native chap, Satchmo.

'And man, peel back your peepers on this,' laughs Zakes, tapping another set of switches. Above his head a TV screen sizzles into life. It's footage of a car bomb somewhere. I find a remote control at my elbow, and zap the off-button, saying, 'Hell, hey – outstanding!'

'Drinks, phone, computer, fax, wash-basin.'

'Fab, unreal, blow your mind!' A bar has opened at our knees. I tuck in.

'I wonder if we can get long-distance?' whispers Angela, lifting the phone.

I look at her, shocked, but before I can speak, Zakes says, 'Angela, the story is – no ways.'

'Oh, right, sorry,' she mumbles, and stares out of the window. I quickly fix her a Buck's Fizz.

'Wanna drink, Zakes?' I ask.

'Well, just a *doppie*, thanky-doodle-dandy, sir,' he says, handing over an empty cooldrink can, with straw. I throw in some Pepsi and Scotch, and pass it back. '*L'chaim!*' he says.

We go quiet, schlurping at our drinks and swaying to Eddie Fisher. Outside the air is milky, and people drive with their headlamps on. I glimpse the broken freeway above us, leading up eerily into the mist. What if someone got onto it by mistake, and accelerated? The foghorn blares, quite close. We're approaching Sea Point. I sing softly.

'Lady of Spain I adore you,

Pull down your *broeks*, I'll explore you . . .'

Zakes laughs. '*Gooi daai nommer, gooi-gooi!*'

'The fifties, hey?' I say. 'Those were the days.'

'*Is mos*, sir!'

'Zakes, my pal.'

'Sir, my master.'

'Where are you hiding Dad?'

He stops schlurping. Ahead, at the Three Anchor Bay junction, the robots turn red, and we drift to a stop. He lowers the volume on Eddie Fisher, then asks, 'How are we doing for time, sir?'

'Need to be back for lunch by about . . . one.'

'Is your watch Swiss, sir?'

I laugh. 'Hell, Zakes, and I thought when we met you were shaking my hand.'

'Mister Leon,' he exclaims, offended. 'So true as anything, I'm jolly damned glad to see you back by us here.'

'Good. And I'd be jolly damned glad to see my dad.'

He jerks up his chin, tilting the loose red eyes back into their sockets. We consider one another in his mirror.

'If a person knew,' he says, 'wouldn't a person be now sworn to keep his *bek* shut?'

'Depends . . .' I say, taking off my watch, leaning over and laying it on the passenger seat, just as the lights change and we move off.

(Jesus – he managed that during one red light!)

Now he pulls up along the Beach Road. 'Has Angela seen the Atlantic Ocean yet, Mister Leon?'

'Huhn? No, no, she hasn't. Come and see the Atlantic Ocean, darling,' I say, shoving a bewildered Angela out of the car.

The beachfront is cold, with brownish sea-scum in the gutters from yesterday's storm. A section of coloured lights has come loose along the promenade, and they dangle heavily in the wind. We stroll over the boggy lawns towards the sea wall. Beyond, the waves are wild. I'd forgotten how wild they get at this time of year. Huge, yellow-green, with the kelp showing like black guts, they rear and rush at you.

'Not sure if I trust Zakes,' says Angela.

'Don't be racist,' I reply, chuckling. 'He had a deprived upbringing. Dad hauled him out of a life of poverty and made a new person of him.'

'What – like you did with me?'

I laugh, but her expression is humourless; tensed against the chill and damp.

(Oh, where's my old Angela?)

As we cross a small playground, I push the roundabout into motion and climb on. 'So, over there we have the Atlantic Ocean going meshuggeh . . . over there, the famous Lion's Head mountain, decapitated by mist today . . . over there, Zakes ringing my dad . . .'

'You gave him your watch.'

'It wasn't one of my good ones.'

'It was, actually. A 1921 Patek Philippe. Your Easter treat two years ago.'

'Oh shit. Sorry.'

EIGHTEEN

The lift seems to be rising forever; slowly, almost grudgingly, hissing with the effort. These flats are let out on a time-share scheme; different people own them for different weeks of the year. Standing right on the beachfront, it's packed during the good months, but during the winter the only takers are a few old couples and maybe a writer or two. So the owners close down some floors, to minimise the cleaning.

One of the cleaners is Zakes's contact here: a toothless girl heading fast for dipso-land.

The lift stops on the twenty-fourth floor, one below the top. There must be a private lift direct to the penthouse. We go outside and climb the fire escape. It's sickeningly high here, with Sea Point flickering into view through the grid under our feet. The Lipschitz mansion is practically the only thing level with us, and from here the turret looks like the dome on a Russian church.

Zakes has his own key to the penthouse's fire-escape door.

Within, the rooms are walled in glass – glass from ceiling to floor. The furniture is sparse and modern, made to last, easy to clean. It's got to survive holidaying families with kids, Joburg playboys with harems of girls or boys, lonely businessmen in town for a week, boozing themselves silly at night and then kotching it up wherever.

Zakes leads us through these glassy rooms, to one where the mirrored door is shut.

I see myself looking scared.

Zakes knocks and enters.

After all the empty rooms, the clutter in here comes as a surprise: suitcases, a big trunk, crates of vodka, a ghetto-blaster. And Dad. Asleep on the floor in one corner, wrapped in his magnificent black coat. His Karakul coat. It seems like he's worn nothing else since I was a kid, and it's always fascinated me. The Karakul lambs have to be skinned exactly one day after birth, and it can take up to sixty lambs for a normal-sized coat. Dad's would've taken three times that.

I stare at him. He's put on even more weight, which is virtually impossible. His Polish features are wide, thick and flat. The hair used to be bushy and red like mine, but now, although there's still a great mane of it, it's a lemony colour. It's unwashed, and stubble glistens on his tortoise-like jaws.

'What happened?' he suddenly mutters. 'Hahh? To this thing. A lifetime. What happened?'

Zakes squats at his side and gently rubs one hand. 'Mister Chaim,' he whispers, 'Leon is here.'

'Leon? Leon died.'

'He means my mom's dad,' I explain, cheerfully, to Angela.

'Leon, Leon,' Dad says, looking up with big boiled eyes, 'all these Leons.' He raises his arms. For a sec it's as though he's going to reach for me. But it's Zakes he grasps.

Getting him up ain't easy, but Zakes is well practised, somehow gripping Dad's huge torso, which is loose and peculiar as a sack of water. The black coat flaps open – he's wearing only his long winter underwear, or *gatkes*, as he calls them. I look away. He and Zakes stagger to the trunk. It makes a cracking noise as Dad sits, but holds.

Now Dad recognises me. Again he raises his arms. Are we going to *hug*? A spook cartwheels through me, stinging my eyes, squashing my bowels. I stumble forward. But we just do the usual – we just shake hands.

'Leon,' he says. '*Jak sie masz?*'

(Polish? He's pissed.)

'No, I'm fine, Dad, and howzit by you?'

'*Nje, jako-tako*. Hey, d'you know Zakes?'

'Dad, of course I know –'

'Hey, come here,' he roars, grabbing hold of Zakes. 'Leon, you see this man here – this man is my saviour. He gets me this flat, the food, he fixes me up with the works.' Dad indicates the ghetto-blaster. 'It's his only one, and he lends it me. Will you drink with me, Zakes?' Dad reaches around for a bottle, and finding none, clicks his fingers.

Zakes darts across the room, fetches a full bottle from a crate and snaps open the screw-top.

I watch, horrified, as they pass it from mouth to mouth. I don't know which is the more repulsive: Zakes's wet brown lips or Dad's harsh beak. He's lost one of the lower teeth, and it's created a sort'f hole in his face, a black gap through which stuff spills: his slurred words, or spit, or the drink. The nightmare I sometimes have – of springing a puncture – it's happened to Dad for real.

'Who's this?' Dad cries suddenly, pointing at Angela. 'Get the newspapers out of here!'

'Dad, this is Angela,' I explain, 'my wife.'

'What – the gold-digger?' Dad asks Zakes. 'He's brought along the gold-digger?'

'I'm uh . . . off back to the house,' says Angela.

'I'll drive you there, Angela,' says Zakes.

'No, Zakes,' says Dad, in a whimper.

'Yes, Zakes,' I insist, tapping my bare wrist. He nods and goes to the mirrored door. Angela hurries after him. The door closes, showing me and Dad. Two balloons in the room. Big and king-sized.

'Where's Zakes gone?' mutters Dad, reaching round like a blind man.

'It's OK, he'll be back now-now.'

'Leon?'

'Ja.'

'What you doing here?'

'I came over for your anniversary.'

'That a fact?'

'Yup.'

'We're not together anymore, your mother and I.'

'I know.'

'It's happening lots these days,' he says, passing the bottle.

I wipe it thoroughly and take a sluk. 'What is ha – ?' I pause, throat on fire – the liquor must be two hundred percent proof. 'What's happening lots?'

'The three D's.'

'The three whats?'

'The three D's is how I call it. Departures, deaths and divorces. That's how we spend our weekends. At the airport, at the cemetery, at friends' houses. Commiserating, commiserating. So, OK, now people can come commiserate with me.'

'So that's why you've done it? As social one-upmanship?'

'Hahh?'

I lean back against the wall. How many times have I heard that noise – 'Hahh?' – that bludgeoning noise. It's not asking you to speak clearer. It deafens everything within reach.

'Put on the music,' he says, clicking his fingers.

'Why did no one tell me,' I ask, kneeling at Zakes's ghetto-blaster, 'about you and Mom?'

'I tried. The Wednesday last I tried. I spoke with your machine. And for days after, always your machine.'

(That message! While Angela and Gertjie were at her show, and I was passed out on the lawn. And, then, during Thursday and Friday, as we three roamed around naked, yes, the phone rang and rang.)

I slip in a tape: 'Trans-Atlantic Hits of the Forties and Fifties'. Benny Goodman is on first, 'Stompin' at the Savoy'. Dad softens, smiles, and the oily eyes go oilier.

'So how's the UK keeping?' he asks.

'It's still there.'

'Grey vests.'

'Sorry?'

'The UK sky. Grey vests.'

'Not these days. Blue, blue. Whereas *here* . . .'

'Here it's winter.'

'Winters never used to be like this.'

'Agh, *idz docholery*! And how's Pallister?'

I laugh. He asks after the weather and his UK accountant. That's how he sums up my life in exile.

(But hang on! *Pallister* – does Dad know anything about our charitable donations?)

'I haven't really seen much of Pallister,' I say, watching Dad closely.

'A good man,' he mutters, 'a good servant. Comes when called.'

'So you've always said.'

He's miles away, listening to Benny Goodman's sounds winging across some rainbow-coloured dancefloor.

'Dad,' I say, 'today is your fiftieth anniversary.'

'Hahh? Fifty years ago the war started. And a lifetime went away. Where?'

(I've always wondered if he had a wife and kids before. I mean, he was thirty-one when he fled Poland. Unless he was a moffie back then . . . !)

'Tell me about it,' I say. 'Life in Poland.'

'Gone. *Zetz!* Get the Commies to tell you.'

'Commies? You mean the Nazis.'

'There's a difference?'

'But . . . wasn't it the Nazis you were fleeing?'

'And why were the Nazis coming? To get the Commies.'

'What? Weren't the Nazis coming to get the Jews? The capitalist Jews?'

'No. Only the Jews in the Communist Party, or in the *Bund*, or in the *Poale-tsion*, or what you want.'

I swig from the bottle, wishing Angela was here, with all the facts at her fingertips. On Zakes's machine, someone's singing about having a lovely bunch of coconuts, big ones, small ones, some as big as your head. 'So,' I say, 'it was all the fault of the Jews in the Communist Party?'

'Correct. These were the troublemakers. Deserved everything they got. The rest of us were innocent bystanders. We knew nothing. Politics – who knew about politics? We were businessmen. And the same thing is happening today in this country. The majority of people are happy. And now I'm talking *shvartze* as well – and nobody must come tell me I don't know the black man, because I'm working with him cheek by jowl, day in, day out. And I'm here to tell you he's happy. He's happy, I'm happy, everybody's happy. Except for the Commies. And who are they?

A handful of delinquent Jews again, *Got vet shtrofen*! Again we'll be ruined by a handful!'

'Maybe. But this life you left behind . . . ?'

'I don't recall it. Who recalls a lifetime ago?'

I sigh. 'Anyway, fifty years ago you married Mom and – '

'She's *kurwa*! Cunt! You know what I'm saying?'

'I'm getting your drift.'

'You also think she's the cunt?'

'Uhh . . .' I shift my position and almost fall over. Jesus, pissed already. Luckily he is too, and forgets his question. We go quiet. Tony Martin has taken over on Zakes's blaster.

> *If I seem starry-eyed*
> *That's a danger in paradise*
> *For mortals to stand beside*
> *An angel like you . . .*

Dad hoists himself up. 'So there we are!' He wobbles over to the huge window. Beyond, nothing but sea, mist and sky, endless and hopeless, the wind pushing, the waves falling. Dad raises his arms and slowly leans onto the glass.

'Should you do that?' I ask.

'*Ja*, I should.'

He rocks back on his heels, then forward again, quite strongly, bumping the window.

'Dad, I'd really prefer it if you didn't . . .'

'It's OK,' he mutters. 'All day I do this. Nobody can spot me from down there. Come look.'

'I'm not worried whether anyone can – '

'Come look!'

I shuffle over.

'Closer,' he says, clicking his fingers.

I put my forehead against the window, copying him. The glass is freezing.

'Scared?' he asks in a dull voice.

'Nope. It's like flying.'

'Like flying,' he repeats softly, contentedly.

I squint round. His face is squashed against the glass, a mass of flesh and steam. Saliva dribbles from the hole in his mouth. I turn back to the sea.

'Is that one of yours?' I ask. 'That boat.'

'Who knows?'

'Dad, it must be very difficult running the business with Moshe gone.'

'Don't talk to me about Moshe. *Kurwa!* You know what this means?'

'Yes, you've just told me. Cunt.'

'Cunt? No – whore. No – womb. Which is it? I can't recall now.'

'Womb? Womb is a swear-word?'

'*Psiakrew!* You know this?'

'Dad, I never learned Yiddish.'

'It's Polish.'

'Polish, Yiddish, what's the odds? I don't speak the lingo, all right?'

He chuckles, heaving against the glass. 'That's a good one. "Polish, Yiddish, what's the odds?" I must remember this one.'

Each time he bumps the window, I feel the reverberation, a tiny blow to my forehead. Way, way below I see Dad's car – his *Royals*-Royce – pulling up. Zakes has taken Angela home and returned. He gets out, looks up at the building, then slopes across the lawns to the beach, schlurping at his cooldrink can.

'Where's our bottle?' asks Dad.

Stepping back from the window is like stepping back onto solid ground. 'Is that why you're staying away from work?' I ask, finding the bottle.

'Hahh?'

'Because it's getting too much for you? With Moshe gone. We've been there this morning, and Adam Gool seems to be –'

'He's a good servant, Adam. He doesn't go to the toilet without consulting me. He's a good boy.'

'I hope so, because he seems to be running the outfit.'

'No, he won't get it.'

'What?'

'I'll give it to Zakes.'

'Give what?'

157

'Where's my drink?' he asks, clicking his fingers.

I pass it to him, staying back from the window.

'Closer,' he says.

I sigh, and lean forward again.

'Scared?' he asks.

'Dad, we've been through this.'

'Scared I'll give it to Zakes?'

'Give *what*?'

'No, I'll give it to Ivan.'

'Who's Ivan?'

'Ivan? It's his bar mitzvah on Saturday. You don't remember Ivan?'

'Well, if it's his bar mitzvah, and he's therefore thirteen, and since I've been away thirteen years, what the fuck d'you expect me to remember?'

'Hey, cut it out!' he roars. 'You don't get smart with me, hahh? I'm not one of your friends.'

'True.'

I jump as the bottle suddenly swings up – it clangs against the window – and he takes a long drink.

'So OK, who's Ivan?' I ask.

'Ivan? Ivan is Moshe's youngest son.'

'Moshe – Moshe, as in your ex-partner, Moshe?'

'Correct. The Moshe who deserted his business and his family for a blonde shiksa in California – the *kurwa*! All clear?'

'All clear. OK, now what is it you're going to give Ivan?'

'The business. What else? I'm going to give it him on Saturday. As a bar mitzvah present, *ja*?'

'You're going to give your business to the son of the partner who deserted you?'

'He deserted the son too. They belong together.'

'But Dad, aren't you giving the business back to Moshe? Can't he come back and *gup* it off his son?'

'So?'

'So? You hate him.'

'So? He's family.'

'Aah!'

That word – another ear-splitting noise – *family*! Dad and

Moshe were the only ones of their lot to escape before the war. No more than first cousins, but nevertheless family. Whatever they do to one another, they're family. Linked forever. I roll my forehead against the cold glass, soothing it, as I sing along to Dad's tape.

'*Daveeee*
Davy Crockett
King of the wild frontier . . .'

'Scared?' asks Dad, in that dull voice.

'You keep asking me that. I don't want the business. I've got my life in London.'

'You don't want the business? No, no, my boy – it's the business that doesn't want you. You couldn't run the business if it stood up and bit you in the face.'

'That's cool. I have no prob with that. I couldn't run the business, and you couldn't do some of the things I do.'

'Like for instance?' he asks.

'Like . . .'

'Like sticking my *shvontz* up another man's backside? No, granted, that I couldn't do.'

'Dad – I am married!'

'To a gold-digger!'

'No,' I protest, blushing suddenly. (Has his UK accountant, Pallister, said something?) 'And even if she was, she's a gold-digger with womb, cunt, you name it!'

'*Ja*? So where's the firstborn?'

'Ah well . . .'

'No. Not well. Not well at all. But now you know why I keep asking.'

'What?'

'If you're scared.'

The entrance hall is ablaze with light. The whole ground floor is. Light from every window, gleaming across the cold garden, picking out the taller plants, the cacti and palms.

Walking up the path isn't easy. I've got five legs. Precisely five:

159

connected at the centre, like the spokes of a wheel. And the crazy-paving doesn't help matters.

Using the banana tree for cover, in case anyone's at those bright windows, I kneel in the flower bed, and – KWUIGSH! – it's fingers down the throat. Again and again. Then I clean my lips and fingers with wet leaves, and rise. Better. Fewer legs.

In the distance, a burglar alarm goes off, and next door the boerbull barks. This gets Jungle going. His howling is rather wonderful, rising through the mist, up over our turret, which looks like the dome on a Commie church. Do they have wolves in Poland? Must do.

Entering the hallway, I shade my eyes against the light. My God – even the chandelier is lit. I can see it through the glowing fat of my fingers.

'*Nee, sies*, Master,' I hear Lizzie say. 'No, it isn't nice for a person to be like this.'

'At three o'clock on a Monday afternoon,' Angela adds, tutting.

Removing my hand, I find them down the other end of the marble hall, both on hands and knees, washing the floor. Angela's wearing her tracksuit, and one of Lizzie's *doeks* tied round her hair.

'I'm OK,' I say, demonstrating a steady walk. Unfortunately I choose a wet stretch, and next thing I'm in a rocking chair next to the phone. Its motion is a bit nauseating, so I ease myself onto the floor, from where I peer at them. ''m fine.'

'No, no, Master,' says Lizzie, 'this isn't nice.'

'Tell him, tell him,' sings Angela.

'Lizzie's not the one to tell me anything,' I scoff. 'She was *poegaaied* right through my childhood. Mom went nuts thinking of new places to hide the liquor cabinet key.'

'Ai, Master Leon – *loop!*' laughs Lizzie. 'That's now all in the past.'

'She's a reformed character,' adds Angela. 'Apparently they've got this marvellous new priest in her township, Bon . . . Bonte . . .'

'Brontë?' I suggest wittily, then burp, savouring a bubble of vodka which survived the upchuck.

'Master?' says Lizzie. 'No – Bonteheuvel.'

'Bon-te-heu-vel,' repeats Angela carefully, 'this marvellous priest –'

'Father Arendse,' prompts Lizzie.

'Father Arendse, who's teaching them how the government keeps down the price of liquor –'

'That's it,' says Lizzie, 'to –'

'To anaesthetise the population,' says Angela, 'and how –'

'Why don't you let her speak for herself?' I ask.

'What?' says Angela, face darkening. '*What?*'

'Nothing,' I sigh.

'She can't pronounce the word.'

'OK, fine. I'm cool.'

'Anaesthetise,' says Angela, 'a difficult word.'

'It is.'

'Can you say it?'

'Nope. Can't say it, but sure can do! Like you can too.'

She glares at me. I smile back.

Lizzie glances nervously from Angela to me, then says, 'Master Leon, I was only telling Madam Angela how this good priest is teaching us –'

'Precious little!' snaps Angela, suddenly rounding on her. 'He's teaching you precious little. My name is Angela. Angela! How many times do I have to . . . ?'

Lizzie freezes, eyes down.

'Sorry,' says Angela, 'sorry, sorry, I honestly didn't mean that. Please carry on.' Lizzie says nothing. Angela grits her teeth and scrubs the floor viciously. 'Lizzie – please carry on.'

'Agh no,' Lizzie says quietly, 'I's only telling how in his sermons, Father Arendse is –'

'Sermons?' I say. 'Should he be using sermons for propaganda? I mean –'

I blink as the scrubbing brush flies through the air.

'Prick!' hisses Angela.

The brush bounces off my forehead and into Lizzie's lap.

'I'll go make Master some nice black coffee,' she mumbles, scurrying out.

For a while, me and Angela sit in silence.

'You OK?' I ask her.

'No,' she says. 'Are you?'

I examine my head. 'Uhm . . .'

'I don't mean that. You deserved that. Can we phone now?'

'Phone?'

'It's three o'clock here – one o'clock his time.'

'Ah.'

'Yes. He'll be having lunch now.'

'How do you know he'll – ?'

'I don't!' she cries. 'But it doesn't exactly push out the boundaries of comprehension, does it – the notion of someone having lunch at one o'clock?'

'OK, OK, let's phone.'

I haul myself onto the bottom of the stairs as she picks up the receiver. Her fingers slip on the buttons and she has to re-dial. Then it happens again. She whispers to herself. It's like watching an addict.

There's no reply from the East End bedsit, so she tries our house. She listens to her own voice asking for a message, then says, 'Hello? Anyone there?'

'You just won't use his name, hey?' I say.

'Hmn?'

'For two days now you've said "he", "him", "his" – anything but his name. Why don't you use his name?'

'Why don't you?' she says, stretching the receiver towards me.

'Gertjie . . . ?' I call, and instantly feel sick.

Suddenly Angela puts down the phone. Someone's on the stairs behind me. I stagger to my feet. A youngish woman in a raincoat, with large yellowish eyes, and virtually no chin.

'My word, hey,' she says, 'but isn't it bright down here?' She's got an Oranjezicht accent, so sibilant even the females sound like moffies. 'So anyway,' she says, 'bye-bye for now, see you next week, same time, same place.'

Ja, see you,' I mutter. When she's gone, I turn to Angela with raised eyebrows.

'Dunno,' she says. 'Something to do with your mother. Her spiritualism, I think.'

'Ah. Mom . . .' I start upstairs.

'Brush your teeth first. A hint of vomit.'

'Right.' I stroke one of the ebony lamp holders. 'And whose idea is the Blackpool Illuminations?'

'Lizzie and me. We couldn't see to work.'

'Mom won't like it.'

'Oh dear, what a pity.'

(*Ai!* This holiday could be in trouble.)

In the bathroom, Gertjie's toilet bag sits alone on one shelf. I wonder if Angela's been sniffing it secretly? Feeling reckless, I get it down. I catch his scent instantly, and have to lean back against the wall. Then I take out his toothpaste and aim it at my brush. Nothing comes out. Odd. It's a new tube: Colgate, family-sized. I try again, then give up, and use our own paste.

And now, with mouth brushed, rinsed and sprayed, I'm finally ready for my mother.

As soon as I enter the bedroom, she reaches for me, almost ecstatically. Are *we* going to hug? I dash over. But again it's only my hand that's taken, and with a look of disappointment, as if she were expecting to touch something more interesting.

Her eyes clear quickly, radiant in her fat moon face. 'Leon was present,' she says.

'Your dad?'

'Hm? Leon – *Leon* was present,' she repeats impatiently.

'Oh, that's good,' I say, feeling vaguely embarrassed and scared.

She lights a Peter Stuyvesant, and watches the curling smoke. 'He's never been present before. Never. He only sent two words today, but oh, *what* two words! "Happy" and "Peace". Isn't that fabulous? Mind you, it doesn't really surprise me. He suffered so much in this world, he was bound to find bliss in the next. He was a prospector here, y'know, in the olden days –'

'*Ja*, I know.'

'*Ja*, schlepping from one mountainside to the next, one river after another, sifting, digging, cracking open boulders with his bare hands. What else could he do? From Russia they came with nothing. And his whole life that's all he ever found – nothing.'

'*Ja*, you've told me.'

'*Ja*. Even after we'd brought him down here, and rented for him that lovely flat in Fairview Mansions, and given him every luxury an old person could need, even then he'd still schlep down to the beachfront with his pick and shovel, returning at sundown with plastic bags full of sand.'

'*Ja* . . .' I stop, suddenly realising something – we had a *tramp* in the family!

'*Ja*, people laughed,' she continues. 'Your father laughed loudest of all. The bigshot Pole laughing at the little Russian prospector – "the little gold-digger", he called him. Shame, hey? And what with all the persecution Leon had already endured in the old country. Boy oh boy, did he pay his earthly dues! I wouldn't be surprised if he's settled all his karmic debts, and never has to enter the flesh again.'

'Is this like reincarnation?' I ask, getting that embarrassed, scared feeling again.

She takes my hand. 'This physical world is designed for one thing and one thing only – to aid our spiritual progress. We only keep coming back to pay off more karmic debts. So, each time, our souls have to find the most unsuitable environment for –'

'*Un*suitable?'

'Of course. The whole idea is to have as many hurdles as possible. And then, once an unsuitable environment has been found, the soul hovers around the new parents-to-be, making sure it's willing to take on their particular set-up.'

'Jesus,' I say, thinking of my rooting bouts with Angela. Was there sometimes a soul or two hovering round, some ghostly voyeurs? If so, why didn't any of them fancy us? Aren't we spectacularly unsuitable as parents? I mean, how many more hurdles does a soul want? Or were they thinking: I know I've got to suffer, but these two are beyond a joke!

Wow. The more you think about it, the creepier it gets. I mean, who's inside me right now? Who's using me as his idea of a bad time? Or Angela? Or Gertjie? Poor, beautiful Gertjie. Some soul has picked a rough ride there – a class piece of torture.

I nod at Mom, as she haks on and on, but now I'm picturing Gertjie against her pillows – the dark trail of hair down his belly, like stitches; candlewax falling on them, plip, plup.

I jump as Mom's hand touches my thigh, emphasising a detail in her reincarnation spiel.

'Mom,' I suddenly say, 'I don't suppose you feel like a party tonight . . . ?'

So my second day back home ends with a cruise round Table Bay. Dark and freezing. Although the ship is vaguely heated, there's no way of holding off the chill. Maybe it's because so few people turn up. You'd've thought that once word got round the docks, there would've been hordes; but maybe word didn't get *all* the way round. Only the office workers are here. Nice to find that there are still half a dozen whiteys; the rest are the Coloureds we saw this morning. There's not one black face to be seen.

I reckon that a dose of good old SA censorship went into the invitation list.

Adam Gool is on the main table, with glamorous wife and kids, and so is the receptionist with her husband and baby. These two families flank me and Angela. We've been given the seats of honour.

Though I say it myself, we do look bloody fab! La has worn an incredible 1947 Lanvin number – the word *unreal* doesn't even do it justice – and I've gone the whole hog in white tie and tails. These are the cossies we bought specially in London for tonight's big occasion.

The caterers have done a fantastic spread, with crayfish thermidor, kingklip in cream and mushrooms, fillet of baby beef, you name it. In fact, there're too many dishes. Actually, there're too many caterers – they almost outnumber the guests.

Even the band almost outnumbers the guests.

Knowing Dad's musical tastes, they've hired a huge Benny Goodman-type crowd, with clarinets, trombones, double-bass, the works.

When me and La take the dancefloor, everyone else scoots. Applause as we shimmy and sashay hither and thither, trying out those steps we've so often giggled over in *Come Dancing*. Normally Angela can be a bit self-conscious about her two left feet, but not tonight – she's high on champers. I've always been a demon of the dancefloor, but I really excel myself now, fired up by the clapping audience. In fact, I think my face only hits the dust once.

I'm almost sure Adam Gool smiles as that happens, and whispers comments. Well, I'm sorry but I don't know who he thinks he is! Sitting there on the head table, working through a bottle of finest Scotch, ordered as soon as they arrived. They get up to dance only once, the Gools, much later, when the guests have tired of Benny Goodman and requested some good old Country and Western sounds! It's now, as Adam dances, leading with the arse, that I glimpse the *gammatjie* I once played with as a kid. Jesus, he was the star of the Coon Carnival at Green Point Stadium one year. Does he admit to that? Or, like Dad, does he say 'I don't recall'?

Talking of recalling, I almost forgot Lizzie.

Ja, we've brought her along – all done up in her Sunday best: little green suit and hat.

Strange thing is, despite the freezing cold, she spends most of her evening up on deck. It's because, as we sail back and forth across the bay, we keep passing the famous jail, Robben Island, where apparently she had a son die. He must've been in for a bloody serious crime, because they never allowed her to visit. Never in the eighteen years he was in that place, that dark hump we keep passing tonight. Angela goes to stand with her towards the end of the cruise, and holds her arm.

Or was it a brother Lizzie had in there? She did tell me. Anyway – son, brother, or anonymous soul paying off a few karmic debts – it's damn sad, hey?

NINETEEN

I t's Friday. We've been here almost a week, and this is the first half-decent weather we've had. It's almost warm, almost sunny, almost like I remember.

Angela's hired a cab and gone to view the townships. She says she's sick of just seeing white suburbs and meeting white people. Don't know what she's talking about; I mean, last night we suffered through yet another dinner with the Gools, and *they're* not white. But Angela says they might as well be – 'they're so divorced from the liberation struggle of their brothers and sisters'. *Ja*, she's started talking in these *farkackteh* slogans. Either that, or it's Gertjie, Gertjie, Gertjie. Day and night she's busy phoning him, without ever getting through. Agh, she's changing out of all recognition. Last night at the restaurant she didn't even wear make-up; she dressed just anyhow, and had on her old specs rather than those contact lenses which cost the earth. I can hardly bear to be with her. She's stopped making me laugh. Worse, she's stopped making *herself* laugh.

So anyway, I've given this morning's sight-seeing a miss. As I said to her, I *know* conditions in the townships are gross – who needs to *see*? Also, last night's dinner has left me with a hangover which future generations will speak of. The Goolish way is to drink whisky, not wine at table.

When I finally stagger down to the beachfront, this morning's drizzle has dried on the pavement, there's nice, salty sunlight on the blocks of flats, and a lovely rainbow showing over the water. The seagulls are plentiful, and there are pigeons too: big clean birds, not like the flying rats of London. Joggers are out, old folk taking their constitutionals, people walking little dogs adorned in little T-shirts, Coloured beach patrol guys patrolling (which is something new), and some teenage surfers congregated against the railings at Broken Baths Beach. It must be the winter school hols. I stroll to a stop alongside.

One or two of the boys are changing, peeling off their gleaming black wet-suits to show white muscles underneath, downy and goosebumped. They look like a whole load of Gertjies.

And yup, here comes that randy buzz – it's a bit like too much caffeine – that randy hangover buzz. I go down the steps into a Gents conveniently placed on the edge of the beach.

Only one character hanging round: an old skeletal thing hunched at the far corner of the weeing wall. He tries to catch my eye, but I ignore him and have a bona-fide leak. My piss sounds like fingers tapping on the zinc sheet, tapping as I wait for something more interesting to arrive.

'Well, I'm damned,' says the old man suddenly, 'it's Leonora Lipschitz.'

I look up. 'Oh my God – it's uh . . .'

'Petrus Spies,' he says, shuffling along.

'Petrus, of course! Howzit?' I say, taking his outstretched hand and then wishing I hadn't – it's damp from his dick.

(This can't be Petrus. Petrus was ten years my junior and one of the fairest beauties of the Cape – and all points north. An air steward, or coffee-moffie, as we say. This balding old skeleton can't be Petrus!)

'You back in town, Leonora?' he asks, as we zip up and he takes my arm, leading me past the washbasin (which I wouldn't've minded using), and out of the lav.

'Just a flying visit,' I say, flinching as we climb the steps, arm in arm, towards the surfing club.

Petrus nods towards a dark, hairy-legged teenager who's just stepping out of his wet-suit, and says, loudly, 'Oh – look at the fuel engine on that!'

The group explode into wolf whistles and a chorus of 'Moffies!
Bum-chums! Plague merchants!'

I cringe, but Petrus laughs, taking it in his stride; this is routine
apparently. 'They're just frustrated little *pielie*-pullers,' he says,
sweeping me off along the front. 'If they can't have your body,
they'll have your reputation. So anyhow, Leonora, how goes life
in the UK? Tell all.'

I start to, but we haven't walked a hundred yards before Petrus
is out of breath and sweating. He flops onto one of the benches,
wraps his long legs into a little spiral, and offers me a ciggie. It's
a Marlboro. I'm so impressed, I accept. 'Hey, I thought the
sanctions . . .'

'*Ja*-no, it's true, but I can get them through the airlines. Go on,
have a whole pack,' he says, producing a fresh one from his
raincoat.

'Hell, that's damn generous of you.'

'Agh, bulldust, man! I've got cartons and cartons up in the flat.
Have it for old time's sake.'

'Thank you,' I say, pocketing it. He lights our ciggies. It's my
first in ten years. Me and Angela gave up together, for the sake
of our child-to-be. I inhale now, smiling at Petrus as the smoke
snakes its funny way through me. (Wowee, it feels like I'm gonna
fall over, or kak my pants!) 'So, you still work for the airlines?' I
ask, wondering if he could've possibly met Gertjie.

'*Ja*, but they've grounded me, doll,' he says in a husky whine.
'The baroness in an office job – can you *imagine*? She who could
straddle a Boeing without stretching!' He blows a smoke-ring,
and looks out to sea. 'Agh, I've had this flu thing for a while. Asian
flu, they think, or outer Mongolian, or Jessie Christ only knows!'
As I laugh, he quickly adds, 'It *is* flu. It's not what you think.'

'I didn't. I – '

'We don't have that problem here yet. It's one of the rare
occasions where *Suid-Afrika* actually benefits from being ten
years behind the times.'

I laugh again, wondering if he's telling the truth.

(I wish I'd washed my hands.)

'In fact,' continues Petrus, 'since you left, we've become the
San Francisco of South Africa.'

'That so?'

'All along here. Day and night. And the Wall, of course,' he adds, nodding towards a concrete enclosure on the shoreline, open to the sea, walled to the world, for nude sunbathing, men-only. In my day, it was shared, uncomfortably, between old Yids and cruising moffies.

'No, well, that was always active,' I say, squinting at the heads visible above the enclosure.

'Not like now, Leonora,' says Petrus. 'On a summer night there are *klomp-pomps* going on in there that you wouldn't believe! Fifteen, twenty guys at a time. Jol on down, doll. Even now in winter, it's still all go.'

I chuckle. 'No thanks – I'm married.'

'*Allewêreld!*' exclaims Petrus, 'Leonora's linked! Congrats, congrats, peal those bells! Is he nice?'

'It's a she.'

Petrus curves a suspicious eyebrow at me, then says, 'So long as she makes you purr, doll.' He flops, puffing, onto another bench, and lights another ciggie. 'Still . . . old habits, hmm?'

I smile nervously. 'OK, let's stroll on down.'

'You go. Too, *too* many steps for the baroness.'

There are no more than ten steps down to the beach, but he's serious. He gives a sad smile, the mouthful of long teeth making his face even more skull-like. 'I'll keep guard,' he says, 'in case your wife turns up.'

I descend the steps, and start along the narrow path which leads over the rocks to the Wall. *Ja*, this bit always felt so conspicuous. You're visible all down the beachfront. You're like an ant on a pencil.

Inside the Wall, the sun beats down quite warmly. There's a concrete sunbathing area, and a rock pool for swimming. Half a dozen guys are arranged on the two shelves which run round the enclosure: a muscly guy wearing shorts and a touch-me-not expression; a plump teenager, storing up pictures for a wire-pull later (this could be me thirty years ago); and surprisingly a couple of Coloureds, or 'chloras' as Petrus would say. So the Wall's gone multi-racial. My, my, times really are a-changing.

One of the Coloureds is asleep on the ground. He's the only

nude bloke, though he's thrown a corner of his shirt over the
vital bits. He's young, cute, but with the odd bruise and scar. His
discarded clothes are grubby. I reckon he lives on the streets,
and comes here to earn a quick buck. I perch near him, smoking
Petrus's Marlboro, which is making me completely bloody
high.

Hell, I'd forgotten how sexy this town is. So long as you don't
mind crossing the colour bar (and these days it's legal), you can
have sex by the bucketful. It's waiting for you, everywhere: these
cute young tramps, guys and gals, hanging round the entrance of
every shop and bioscope, or in the parking lots, guiding you to
an empty space; mongrel kids who don't pass a dustbin without
having a quick snuffle. In this town, no matter how old, ugly or
vrot you are, you can pick up living, breathing porn on every
corner.

But now I hesitate. If this boy is here to earn some bucks, why
has he fallen asleep? And it's a strange sleep; a kind of shiver goes
through his belly with each breath. I look round. Why are the
other guys steering clear of him, when he's the dishiest thing in
sight? What do they know that I don't?

I glance from the boy's shivering belly to my hand – which
Petrus touched. I throw his ciggie away, and hurry over to the
rock pool. It's covered in brownish scum wobbling in the air
currents. Kneeling, I try to wash my hands, but – *siss!* – the brown
sticks to my fingers. Oil maybe, from a tanker which has pranged
somewhere along the coast?

Looking out to sea from this angle, the waves seem as high as
blocks of flats. The noise as they fall is terrifying; likewise the way
they rush towards the rock pool, smashing apart only at the last
moment, while another wave rises behind, even bigger.

When I was a kid, I remember seeing a picture of a tidal wave,
and thinking how easily Sea Point could be blatted in one stroke.

Suddenly, the next wave crashes into the rock pool. The brown
scum rears and rolls, and my shoes fill with water. Behind me,
the other guys laugh. I blush and turn. But it's not me they're
mocking. The wave has reached all the way to the naked boy. He
tries to rise, but slips and travels back with the wave, legs paddling
the air. His shlonger is for fainting, but his face is blank; pissed

171

or sick, who knows? He comes to a stop against my legs, muttering, 'Sorry, my master, sorry, sorry hey?'

I flee.

Beyond the enclosure, all is normal and calm again, with a fresh rainbow above Sea Point, a really incredible, picture-book rainbow.

I climb the steps back to the beachfront, only to find Petrus gone. The bench is empty, with just a couple of Marlboro *stompies* littering the ground.

Just as well – he was starting to give me the creeps.

To my surprise, Angela's cab is pulling up just as I reach the house.

'Back early,' I comment, thanking my lucky stars I didn't bring along the grubby chlora boy.

'Yes.' She sways suddenly on the steep incline.

'You pissed?' I laugh.

'Oh good idea,' she says. 'Oh yes, let's get legless!'

Sighing, I follow her into the house. From upstairs, I can hear Mom hacking her guts out. We go into Dad's bar, panelled with dark wood.

'So it was bad?' I ask, twiddling open the staff-proof combination lock on Dad's liquor cabinet.

'It was much worse than bad. Much worse.'

'Told you,' I say, fixing us a couple of massive vodka tonics.

'Yes, you did. You knew. You know it all.'

We stare at one another. Her face looks bloated. It isn't just the missing make-up. This morning's sight-seeing has filled her with something new – anger or shame? – something blood-red anyway, something which leaves me out completely. It reminds me of that night I didn't go to her school concert, and she came back on fire. And it reminds me of rooms disappearing when you walk out of them.

'So where did you go?' I ask.

'Langa. Guguletu. Crossroads. That was the worst – the squatters' town. In the drizzle.'

'Oh? It was sunny here.'

'Yes. It was sunny there later. With an astonishing rainbow.'

'*Ja*, I saw that too.'

'Looked like jewellery,' she mutters, grimacing.

'Jewellery?'

She goes silent, and drinks. I walk to the window. 'Another rainbow,' I say, gazing down across our spectacular view to where a vivid beaut rises from the sea, completing only a third of its arc, before abruptly vanishing. Above, a stormy sky is moving in: vivid blues and mauves. 'Talk about jewellery,' I laugh, 'God's really queening it today.'

'Refill!' says Angela holding up her glass.

'Already?'

'Oh, isn't that the idea? To get legless?'

'Angela –'

'To get completely out of our stinking heads?'

'Angela, it really isn't nice seeing you like this, y'know.'

'Tough shit. Lots of things aren't nice. I feel sick, my life feels sick. That isn't nice. I don't know if I can cure it. Well, I probably can, but do I have the courage? Not a nice feeling.'

'I'm not following. What d'you mean?'

'I mean you.'

'Me what?'

She chews her lip. I wait. She goes to rub her eyes, forgetting that she's wearing specs, and bashes them against her nose. She swears and puts back her head, determined not to cry.

I fill her glass. Outside, it's started raining, the water brushing the window in little bursts, like a swarm of insects.

'So,' she says, 'what d'you want to do this afternoon? Fuck?'

'Oh. Uhm . . . ?'

We trail upstairs, taking our drinks along.

'Y'know,' she says, as we close the bedroom door and start to strip, 'in the taxi, I was thinking about Gertjie.'

'Gertjie, ahuh?'

'How he could explain it all. Everything I'm feeling . . . about South Africa.'

'*Ja*, probably,' I mutter, hurting vaguely, somewhere. I pull closed the venetian blinds, and get into bed. The sheets are cold, almost damp. Now Angela climbs in, and we sit apart, schlurping at our drinks.

'On the other hand,' she says, 'I was wondering if he's entirely stable.'

'Gertjie? He isn't. You've always said he isn't. He says so himself. That it'll take a while before he comes completely right –'

'Yes,' she snaps, 'but what I'm wondering is – should we have trusted him with the keys of the house? Who's to say he hasn't been stoned when he's there, with Charlotte and her friends? D'you see?'

'No. What exactly are you –'

'An unlocked door. A window open. The alarm left off. Burglars, squatters . . .' She laughs grimly. 'We could come back to find a little squatters' camp.'

'Ah, squatters,' I echo, finishing my drink. I'm feeling better now, nicely fuzzy in the half-darkness. I peer into the shadows. Ever since Mom's spiel about reincarnation, places seem so much more crowded. Right now in this room, there's probably a Russian gold-digger or two, some parcel-cutting boys from an Ottoman palace, a few surfers who took a fatal ride on a tidal wave, and so on. A throng of ghostly voyeurs, homeless spirits. And among them all, surely there must be *one* eager to move in with me and Angela? 'Squatters,' I murmur, as my fingers dig through the soft, moist hair in her lap.

'So d'you see?' she says.

'Mmmh.'

'Why I'd better go back.'

'Mm . . . *what?*'

'Well, I should, shouldn't I? Fly back. To take care of the house.'

I prop myself up on one elbow, lust draining fast. 'Or we could risk it,' I say, after a moment.

'Risk what?' she asks, also lifting onto an elbow.

'Everything. The house. Gertjie there. Charlotte and her cronies. Squatters maybe. Just leave them.'

'I'm sorry? What? With all my books. My garden. My –'

I laugh. 'You're full of shit, man! Why don't you just chuck a few more thousand bucks at the ANC? Hey? Then you can lie back and enjoy yourself. Like you used to.'

She goes very still.

'Sorry,' I mutter. 'But just lie back, hey?' – and I heave myself on top.

With a sudden cry, she brings her knee up between my legs. Luckily, both of us are so well-padded, my gear escapes with just a medium bump.

'You kakking bitch!' I hiss, clipping her mouth.

We glare at one another, nose to nose, then I clamber off, throw on some clothes, and stalk out.

I pace the corridor for a bit, before stopping to sniff the air. There's a strange, giddy fragrance. It's coming from Mom's room. Oh *ja*, she's got her aromatherapist here this arvie. The door's open a fraction. You can just see a corner of the bed, with Mom, face-down, one greasy, naked shoulder rolling back and forth, like she's being buggered. I watch, digging my hands in my pockets. My fingers touch cardboard, covered in cellophane. Petrus's gift! The pack of Marlboros. I fondle it, wondering if germs can live on cellophane – or penetrate it? Shrugging, I knock on the door. 'It's me,' I call.

'Just a mo,' comes the reply. Through the crack in the door, I watch a re-arranging of towels and sheets. 'OK.'

I enter. The aromatherapist is a plasticky brunette in a white jump-suit. I nod at her, then kneel at Mom's bed, and whisper, 'Got you a pressie.'

As I place the Marlboros on her bedside table, she frowns – a frown full of wonder – as though she's witnessing some other-worldly visitation. Then she rips off the cellophane, and lights a ciggie, sucking on it deeply.

I watch, holding my breath. Although her eyes are closed, her lashes start to glisten. I've never seen this before – never seen her really moved before.

'Thanks,' she whispers, taking my hand. Will she smell Angela on my fingers? Probably not, with all the exotic oils saturating her own bod. We stay like this, me and Mom, holding hands for a long moment. From the wireless on her bedside table comes the signature tune of that afternoon programme, whatsitcalled? – it reminds me of when I was a kid, and had a cold, and Mom let me stay home from school, and, for a day, life was a hundred percent luxurious and safe.

Suddenly, we hear Angela's voice. 'Leon! Leon!'

'*Oich*,' Mom groans softly, 'that woman!'

I dash into the corridor. Angela's *kaalgat* nude and white-faced. 'He's here,' she gasps, 'he's here!'

'What?' I ask, a shiver going through me.

'Gertjie. Here. In South Africa. He's had to come back. Something about his mother being poorly.'

(I feel myself falling.)

I shoo her back into the bedroom. The telephone receiver is lying on the bed, with a tiny voice going 'Hello? Hello?'

'Charlotte,' explains Angela, 'I finally got her, and not her machine.'

'Ask,' I say, 'if she's got his Joburg number.'

Angela speaks to Charlotte, then turns back. 'He hasn't gone to Joburg. He's gone to his parents.'

'*Ja*, and they're in Joburg.'

'Apparently not.'

I take the phone. 'Charlotte, hi, howzit?'

'Tickety,' she says. 'You? How's –'

'No, can't complain, listen, did Gertjie mention where he was going? Was the place *Suurvlei*?'

'Could be. I didn't get very far with his Afrikaans. But yaah, that sounds like –'

I wham down the receiver. 'She thinks they're in Suurvlei,' I tell Angela.

'Maybe his parents moved back.'

'What, his dad retired, maybe? Strain of work.'

Angela leans forward, hugging herself, then walks into the bathroom.

I dial the exchange and ask them to get me a number in Suurvlei – the van der Bijls. There's no one of that name in Suurvlei. The police station, then? The operator dials. The line gulps, stretches and travels away.

(I'm falling, I'm falling.)

'*Ja, goeie middag, Suurvlei Polisiestasie, kan ek help?*'

'Afternoon,' I say, brisk and official. 'Can I please have Gertjie van der Bijl?'

'*'skuus, meneer?*'

'Yup, Gertjie van der Bijl please.'

'*Nee, meneer, jy het die verkeerde nommer.*'

'D'you not speak English?'

'Yes, meneer.'

'Ja – then kindly do so!'

I hesitate. I've just shouted at an Afrikaner in uniform.

'Meneer,' he says, 'I am telling meneer that he has the wrong number. No one of that name is here.'

(Hang on, the voice isn't an Afrikaner's – it's a black man's.)

'He's the son of one of your policemen there,' I say.

'No, meneer. Not here.'

'Maybe a policeman who was there before?'

'Well, Sergeant Landsman, meneer, he has been here all his life, meneer.'

'What, and there's just him and you?'

The line goes quiet. When the man speaks now, his voice is drier, thicker. 'Who is this?'

I slam down the phone.

Now a knock on the bedroom door, and Lizzie comes in. She glances round the dark room with its rumpled bed, grins approvingly, then says, 'Excuse me, Leon.'

'*Ja?*' I say, flexing my jaw. (I'm not yet that crazy about this 'Leon' business.)

'There's someone downstairs that you is going to be very, *very* glad to see.'

'Very, very glad to . . . ?' I blink at her and pop my ears. In a tiny voice, I ask, 'Who?'

She leans forward and whispers, 'Zakes.'

'Zakes?'

'Agh, Leon must now remember Zakes.'

'Of course I remember Zakes. He's been carting us around all week.'

'Is it so? Then why's the damn old *dronklap* never popped in before to say his hullos to old Lizzie?'

'I don't fucking know! Why has he come in now?'

'To pick you up, Leon. He says it's all arranged and you're late.'

'Right,' I say, frowning. 'I'll be down in a sec.'

I go into the bathroom. Angela's at the basin, still naked, with her face buried in Gertjie's toilet bag.

'For shit's sake!' I say, snatching it off her. 'Look, have we arranged to go somewhere? Last night – at dinner with the Gools.'

'Oh . . . yes. Adam wants you to come to the harbour. On your own. There's some problem.'

'Really? Why don't I remember this?'

'Because you'd just fallen off your chair. For the second time.'

'Hn.'

'Did you get through to Suurvlei?' she asks.

'Naa,' I say, retreating to the door, 'you've got to book a call. The town's in the middle of the sticks. I'll try again from the office.'

Downstairs I go, out across the rainy garden, and onto the amazing incline of the road, where the Rolls leans, waiting.

'Hi Zakesie-babes,' I say, flopping into the back seat. 'And howzit by you this arvie?'

'Nay sir – sweet!'

'Good boy.'

I've still got Gertjie's toilet bag in my hand. God, he's in the country, he's actually here! The thought fills me with as much dread as craving. If it wasn't for Angela, I could be over Gertjie by now. Listen, I have affairs like the Gertjie thing as regular as Angela has her periods. I sling the toilet bag onto the seat next to me.

'I took the suit to the cleaners, sir,' says Zakes.

'Sorry?'

'We'll make him look smart like a king again, hey, Master Leon? I reckon, I reckon.'

'Uhh . . . ?'

'What we now said. Last night. When I drove you and Angela back after your supper with that Adam Gool wise-arsed bugger.'

'Oh *ja*. Must've been a bit slammed,' I chortle. 'Just remind me.'

'Making your dad look smart, like a king. *Ag, kyk die style daar!* Tomorrow at the barmitzvah.'

'Oh *ja*, for sure, right on!'

Jesus – Ivan's barmitzvah. I forgot. What will that be like? With

Dad downstairs in the shul, and Mom in the women's gallery?
Maybe they'll have a reunion.

I am a happy wanderer
Along the mountain track

– goes Dad's six-speaker stereo. I fix me and Zakes a drink,
and settle back, singing along.

Val do Reeee
Val do Ra-ha-ha-ha-ha . . .

TWENTY

'L eon,' says a small man, turning from the window.
        'Pallister!'

Dad's British accountant – here, in Dad's office? Pallister is wrapped in coat, scarf and gloves, but a bright red sunburn glows on his balding forehead and hairless wrists; sunburn from that fab London summer back home. The good servant has been called, and has come. But why?

'And this is our internal auditor, Barney Lieberman,' says Adam, 'but you know one another.'

'No,' I say, shaking hands with a chubby man, whose intensely black beard frames a permanent grin.

''course you do,' says Barney. 'I'm Ashley's younger *broer*.'

'Ashley?' I murmur.

'*Ja*, gone to Canada. You remember now? I married one of the Goldblatt girls.'

'The Goldblatt girls?'

'Phyllis. Selma's sister, who's an in-law to your Mom's cousin, Ethel.'

'Phyllis, Selma, Ethel?'

'So we're practically family.'

'Family?'

Barney roars with laughter. 'A real Lipschitz sense of humour!'

Everyone laughs politely, then Adam gestures us to sit. I try to avoid Dad's place, but after a brief game of musical chairs, with everyone lifting their elbows and shifting round the desk, I end in it anyway. The receptionist brings in coffee, and Adam aims his tinted specs at me, imploring me not to go for Dad's liquor drawer. I smile sheepishly and fold my hands on my tum.

Now Adam says: 'OK, gents, who wants to kick off please?'

'May I?' says Pallister, and, without waiting, turns to me. 'Leon, I've had a visit from the Inland Revenue back in London, the 734 Office, I'm afraid.'

I lean forward, eyebrows raised. I can tell already I'm not going to understand much of this.

'Gentle enquiries at this stage,' continues Pallister, 'but once these fellows start – '

'You don't get rid of them, hey!' laughs Barney,.

'Who are they?' I ask. 'And what do they want?'

Everyone laughs. I look round, bewildered.

'I reckon they want all the shekels you've been hiding from them,' beams Barney.

'Have I?' I ask Pallister.

Again it's Barney who answers, chortling: 'I should damn well hope so! With no visible income or investments of your own, you're practically off the system. Boy, if you were paying the full ransom, Mr Pallister here would have to hand back his B. Comm. Honours!'

Everyone bellows at this one.

'*Ja*, well,' I say, trying to join in, 'I just sign whatever he sends me.'

The laughter dies. Everyone looks at me with pitying eyes for a moment, then Barney says:

'Let's just hope you can trust your accountant!'

The laughter is deafening. Thighs are pummelled and handkerchiefs appear.

'Oh dear . . .' says Pallister, wiping away a tear. 'All right – so far so good.'

'Yes?' I say, starting to relax.

'But now we come to your charity work.'

'*My* charity work?'

'I use the term loosely. The organisations range from political extremists to homosexual help-lines.'

For a sec everyone drops their gaze. Mine lands in Adam's lap.
I look up sharply.

'Thousands of pounds,' says Pallister, 'so the 734 Office tell me.
Expenditure which doesn't tally with your annual declarations.
How could it? I had no idea you were making these donations.'

'Then how does the 7 . . . whatsit office know?' I ask.

'We're not sure.'

'Though there's a suspect, hey, Mr Pallister?' says Barney.

'There is,' says Pallister, taking a newspaper clipping out of his
pocket. I twitch, remembering the day we left for South Africa –
those reporters waiting outside our house! Without unfolding the
clipping, Pallister continues, 'However – so far so good.'

'So far, still good?' I ask nervously.

'Oh yes. We could offer the Inland Revenue a deal. Their
Commercial Office is keen on deals. Saves paperwork. We could
assure them there was no wilful neglect, and offer to pay up, plus
interest and penalties.'

'Which will be, by the way – ?' asks Barney.

'Just over half a mill,' says Pallister.

'No problem,' say Barney and Adam in unison.

'Good,' says Pallister, sitting back. 'Mr Lieberman?'

'*Ja*, thanks, Mr Pallister,' says Barney, plonking his elbows on
the desk and giving me his beardy smile. 'Leon, the thing is this
– the UK Inland Revenue don't give a stuff about your dad's
Guernsey account. Why should they? It's money in their pocket.
But our blokes here naturally take a different view. And I'm afraid,
I've had a visit too. From our version of this 734 outfit. We call
ours the Hit Squad.' He produces some notes, scribbled on
fragments of thin paper, which look like they could be eaten in an
emergency. 'A query here, for instance, about our simultaneous
acquisition in '86 of a new vessel for our local fleet and a
second-hand one for the South American line. The implication,
Leon, is clear. Were we diverting profitable cargo? Were we
transferring pricing? Were we charging central overheads in
different directions?'

I gaze back. (Was he talking English?) Unable to think of
anything else, I ask, 'And were we?'

'Of course we were!' all three say together, and guffaw.

'These are unpredictable times here, Leon,' says Barney, jovial as ever. 'Everybody has to think about making offshore provisions. Moshe has already taken advantage of our American provisions. Likewise you in the UK. Your folks – and me for that matter – might still have to follow suit. If these unpredictable times ever become predictable.'

Again, laughter round the table. Why is Adam joining in? Where has he made his 'offshore provisions'? Mauritius?

'Quite naturally,' Barney continues, 'our authorities here are trying to discourage people from "taking the gap", as we used to say in my rugby-playing days. The Exodus, the Chicken Run, call it what you will. Now, I've always had a good relationship with the tax crowd here, Leon. I mean, dammit, your dad's been a loyal son to South Africa – loyal and profitable.'

'So, why are they suddenly giving you a hard time?' I ask.

Barney smiles. 'Mr Pallister?' he says.

'Thank you, Mr Lieberman,' says Pallister, sitting forward, and unfolding the newspaper clipping. 'You may not have seen this, Leon. I think it came out after you left . . .'

SCHOOL OF SHAME – reads the headline, and – TEACHER IN HIDING. There's a photo of *our house* with all the curtains drawn (taken, my God, during our threesome with Gertjie), and underneath the photo of *me* as we were leaving for Heathrow. Me with startled eyes and open mouth. A third photo shows Nat Roshney. I skim over the article: 'South African dissidents, the opera star, Nathaniel Roshney and the millionaire, Leon Lipschitz . . . part of a conspiracy to turn a London school into a hot-bed of leftist brain-washing . . . Mr Lipschitz's wife is a teacher at Hadsworth House . . .'

'What's this shit from?' I ask, before glancing to the name at the top, and realising it's one of the few papers I don't mind browsing through.

'Leon, let's make one thing clear,' says Barney, 'your politics are your own affair.'

'Absolutely,' says Pallister, with that politeness the British use when they're very angry. 'From our point of view, we simply regret that you saw fit to involve such formidable opposition.' He points to a fourth photo in the paper. 'Here's the chap behind it all, we think. The chap who's tracked down your charitable donations, your father's Guernsey account, and alerted the tax people on both sides of the Equator.'

I peer at the newsprint again, at a brutish-faced man standing with a boy in front of Angela's school.

'Paul Chagbury, yes?' says Pallister. 'An undistinguished career in Parliament, but very big in the City.'

'Very big here too,' adds Barney. 'Several big, big factories over Port Elizabeth way.'

'Hnghh,' I murmur, reaching down to Dad's liquor drawer. Adam watches with dark, disappointed eyes as I throw a slug of Irish whiskey into my coffee. But I don't think it's just my day-time boozing that depresses him. It's the damage I've done to the business – the business he's set his sights on, this upwardly mobile Coloured boy. Have I ruined things with my anti-Apartheid stance in London? Me, the famous South African dissident. I bite back a smile, then say, 'So . . . what d'you all want me to do?'

Everyone chuckles.

'No, no, *you*'ve done quite enough,' laughs Barney, slapping my back.

'It's your dad we need right now,' says Adam.

'Ah,' I say.

'Any luck yet? Making contact?'

'No.'

'Agh – pity.'

'*Ja.*'

'In any case, it's Ivan's bar mitzvah tomorrow. Moshe's son.'

'Is it?'

'Moshe was the only other survivor of your dad's family in Poland. Now I reason it this way – your dad won't miss the bar mitzvah tomorrow.'

'Won't he?' I mutter.

Barney reaches for the Irish whiskey. 'What we'd like to do, Leon, is come along to the reception afterwards. Have a word with your dad. We wouldn't dream of suggesting it, if it wasn't so serious. Oh, classy!' he comments, tasting the whiskey. 'I mean, if it was a do on your mom's side, I'd've been invited anyway. We're practically family. Hey?'

He reaches across and gives my arm a little rub. This makes me feel suddenly tearful – until, looking up, I see his face. The smile has dried into a little sneer.

'No, don't come to the reception,' I say quietly. 'Wait here, and I'll bring him to you afterwards. Me and Zakes will bring him.'

'You OK, Mister Leon?' asks Zakes.

'*Ja.* Fine. Why?'

I suddenly realise I'm in the front seat, next to him. I've never sat here before.

''m fine,' I repeat. 'D'you want me to move back?'

'Hey gee, you can't,' he laughs. 'Your dad's there.'

I swing round. Dad's best suit is propped on the back seat; acres of silver cashmere, glimmering in cellophane from the dry-cleaners.

Zakes laughs again, and gives me an odd handshake, a bit like the Romans do in *Ben Hur*; maybe it's also something to do with Black Power, who knows?

'Zakes, my friend,' I say.

'Sir, my master.'

'Dad's in trouble. Shocking trouble. The business is in trouble. We're all in trouble.'

Zakes goes still. For a long moment. Then he sighs, starts the car, and we head off across the windy docks. Only five o'clock and it's already going dark, a soggy mist falling. On the stereo, Satchmo is mid-way through Blueberry Hill.

'*Ba-du-dah, buzz buzz, ba-da-day* . . .'

Our route takes us round the corner of a warehouse, close to the edge of the jetty. Suddenly we lurch over, one wheel in mid-air. Zakes pulls us to safety, then slams on the brakes.

He's blind with tears.

'Sorry,' he gasps. 'Never have I done that. And I'm now driving forty years.'

'It's OK, we're OK.'

'Your dad's been like a dad by me too. It's going to be hard, man, hard, to watch that good master in the shit. Who's behind it, hey? This bastard must now *uitkyk* because the shock is heading his way. Zakes will get fokken busy with him now. I'll *sommer* stick him with a knife! *Ek trap vir djou binne in djou djina!* I'll *moer* him backwards there through hell! *Die fokken naai!* Who is he, hey?'

'Dunno,' I mumble.

'*Eina!*' he cries, wiping his face with his windscreen shammy, 'it's going to give me bad heartsore, man – *nee, eina!* – to see people shitting on the head of my good master. *Eina, eina!*'

He sets off again, only to brake immediately. I fly forward, knuckles banging the dashboard. Zakes is sobbing again. Deep, ugly sobs.

'Zakes, d'you want me to drive?' I ask.

He nods helplessly.

I help him out of the car. He tumbles into the back, moves Dad's suit to one side, and opens the bar.

I climb into the driver's seat, praying that no one is watching.

TWENTY-ONE

As Mom comes down the stairs, I suddenly remember something from when I was a kid – a vague image of her like this: all dolled up, spectacular and huge, making some grand descent. A gangplank, yes, it was down a gangplank. The sun was shining, a band was playing, and my mom was leaving a ship – yet somehow bringing the ship with her. Which seemed perfectly logical. My dad's in shipping, I thought, so natch, he married a ship.

She's been awake since dawn today. The hairdresser, beautician and manicurist came then. They've got a local salon, and operate a home service. For two hours they worked, curling, painting, filing. Then, at nine, Fatima, the Malay dressmaker, arrived to help Mom into a newly stitched cossie, and to do any last minute turning-up and easing-out.

I reckon Mom's pretty happy with the results, because she flicked on the chandelier before starting down the stairs. I'm watching from the marble hallway, hands clasped under chin, head to one side. 'Mama,' I feel like crying, 'bravo, Mama!' (don't ask why the Italian) – I so love seeing her up on her feet, and painted in healthy hues. But I won't tell her, or she'll think I've got a crush.

So instead I say, 'Agh, come *on*! Everyone's waiting for you. As always.'

'*Ai-yaich!*' she says, 'Lizzie's still using the wrong polish on these stairs. A person could break their bloody neck. If I've told her once . . .'

It's incredible that she's agreed to attend the bar mitzvah today – I mean, Ivan isn't from her side of the family. But Dad will be there, and she doesn't want people talking (she thinks no one has heard about them); she doesn't want people pitying her, like they'll do today with Ivan and his mother, deserted by Moshe.

I just hope Dad goes along with the pretence. Me and Zakes are his minders today, while Lizzie and Angela will look after Mom. A limo-taxi awaits the ladies in the drive.

'Angela,' I call, 'c'mon. Mom's *finally* ready.' I look round. 'Angela?' I bellow, striding to the kitchen, wondering if, as per usual, she's helping Lizzie wash up the breakfast things.

'No, Master,' I hear, as I fling open the door, 'Master – Leon – no!'

Lizzie's saving electricity in here, so all I see is a shadow breaking loose from the gloom, and moving across the lino with a thumping, scratching noise.

'No, Master!'

The shadow charges past me, banging my knees. And now Lizzie is shoving through as well, screaming, 'Madam, quick, go upstairs!'

I retreat into the kitchen and peer round the door.

Jungle is in the middle of the brightly lit hall, spinning on the marble. Who's he going for first – Mom on the stairs, or Angela in the lav doorway?

'Madam, get upstairs,' screeches Lizzie, grabbing Jungle's neck as he lunges for Mom, jaws chattering.

But Mom holds her ground, with a surprising expression – almost disdain – as Lizzie fights with the dog below her. The great ship has come this far and isn't turning back.

'WAAA!' shrieks Angela. 'HAAA-WAAA-HAAA!'

Old Lizzie goes down, losing her balance, still clutching Jungle's neck. His paws churn the air, Lizzie's face, her clothes.

(I've just realised she's wearing her best suit, her green church suit – for the barmitzvah.)

'HAAA-WAAA!' shrieks Angela.

'Get upstairs,' pants Lizzie. 'Madam, please – Ruth please – please Ruth, go upstairs!'

(*Ruth?*)

A tiny quiver goes through Mom, but she doesn't budge.

For a long time Lizzie tugs at the dog's neck, until he slows, choking, and rests his head on the stairs, spine still arched. And finally that slackens too, and he sits back, panting wildly.

Making the same harsh, painful noise, Lizzie gets to her feet. 'Ai, f – father,' she whispers, seeing her wrecked suit – and releases her grip on Jungle.

'Take him away,' says Mom quietly.

Dazed, Lizzie looks up. So does Jungle.

'Quickly now,' says Mom, still without raising her voice, but crosser.

It's Lizzie's turn to stay put, one hand dangling near Jungle's scruff, but not taking it. She frowns at Mom, almost scowling; that raw scowl you sometimes see on the non-whites here. (I never know if they're hurt or angry.) But hell, it's so unlike Lizzie.

(I wonder why her son – or brother – was on Robben Island?)

Without warning, Jungle snaps at Mom's leg, just missing – though he could easily have reached.

'WAA!' goes Angela.

Mom catches her breath, then, calmer than ever, says, 'This will make me late.'

''s, Madam,' mutters Lizzie, and suddenly hauls the dog into the kitchen, beating it – vicious blows that shudder through its body. It takes each with a funny half-cough.

'Well, I'm blessed, hey!' laughs Mom when they're gone. It's her first show of fear.

I sink onto a chair, puffing.

'OK, folks, let's make a move,' says Mom, lowering herself off the last stair. Without the banister for support, she loses her buoyancy, and moves with a lumbering shuffle, very like Dad, but more bent.

'Ruth,' says Angela, coming forward, trembling, 'don't you need to ...? Are you all right?'

'Fine, thank you dear,' replies Mom sharply. 'And yourself?'

'Mom ...?' I say.

189

'It's the new dress,' she says, 'and the new scent I'm wearing. He didn't recognise me. Only doing what's he's trained to do. At least we know we're safe from intruders and such-like. Now, come along.'

'Madam,' says Lizzie, reappearing at the kitchen door, 'Madam, I don't think I must come to the shul like this –' She fingers her torn clothes.

'No,' says Mom coldly. 'Ah well.'

After the limo-taxi drives Mom and Angela away, I wait another fifteen minutes, and then, when Zakes still hasn't shown up, I walk down to the beachfront.

Should've brought an umbrella; there's a drizzly breeze this morning.

Dad's lime-green Rolls stands on the road outside the flats. It's unoccupied, one door ajar.

I guess Zakes just forgot to pick me up.

I look round. Which direction has he strolled in, schlurping at his cooldrink can? I start to cross the road, heading for the beach, then stop. There's something about the way the wind is nudging that open door on the car.

Odd to leave a door open in this weather.

I go closer. The door squeaks. I reach out and touch it. It's wet and cold; even the inside rim. The interior looks normal, but not quite. I sit in the driver's seat. Ah. A big gap in the dashboard, with wires hanging out, neatly cut. Below, the tape and CD shelves are bare. I stretch up to the roof. The TV's gone. Round, behind me, to the phone, the fax. Gone. And the counter is open on the bar. It'll be empty.

I sit there, touching the surfaces, tracing my finger through the dew, letting drops gather and run into my palm.

For a long time I do this.

Now Dad appears, wobbling round the corner from the staff entrance, dressed, as before, in his massive Karakul coat, with only his long winter *gatkes* underneath, and a pair of shoes pulled onto bare feet. But his hair is brushed, and he's shaved. He's talking to himself. I watch that funny hole in his mouth, from the missing tooth; it winks blackly in his face.

'And what's going on here?' he asks, arriving at the car. 'Where's Zakes? First thing this morning, I'm looking down – the street-lights are still on, and I see the car. I'm thinking – Zakes is blinking early! Probably to come shave me . . .'

(There are little nicks all over his jaws, with blood smudges.)

'But he doesn't come up. He's not up and he's not down. For hours he's nowhere. Just the car. And then you. What's the big idea, hahh?'

I shrug, and shift over to the passenger seat. Using the car roof as support, he swings deftly, like a giant ape, into the car. It sinks under him, magnificently, sadly.

The big boiled eyes watch my fingers trace the hole in the dashboard, the empty tape shelves, the wires hanging from the roof.

Then he pulls open the ashtray, feels inside, and extracts a key.

'He leaves it here,' Dad said quietly, 'whenever I'm driving myself.'

'*Zakes?*'

'*Ja.*' He rubs the key between thumb and forefinger. 'But not the car. He left me the car.'

I sit, blinking. 'Why not the car too?'

'Becaaause . . .' sighs Dad, 'if he took the car, then I'd have to go after him. He knows me too well.' Dad bunches his fist and presses it, softly, against the gap in the dashboard. 'He knows I won't go after a man who takes these things. A small man takes these things, some piece of walking rubbish. Not worth running after. You must love someone to run after him. You think I could love rubbish? Zakes knows me.'

The wind suddenly jerks the door. Dad pulls it shut. We sit silently in the cold, damp car.

Zakes must've got pissed after driving me back yesterday arvie, and then decided it was time to move on. What did he say? – that it would hurt his heart to see Dad in the shit.

It would maybe comfort Dad to hear this – except then I'd have to tell him about the shit he's in. And that's for later.

'So, there we are,' Dad says slowly. His eyes are blank. I wish

191

he'd cry. It would sort of balance things; him sitting where Zakes did yesterday, howling his eyes out.

'Well, well, what a morning,' I say. 'Up at the house, when the ladies were leaving for shul –'

'Shul – oh *ja, tak, tak*,' he says, checking his watch, 'let me just jump into my suit and then we . . .'

He goes quiet.

I give a little groan. 'What – he never brought the suit up to you yesterday?'

'It went to the cleaners.'

'And came back. I saw it. Did he not . . . ?'

'So. OK. The suit too. Where's the sense in that? You think it'll fit him? Maybe as a tent for his flight into the wilderness.'

Dad puts back his head, and closes his eyes. Quick little breaths, like *phew, phew!* come through the hole in his mouth.

'So – *Alivei!*' he says, switching on the ignition.

'Dad,' I say, 'you're not wearing any clothes.'

''s OK,' he mutters, driving off.

'You're going to shul in your undies?'

''s OK.'

'But you must have a dozen other suits –'

'Ten dozen! Who you think you're talking to?'

'So?'

'So? Forty year or so!'

'What?'

'Me and Zakes. Forty year. Never took a thing. A hundred times my briefcase is in the car, my wallet, your mother's jewellery and riches. Wages for the whole of Lipschitz and Son – a hundred times over he's a made man. I'd've given him anything. Anything and everything. And what does he take? He takes my music. So?'

I look at Dad. His flesh hangs, white and moist, like on a plucked bird, with razor nicks and tufts of white.

'OK, sing,' he says.

'Sorry?'

Ja, we're all sorry,' he growls, snapping his fingers. 'C'mon!' Then, softer, he adds, 'Please.' Covering my face, I quietly sing:

I found my thrill
On Blueberry Hill
On Blueberry Hill
When I found you . . .

I haven't been to shul for years. Even before I left South Africa
I used to give bar mitzvahs and marriages a miss, just rocking up
for the booze afterwards. *Ja*, me and the faith, we parted company
a long time back.

Angela once asked me why.

Who knows why? I could only think of one reason: it's boring.
The faith is boring.

Why, she asked, why is it boring?

Don't know, I said, maybe because it's no better at answering
questions than I am.

The service has already started by the time me and Dad reach
the shul in Montagu Road. Donning yarmulkas and tallises, we
slip into the rear pews, way behind the small congregation. Just
two other people back here; servants from Ivan's house, an elderly
chauffeur and gardener. They're both wearing ludicrous old suits
– probably Moshe's hand-me-downs – so I don't know how they
have the nerve to stare at the way Dad's dressed.

Angela, in the women's gallery, glances down when we come
in, but Mom doesn't. She's staring ahead, grimly. She's another one
who doesn't observe the faith anymore. Not since she discovered
spiritualism. Then the faith became meaningless: who needs to
worship enigmatic forces, when you've got your own dearly
departed?

Places are usually smaller than you remember. The shul isn't.
It's bigger, and weirder – from another age, and a dozen other
places. I never realised before, but our own Great Trek is scrawled
all over it. The Middle East still hangs on in the beaded silk
brocades round the Ark; Spain in the sequined curtains; Germany
and Poland in the hefty velvet tablecloths; Russia in the onion
domes with their fruity plaster swags; and then, in the whole

voluptuous over-the-topness of it all, in the columns painted marble, and the panelling that's only faced with mahogany, there's Hollywood and journey's end. Now turn round and go back. *Plant a tree in Israel*, say the collecting tins; and everywhere, words in Hebrew, Hebrew . . .

Don't know where the shul chandeliers hail from. Dark, spidery things, draped with beads, they take the eye up, past the women's gallery, to the great domed ceiling, where God sits, or flutters, or hangs like a bat.

Hey Batman, I'm in trouble, come help!

And did He ever?

Maybe that's why I left the faith: I didn't feel protected. So I ran. Perfectly natural reaction, and one that I'm familiar with. It's safer not to be anything too specific – in sex, religion or race. Safer, and more forward-looking. You could say I was the first global citizen.

They're taking the Torah out of the Ark now. As the congregation rises, the shul seems to darken. I'm trying to remember what the ritual means: the hoisting up of those cloaked scrolls; and their procession to the bima, people crowding forward to touch with their tallises, which they then kiss; and the stripping of the scrolls on the bima – they ring and tinkle as they're stripped – and all the time, the choir singing a great, beautifully sad number, like something out of an opera.

I glance up at the gallery. Angela's studying the alien service, her face open, fascinated. She almost looks like the old Angela, marvelling at the craziness of the world. (I haven't told her about the meeting at the docks yesterday, or about the one planned for today.) Both she and Mom look so small up there, like banished people, hardly anyone around them.

In the old days, this whole joint would be overflowing on a Saturday morning, people popping in and out, seeing who's here, doing a quick deal or two, a babble of prayer and gossip.

So where's everyone today? *All* in Israel?

The ones who are left are a raggedy old crowd, scourged by strokes or booze. Purplish drowned faces, or yellowy with winter tans. The men are bald and have damp moustaches. The women wear wigs or hairdos like ice sculptures, with turquoise daubed round their eyes, and smudged carmine on their lips. Their necks and wrists are bound in platinum, ivory, bone and plastic; and huge rings bulge on knuckly fingers. It's cold in here, so everyone's worn furs and hats, and dark overcoats. They look like travellers – travellers waiting in a huge shadowy hall.

'Dad,' I whisper, 'why don't we go have a drink?'

But he's miles away. He's not looked up at Mom once. For the whole service he's sat forward, elbows on the pew in front, the great black coat bunching round his shoulders, bison-like, and his eyes fixed on the back of Ivan's head.

That's all we can see of the bar mitzvah boy down at the front: an ironed, satin yarmulka on brushed hair, and the tips of specs over his ears.

(Is Dad still planning to give the business to Ivan today? Mind you, does Dad still have a business to give?)

On one side of Ivan sits his bar mitzvah teacher; on the other it should be his dad, Moshe. Instead it's an uncle maybe, or a grandfather. I can't recognise anyone. Yet I'm probably, almost definitely, related to half of these people – these anonymous necks and ears.

Then one turns and waves.

Barney – Dad's accountant!

But he said he wasn't coming!

My sphincter unlocks. I tweak it shut. Ignoring the waving Barney, I lean over to Dad again. 'D'you remember that bar open down at –'

'*Hust, sha*, shush,' he says.

Now I realise that everything has gone absolutely silent; like the whole congregation breathed in together. All you can hear are the seagulls circling the shul's dome, giving mad toy-like yaps.

Ivan's big moment has come. He climbs the steps onto the bima, and joins the scrum of men up there: the balkorah, the cantor, the shul president and vice-president, the shamas; all wearing tallises of biblical proportions, thick and cream-coloured.

When Angela did World Religions for a previous school concert, she found out that the bar mitzvah is meant to coincide with the sprouting of pubic hair. I never knew that. Two hairs specifically.

Ivan's body must surely be smooth and white as soap. He looks like he has eczema, and is good at maths. His singing is virtually inaudible; you hear only a distant shiver in the air.

When he's finished, the scrum mills round him on the bima, consulting one another. I remember this bit: it's something they won't be able to do today. Moshe should step forward now and say 'Blessed be He who hath freed me.' *Ja*, the father thanks God for taking the kid off his hands. From today on, the boy's a man; he can fend for himself.

Now, as Ivan descends the bima, his main ordeal over, and sweets plop down from the women's gallery, Dad suddenly murmurs, 'Moshe.'

'No,' I whisper, 'that isn't Moshe. That's Ivan.'

'Moshe,' says Dad, louder.

'Dad,' I say, glancing round, 'Moshe's in California.'

He checks himself, nodding, and goes silent as the service continues. But the moment Ivan is fetched up to the bima again, it sets him off.

'Moshe ... *spierdalaj stad!*' he growls in Polish. '*Kurwa!*' Turning to me, he asks, 'You know what this means, hahh – *kurwa?*'

'Yes,' I sigh '– cunt.'

'What?'

'Cunt,' I say louder, blushing, as one or two heads turn.

Dad leans towards them. '*Chazzer!*' he snaps, changing to Yiddish, '*Farkackteh dreykop!* Only good for shitting out. Only good for the fowl sacrifice! Moshe, you hear – *geyt kacken ahfen yam!*'

'Dad,' I mutter, 'none of these people are Moshe.'

He turns to me with a terrible look, and says, 'He took my music.'

'No Dad, that was Zakes. Moshe only took your American funds.'

Dad clambers to his feet. 'My music,' he cries.

Luckily, at this very moment, everyone else stands too. The Torah is going back to the Ark. A clamour of song and chattering of prayers starts up, coming in waves, as people *duven*, rocking and swaying.

'Jub-jub-jub!' grunts Dad, catching their rhythm. 'Kak-kak-kak!

Buzz-buzz-buzz!', and now, shaking his head, he half-sings, half moans:

'Za da day
I love to go a-wandering
On Blueberry Hill
Val do ra-ha-ha-ha-ha . . . '

Again people glance over, but they can't tell if he's praying or what; everyone's making such peculiar noises. The more they stare, the harder he rocks, and the more passionately he chants:

'And c'est si bon
And Mona Lisa
And val do ra
And Davy Crockett . . . '

I clutch his sleeve, unsure whether to let him finish, or drag him out, scared any moment he'll put back his head and bellow. Now each of his heaves takes me along, rocking me with him – oh, oh, oh Dad. When last, hey?

For a sec, joined to him like this, and to the rocking assembly, it all makes sense – religion. It's so reassuring, the harmony, the rocking together, parents and kids, and ghosts from the past.

But only for a sec. Then I notice Barney watching through the bobbing crowd. The rabbi has noticed us as well. And the president, who whispers to the shamas, who now scoots over.

Time to go.

Dad follows me without a struggle, almost eagerly. We rush through the swing doors – *WHUP*. It's cold in the foyer, with puddles under the umbrella stands. Dad stands, rocking himself, chanting quietly.

'Is he all right?' asks Angela, coming down the stairs.

'Dunno,' I say. 'Probably not.'

WHUP – and Barney hurries through the doors. 'Is your dad OK?' he asks.

'*Ja*, fine,' I answer, listening through the doors, as the rabbi addresses Ivan. 'A glorious future' – *WHUP* – 'your children's children' – *WHUP*.

'Chaim,' says Barney, going to Dad and giving him a beardy grin, 'hell, where've you been, man?'

'Who's this?' Dad asks me.

'It's OK, it's cool,' I reply, and then, taking Barney aside, I whisper, 'Listen, let's go to the docks now. Immediately. Have you got a car here?'

Barney looks at Dad, then slowly, almost pensively, says, 'He's not wearing any trousers.'

'No, he isn't. Your car?'

'Just outside.'

'We'll follow you then,' I say, grabbing Dad with one hand and Angela with the other.

'Your mother,' says Angela. 'Are we just –'

'She'll be OK. Everything's cool.'

I get them into the Rolls: Dad at the back, Angela alongside, then set off after Barney's maroon BMW.

'What happened in here?' asks Angela, looking at all the hanging wires. 'And where's Zakes?'

'He's cool,' I say. 'Everything's cool.'

'But where are we going?'

'We're going where Barney's going.'

'And where's that.'

'Look, it's cool. Just relax.'

It's a darkish day. We quickly pass the tennis courts and stadiums of Green Point Common, and zoom onto the freeways. One of these routes must lead onto the unfinished fly-way – over there probably, where a row of barrels blocks the way. What if someone moves them one night as a joke?

(I'm flying, I'm flying.)

On the Foreshore, the road keeps turning to face the docks. Any moment Dad'll catch on and say something. I glance in my mirror. His eyes meet mine, blankly.

Barney's BMW turns into one of the harbour entrances. It's manned by a black security guy. Barney shows his ID, then gestures back to us. The security guy nods – Dad's Rolls is well-known. The swing-barrier lifts and Barney drives in. The security guy turns to us, waving us through.

I take a deep breath, then reverse at speed, swerve back onto the main road, and hit the accelerator.

'And where now?' asks Angela in a calm, almost indifferent voice.

I shrug.

In the mirror, I see Dad smile. I glance to the road behind him, expecting Barney's BMW to be giving chase – but no. Not yet. A road-sign says LOOK – THINK – STAY ALIVE. Now there's another bewildering choice of freeways. I'm swept off towards CITY / STAD, with Table Mountain and Devil's Peak looming into view. Still no sign of the BMW in my mirror. A billboard says OK – GRATIS. We're in Woodstock; the Saturday morning streets are crowded, slowing us down. But surely we're safe by now. Even if Barney realised straightaway, did a fast U-turn, and shot back, through the security gates, he can't have kept up – can he? On one shop, the lettering says ARROW, on another, 24 HOURS. I turn off the main road.

I'm suddenly on more familiar territory – De Waal Drive – climbing up towards Varsity, past enormous fields (belonging, I think, to the Zoo) where small herds of zebra and wildebeest huddle in the drizzle.

'Oh look,' says Angela, almost to herself, '. . . Africa.'

Heavy rain starts to fall, slushing on the windscreen, and spraying off passing cars. Feeling braver now – now that the world is blurred – I accelerate like crazy, and we zip past signs for English-sounding places like BISHOPS COURT and PLUMSTEAD, then Afrikaans ones, DIEPRIVIER, BERGVLIET, the Coloured area, RETREAT, faster and faster, and eventually – let's hear it for the Jews – MUIZENBERG!

We used to trek here every Sunday. It was a refuge from the Christian Sabbath: looking like a cross between Blackpool and Coney Island, with spans of packed beaches, playgrounds, putt-putt greens, cafés with jukeboxes, and one or two posh hotels, where we always 'took tea'. I remember my bare feet on a grand carpet – a Turkish carpet? – and the sandy prints they left.

On south, to less familiar places, Fish Hoek and Simonstown, and now the landscape is changing. A coast road with orange cliffs and stunted trees. We go through a toll-gate (NO DOGS OR FIREARMS), and onto flat bushland with distant *koppies*.

'Africa . . .' murmurs Angela again.

'Dad,' I say, 'have you ever been here?'

He looks at me in the mirror, blankly.

199

'I don't think so,' I say, answering for him. 'I think the only time I came here was on a school outing.'

'Where is it?' asks Angela, as the road ends finally, very finally, in a parking area.

'Cape Point. The southernmost tip of Africa.'

'But . . . it can't be,' says Angela.

'What?'

'Think of the map. We've gone down the thin, squiggly bit, yes? South of Cape Town?'

'Yes.'

'Yes, well, think of the map. Africa bulges beneath this bit.'

Before I can argue, Dad says:

'Zakes, d'you want to drink with me?'

I twist round. 'Dad, I'm not Zakes, I'm Leon.'

'Leon died.'

I sigh. 'Not *that* Leon.'

'So why won't you drink with me?'

'Dad, there's no drink. No Zakes and no drink. He took the drink.'

'Hahh?' says Dad, searching the bar. 'My music *and* my drink?'

'Dad, have you seen Cape Point before?'

'And yet left me his toiletries.'

'*What?*' me and Angela say together, swinging round, to see Dad lift Gertjie's toilet bag out of the bar. (Oh *ja* – I put it in the car yesterday, then forgot to ditch it.)

Dad rummages through it. 'Isn't this alcohol?' he asks, uncorking Gertjie's after-shave.

'No,' cries Angela, snatching the bag away.

'Hey,' Dad shouts, 'who you think you're – ?'

'Dad, Dad,' I say, leaping out of the car. 'I want you to see the southernmost tip of Africa –'

'It isn't,' says Angela, climbing out her side, cradling the toilet bag. 'I'm sorry, but it isn't!'

'Come and look, Dad,' I say, leading him across the parking area, 'come and look at the southernmost tip.'

Shaking her head, Angela follows.

The last time I was here, on that school outing, I was terrified of the baboons on the surrounding rocks. We'd been warned about them: how a boy had a finger torn off, how a baby girl had been kidnapped, disappearing forever. And they were even worse than we imagined, with their caveman brows, wolf snouts, pink and blue arses. So we shrieked and laughed. A tuck shop was selling cooldrinks, and that made us laugh even more, can't remember why. Red and green drinks, pink and blue bums, baking sunshine.

The tuck shop is closed today. No schoolkids, no baboons. Everywhere wet and silent.

We climb a steep concrete incline; all three of us quickly out of breath, but lumbering on. At the top there's a winding stone-slab stairway leading even higher. We climb on, past block-houses ticking and whirring with weather instruments, to a lighthouse. Every surface is covered with tourist graffiti.

Panting, we reach the railing.

And now below is Cape Point: an ugly snag of land, really just a giant rock with a grassy spine. On the left side, there's the calmer, silvery Indian Ocean; while on the right, the Atlantic is pitching about, flashing turquoise one moment, bottle-black the next. Round the rock's base, all is white, an insane foaming white. The body of water is so immense it can only heave itself at the rock in amazing, terrifying slow-motion.

'The Atlantic and Indian Oceans,' I say, in a sing-song voice. 'Gosh, hey? Quite something, hey? Here the two great oceans meet . . .'

But nobody's interested, or even listening. Dad's quietly singing 'Val do raa', Angela's cradling the toilet bag, both gazing out to sea, their clothes wrinkling in the spray and drizzle. The wind comes in sudden, alarming attacks, shoving you closer to the railings.

Now I remember.

The day before the school outing, we'd learned a frightening thing in history class. The story of a native girl in the middle of the last century. She'd seen a vision in a pond. Her ancestors promised to drive the white man into the sea on condition her people destroyed all their cattle and crops. Witchdoctors confirmed her story. People went to the pond and saw armies of warriors waiting to emerge, and heard the horns of magic oxen clicking among the reeds. So everyone killed their cattle, burned their crops, and waited for the big day. The sun would rise, blood-red, and hurricanes would blow the white man into the sea.

Nothing happened. Except that millions of natives starved to death.

If the story was meant to make us kids feel secure, it didn't work. Not on me. I was too thunderstruck by the news that the natives wanted us gone; they wanted it so badly they were prepared to risk losing everything. Which they did – they wanted it *that* badly.

Then, just twenty-four hours after hearing the story, to stand at Cape Point – like we're doing now.

We're on the edge of everything solid, with the whole of bloody Africa behind us. And in front, what? One last rock, streaming wet, and two oceans going nuts. The size – the *weight* of those waves! And nothing to stop us slipping in, if a strong enough hurricane blew, or ghostly armies arose, or magic herds stampeded. Angela said think of the map. *Ja*, OK, I'm thinking. The whole of that continent, the most beautiful continent, beautiful as sin, the male continent! Think of him posing there – the monster male, with humps and horns and ridges, and all of him balanced finally on one toe, or a claw, or tail; and you – you on the very tip.

'So *ja*, this is the southernmost tip, Dad,' I say, teeth chattering. 'Down there, down south, there's bugger-all. Bugger-all till the South Pole. Now howzabout that, hey, to think that – ?'

'No, I'm sorry,' interrupts Angela, 'but let's get our facts straight here. I mean – '

'Oh, La,' I say, hugging her tight, 'please don't let's get our facts straight. On the day they brought us here, I'm sure they told us it was the southernmost tip. I'm sure they did. And even if . . .' I hear my voice start to go, so I stop.

'All right, shh,' says Angela, rocking me. 'Sh, duck, sh.' Her specs are misted over, so she shoves them in her pocket. She's soaking. So is Dad; his yellowish hair is streaming down his cheeks, and his coat has flattened, halving his bulk.

'*Ja*, I have come here before,' he says suddenly, 'but I never knew it was the southernmost tip of Africa. The whole of Africa? That's quite something, hahh?'

'Yes,' says Angela, eyes shining, 'isn't it? Isn't that something.'

TWENTY-TWO

'W here are we now?' says Angela, handing over the brandy bottle, then steadying the wheel while I drink.

'You keep asking,' I murmur.

'Only 'cause you keep not answering.'

'Untrue. I keep answering that I don't know.'

We laugh. I take the wheel again. Angela passes the bottle over her shoulder to Dad, and leans her face on the window, watching the sunset.

It's now, at dusk, that the veld shows its true size. The dipping sun makes you constantly check out the horizon, and you suddenly notice how far away it is – on every side. The land seems to fill and lift, like lungs, before plunging under for the night. And boy, is it shocking – your car left alone on this endless road in the dark. For long, long stretches you don't see other headlamps, or lights from dwellings. When a cluster appears, from a farm or *dorp*, you watch it for several minutes, slowly travelling past you. With so little illumination coming off the land, you can see the whole sky above you, the whole bloody bowl, and everything in it, stars, planets, what-have-you.

I switch off the headlamps and drive by moonlight. The land is like the sky – a kind of bowl, a kind of transparency; everything visible, on and on.

'They can't take aim now,' giggles Angela, as we zoom on without lights, 'the flying pigs.'

203

'Safe at last!' I say.

We've been laughing about this for hours. Ever since we stopped for booze and petrol in a *dorp*, and they warned us about these big buck called kudu – big as horses. Apparently as darkness falls, so do the kudu. They stand by the roadside, mesmerised by your headlamps, and then, the instant the lamps pass, they jump – crashing into what's just behind the lamps. You. We thought it was all a leg-pull until, leaving the town, we started seeing these roadsigns with pictures of kudu in mid-air. 'If pigs could fly,' said Angela, and, although kudu look nothing like pigs, it tickled our fancy then, and it's still going strong.

(It's nice to be friends with La again. Nice to see her happy again, well-pissed and a bit wild. She's like someone who's escaped from prison.)

The bottle comes round to me. This time I stop Angela from steadying the wheel, and leave the car to look after itself. No lights. No hands. No big deal. The road's wide, flat, and drawn with a ruler.

Each time I throw back my head to drink, I see Dad in the mirror. He's wrapped in blankets, although his coat must be dry by now, after its soaking at Cape Point. When was that? Hours ago. I keep expecting Dad to sleep, but since we hit the bundu, he's been holding the roof strap with both hands, nose resting in the crook of one arm, big eyes gazing out of the window. It makes him look brainless, like a caged gorilla hanging on a strap, idling away the day, waiting and watching, with nothing to see.

Maybe he's curious to see the veld at last. He's only ever viewed it from the air, flying to business meetings in Joburg or Bloemfontein. For the rest of his life in this country, he's stayed where he first landed: on the coast, on the edge.

Mind you, before this afternoon, *I*'d never seen the veld either. The blonde grass, fields of cacti, dust-snakes blowing across the tarmac. The first sight made me quite nostalgic. Not for my real childhood, but my Saturday morning childhood – at the cowboy flicks, *yaaaay*! The veld looks exactly like the prairies.

So it was wonderful to see it – for about five minutes. Then monotony took over. The endless telegraph poles and farm fences, the endless litter along the roadside. I thought it was a local stone at first – the constant glint – until, looking closer, I realised it was this trail of broken bottles, tins and ciggie packets.

The other thing you see along the roadside is lone blacks or Coloureds (some with blond hair) trekking on foot. Hard to tell which are tramps, they're all so dusty. The dust is reassuring. It makes you feel this is the way things have always been, and always will.

They all stop to gawp at us. *A Rolls-Royce!* – itself getting dustier as the day has worn on.

'Leon!'

I'm suddenly aware of a moonlit road, the Rolls driving itself – and wandering. I grab the wheel and flick the lights back on.

'Leon,' Angela shrieks again.

A pair of eyes in my headlamps. A flying pig? Too late to swerve.

'Oops,' I giggle, as the car bumps over something.

'Stop,' cries Angela. 'Stop the car!'

'Too late. Sorry.'

'But wha'ifsh . . .' She pauses, regains control of her tongue, then says, 'What if it's still alive?'

'Won't be for long. There'll be jackals around. Hungry in the winter. Hey, maybe it *was* a jackal.'

'Maybe,' she sighs, settling back. 'Or a little springbok. So attractive – springboks.'

'Mm. Specially the kind that play rugby.'

We howl with laughter, and drink more brandy, Angela finishing the bottle.

Now something else in my headlamps. A vague, luminous arrangement. It slowly forms into a klomp of whitewashed rocks on the roadside, spelling out the words: HOTEL – 1 KM. I start braking.

The hotel is alongside a small railway station, though God knows why anyone would stop here. We pull into a yard surrounded by corrugated-iron-roof bungalows, a couple of petrol pumps, a shed with the generator, giving off a low boom-boom noise. This syncopates with the click of a windmill that's turning somewhere in the dark. Across from us, there's a bar, with signs advertising Coca-Cola and Lion Beer.

Opening the car door, I gasp. The cold's unreal. Not like the soggy chill of Sea Point, this is kosher, inland cold, almost sticking to your skin.

Maybe I've had much less to drink than Dad or Angela – they both fall over when they get out of the car. Dad heaves himself up, and tumbles towards the bar, pulling on his coat. I lift Angela, and we hurry after.

Inside the bar, a strip of neon throws its terrible light, which is more like dimness, like time has stopped at three a.m. I check my watch: just past nine. A winy reek comes off the unmanned counter, and off the tables and chairs, whose foam seats have burst like overcooked puddings. On one wall, there's an odd collection of pin-ups: bathing beauties from the fifties, a prize Merino sheep, all of South Africa's prime ministers and presidents, and, most prominently, a colour photo of Jim Reeves.

Three white men are sitting down the other end, near a paraffin stove. Two of them are in sheepskin coats, farmers I reckon, and the other wears a dressing-gown. He rises. Although very tall, he can't be more than a teenager, with narrow shoulders and long arms. On his feet are socks and plastic slip-slops.

'*Naand menere, mevrou,*' he says, '*en wat kan ons julle aan-bied?*'

'*Nou ja,*' Dad says to us, '*wat wil julle drink?*'

(It's funny hearing him speak Afrikaans; he learned it off Zakes and Adam.)

'Shouldn't we stick to brandy?' I say.

'Lawks, no,' cries Angela. 'We must try the local tipple. Good tapster,' she says to the boy, 'your most famed cordial, if you please.'

I lean on the counter, giggling.

Dad gives us a bleary look, then asks the boy to pour us whatever the two farmers are drinking.

'*Spook en diesel,*' grins the boy, filling three glasses with cane spirit and Coca-Cola. Me and Angela exchange a grimace, then start giggling again.

'*Nee, gooi man – gooi,*' says Dad, snapping his fingers at the boy, who grins and tips the cane spirit round our glasses again.

Each finger snap makes the farmers look up. One is pot-bellied, about my age, but without teeth, a stringy moustache somewhere in the bunch of jaws. The other is older, bonier, with foggy specs, and a plaster on his hand.

Dad tells the boy we need toilets, some graze, and two bedrooms – in that order. The graze seems a bit of a prob, but, after giving Dad the key to the lav, the boy goes off to investigate.

Now we're left alone with the two farmers.

'Greetings,' says Angela. 'We're from England.' She picks up her drink, and (*ai!*) lurches across to them, hand outstretched. 'Angela Lipschitz.'

'Henning Jooste,' mutters the older man.

'Arrie van Blerk,' squeaks the one with no teeth.

'Henning, Arrie,' says Angela, 'please meet my dearly b'loved, Leon.'

There's nothing for it but to go over. Their hands feel like lizard-skin. Two empty bottles of cane spirit stand on the table, among a collection of Coke bottles, packets of Lucky Strike, and heaped ashtrays. They've been here for hours. I start to retreat, but Angela sits, saying:

'May I? Now tell me, are you chaps Afrikaners? We haven't met any Afrikaners yet.'

The one called Arrie grinds his gums, maybe smiling, then says in his high-pitched voice, 'Yes, lady. Boers.'

'Oh, you don't mind the word "Boer". How fascinating. I've been researching your history for a show, y'see. D'you get much theatre round here? Is there a local rep, a ... a thriving Boer rep?'

She catches my eye and winks. I stare back, anxiously. (Is she looking for trouble – deliberately taking on 'the enemy'? Her mood is wild enough.) Casually laying my hand on her shoulder, and pinching hard, I whisper, 'Howzabout a wash before supper, Angela?'

'Angela, Angela,' echoes Henning, taking off his glasses and spitting on them. '*Sy's darem 'n lekker groot ou teef, nè?*'

'*Hoeka!*' laughs Arrie. '*Haar poes is seker so groot soos 'n waenhuisdeur – wat sê jy?*'

I listen fearfully; *poes* means cunt, *groot* means big. They smile at her as they talk, and she smiles back.

I pinch her again. 'Angela – a wash?'

'Hmn?' she says muzzily, then notices Dad returning. 'And this's Chaim, my papa-in-law. Chaim, come over here and meet these two charming Boer gallants, Henning and Arrie.'

Dad nods at them, but stays at the counter.

'*Maar wie de fok is dié mense?*' whispers Henning as they light some ciggies.

'*Nee, fok weet!*' answers Arrie.

'Pardon?' says Angela.

'No, no, lady, we's talking of our sheep,' says Arrie.

'Sheep! How 'tterly fascinating!'

'Yes, lady . . .'

Suddenly the neon light dims, almost to nothing. Outside the boom-boom of the generator has vanished, leaving just the click of the windmill. In the dark of the bar, I hear the men shifting – their chairs creak like bed-springs. Then, as suddenly, the generator comes back to life, and neon returns. Arrie is grinning at Angela.

'Fas-ci-na-ting,' he squeaks softly. 'Sheep.'

'They certainly are,' says Angela.

'*Sê vir my – is jou poeslippe ook so vol wurms soos 'n skaap s'n?*'

As they laugh, spluttering on the ciggie smoke, Angela views them calmly (has she caught on?), then says, 'Now tell me, do you have many labourers on your farm? To help with these fascinating sheep. 'Cause 'm also fascinated by your labourers.'

'Angela!' I say, gripping her arm.

'Why's he say "Angela", "Angela" all the time?' asks Arrie. He takes my hand. 'My friend, we's not going to bite yous people.' He suddenly pulls back his lips to give a gummy grin – a pink cleft – it's like he's flashed his arse. 'We don't mos bite the English any more.'

'Actually, Leon's South African jus' like you,' says Angela, 'aren't you, darling?'

I nod cheerfully, my heart stopping dead.

Arrie slaps the table, overturning an ashtray. '*A ware Boer! Welkom tuis jong, welkom terug na die land van die lewendes!*'

'I'm sorry,' I say, with a puffing laugh, 'I don't speak much Afrikaans.'

'Bullshit, man. You must now learn him at school. Like we have to learn your lovely English. Not so?'

'Yes. Just don't remember much.'

'You now sure?'

I laugh. 'Sure I'm sure.'

'OK. *Weet jy hoekom jou vrou se poes gesplete is, hè? So dat almal dit kan deel.*'

(Cunt again – my wife's cunt – everyone sharing.)

'OK?' asks Arrie.

'OK what?'

'OK by you?'

I stare at him helplessly, then shake my head. They explode into laughter, coughing, slapping the table, knocking things off.

Luckily, dear God, the young guy returns now, with news of graze. Angela says she isn't hungry and tries to order a round of drinks for the men. I yank her up, and steer her after Dad and the boy.

'I'll be back,' she sings to the men, 'I want to hear all about your labourers.'

'*Ja, kom gou terug, jou groot, ou Engelse wurmpoes,*' laughs Arrie.

Out in the yard, I clout her shoulder. 'Do you have any fucking clue what they were saying about you?'

The blow sends her stumbling away. ''Course I do,' she snaps, steadying herself against the petrol pump. 'But how else is one to ... to learn anything? She's a dirty nurse, experience.'

The young guy shows us our rooms – they're cramped and cold – then leads us to the restaurant: a sort of Golden-Egg-type roadhouse. It must've been closed for the night, because the neon is still flickering back into life as we enter, and a sleepy native woman is tying on an apron. The young guy gestures grandly round the tables, covered in yellow PVC, offering our pick. We sit next to the window. It's freezing, but the others are too pissed to notice. I'd better catch up. Grabbing the bottle of cane spirit that someone's brought along, I splash it round our glasses.

Angela squints at the perspex menu. 'Any local game on?'

'Chicken and chips,' I answer, 'chops and chips, steak and chips.'

'What do I want?' asks Dad, nudging the menu over to me.

'Sorry?'

'What do I want?'

I drop my gaze, blushing. Mom always orders for him in restaurants. 'Have a steak with me,' I mumble.

'No. I fancy chicken.'

'Then why ask?'

He flares. 'Don't start, hahh? I'm not one of your friends.'

'And bubbly,' cries Angela. 'I must have bubbly.'

'Here you are,' I say, adding some Coke to her glass. 'We'd better get some solids in us pronto.' I summon the young guy. He stays put, and summons the native woman. She's a bulky old girl, moving with a lazy swagger.

As she plonks down a basket of bread rolls, Angela chirps, 'Hello. And what's your name?'

'Jessie, Missus.'

'No Missus please. I'm Angela, and this's Leon 'n Chaim.'

Dad splutters in his drink. I quickly give the woman our order. As she starts to swagger off, Angela calls after her, 'Jessie – gi's a shout if you want a hand, won't you, love?'

The woman frowns at Angela, and goes.

Dad sits back, contemplating Angela. 'So, my dear.'

She smiles, cheeks bulging with bread roll. 'So, my papa-in-law.'

'They tell me you're not a Jewess.'

'I'm not, no,' she says. 'Catholic. Is that a problem for you?'

'Not at all.' He smiles gently, powerfully. 'Your Pope's a Catholic.'

She hesitates. 'Yes, we like them that way.'

'Ah *ja*,' he laughs. 'You must excuse my bad English. I'm meaning to say, he's Polish Catholic.'

'Ah. Yeah.'

'So I know what I'm talking about.'

We wait. Eventually he says:

'Guilt.'

'Indeed,' says Angela, ''s something we share.'

He raises his eyebrows.

'Oh yeah,' she says, tearing up another bread roll, 'though I always think there's one major diff'rence. Sex, sex, sex.'

His eyebrows lift a tidge more.

'Sex accounts for so much of our guilt, but ... sex seems to be the only thing you're *not* guilty about.' She turns to me – cue for a laugh. I rub my mouth, buying time. I don't want to choose sides here. I don't even want to referee.

Dad regards her steadily. 'You're guilty about sex?'

'Not me personally.'

'Who then?'

'Catholics in general.'

'The Pope?'

'Well, no, certainly not the Pope.'

'Not you and not the Pope?'

'No.'

'Just all other Catholics.'

She shrugs, and attacks her third bread roll. Dad drinks, eyebrows still raised and aimed at her. The silence stretches, until nobody can remember whose turn it is to speak.

Over at the cash desk, the young guy suddenly turns a switch, and a Country-and-Western number yodels through the restaurant.

Dad glares at the speaker above us, and then, as though in mid-conversation, says, 'But would he help us when we needed him?'

'Sorry?' says Angela. 'Who?'

'Your Pope.'

'D'you mean during the war? Pius, the ... whichever?'

'I do. Turned a blind eye to the Nazis. A blind eye to the Nazis! Can you believe it?'

'Actually, I can,' says Angela, laughing, 'after a week in this country. Lots of blind eyes and lots of Nazis.'

Now Dad laughs. 'My dear, you mustn't believe everything you read in your papers.'

'I don't. I've just met two in the bar.'

'Agh, c'mon, Angela,' I chuckle, 'those blokes were just after your pussy, not any –'

'Oh, Leon's still here!' she says, 'Chaim, did you know you fathered a dickhead?'

Dad watches her closely. 'Like to talk dirty, hahh? Guilt, hahh? Catholic guilt.'

211

'I beg your pardon?' she says.

'Those men out there,' he says, 'they were after you, *ja?*'

'Which I knew perfectly well.'

'You knew?'

'Absolutely. And I was leading them on.'

'Leading them on?'

'Sure. So I could get them onto the subject of – '

'Excuse me, my dear,' says Dad, then turns to me. 'Your mother was no prostitute.'

'Pardon?' says Angela, *'Pardon?'*

Dad raises his hands in surrender. 'I'm telling Leon that his mother was no prostitute. A son should be assured of these things. Forgive me if the subject is a bit vulgar. For a Catholic.'

Angela breaks into laughter, and, in deepest Dudley, says ' 'ere cocker, yer head's full 'a fuckin' saftness!'

Dad turns back to me. 'Your mother. Did I ever tell you how I loved her?'

I stare at him, then shake my head, wishing I could focus better. 'No. No, you didn't.'

'In the fifties. When we took a luxury cruise to Europe on the mailship. The *Pretoria Castle*. You came along. You remember?'

'Vaguely.'

'She was no prostitute. Onboard. Black hair, black eyes, but inside – driven snow. *Ai gut!* We were treated like royalty. I'd done favours for the Union Castle crowd, so it was you scratch my back, I'll do yours and so forth. For eight weeks we sailed, first to Southampton, then onto another cruise ship, and into the Mediterranean, all round the Greek Islands, and Turkey of course.'

'Turkey too?'

'Turkey was the whole reason for the trip.'

'Why so?'

'It's where we're from. In the olden days.'

'Turkey? We were Turkish?'

'For a while.'

'Lipschitz is a Turkish name?'

'Maybe El Lipschitz. Who knows?'

He goes quiet. I lean forward. This is familiar. But from when?

I was sitting like this, drunk at a restaurant table, waiting for a meal to arrive, listening to something about Turkey.

'At last – our feast!'

Looking up, I see Angela climbing to her feet and helping the native woman unload our plates.

'Dad,' I say, 'how d'you know we come from Turkey?'

But he's oblivious, already busy with his graze, bits spilling out. After several mouthfuls, he suddenly stops. 'What's this meat?' he asks.

'Chicken,' I say.

'Never,' he says. 'No, no. No chicken that's ever visited Cape Town. Anyway, I fancied steak.'

'Do you want mine?' I ask. He goes shtum, sulking out the window. Sighing, I swap our meals. Without hesitation, he falls onto my steak, while I grimace at the mess on his plate: the droplets of chewed chicken.

'So,' I say, nudging the plate away, 'tell me about Turkey?'

'Turkey maybe,' he says, 'but never chicken.'

'*Ja*, very funny. Come on – the Lipschitzes in Turkey: tell me.'

He finishes eating, taking his time. Then, finally he looks up and says, 'One of the only things I brought from Poland was this brass belt-clasp. Nothing valuable, but it belonged to my father, and his father, and so on back. So anyhow, you remember Mikey Unterman? – they're living in New York now – anyhow, he was a bigshot jeweller in Cape Town, and he tells me this belt-clasp is probably Turkish, from the olden days. Their empire, you know.'

'Ottoman, yes,' I say, looking at Angela. She's stopped eating and is also listening carefully.

'So Mikey Unterman has a friend who has a friend who arranges for me to see an even bigger-shot jeweller when we're in Istanbul. And this man says yes, this belt-clasp is from early seventeen hundreds and it maybe belonged to a servant in one of the big palaces – a sign of office type of thing. And that's that, as much as he knows. Hold your horses, I say, this servant – he could've been Jewish? Oh, for sure, he says; lots of Jews in Constantinople then, from every whichway, Sephardic and Ashkenazi. And got on very well with the Emperors or whatever you want to call those guys.

Though if they worked in the palace, they'd probably have to convert for a while.'

'A non-Muslim boy,' I murmur, 'given to the master, to educate and cut parcel with.'

'To educate and what?' says Dad.

I pause, blinking at him. 'Their job was to . . . wrap things. Gifts and so on.'

'You know about these servants?'

'If we're talking about the same servants.' I turn to Angela, 'D'you remember any more?'

'Falconry,' she says, 'they learned falconry.'

'Falconry,' Dad repeats, amazed.

'And turban-dressing,' she adds.

'Hn,' Dad comments. 'Turban-dressing I can take or leave, but falconry's good. Sounds more like a Lipschitz.'

'Really?' I say.

'So that's it?' Dad says. 'Wrapping gifts and turbans, then the falcons, and that's a day's work?'

I shrug.

'*Ja*,' sighs Dad, 'still none the wiser. Like that morning in Istanbul, as we're travelling to the jeweller – *ei!* – so full of hope, y'know. And when he started to speak – early seventeen hundreds – incredible! You only have to go back four times. My great-grandpa could've been born then. Only four times. On one hand you can count. With one hand you can reach back for some answers. How did we land in Turkey, why did we bugger off, and why eventually to Poland? Everything would fall into place. But instead? Nothing. One or two small facts. A servant in a palace. And only maybe.'

'Dad, I bet there's more,' I say. 'I bet Mom remembers more from that morning in Istanbul.'

'Maybe,' he says. 'But here's another thought – who can guarantee the belt-clasp is even ours? We treasure it for centuries, but who says my great-grandpa didn't buy it, or receive it as a gift, or find it in the street? You can't hold onto your history: this is the terror. People wake in the night. They're wealthy, happy people. Why are they crying? They can't tell you. They just want to hold you. Hold onto *something*.'

'Where's the belt-clasp now?' asks Angela.

'At the place I was staying in Sea Point. The penthou –' He stops, and closes his eyes.

'What?' I ask.

'The penthouse. Zakes has a key. As soon as we went to the barmitzvah, he was in there! That's why he left the car. He knows me, and I know him. You see?'

'So . . .' I say after a while, 'Zakes inherits the Lipschitz belt-clasp. Which maybe belonged to a servant in an Ottoman palace. Who was maybe a Lipschitz. Or maybe not.' I laugh. 'At least the mystery is out of our hands.'

The others look at me solemnly. We lapse into silence, drinking and listening to the music.

> *Oh give me a home*
> *Where the buffalo roam*
> *Where the deer and the antelope play . . .*

The young guy notices me singing along, and calls over, '*Hou meneer van die musiek?*'

'Cowboy music, hey?' I call back.

He grins back, overjoyed that he's done the right thing. Shy, innocent. For a sec it's Gertjie sitting there. If only this boy was prettier . . .

'Leon,' Dad says, 'will you do me a favour?'

'Sock it to me, Pops.'

'Ask him if he's got any Benny Goodman.'

'Sure thing, Pops.' I rise, taking the change of altitude on the chin (shit, I'm well gone!), and I'm about to move off, when Angela says:

'Chaim, what *is* it about the fifties? For you?'

Dad looks at her for a long moment, then softly, almost sexily, says, 'Peacetime.'

'Where?' she asks.

'Here.'

'Peacetime?' She takes off her specs, rubs her eyes, and then returns his smile, confident and sassy. 'Do you know the date of the shootings in – ?'

'No,' he says immediately, in a thick voice. 'And I don't want to know. But here's something I *do* know – we were all happy then.'

'Not all of you,' she says, laughing harshly.

'*All*! Don't talk to me about the black man, my dear, because I'm working with him, day in, day out, and he's smiling at me. And when the black man smiles it's a lovely thing, hahh? It shines like a light. You want to tell me he's breaking his heart at the same time? Do me a favour! I had just fled the terrors of the earth – you think I'm going to come here and hurt people? You think that's possible? No. My conscience is clear. All I did was hold up my hand with the majority.'

'The *majority*?' laughs Angela.

'OK, folks,' I say, 'break it up.'

'Yes,' bellows Dad, 'the majority! The majority that I can see, that I can touch, that I can belong to.'

Angela just laughs at Dad; laughs and laughs.

He smiles back. It's a small, rude, man-to-woman smile, appalling on his mouth with its black hole. 'You're a schoolteacher, *ja*? OK, so educate me, please. Tell me this thing – when everything changes here now, as it will, and your so-called majority becomes *the* majority, what will you get? A majority of heroes? Or . . .' He reaches over, and slowly twiddles the wedding ring on her finger, 'or a majority of people trying to live as comfortably as they can. Knowing they won't always hold onto it, and waking now and then in the night. You know how it is.'

'No,' she says, pulling away her hand. 'I've no idea how it is. I sleep fine.' She's still trying to laugh, but her eyes have suddenly filled with tears.

He smiles at her again, then turns to me. 'Ask if they've got Benny Goodman. Please.'

I wave at the boy. 'Benny Goodman – yes?'

'Meneer?' he asks, grinning and shrugging.

'Nope,' I tell Dad, 'no Benny Goodman.'

'No Benny Goodman . . . ?' He thinks about this, chin on chest. In a sec he's asleep.

'Jesus, La,' I whisper.

'Yes,' she says, mopping her face. 'Jesus.'

'We were Turkish! Maybe.'

'What?' She puts back her specs, and sighs. 'You find that interesting?'

'You betcha bottom dollar!'

'Why's that?'

'Because I thought we were Polish. And Russian.'

'You thought the Bible was set in Eastern Europe?'

'No. But –'

'Turkish, Polish, Spanish, Ethiopian, so what?'

'So what? It's incredible!'

'No, it isn't. My people can't remember further back than yesterday – something about Mum's lot coming from Ireland; something about my dad's grandad doing farm labour. So what?'

'But at least you know what part of the world you're from. At least when you stand on UK soil, you know you've got some roots down there.'

'Not necessarily. Who says I'm not the result of a one-night stand some Roman legionnaire had in Bath? It doesn't matter, Leon. All that matters is *now*. And what are the Lipschitzes doing *now*?'

'We're existing! Still – after thousands of years – we're still here, we're surviving!'

'At what cost? The majority in this country –'

'Here we go again with your majorities! Didn't you hear my dad? *We* are the majority. To a Lipschitz, the Lipschitzes are the majority. That's all a Lipschitz can reach out and touch. The rest is just newspaper stuff – commies, fascists, black rule, white rule – today they're terrorists, tomorrow they're heroes. The only thing we can rely on is ourselves. The Lipschitzes! Back and forward we stretch. Forward to a Lipschitz that we're going to send into the future, me and you – and back, back to a Lipschitz who was a servant in an Ottoman palace. Isn't that incredible? Look at the Lipschitzes now, and just think – we were servants, La, servants!'

'Well, yes, *that* is incredible. Although posh servants. And catamites. Trust the Lipschitzes. But yes, you were servants. All right then . . .' She collects our dirty plates, and offers them to me. 'Wash these, please.'

I stare back. 'What are you trying to prove?'

She smiles and carries the plates to the kitchen.

'You're proving nothing,' I shout after her.

'Proving nothing perhaps,' she calls back, 'but doing something.'

'No, nothing! Liberal wank – it's insulting!'

The young guy runs after Angela, while the native woman bolts out of the doorway to meet her. Then the three of them disappear into the kitchen, tussling with the plates.

I rest on the table, catching my breath. I can hear rain. Leaning against the window and shielding my eyes from my reflection, I peer at the night. Clear and dry; the generator and windmill going boom-click-boom. I sit back, puzzled. In here, the noise is plip, plup. I hold out my palm in different directions. Then I see it on the floor. A trickle coming round the leg of the table toward my shoe; a bright yellow trickle.

'Come on, Dad – quick!' I say, shaking him awake.

'Hahh?'

'Just come with me.' Without looking under his chair, I hoist him up, and lead him out quickly. He's docile, completely bloody out of it.

In his room – a neon light again, three a.m. again.

Dad stands, snoring, as I unbutton the great Karakul coat and ease it off him. Now he's just in his *gatkes* and shoes. The *gatkes* are yellowish, getting yellower in the armpits, and bright yellow in the crotch, almost transparent.

Shutting my eyes, I start to undo the buttons. As each yields, I hear myself making a funny noise, like a dry sob. I must shut up – he'll hear. I unbutton to his navel, then fumble for the neck-line of the *gatkes*, and slip it off his shoulders and arms, down his back and sides, over his belly, and down.

'Yaah!' I cry, clutching the cloth, and falling with it, so that now I'm staring at a giant puddle of *gatkes* over his snakeskin moccasins.

Crouching there, looking no higher, I free his feet.

Now, with a huge sigh, he sits on the edge of the bed and sprawls back. The springs shriek. From my viewpoint, I watch them stretch and sink, then finally steady, inches from the floor.

I should wash him, but I can't. I should get him under the blankets, but I can't.

Suddenly the light dims, flickers, then goes out completely. The generator has packed up for real this time. The darkness makes me feel even worse – crouching here, near my naked father.

I jump up, then stop. On the dressing-table, I can just make out a candle in a white enamel holder. I light it. Nearby is a Bible. There's something in here, one of the stories: a father naked, a son having a good look. The son is cursed for evermore – a servant of servants. The Afrikaners quote it a lot.

A servant of servants.

Just for looking at your father's dick?

I lift the candle and carry it to the bed.

Amazing to see the thing at last: where it all began. Bigger, browner than I expected, speckled with age. I kneel, bringing in the candlelight, to memorise it better. I peer at it so closely I could kiss it; so close the shape stops making sense. This is a leftover from before, a darker age – this darker, looser flesh, the animal still hanging on, changing shape with the changing climate. Air, water, a touch, a memory, and it's BEZOING! or SQUIG. And women think we're always scratching ourselves? Not at all – we're just checking out the latest.

So – my father's. While he snores.

On the eighth day after his birth, the men of his family would've gathered round, uncovered him like now, and looked down, perhaps also by candlelight, while the *mohel* took hold of it and sliced some off. Who was in that circle of faces? Were any of them moffies? With Turkish, parcel-cutting blood still in their veins. And when the *mohel* bent right close, like I am now, and sucked it clean, like I could now, did any of them blush? And in a hundred, million years, would any of them have pictured the baby as a colossal old man, in a dusty hotel room, with his son studying his nakedness?

'Leon?' I hear Dad say, 'what you doing?'

I slowly lift the candle, up, up over his stomach, like sunlight rising over the brow of a hill, until I see him looking back.

'What's going on?' he asks.

The candle goes out as I drop it, and run.

Down the dark corridor, into our dark room, fumbling over to the washbasin. I open the tap, and then have to stagger back. A smell like *vrot* eggs fills the room. I put my hand under the icy trickle, sniff it, and gasp again. It's the water! The *brak* water, full of sodium. I run again: into the dark yard, into the car. Gertjie's toilet bag – that's got some sweet English scents. I'm about to open it, when I see something scrawled in the frost on the windscreen. I scrabble to the front of the car. The writing says: ENGELSE POES.

(My God – those men!)

I run. Stumbling into the dark restaurant, finding my way to the kitchen. Angela and the native woman are at the sink, washing up by candlelight, the bottle of cane spirit at their side.

'Are you all right?' asks Angela.

'Are you?' I say, panting. 'Those men?'

'What men?'

'No? OK, come – be with me, please.'

Angela hugs the native woman, and bequeaths her the rest of the cane spirit. The woman accepts with a nervous glance in my direction.

In our room, I lock the door and test it several times. Angela undresses and falls into bed. In the dark, I search through Gertjie's bag. I open his tube of toothpaste, wanting to rub some on my gums, but, like before, nothing comes out. I spray his deodorant on my palms, then dab on his aftershave, and clasp my hands over my face, taking deep breaths. But the smell's too sweet, too synthetic, nothing like him anymore. Dazed, I strip off and climb into bed.

Angela crawls into my arms, humming, 'Cosy sick old lady' – then suddenly freezes.

'Gertjie?' she whispers.

'Oh . . .' I say, then, *'ja.'*

Within a sec, we're rooting like maniacs.

We wake just before dawn. While Angela washes Dad's *gatkes*, I stagger outside. It's freezing. There's a bluish mist, like woodsmoke, round the feet of some distant bluegums. The land smells of wet straw. I can hear roosters, dogs, and native voices calling somewhere.

At last the *gatkes* are dried, Dad's dressed again, we've paid the bill (there wasn't enough cash, so Angela gave some jewellery), and we're climbing into the Rolls.

'What's that way?' I ask the young guy, noticing a side route, off the national road.

'No meneer, that's the old King William's Town road, but now it goes into the Ciskei. Just a few farms and *dorps* before the border. Baakens Plaas, Suurvlei, Nelshoek.'

'Suurvlei, did you say?'

'*Ja*, meneer. Forty k. or so. Close.'

I stare at him.

But of course it's close.

TWENTY-THREE

At last someone is coming. A tiny silhouette stepping from the
police station and starting across the compound. Despite the
distance, I can hear each of his footsteps; each step gently crushing
the gravel. It's very clear. Like the ticking of the cord on the
flagpole; each tick, very clear. It's practically desert round by here,
so there's nothing to stop sound from travelling on and on. Even
Suurvlei, in a shallow vale behind us, doesn't cause any barrier.
But then Suurvlei is a ghost town; hollow buildings, rusting jeeps,
plastic bags chasing themselves in little whirlwinds.

We wait, listening to the man's footsteps. I narrow my eyes.
The guy's a cop, obviously – and black. Must be the one I spoke
to on the phone. I lean forward onto the gate, then jump back.
Did I get a shock? No. It's frost still on the wire. A high fence
surrounds the compound, with floodlights and surveillance
cameras at each corner. The police station itself is built as a
block-house, two-storied and dazzlingly whitewashed.

'Ask if we can use their loo,' says Angela at my side.

'And booze,' Dad calls from the car. 'Ask if they can supply
some booze.'

I reply with a scowl.

(Today's hangover is like that: it's given me a temper, Dad the
shakes, and La the runs.)

The policeman stops, still some distance from us. He's thirtyish,
with big muscles and a big gut. The peaked cap is pulled down

222

over his nose, so that only his great muzzle of a mouth shows, the lips not quite closing over long ivories. It makes him look like he's bitten onto something hot, and it's taking a while cooling.

I smile. 'Hi – we spoke on the phone. I'm trying to contact Gertjie van der Bijl.'

He ponders this, hands in pockets, which tilts his holster to one side. Then he sighs. 'But I told you, meneer, this person – he is not here.'

'OK. But you also told me there's another policeman, am I right?'

'Sergeant Landsman, *ja*.'

'OK, can I talk to him, please?'

'Why?'

'He may know something about Gertjie van –'

'No, he does not. No one of this name is here.'

'The loo,' whispers Angela, jigging at my side.

'Shush,' I mutter, then, still smiling at the man, I say: 'OK, look – where will I find a register, a . . . voters' roll or suchlike?'

'How would he know?' says Angela, 'he's not allowed to vote.'

'Angela,' I hiss, then to him: 'Where can I –'

'Excuse me,' Angela says, shaking the gate, 'may I use your facilities?'

He turns his head – the cap, the deep shadow and the muzzle jaws – towards her, and watches her mark time.

'Please,' says Angela, '*please!*'

Now Dad leans out of the car. 'Hey, Constable, have you got a staff canteen here? With a bar?'

The man gives us a long look – our crinkled finery, the dusty Rolls – all of this he gives a long look, while my insides slowly rearrange themselves.

Then, in the silence, we hear the sound of someone running.

Way below, a figure is jogging through Suurvlei. He almost sparkles in the chilly sunlight. We wait, again listening to clear footfalls while we watch a distant figure take shape. This one's a white man wearing a grey track-suit. He has cropped, silver hair. Something familiar about his build: flat and sinewy. As he comes up the slope, he pants with each stride: a regular thumping heartbeat. I feel my chest (I hate touching it, that movement, so close to the surface.)

As the man reaches the Rolls he stops, and immediately presses a button on his watch. With a puff of disappointment, almost fury, he leans onto his knees, then right back, stretching his spine.

Although only in his mid-forties, his face is very wrinkled. A lifetime of squinting into the sun has tightened his expression, and half-closed his eyes, one more than the other. His is not a face you'd ever see in the UK. Baked and grim, it's a warrior's face. An African warrior. A white African.

But he can't be the warrior Gertjie told me about: the one fighting the holy war. With 'sensitive' duties – questioning prisoners until they answer.

He can't be. I don't want him to be.

'*Sersant* Landsman,' he says, offering his hand.

'Hi. Leon Lipschitz.'

'Oh,' he says, 'then this must be Angela.' His voice is low and dry.

I give a spluttering laugh. 'You know us?'

'Excuse me,' says Angela, 'could I use your toilet? It's a teeny bit urgent.'

Landsman turns to the black policeman. 'Zwane, *maak oop die bek en wys vir Mevrou Lipschitz waar die toilette is.*'

Zwane taps a code into a panel, and the gates open with an odd, swift, human noise, like a sigh. Angela scampers through and dashes for the building, with Zwane at her side.

'Come,' Landsman says to me.

I jump into the car and drive in.

'What are we doing here?' asks Dad from the back seat. 'Who are these people?'

'Not sure,' I say, watching in my mirror as the gates automatically shut behind us. 'The white cop may be the father of a pal of ours.'

'A pal? *Danken Got!* At least we'll get a drink.'

Stepping into the building, we find ourselves in a large reception office. A motionless fan hangs from the high ceiling, and the walls are thick and whitewashed. What with the sunlight falling through slit-like windows, it could almost be a Mediterranean villa. Except for the iciness. And the furniture – in canvas, iron and hardboard.

Landsman pulls the tracksuit hood over his head, lights a Camel Untipped, and checks through messages at the phone, studying each with a blank expression.

I look round, wondering which door Angela's gone through.

Landsman smokes. We wait.

When he's finished his ciggie, he puts the messages aside, and checks his watch. 'OK,' he says, 'I must now complete my PT. In this part of the world, a person must make strict routines. And thereafter he must keep to them. You understand?'

'Yes,' I say, laughing for no reason.

'*Bring daar koffie vir die mense*,' he says to Zwane who's popped up behind us, and now vanishes again. 'So. The constable will bring you coffee. I will do PT. Then we talk. What time is Marius due?'

'I'm sorry?' I say.

'When did he say he's coming through?'

'Who?'

'Marius.'

'Who's Marius?'

Landsman stares at me. A long silence.

Now Angela returns, saying, 'Oh, dearie me, blimey, thank you so much.'

Landsman looks from her to me. 'Are you not Mr and Mrs Lipschitz from London?'

'Yes,' we both answer.

'Mr and Mrs Lipschitz who was there with Marius?'

'Who's Marius?' says Angela.

'Gertjie,' I say.

'Who's Gertjie?' says Landsman.

We all look at one another. Then Landsman clears his throat, and, quietly, cautiously, says, 'Before he came to London, he was – how must I put it – so on his nerves. For a few months. Did he tell you?'

'Yes,' I answer, surprised how dry my mouth is.

'So. He gets mixed-up. And that type of thing.'

I laugh. 'Mixed-up about his own name?'

225

'He gets mixed-up,' repeats Landsman quietly, finishing the discussion.

'You're not his father,' says Angela, very definitely. 'You're not.'

'Of course,' says Landsman.

Angela makes a funny noise, a splutter, as though winded. I dare not look at her. For some reason my gaze rests on Landsman's hands; his fingernails. A memory comes back, don't ask me why, of a TV documentary on autopsies: a close-up of fingernails being cleaned.

Landsman's are close-cropped, and oily from his ciggies.

'Marius is due to come through,' he says slowly, 'from Joburg. We're waiting on him today or tomorrow. Isn't that why you people have turned up?'

'No,' I say. 'Well – yes. On the offchance. If we can, yes please. But no, we didn't uh . . . strictly.'

Landsman frowns. 'Pardon me, it must be my English . . .'

'Your English is excellent,' says Angela, coolly.

He gives a minute shrug. 'My wife,' he says, 'like you – a schoolteacher. English to a T. But mine – not so good.'

'How is she, by the way?' I ask. 'Your wife.'

He rests his inanimate, half-closed eyes on me. (Again I'm reminded of that programme on autopsies.) This time I swear his silence lasts for a minute or more. Then, without emotion, he says:

'My wife passed away five years ago.'

'I'm sorry,' I say, blushing, 'I thought Getj – Marius said she wasn't well. I must've heard wrong.'

'He gets mixed-up,' says Landsman slowly, as though reminding me for the last time.

'Yes.'

'It makes others mixed-up.'

'Yes.'

'Me, for example,' says Dad suddenly. 'I'm very mixed-up. Gertjie, Marius, the *schvartzer* cop, this man and his wife, the world and his. Strangers, the lot of them!'

'Yes, pardon me,' says Landsman, 'we haven't met . . .'

I watch them shaking hands; Landsman's baked fingers against Dad's, damp and trembling.

'Marius will no doubt explain it all when he comes here,' says Landsman, checking his watch again. 'Now I *must* do my PT. I'm very far behind now.'

As soon as he's gone, I turn to Angela. (I wonder if I look as pale as she does.) 'OK,' I whisper, 'so what do we do?'

'We wait,' she says. 'If Gertjie's coming, we wait.'

'If who's coming?' I ask, smiling grimly. 'D'you mean – ?'

A door opens. I go shtum, wincing as I nip my tongue. It's Zwane with a tray of enamel mugs.

'OK, Constable my boy,' says Dad, lumbering over. 'Your coffee looks terrific. This is million dollar coffee. But we'll have something in it, if you don't mind.'

'Meneer?'

I cringe as Dad starts snapping his fingers. 'Whisky, brandy, *witblitz*, whatever you've got.'

'No liquor here, meneer.'

'No liquor – my God! What do you people drink?'

'Coffee, meneer.'

'And after hours?'

'Coffee, meneer.'

Dad smiles at him. 'It's OK, pal, you can relax. Back in Cape Town, the head of Harbour Police, he's my best bedfellow. Cops I know inside out and I've never met a dry one yet.' Zwane is motionless; he can stay as motionless as Landsman. (Maybe they do yoga together?) Dad smiles again. 'Fair enough, Constable – we play it your way.' With hands shaking terribly, he feels in the pockets of his coat – then, remembering, gives a snort of irritation and snaps his fingers at Angela. 'Hey, got any jewellery left?'

The shadow under Zwane's cap darkens. 'I do not drink, meneer. And Sergeant Landsman, he does not drink. And, meneer, nobody will drink here – not on the Sabbath.' He strides out.

'Pretty high and mighty, hahh?' says Dad.

'Oh, that's right, cocker,' says Angela. 'You prefer blacks when they *smile* at you.'

'Shut up,' I say to her.

'Hahh?' says Dad. 'What did the gold-digging shiksa say?'

'And you,' I say, rounding on him, 'you shut up too. You're bloody nuts! Where do you think you are? This isn't a bottle-store.

It's a police station. A *South African* police station! From now on everyone shuts up, OK? I'm the only one who gets to speak. Is that clear?'

They both just laugh, and move over to the coffee tray.

'Oh,' says Angela, after a couple of sips – and, gripping her stomach, she charges out.

I go to the window. Landsman has built himself a small assault course outside, with logs and concrete blocks. Here he's doing his exercises, double-time: press-ups, sit-ups, chin-ups. I'm dead just *looking*.

Amazing to think we're roughly the same age. (*Ja*, Gertjie used to call me 'Pa'.) Landsman is so fit, yet his face is so wiped-out. Mind you, whose wouldn't be? – after what he's seen, and *done*. The thought goes through me like a charge. Now he strips off his tracksuit top. In the tight white T-shirt, his muscles could be made of marble. I feel giddy. It's like watching those newsreels of gymnastics in Germany before the last war. That new race of Aryan supermen perfecting their bodies; bodies designed for love, but trained to kill. And the object of their attentions? *Me*.

I don't recall sitting down for a zizz, yet here I am waking. I open my eyes. Twitching, swaying, sperm-shaped thingies swim across my vision, and die. Brain cells? I raise my head, listening to the grit in my neck, and look round the office. Must be about midday. Angela's not here. Dad's over in one corner, trembling, smoking a ciggie. Funny – he doesn't smoke. But I know how he feels. Each day, by now, he and me – we'd've had a drink already; so we never get the full force of any one hangover. But today – you could say this is a lifetime's hangover. Nothing for it: I need to graze or cum, and like urgent! (Ooh, *lekker* thought – rooting in a police station.)

'Dad,' I whisper, 'where's Angela?'

'*Oifen balkon ken kain korn nit geroten.*'

'What?'

'*Tak, my chcemy zapomnic.*'

'Oh Dad,' I sigh, 'why can't you just speak English, like everyone else's parents?'

'*Wie laaste lag, lag die lekkerste.*'

'Sure – glibbidiglomble.'

I go to the front door. No one about. Just the flagpole ticking away, as if charting some countdown.

Now footsteps join in, keeping the beat.

Zwane comes into view, patrolling the fence, head turned away, the cap and its shadow aimed at the veld. I follow his gaze. Nothing. What's he expecting? The hordes from that flick, *Zulu*, to suddenly come over the horizon? You heard their drums first, hey? – or was it their singing, in deep hoarse voices? Anyhow, something thumping away, like now.

BOMP, BOMP, BOMP.

I turn, as Angela charges, heavy-footed, into the office.

'What?' I cry.

'Landsman . . .' she sobs.

'*What?*'

'He's in there.'

'Where? What?'

'I need to go again. I've just been, but I need to go again. It keeps coming – from every end. Oh Bubs, please make it stop! I must go again. But he's in there, he's in there!'

'The lav?' I say, laughing. 'Jesus, I thought –'

'Go and see if he's through. Please.'

'O K, sure, but just take it easy, hey? It's only a hangover. You've got to lean into a hangover, make it your friend.'

Taking the exit behind the desk, I find myself in a long corridor with no windows, and all the doors shut. No signs or nameplates. I go to each, listening. Now I hear water behind one, and enter.

A white tiled room. On one side, a weeing wall and lavs; opposite, an open row of showers. Landsman stands with his back to me, under a gush of brown water. Again, that unbelievable stink of *vrot* eggs! Yet he's washing himself in it. Just like Gertjie said: washing, always washing. The thought – and smell – makes me sick, but the vision before me, that's a different story. It could be Gertjie's naked back – Gertjie at the Turk's shower party: soap running down the arrow of his spine, into the cleavage of his arse, down through the fur of his legs.

Without warning, Landsman turns, and peers through the pouring water.

'Sorry,' I mumble, 'I'm just . . .' I hurry to the weeing wall.

I hear him turn off the shower and step onto the floor. (This is familiar too: Gertjie behind me in a lav somewhere.) Wet footsteps approach. I try to glance over my shoulder without turning my head. I can't see him; he's right behind me.

'So,' I say, zipping up and swinging round.

Oh. The towel rail is here, next to the weeing wall – he's only come this close to reach it.

He says nothing, and starts drying himself. Determined not to stare, I keep my head back, like with a nose bleed.

'Uh . . .' I say eventually, 'this your day off?' He gives a small nod. 'Sunday,' I add, vaguely. He says nothing. 'Uhm . . . my wife. Needs to be in here.'

'She's not feeling right?' he asks quietly.

'No. A few drinks last night, and uhm . . . out of action today.'

'O K then, come,' he says suddenly, wrapping the towel round his middle, and taking my arm. Amazed, I just trot along.

Down the corridor we go and through another door. A big whitewashed room like the office, but with older, warmer furniture. On the floor, some buckskin rugs; in one corner, an old-fashioned wireless. A tiny bed, with his sweaty tracksuit thrown across it – his underpants, too.

'Sport on Sunday,' I say, laughing nervously. 'Wasn't allowed when I was growing up. Never on a Sunday, hey? Did you ever see that flick?'

He says nothing, lights a Camel Untipped, opens a cupboard, and takes out a wooden box. As he flips up the lid, I catch a glimpse of metal instruments.

'What's that?' I ask, with a numb giggle.

While he searches through the box, he shows me the lid.

'Oh,' I say, seeing the red cross, 'safety-first, hey? Damn important. In the middle of nowhere. Have you cut yourself?'

He looks up.

'Cut yourself?' I repeat. 'Doing PT?'

'Your wife. Her stomach.'

'Of course.'

He sits on the edge of the bed, reading the labels on the various bottles.

Now that his head is bowed, I can stare. *Ai!* Naked fathers – for the second time in twenty-four hours. Except the bod on this one is amazing. A stitching of dark hair trails from his navel, like on Gertjie, over the ridged stomach, and dips under his towel.

I feel a groiny prickle. (It's not me, it's the hangover!) I walk, fidgeting, around the room.

On the mantelpiece, there's a small Bible, an ebony cross and a framed black-and-white photo – Landsman as a young man, standing next to a dark-haired woman, beautiful but emaciated. They're each resting a hand on the shoulders of a small boy, who's wearing a school cap.

'Marius?' I ask.

Landsman nods.

'Sweet.'

'In London,' he says, 'you kept your eye on him.'

'Sorry?'

'In his letters, he said you and Angela were like parents.'

'No, no. Well. It was nothing. Really.'

'You are interested in him?'

'I'm sorry?'

He balances his ciggie on the first-aid box, then kneels and reaches under the bed. The wrapped towel opens along his thigh, right up onto the hairless, untanned side of his hip. I shut my eyes.

'This was my hobby,' he says, pulling out a cardboard box. 'In this part of the world, a person must have hobbies.'

The box is filled with photographs, strips of negatives, old Kodak photo-wallets, and little khaki ones saying '*Ilford – die film vir Suid-Afrikaanse toestande*'. Landsman hands over a stack of albums, then returns to his ciggie and the first-aid box.

Each of the albums is labelled and dated in Afrikaans. The handwriting, in fountain-pen, is meticulous. As I open the first, I catch that whiff of old photos: that cool mustiness.

231

First, in small, square Brownie snaps, there's Landsman in his late teens courting his future wife, both very dishy – although she's already weirdly thin. Their wedding reception on a farm, an ox roasting, Boers dancing to a squeeze-box; dancing the *tiekie-draai*! Now, the Landsmans' old home-cum-police station, the gables in shade from a bluegum. Gertjie as a baby: adorability you could die for, but an odd laziness in his eyes. Growing into a shy angel with very bright hair. His first day at school – Mom, the teacher, holding his hand. The black-and-white snaps expand. Glimpses of Suurvlei, a busy farming community; donkey-carts, bakkies, a sheep drive. Gertjie in rugby shirt and shorts, but bare-footed, a grim look on his face. (He never meets the camera's gaze.) Now, as the snaps turn into colour, Suurvlei's looking quieter, and Landsman's wife is looking thinner. A breathtaking shot of Gertjie, aged about fifteen, in a bathing costume, perched on the water tank alongside a windmill. Fearful, eternally fearful. His nose is still unbroken. I page urgently through the books. Gertjie's finished school, he's off to the army, he's back on leave – in uniform. And for the first time, he stares straight into the camera and grins. His looks have opened like a flower, and with the dead straight nose, he is perfect: a classic, Aryan beauty. Then he vanishes. 1985. I flick through the rest, but he never reappears. Suurvlei becomes more like it is now: deserted streets and buildings. Landsman's wife shrivels. One last snap of her: a skeleton trying to hold down a hat in the wind, then – ZAP! Now shots of a building site: the new police station taking shape. Zwane appears, his great muzzle of a mouth lifted arrogantly to the camera; hat off, but eyes still in shadow from a thick, fierce brow. And that's it: the last photo.

I sit back.

Landsman has changed into a fresh grey tracksuit, and is lighting another ciggie. He's miles away, not looking at me, not awaiting any comment on the albums. '*Aanstap, aanstap,*' he mutters to himself, noticing his watch. 'You must please pardon me.'

'Of course,' I say, and hurry to the door.

'Hang on,' he says. I stop. He holds out a small brown bottle.

'Oh *ja* – thanks,' I say.

'*Nee-wat,*' he says, smiling for the first time, 'I must thank you.

232

For keeping an eye on Marius there in London. I'm ... rather very grateful to you.'

'It was nothing. Really. Nothing.'

Walking back to the reception office, I rub my head, easing out the thought bubbles:

Gertjie's family never went to Joburg. They never left Suurvlei. Unless there are missing photos. Yet there can't be. Year after year documented in absolute detail. So what's been going on? And – do I tell Angela?

In the office, she's bent double on a chair, and Dad's asleep in the corner.

'How you doing?' I say to her.

'Bubs, why do I feel so frightened?'

'It's just a hangover.'

'You mean Landsman doesn't exist?' she laughs. 'Just part of the DTs?'

'Huhn? Oh, he gave me this. For your tummy.'

She stares at the brown bottle, then at me, and laughs again. 'Oh love, you honestly expect me to drink this? From *him*?'

'What? Oh. No, I don't think –'

'No. You don't. That's why I get so frightened.'

'If you're frightened, let's go.'

'No. If Gertjie's coming, we're stopping.'

'Fine. Then we're stopping,' I say, reflecting on the Dudley turn of phrase.

'Come with me to the loo,' she says. 'Stand outside while I go.'

'Okeydoke.'

She hurries down the corridor and into the lav. I pace outside. Through a crack in Landsman's door, I see him kneeling next to his bed. He's praying. His feet are bare, the yellow soles angled towards me. It makes a man look so defenceless, hey? So innocent. Like a kid. Even Landsman – except for the ciggie in his folded hands.

That isn't nice – talking to God with a ciggie on the go.

*

233

We're having supper.

Angela sits, staring at Landsman.

She's refused his food: a Boer speciality, sheep's tripe and trotters. When he summoned us into the kitchen, and she saw his apron smeared with blood and fat, she had to charge for the lav again.

Now she just sits, staring at him.

I keep expecting her to say something, but the silence from Landsman and Zwane (who eats alone, nearer the fire) is too powerful. Apart from grace, whispered in Afrikaans, they've said nothing. A silence only has to go on for a few minutes and it becomes hard to break. These blokes have spent years in silence. Eating in silence, living in silence. They're practically in a trance. Landsman doesn't seem to notice Angela staring, or the pellets of stew which Dad's shaking fork sends zipping round the table.

Maybe it's something else, his trance. Maybe he's dwelling on a question that's worrying us too: why did his son use a different name in London?

'*Nou-ja*,' he sighs, when we've finished grazing, 'let me show you to your rooms.'

I glance at the clock above the mantelpiece. Seven thirteen. *Bedtime?*

Seeing my expression, Landsman says, 'Marius won't come through now. Not after the light goes. We keep farmers' time. He'll come through in the morning.'

We follow him up some concrete stairs.

The upper landing is freezing. A warren of corridors lead in different directions, lit only by the floodlights outside in the compound: squares of light falling at broken angles along the walls.

Landsman leads down a corridor lined with doors.

I chuckle nervously. 'Are these the cells?' He shakes his head. 'Then why so many rooms?'

'In the event of emergency.'

I'm about to ask what he means, when he opens one of the doors. A narrow barrack-room, deserted but expectant – with cellophane-wrapped blankets on the wrought-iron beds. 'Take bedding, hey?' he says, 'as much as you want.' He opens another. 'Except from here. Marius' room.'

Angela and me both leap to the doorway. The room is smaller than the others, but as featureless – apart from a suitcase and trunk in one corner.

'So, he still lives here?' I ask, confused.

'No,' says Landsman, 'but when he visits he likes sleeping up here. And when he was sick last year, he stayed a bit thereafter. That's when he brought back some things.' He walks over to the luggage. 'It's still unpacked.'

'How so?' I ask.

Landsman goes stiller than ever. After at least two full minutes, he says, 'He had no energy. And I don't . . .' He hesitates. 'I don't want to know about the things he's busy with in Joburg.' He sits on the trunk. Another minute or two passes, with no one daring to move. Then Landsman says quietly, 'I've led a simple life here. Here the only crime we get is drunkenness, or trespassing on grazing lands. But this is unfortunately not the case in Joburg. Not there, nor in the other cities. *Nee man, dis nou weer 'n hele ander storie.*'

'There you're right,' says Dad, lumbering over and joining him. 'There was a morning. The day I arrived from Poland. I sat down on a suitcase – just like we are now. At the docks. I said, *Baroch Ashem*, thank you, God, you've brought me to a simple place this time. The sun is shining, the air is clean, life will at long last be simple . . . But I was wrong.' He pulls his coat tighter round him.

'Why? How? What happened?'

'What happened?' echoes Landsman, 'I wish somebody could explain it to me.'

'Got a cigarette?' asks Dad, and then, as they light up, 'in the fifties. It was good in the fifties.'

Angela groans and leans against the doorway.

'Please shut up,' I whisper to her.

'And in the sixties,' Landsman says to Dad, 'it was still good in the sixties. Isn't it so? The whole land went *deurmekaar* in the seventies. That's when the growing lawlessness started. Just as Marius is coming into manhood. Him and the land – together, they turn into strangers.'

'My son too,' says Dad, 'that's when he packed his bags and became *tahkeh* a stranger.'

'Marius was too lonely.'

'Lonely Leon, yes.'

'His loneliness made him different.'

'Different? Don't talk to me about different!'

'Obeyed no rules. Of truth. Of compassion.'

'Of the sex business. Not a single rule.'

'He wouldn't do like what I do.'

'Nope. Wouldn't follow me into the business.'

'I have served our country – decently.'

'Our country,' repeats Dad. Then he closes his eyes and starts to sing: 'Ringing out from our blue heavens . . .'

Landsman joins in: *'Uit die diepte van ons see . . .'*

'Over everlasting mountains,' sings Dad.

'Waar die kranse antwoord gee.'

Angela turns to me, puzzled. 'The anthem,' I whisper. She gasps, then giggles.

Dad's voice lifts: 'From the plains where creaking wagons cut their trails into the earth . . .'

'Ruis die stem van ons geliefde,' sings Landsman, and then they join together:

'Van ons land, Suid Afrika.'

Angela giggles again. Mistaking the noise, Dad says, *'Ja,* it touches the heart, hahh? One of the first things I learned when I arrived. I didn't know the meanings yet, but by God, it felt good.'

'Ja, wel,' says Landsman, *'wat het gebeur?'*

'What happened?' echoes Dad.

'Wat het met Kanaän gebeur?'

'Canaan, the promised land, the paradise. For our children and our children's children. What happened?'

'Ag, my seun, my seun.'

'My boy, my firstborn.'

'O' Marius!'

'Beloved Leon!'

I stare at Dad. He keeps saying my name: I'm here in front of him – why doesn't he look at me? But both men have their heads lowered, dragging mournfully on their ciggies.

Angela's giggles are getting worse. 'Oh dear,' she cries suddenly, then dashes away, throwing open doors till she finds a lav.

I wait in the long, weirdly lit corridor.

The two men come out of Gertjie's room. Landsman mutters, 'Pardon me,' and hurries downstairs.

'You're pardoned,' says Dad, dazed and shivering. 'We're all pardoned' – and he wanders into the nearest room, shutting the door.

Now another door opens, and Angela reappears.

'OK?' I ask.

'Oh sure,' she replies grimly. 'The loo paper here! It's so hard you can't flush it away.'

'Designed for policemen's bums,' I say, chuckling. 'We don't call the Boers *crunchies* for nothing.'

I follow her back into Gertjie's room. She walks over to his luggage, and stands looking down at the suitcase. With one foot, she nudges the lid. It lifts slightly.

In the semi-dark, we look at one another.

'No,' I say.

'No?' she says in a detached voice, raising the suitcase lid again and this time keeping it open.

A jumble of clothes, packed in a rush. She kneels and lowers her face. 'Not his smell,' she says, more to herself than me. Then, casually, almost lazily, she digs among the clothes and finds a small, oval bottle. She holds it in a patch of light from the window. It illuminates with an amber glow. She opens the bottle and sniffs. 'No,' she says, 'not his aftershave.'

'He'd've bought a different one here.'

She lifts out a shirt and examines it in the light. It's a grey-blue colour. Although rumpled, you can tell it was crisply starched before. She slips her fingers into shoulder lapels. 'This isn't a student's shirt.'

'No,' I say, 'it's not even a civvy shirt.'

'Perhaps from when he was in the army?'

'Wrong colour. Air force maybe. Or navy.'

'I thought he said he was in the army.'

'I thought so too.'

She sighs – a quiet, remote sigh – then moves over to the trunk.

237

Inside, another jumble, with books and music cassettes on top. She lifts some paperbacks to the light. 'American pulp,' she says, 'yet Primo Levi too.'

'Prima what?'

'Oh, Leon – he was an Italian Jew in Auschwitz.'

'Ah-huhn? Well then, that's nice.'

'Nice?'

'Nice that Gertjie should be reading up about Jewish history.'

'Nice . . .' She lifts a music cassette. '"*Net Vir Ons Mense*". What does that mean?'

'Uh . . . "Just For Our People". Folk songs.'

'Just For Our People? That isn't very nice.'

'OK, La, let's stop this.'

'Oh, but *this* looks nice,' says Angela, lifting out a neatly folded jacket with braid and insignia. Again the cloth is blue-grey. 'We must've heard wrong,' says Angela. 'He definitely wasn't in the army. Or in the air force. Or navy.'

I stare back at her.

'Come on,' she says quietly. 'Come on.'

'OK,' I mutter, 'OK. Police.'

She thinks, then says briskly, 'Fine. This is Landsman's stuff. Not Gertjie's. All settled.'

'No, I'm not –'

'It's Landsman's stuff. From when he was in the Johannesburg police.'

'But he wasn't. He never left Suurvlei. I saw photos this arvie. Of him here. Year after year. It's Gertjie who went away, not him.'

'No,' she says calmly, 'photos can be faked.'

'La . . .'

'No. I'm sorry. These are policeman's things, not Gertjie's.' She lifts out more uniforms, laying them on the floor with peculiar precision. 'Do these look like his things? No. Do they smell like him? No. Do they – ?' She stops, and carries one of the uniforms to the light. It's different, brown in colour. As she holds it, one sleeve slips out. On it is a circular white badge, with a black symbol – three sevens attached by their tails, whirling round, and looking, as someone once said, like a swastika that's been given a hard klup.

Angela is motionless.

'Three sevens,' I say softly, touching the badge. 'Isn't it funny, but there's something in this which . . . I dunno. It's terrible. Like this morning when I was with Landsman, before I realised he wasn't what we thought, and there was this . . . sort'f terrible excitement. Yet I've never been into any of that S-M stuff. I mean, *me*? Me and pain? C'mon! But there's something . . . I'm almost turned-on now. Why?'

'Well, all settled,' says Angela, as though I hadn't spoken. She starts folding the brown shirt. 'Landsman's stuff. Not Gertjie's.'

I give a little laugh. 'You keep saying that. Landsman's stuff – not Gertjie's. Landsman – not Gertjie. But . . .' I walk to the door, check out the corridor, then turn back, and whisper, 'Landsman *is* Gertjie. Landsman is his real surname. Don't you see? *We* thought – '

Don't ask me what the fuck happens next.

Angela comes across the room like a rugby forward, the brown shirt clutched to her chest, shoulders bunched, head down. For a sec, I think she's dashing to the lav again. Until her head hits my belly. I fly backwards into the corridor. The back of my skull hits the wall. Something whips my face. Her hand? No, the folded shirt. Can cloth be so sharp? I stagger away from the wall, coughing, eyes pouring. She hits me from behind. I smash into the opposite wall. Every bone's got to be broken in my face. It's holding together, but only just, like a shattered windscreen. Hoarse panting somewhere. Is that her? Or me? I've got hold of her hair and I'm swinging her round the corridor. Her wrists and ankles keep hitting the walls. That must hurt. Poor Angela. Her poor family. Poor labourers. So easy to push around. Like the way I'm pushing her into this barrack-room, and onto this bed where the blankets are wrapped in cellophane bags. Kids suffocate in cellophane. Even Angela could – and will – if I keep it pressed to her face much longer. Something hits my chin. Her knee maybe. And now things are a bit blurred again, as though we're dancing very fast. Round and round. Dervishes. Are they Turkish? Stairs – where did stairs come from? Actually, sorry, it's an escalator. A concrete escalator. Moving up to meet us. Angela hits the floor first. Me on top of her, kotching up Landsman's tripe and trotters. And abracadabra, Landsman's boots are here too, scurrying around. And Zwane too. Hullo, Zwane. Scurrying around – and slipping. Hang on, I don't remember the tripe and trotters being so red. Oh no! Oh dear, oh dear! Is it *strictly* necessary to show blood? Tsk – modern entertainment! Back in the golden age of the silver screen, the gods and goddesses couldn't even smooch without one foot on the floor. Those were the days, hey? The bioscope. Saturday mornings. Swapping comics in the queue, and then squealing in the dark. Bugs Bunny, Tom and Jerry. Flattened – CRONCH, OOF! – but always OK in the end. Always smiling as they vanished into that twirling black hole.

TWENTY-FOUR

'Is it sore? Must be. Here – is it sore?'
So this is what it feels like. Strapped to a bed (a *bed*: how
horrible it should happen on a *bed*), with someone carefully,
almost gently, hurting you.

Look at him – so attentive. I wonder if this job of his, this
unusual career, if it eventually becomes boring? Are there days
when he thinks, Agh, I don't feel like work today? And what's it
like to come home from work and touch the people around you?
Friends, lovers. I mean, you can wash yourself, and wash and
wash, but what about other people – can you bear to touch them
once you've discovered how easily they come apart? How easy it
is to slice and peel them like food. Bad food by now – they're
rotting in front of your eyes, yet they're still talking, struggling,
planning to get through it. After seeing this, can you still find
people attractive? Maybe it just heightens your awareness. A sense
of relief even? Hey, we *are* just mortal! The poets and priests were
lying! Hey, at least the bloody mystery's over!

'And here? Tell me if this is sore.' He bends closer and kisses
me lightly. 'Is it?'

'Yes.'

'Then I mustn't.'

'No. Please.'

'Then I won't.'

'Thank you.'

241

'My pleasure. Hey, we're being very bloody English. Very polite. For boyfriends.'

'Boyfriends – are we still?'

He shrugs. 'Sure.'

'But what must I call you? Gertjie or Marius?'

'No, Gertjie definitely. Marius would sound funny on your tongue. I wouldn't know who you meant.'

'OK then. Hullo, Gertjie.'

'Hi.'

'I didn't think we were going to meet up again.'

'Me neither. But it's good, *nè?*'

'Ja . . .'

'You don't sound sure.'

'No, no, I am. But can I ask a favour?'

'Anything.'

'Would you release me?'

'Oh, I'm sorry.'

He sits back and, to my surprise, I can move my arms, my legs. I'm not strapped down. It was the weight of the blankets, and him leaning on them.

I'm in his room, upstairs in the police station. His uniforms and stuff have been packed away. The bright patch on the wall, it isn't from a floodlight anymore – it's early sunlight: softening his features, his hair, the stubble on his cheeks. I'm looking up at a gorgeous, vaselined close-up in one of those old flicks.

'My pa,' he whispers, giving me that fab blushing smile, and kisses my palm. I wince. 'Sorry,' he says.

I look at my hand. It's so swollen, I could be wearing a rubber glove. And from what I can see of my face, squinting here and there, it looks like the corners of a sponge. All sorts of colours. Running my tongue round my mouth, I find new shapes to my teeth and on my lips.

'Where can I kiss you that won't hurt?' he asks, nuzzling his head under the blankets. I peer down. My shirt front is patterned with dried blood. I lie back, listening to his muffled voice giggling. 'Where? Here? Is here sore?'

(Help. I don't want this to be nice.)

'Gertjie,' I say, lifting his head, 'we must have a talk.'

'I'm dead,' he says, standing abruptly, and stretching, 'I'm dead, dead. Travelling all night. Must liven myself up. Did you like my present?'

'Your present?'

'Toothpaste. Got any left?'

'Oh. What? No, I haven't used any. Couldn't get it to work.'

'Is this now true? Where is it?'

'In the car.'

'The Rolls, is she yours? *Yirra*, she's a beaut, hey? Will you take us for a spin?'

'Sure –'

'Right now? My pa got called out to van der Walt's farm. D'you want to? Before he gets back?'

'Uh . . . *ja*, if . . .'

He closes his eyes, and whispers, '*O' ja*, I *smaak* this! Come. Quick.'

He pulls back the blankets and I cautiously lift myself onto the side of the bed. I'm fully dressed, even my shoes. Dried blood in my socks, on my cuffs. The bed as well – covered in blood.

'Sorry about this,' I say.

'Hey man, no big shit – the laundry van comes through tomorrow. See if you can stand.'

It's surprisingly easy. As long as I keep my swollen hand from touching anything, there's no pain. The opposite almost. I feel rested, alert; more and more alert with each sec.

'How did I get here?' I ask. 'We were on the stairs. The bottom of the stairs.'

'You walked. Pa says you wouldn't let them help you, or even touch you. So they left you. They could see you weren't hurt too bad.'

I look at all the blood. 'This isn't too bad?'

'Naa,' he says, 'it's healing already.'

'Amazing. You can lose all this blood –'

'And the body just closes up and makes some more. We are miraculous creatures.'

I stare at him. The sunlight round his head is like a halo. 'And Angela?' I ask, limping into the corridor, 'where's Angela?'

'Downstairs.' He hesitates, suddenly upset. 'She won't see me

243

. . . my *engeltjie*'s the hell-in with me.' He clamps one finger over his lips. Then, after a moment, 'Will you go talk to her, pa? See if she'll come with? For a spin. The three of us together again.'

I nod. (It's funny. My head's so clear, it's like being on some drug.)

'But now!' he says. 'Before Pa comes back, and makes me sit down for a long *ou geselsie* with him. You know parents.' He smiles. The tears are gone.

'Parents,' I say, opening the door to Dad's room.

He's on his back, snoring softly, with his coat wrapped round him. In sleep, his face has lost all its fury, all that puff and colour. It has gone into its true shape, like it will again, quite soon, when he dies; his jaw sagging back into his skull, emptying his cheeks, just leaving a puzzled scowl.

'He's magnificent,' whispers Gertjie.

'Really?'

'Oh definitely.'

'Turkish, y'know.'

'Polish, I thought.'

'Turkish originally. Like that bloke we met in London. The singer. Y'know, who'd been in a Turkish prison, where they'd –' I stop, remembering how the singer had recognised something in Gertjie. 'Anyway, the Lipschitzes are Turkish. Maybe. Isn't that incredible?'

'No. Why?'

'Hey, that's what Angela said! Well, *I* think it's incredible – that in the past we may've –'

'No. *Now*. Now is the only incredible thing.'

'Just what Angela said.'

'She's wise. She's magnificent. Like your dad. Like you. Magnificent, miraculous.'

I turn to him. 'Are you stoned?'

He grins. 'Just haven't slept all night. Some brandy on the train. Watched the land passing. Fokken breathtaking, man! Specially at night. Heaven on earth – literally. Miraculous!'

We continue down the corridor to the stairs.

'So,' I say, 'why are you back?'

'It's thanks to you and Angela. I feel so much better. Thought I'd try again.'

'Try –?'

'Work. London was OK. Charlotte. Her amazing old raves. Your goodness. But work gives a man purpose. So I've asked them for another chance. I took a full medical, there in Joburg on Friday. The signs are good. They'll let me know this week.'

'We thought you were, y'know . . . a student.'

'*Ja*, well. In London, people wouldn't understand. You know how we're misunderstood in the outside world. Here I can explain better.'

We've reached the ground floor corridor. He indicates stairs at one end. 'Angela's down there. Please make her come with. I've so much to say.'

'Okeydoke.'

Another concrete stairwell. Me on my ace, feeling fantastic. And I've just realised why – no hangover! Yesterday was the first booze-free day since – when? – since birth, I think. Right, that's me and booze finished with, like I finished with the ballet. Who needs it? Today is so wonderful. Exciting, clear, easy to follow. Made of bright, comic-book dots, or celluloid. All it needs now is music. Leon's theme. Something huge and inspiring, like, I dunno, the theme from *Born Free* maybe, or *Superman*. I am, after all, a magnificent, miraculous force.

In the basement, there's a single long corridor with cells on either side; clean and modern. No privacy though. I'm walking between walls of mesh; you can see to every far corner. Must be sexy when the cells are occupied. Studying people; seeing their every function, every feeling – their thoughts even.

Zwane stands halfway down the corridor. Today *he's* wearing a grey tracksuit; today must be his day off. He's leaning against the mesh, talking to someone in that cell. From this angle the mesh is opaque, but as I approach, the light sweeps across, wiping it clear, just like in the movies, and lo and behold – Angela. Propped on one of the bunks, and *also* wearing a grey tracksuit.

'No, hang it all, man,' I say to Zwane, as I test the cell door and find it locked.

He turns his back on me and strolls away.

'Hey,' I shout, but he doesn't stop.

'It's all right,' says Angela.

'Damn cheeky, hey?'

'No. It's shyness actually. He's rather sweet when you make the effort. Look what he's lent me . . .'

She feels round her bunk, hardly able to turn her head. She's a mess. A gross black eye, and plasters criss-crossing her swollen face.

'Listen,' I call, 'Landsman will be back now-now. He'll let you out. This is ridiculous!'

'No, it's fine. I asked them to do it.'

'You asked them to lock you in?'

'Gertjie's here.'

'Yes.'

'When he leaves, then I'll come out.'

I laugh, but she doesn't. She finds what she was looking for, and holds it up for me to see. A large book: *An Illustrated Guide to Greek Mythology*.

'Just coffee-table stuff,' she says, 'but isn't it surprising he's reading it? Constable Zwane.'

'Very. Now listen, Gertjie wants –'

'Apparently there's a travelling library which arrives every month, and he takes out everything he can. Why? Just out of boredom, or something else? Did you notice him patrolling the fence yesterday? Is he watching for enemies or friends? I haven't got round to asking him yet, but it's interesting, yes?'

'*Ja*. Look, Gertjie's asking for a chance to –'

'I don't want to know.' She strokes the book. 'Education, d'you see? That's the cry here and now. Education, education! Who was it that called human history a race between education and catastrophe?'

'Give up. Who was it?'

'Can't remember.'

'Yes, you can.'

'What?'

'You always do this. Pretend not to know things. For my sake. But I don't mind being the barbarian of the family, I promise you I don't. So who was it?'

Angela gives her self-mocking giggle, and says, 'All right – H. G. Wells.'

'Really? Hey, I know his stuff. *The War of the Worlds, The Invisible Man.*'

'Leon! – why have you never told me? You've read two whole books?'

'Sure. The Classic Comics did both of them.'

'Oh chuck,' she gasps, and clutches her face. 'Don't! You mustn't! Aaa-a-ah . . . !' she cries as her laughter rises, opening her wounds. 'You're right – right not to be ashamed of your mind. It's like one of the elements – untamed, natural, free! A Leon blew today, a Leon fell. But tomorrow will be fine and mild again.' Her laughter suddenly changes to sobs, which open her wounds even more.

'La,' I say, 'c'm here. Give me your hand.'

Flinching with pain, she heaves herself off the bunk, shuffles over, and puts her fingers through the mesh. I gently kiss the ends. Her nails are torn from our fight.

'Come on,' I say, 'let's get you out of here. You mustn't worry about Gertjie. He's –'

'I don't want to know,' she says, and then immediately – 'How is he?'

'He looks well. Beautiful. Like an angel.'

'Naturally! Naturally he does! "As beautiful as was bright Lucifer before his fall." D'you remember the night – oh, long, long ago – when we went to see *Faustus?*'

'Angela, Gertjie isn't the devil.'

'Of course not! The devil doesn't exist. Didn't they mention this in the Classic Comics? No official devil. Just each to his own.' Holding the mesh, she leans back and rocks herself. Her matted hair falls over her face, reminding me of her at home, reading, working, being there – always.

'I love you,' I say.

'Crikey,' she laughs. 'Love?'

'That's for damn sure! Whatever's happened, my feeling's always been the same. Great love.'

'No. Loneliness. Me too. Loneliness, not love.'

I smile. 'So, *nu?* Words. Who's fussy?'

She smiles back, her swollen mouth twisting. 'I am.'

247

'La, I'm sorry about last night.'

'Oh . . .'

'I am. I'm really sorry.'

'Oh, don't be!' she says passionately. 'I'm not sorry. I'm grateful. I can leave you now – I can leave you at last.'

'Huhn?'

She reaches through the mesh, and touches the dried blood on my cheek. 'They haven't cleaned you. They cleaned me, changed my clothes, cleaned all of him away.'

'Him? Who's him?'

'Or her. But somehow I always thought it would be a *him*. Somehow you'd've made sure it was a *him*.'

'La, what are you talking about?'

'Oh . . .' She takes a deep breath. 'The week before we left London I was late, period-wise. You never noticed, you were too drunk on Gertjie. I stopped myself from getting excited – I mean, I was so uptight about my show, it was perfectly feasible to be late. Then we arrived here, and it still didn't come, and still I didn't get excited. A long air flight – still made it feasible. But by the end of last week . . . well, it was no longer feasible.'

Without warning, my legs give way, and I land, cross-legged, on the concrete floor, staring up at her.

After a while I say, 'Uhm, I wonder when we – ?'

'On your birthday,' she says briskly. 'The birthday weekend. I'm almost sure.'

Jesus. That incredible sesh round the hotel room, over the furniture and under the shower. Jesus. I think back over the last week. That strange, new, weary Angela. Jesus. The amount she drank at the motel joint on Saturday night, filling her blood with booze, and then making herself sick all yesterday. And then . . . I look at the blood on my clothes, hands, socks. Jesus.

'Why?' I ask, 'why didn't you tell me?'

'Yes. Good question,' she says quietly, professionally, as though in class, 'very good question. Why didn't I tell you? OK, at first I didn't tell you because I wasn't sure. I didn't want us to get excited. And then later, when I was sure – about *it*, I . . . I was suddenly no longer sure about us. Incredible. We'd been trying all this time, seven years, and I'd never stopped to ask – is this a good idea? And when I did, the answer was no. No. I shouldn't tie myself closer to you. The opposite. Quite the opposite. Being with Gertjie has shown me . . . well, different things. D'you see?' She hesitates, thinking deeply. 'I was just so, *so* in love with him.'

And now it happens. The thing I've been fearing all my life. Time stops. This sec is the last. No pulse. No heartbeat. No blood running, hot or cold. But I don't know why I ever feared this. In this kind of stillness, things are absolutely clear. The cartoon bubbles are clear as can be:

I've lost La, and I've lost my kid.

I'm not to blame.

Gertjie is.

And Gertjie will pay.

I climb to my feet – everything's working again – and charge down the corridor.

'Yes, run,' laughs Angela. 'As usual – run!'

She's got it wrong, but there's no time to explain. I must do it now. And I *can* do it. I am magnificent, I am miraculous, I am one of the elements!

You can hear the music starting now, hey? My theme. Leon's theme. Starting quiet, but there's got to be a hundred violins in there at least, a giant harp or two, and oh, such colossal drums waiting to be thumped!

Upstairs, Gertjie stands in the office, eager and flushed.

'Will my *engeltjie* join us, pa?' he asks.

I gaze back silently. (OK, now the only question is – how? How to do it? With what?)

'Pa . . . ?' he asks, frowning.

'Sorry. No, no, she isn't.' I glance round the office – there's got to be something in here I can use. 'Must just ask my mom something,' I say, picking up the phone and dialling urgently. 'It's a bit private. Can you wait in the car?'

'A Rolls,' he cries, scampering off: '*Wie die fok sal dit glo! A fokken Rolls!*'

I glance round again. In a police station surely there must be something, hey?

'Yes,' says Mom.

I jump, almost dropping the phone. 'Oh, hi. I was expecting Lizzie to answer.'

'Don't talk to me about Lizzie, please. I've had to get rid of her.'

'Get rid of – ? My God!'

'*Ja*, I know. Shame, hey? But she started with the drinking again.'

'God! How will you manage?' I ask, meanwhile looking round the desk. A paper weight? Not heavy enough.

'Manage?' laughs Mom. 'Agh, you spend so long training staff, you might as well do it yourself.'

'Mh-hn,' I murmur, searching the desk drawers. Pack of cards. Ciggies. Matches . . . '*Matches*?' I say out loud, ' – no.'

Mom pauses. 'Who is this speaking, please?'

'What? Who d'you think it is?'

'Is that not Herman Katz, the reflexologist?'

'The reflexo – ? It's me, Leon!'

'It's Leon,' I hear her whisper excitedly.

'Who are you talking to?' I ask.

'Miss Shapiro. We've just finished one of our . . . But by God, how extraordinary to hear from you!'

'*Ja*, I'm sorry we haven't been in touch.'

'It's *unreal*! Leon's just been present and then the phone rings. And it's you, Leon.'

'*Ja, Ja*,' I say, opening a cupboard behind the desk. *Nothing* – just files! 'Listen, Mom, d'you remember a trip overseas, in the fifties, on the *Pretoria Castle*?'

'Remember? Man, you're talking about the highspot of my life. First-class saloon accommodation, the games on deck, the dances, the fancy-dress . . . have I ever laughed so much? Little Leon came along.'

'Me, Mom, that was me.'

'Yes. And I'll tell you something else for free – your father and I were never so much in love as on that voyage.'

'*Ja*,' I say, stretching the phone towards a metal trunk (an armoury?) against the wall, '*ja*, he told me.'

'He remembers? Well, well. I'm surprised. Tell him thank you.'

Opening the trunk, I see more papers. This is a police station, for shit's sake! What will they do if they're attacked? 'OK, Mom, listen, when we went on to Istanbul –'

'Istanbul? Did we go to to Istanbul?'

'That was the whole reason for the trip. A brass doodah. In Dad's family. He was telling how, in Istanbul, we went to this jeweller's – except he says there wasn't like . . . much information, or any definite proof. About our past. But there must be, I said to him, there must be! I said, I was sure *you'd* remember more. Hey?'

'Oh *ja* . . . I remember, *ja.*'

'Thank God,' I say, sitting on the floor, the phone cord stretched to its limit. 'Tell me. Tell me everything you remember from that morning.'

'Well, I will. People had warned me about Istanbul. A nice view from the harbour, with the golden domes and what-nots, but a bit smelly in the actual streets, and the people a bit like Arabs. That's not for me, thank you very much, I said, so I stayed by the pool on deck. And – oh, that's right! – little Leon stayed too. Chaim wanted to take him along into town, but I wouldn't allow it. Who wants a child to look upon muck and despair? A child must grow up trusting the world. You'll understand this when, please God, you have children of your own.'

'Oh Mommy,' I whimper. Looking up, I see Gertjie beckoning through the doorway; the cold sunlight round his face, his white, white smile. 'Mommy?' I cry, 'I'm frightened.'

'Don't be,' she says gently, 'there's nothing to frighten us in this life. It's unimportant. It's only a stepping stone – to the higher plateau we shall reach. Matter of fact, I asked Leon to give me a picture of the plateau when he was present today, and you know what it sounded like? It sounded just like the end of that cruise – the one we've been talking about. The docking when we finally reached Cape Town again, reached home – journey's end. Stepping down the gangplank, the ship band playing, the sun shining. The best summer in years. Even with sunglasses you couldn't see straight. We were young, we were prosperous, and the future was gold, man, pure bloody gold! And this is –'

I slam down the phone as Gertjie suddenly puts his head

through the doorway. 'The dust from Pa's *bakkie* is on the horizon. If we want to go, we must go now.'

'Right,' I say, running towards him.

I'm empty-handed.

Oh well. It'll just have to be the old-fashioned way; like in the Bible. With a rock.

TWENTY-FIVE

'D amn dry round here, hey?' I say, as Gertjie drives the Rolls down into Suurvlei.

'Like being born on the moon,' he replies. 'Agh, the veld round here has had a lot of bad, bad over-grazing – from Bantu herds. And then you get erosion eating the land, deeper and deeper, until nobody wants it. So when the boundaries of the Ciskei were being drawn up, the pencil drifted over our way. It was the kiss of death. Suddenly we're a border town. Everybody packs their bags and leaves.'

Our Rolls glides into the main street of Suurvlei.

'So who are these people?' I ask, spotting a few figures in a broken doorway.

'The ones who couldn't afford to leave.'

I put my face closer to the window. The glass is dusty, dreamy. I glimpse more figures in the abandoned homes and shops. A town of tramps! Alert and nervy as veld creatures, they straighten their spines to watch our Rolls pass by.

'What colour are they?' I ask, narrowing my eyes.

'White.'

I chuckle. 'How can you tell?'

'They're white,' he says impatiently, 'poor white,' then hits the accelerator.

'Careful,' I laugh, as the car takes a deep breath and lifts off.

He grins. 'No, no – we must see how well a Rolls can go on these roads.'

On the edge of the town, the tarmac finishes abruptly and gravel takes over – with a new slushing sound, while tiny stones zap the chassis.

Then, as soon as we're out in the veld, Gertjie suddenly brakes. Neither of us are wearing seat belts, and the abrupt, slithering, gritty halt heaves us forward. The dust cloud we'd been trailing engulfs us, and carries on past. 'Not so hot, hey?' laughs Gertjie, 'Rolls-Royce brakes?'

'I guess they're not really designed for –'

'Of course not,' he laughs again, ruffling my hair. 'Sweet brain. It thinks sweet and straight. Where's the toothpaste?'

'The what?'

'Toothpaste,' he says, smile vanishing. 'You said it was in the car. Where?'

'Oh.'

'Oh. Oh. Oh,' he mimics. 'Sweet brain. Sweet and slow.'

As I stare at him, something goes. Snaps, as they say. A thread, the first thread. 'Don't,' I hear myself say, fairly calmly – 'Don't.'

Gertjie hesitates, then cries.

'*Jammer Pa, verskoon tog Pa*. I didn't sleep last night. You don't have to give the toothpaste to me. It's OK. You don't have to.'

'But of course I'll give you the . . . what's the big deal with this toothpaste anyway?' I reach behind to the bar, pull out his toilet bag, and produce the tube of Colgate, family-sized.

He wipes his nose on his hand. His voice is small, cautious, eager to please. 'You swear you don't know?' He watches me shake my head, then smiles, undoes the toothpaste cap and squeezes. Nothing comes out. He shakes the tube, bangs it lightly on the dashboard, then harder. He stops himself – 'No, mustn't, hey?'

'What?'

'Hurt him.'

I frown. He leans across and kisses my hair, then climbs out of the car. I follow. It's a bright day, cool when the air's still, an icy edge when it shifts. Gertjie opens the boot. Inside there's a super deluxe tool kit, immaculately kept by Zakes.

Gertjie selects a small pair of pliers. 'Perfect.'

'Perfect,' I echo quietly, my eye on the range of big spanners, and the hefty jack.

Gertjie uses the pliers to nip into the Colgate tube. Plasticky white paste starts to spring from the openings, flopping over his fingers and falling in thick soft drops, turning dull as they hit the veld, like candlewax or cum. Now Gertjie places the Colgate tube on the car bonnet and carefully opens it out, as if dissecting a small white bird, easing the sides away, wary of being too rough with the innards.

A fat McDonald's straw is embedded in the paste. Gertjie uses his hanky to clean it. It's plugged at either end with bluetac.

'What can we put him on?' he wonders aloud, sticking his head into the car.

Now! Just with a fist – my good hand – on his spine! He'd jerk up. His head would hit the door frame. He'd be dazed. People say the rest is messier than you see in the flicks, but at least it'd be guided by this music, this heroic music I keep hearing. I glance to the boot. How long to run there, grab a spanner and run back?

'Ah – *daar's hy*,' says Gertjie, climbing into the back seat and lowering the bar counter. He wipes it with his hanky, then unplugs one end of the McDonald's straw and pours out a little white heap.

'Who'd've thought, hey?' I say, getting in next to him, 'in the middle of the veld – we'd be visiting the ballet!'

Gertjie laughs and, exaggerating his accent, says, 'Agh, man, we's now much more blerrie fokken cultured than what yous think.' He grins at me, waiting for a pat, a stroke, a tickle round the ear.

I give a little smile.

(My guts are doing back-flips and my sphincter's blowing bubbles.)

'You never guessed?' he asks.

'Never did.'

'What did you think my note meant? "A balm for you to sniff in Africa – for the cosy sick old lady."'

'We thought you meant your scent. Your smell.'

'Oh my smell...' He grips my head and pulls it towards his chest, unzipping his anorak.

'Careful,' I squeal. 'My face!'

Ja, sies tog,' he whispers, tenderly placing my head inside his anorak. A wonderful space; dark and warm, daddy and mommy, sweat and nipples. I touch one with my tongue, and stay there, just breathing for a sec, just breathing.

'First things first,' he says, lifting out my purring face. 'Got any credit cards on you?'

'Huhn?'

'Hey, *wag 'n bietjie,*' he says, finding an ID card in one of his pockets. It's sealed in a rectangle of hard plastic. He uses the edge to chop the gritty heap. I listen to the fast, impatient tapping, my eyes fixed on the ID photo – him in uniform.

'Lieutenant,' I say. 'Is that high up?'

'So-so.'

'For your age.'

'Suppose so.'

'How come the brave comrades were fooled?'

'How d'you mean?'

'In London. Angela's pals. They checked you out with Lusaka. Didn't you – ?'

'Oh sure. But they only check out names. Gertjie van der Bijl? OK. Real person. Son of a colleague of mine. A student who got depressed by his father's job, and committed suicide ... or is he still in the nursing home? Can't remember. But no, no, they only check out names, not faces. And even if they did, I'm not known. Not one of the famous ones.'

'So then why change it – your face?' I ask, touching the odd, negroid flatness of his nose; feeling how the broken bone leads your finger to one side.

He laughs, lifting his chin and gently biting my poised finger. 'My nose? That wasn't deliberate.'

He's finished chopping the stuff, and scrapes it into two massive lines.

I look away.

I can see my face in the wing mirror – the first time this

morning. Much worse than I thought. Seeing the blood, the splashes and trails of it . . . or of *him*, as Angela said. The Lipschitz future down the drain. The red-and-black patterns on my face, and the swellings, have created a new expression. A sort'f clown-like terror. But it's not how I feel. Or wasn't – till I saw the ballet tickets.

Gertjie bends forward, and snorts his line through a rolled-up R20 note.

Now! Now's the time to do it! Before anything goes any further. My foot touches a hard object on the floor. The empty brandy bottle from our flight out of Cape Town.

I reach for it.

'*Magtig!*' says Gertjie sitting up abruptly, 'Needed that! Awake all night. I was so on my nerves, man! The medical on Friday. And coming home.' He hands me the rolled-up note.

'Well, well,' I say, twiddling it. 'Glad I didn't know I was carrying ballet tickets through Customs. We had this real gorilla of a guy – '

'Naa, no prob. They're not looking for ballet tickets. And bombs don't fit in toothpaste tubes.'

'Oh really?' I laugh tensely, viewing the big white line before me. 'Anyhow . . . a nice surprise.'

There's no way out. But now, as I lean forward to the line, Gertjie leans back, clamping both hands over his nose, and his eyes close. I blow the line away.

'Oh *lekker*,' I say, going sniff-sniff. 'Thanks.'

'One for the road,' he says, pouring another, bigger heap from the straw.

'My God,' I laugh. 'Straightaway?'

'Loads to get through,' he says, chopping with his ID card, 'we mustn't stay out too long. Pa will want to talk. Hasn't seen me since I went over to London.'

'London,' I sigh. 'Seems a world away. That morning we met. At Air South Africa.'

'*Jsss!* The Airways. Hell no, that was a *kak* idea. My uncle's idea. A change of job – after my bad time here. Did I tell you I had an uncle there by the Airways?'

'Oh – so that was kosher? You were working there for real?'

He looks up, his brow severe. 'Of course.'

257

'Good,' I laugh, 'I'm pleased. I wouldn't want to hear that the Airways was actually, y'know . . . a cover for uh . . .' My laughter's drying as he stares at me. 'Y'know, for your people.'

'Well, it isn't.'

'Good.'

'Not officially.'

'Not – ?'

'Leon, we're at war. *Waar was jy, boetie*? This poor befokked country is . . .' He swings his fist at the landscape – it hits the car window, which shudders. I jump. 'Man, it burns me up,' he says quietly. 'This land is holy, OK? We don't want it changed into a Third World slum, OK? So nobody – *nobody* – gets to make that change, OK?'

'OK,' I mumble, glancing at myself in the wing mirror. Despite the bruises, my face has gone white.

He scratches his scalp. 'Haven't slept, haven't slept . . . you mustn't worry. So – what were we saying? London, the Airways. No, when we met I was just intrigued. Checked you out. Big donations to the ANC in your name, yet . . . how come? You were obviously the type of South African who only opens his newspaper to see what time *Dynasty* is on, so I couldn't work it out. Until I met Angela.'

'Ah.'

'*Ja*. But I wasn't expecting to meet Moses, Johnnie Lunguza, Nat Roshney. Hoo boy, I couldn't believe it! A who's who of the opposition network in London, and I'm suddenly moving round with them. And round their homes, their bookshelves, their filofaxes.'

'Jesus!'

'No, not Him. He's on our side.' Gertjie smiles. 'Anyhow, I must thank you. Because of you, my chances are much better – of being accepted back at work. So, thank you, pa.'

Again I see myself in the wing mirror. 'Fucking hell,' I whisper.

Gertjie shrugs, then takes his new line with stroking snorts, precisely half in each nostril. Now one finger skims over the bar counter, and he rubs the residue into his gums. The weeks with Charlotte have made him a professional. He hands me the rolled-up note.

How do I get out of it again? He's watching me, while he twitches his face with quick, violent sniffs, left to right, exercising each nostril.

'Don't look so worried, pa,' he says. 'You didn't make an arse of yourself in London. You believed me. Easy mistake to make. You believed I couldn't speak the lingo, believed I was a dumb blond hairyback. Easy. A guy can be anyone he wants in a foreign land. People will put you into a box without you even saying "Yes please". This bloke's an Arab – he's going to be rich. This one's British – he's either going to be fancy-fancy or pissing lager in the gutter. And this *ou*'s an Afrikaner – so he's going to be a Bible-punching bigot.'

'But ... he wasn't. In London. He was gentle, confused. He blushed, he cried. He told me –'

'Hey, *sowaar*, that's right! A varsity student! A freedom fighter! OK then – put this guy in a box marked "Born Again Boer".' He points to my line on the counter. 'All yours, and let's roll.'

He leaps out of the back seat, and into the front. I blow away the line, and clamber after him, pausing only to watch, mournfully, as the little white cloud falls into the thick pile carpet.

I hardly manage to get into the passenger seat before we're off, accelerating like crazy. A wild flapping noise, like from a monstrous vulture, comes with us. I glance in the wing mirror. The boot's still open. Now a ferocious riff of clunking metal – the spanners, the jack. We go over a bump in the road, and the massive lime-green boot, caked in dirt, rears to its limit, straining, shuddering; huge jaws kotching everything up. I listen. No more clunking metal.

'OK?' Gertjie asks. His face is open, excited, a kid at the amusement park.

'Sure thing,' I say, clutching the hand grip on my door. I want to press down the doorlock, but wouldn't that be a bit sissy?

'Don't be scared,' he says.

'Where from!' I say, copying his sniffs and gum-licking.

'Nothing to be scared of. We used to do this on weekends off. Just drive out of the city on a Friday night, leave old Joeys behind, and bomb out into the veld. Out, out, out. Sleeping bags, tins of chow, a crate of whisky, our rifles. Whole fleet of *bakkies*.

Paragraph one, rule one: no wives! Girlfriends and *hoere* only! Weekend in the veld, bundu-bashing! Hunting, screwing, *bakkie*-races, getting completely bloody wasted!'

(When he says screwing, does he mean it? Him – who could never get his lust up, not with me nor with La? Maybe he just hugged these girlfriends and whores? Hugged them tight, like there was no one else in the world. While his pals stood round and jeered.)

'So don't be scared,' he says gently, 'I'm used to it. Nothing to prang into, you see. Just bumps.'

We go over one. The car takes off for a sec.

'It's the fokken rodeo show!' he cries.

'Yaaay!' I say, my voice shivering.

'Fokken ride him!'

'Heigh-ho Silver!'

'*Trap hom, looi hom!* Fokken British, hey?'

'Sorry?'

'They think they can make cars. The king, hey? The king of cars.'

'Well, probably not designed for –'

'I love you, Leon, I love you – you're so thick.'

'Don't,' I say, as another thread snaps.

'Of course he's not fokken designed for here,' Gertjie says, ignoring me. 'That's why he fokken lost the fokken Boer War.'

'Rolls-Royce?'

'The king. The British king.'

'I thought they won the Boer W –'

'No, really? But who's got the fokken goldfields, the diamond mines, the loveliest country on earth? Heaven on earth – who owns it, please? Who's got the Cape of Good Hope? Your father's in shipping, ask him, please – civvy shipping, but he'll know. A strategic port? Fok me! We're the crux of the world, look, look, look at the map.'

'Jesus – funny you saying that, 'cause we were down at Cape Point on Saturda –'

'Leon, sh, sh, your brain is sweet but sh, sh.'

'Don't,' I say, louder this time.

'What? Man, I'm saying just look at the map, the world, spread it out. Where does your eye go first, which continent's in the centre? And now where does your eye go, where's the whole shape leading? Down. Down to where all the goodness settles, all the strength, all the richness. The Republic. And whose is it? So tell me again, please – who won the war?'

'Whoever you like,' I mumble, squeezing the door-grip, as he accelerates and the car starts to quake. The boot is bashing up and down: a colossal paddle thwacking the back of the car. Gravel churns round the wheels, shlushing and crackling so noisily we could be driving a bloody Magi-Mix. From underneath, stones are striking with real, ugly, sharp blows; others fly up through the dust-clouds, thrown from the spinning wheels. One boomerangs back and clips the windscreen, leaving a milky bruise.

Gertjie hits the gas again, putting his tongue between his teeth, just the tip showing. If we went over a bump now, he'd bite it off. And then, while he's stupefied with pain, I could do it. What? Dunno. Some fabulous stunt. Twirling in my seat, knees up, kicking him with both feet, wrestling the wheel away, opening his door, kicking him out.

I glance at the speedometer. The needle's at 160K. It moves to 175. If we carry on like this, I won't have to do anything. My dream – a terrible explosion somewhere inside – it's going to happen. But not to me – to the car. Well, both. If it goes, I go with it.

And that, as they say, is the prob.

I reach behind with my good hand and ease the seat belt across my chest, casj as poss.

Without looking, Gertjie smiles and says, 'It'll spoil it. Don't.'

'I wasn't.' I let the belt go – it smacks my shoulder. 'It was just something to play with.'

'Play with me.'

I give a spluttering laugh. 'Can't.' I show him the hand closest to him, the rubber-glove hand.

'*Ag, sies tog, het jy nou seergekry?*'

'Sorry?'

'Let me kiss it better.'

'When we stop.'

'Incorrect. *If* we stop.'

261

'Ah.'

'*Rolls-Royce se gat!*' he cries. We're touching 190. The car's actually travelling better, but there's a new noise – like a giant breath hissing with caution. I lean towards the window. We're skimming across a strange land crust, salty and grey, without vegetation. Even the sky is blank: a perfect blue, but frightening. The speedometer nervously touches 200, shies away, touches it again. Gertjie rocks himself, urging the car faster, licking his gums, one hand on the wheel, the other rubbing round his body. He reaches across and digs in my crotch.

'OK, pa?' he asks.

'OK, boy.'

'*Voet-in-die-hoek?*'

'Translation, please.'

'Flat-out.'

'Uhm?'

'Too late – we're there!'

He brakes. I lunge for the seat belt, but it's hardly necessary. We go into a long, slow-motion skid, hugely graceful, courtesy of Rolls-Royce, and for one incredibly stretched moment, my side lifts off and we're on two wheels. It's suddenly so easy, so high, there's oceans of space, the car is fantastically big and dirty, streaked with fluid greens, whites and browns – I'm riding a whale! Looking down from my floating throne, I can see Gertjie, face bright with excitement, and beyond, in the wondrous clarity of today, an extraordinary, deep black nothingness. What happened to the land? The sickly flat crust has gone; in its place this beautiful, steep, tumbling darkness. Before I can work out where or how, the car rights itself with several vicious, massive thumps, rattling through even my cushions of flab; and now, as we travel to a standstill, upright yet somehow cartwheeling, tyres shredding, posh machinery wailing and shrieking – now there's land again, all around: flat, pale land.

'*So pa,*' says Gertjie, grinning and panting, 'were you expecting that?'

'Nope,' I say, in a tiny voice, 'can't honestly say I was.'

'Go look. I'll make us a line.'

I climb out of the car, and instantly reel back.

We're on the edge of a gully. Quite narrow, no more than thirty feet across. The road has led straight to it and continues on the other side, endlessly, peacefully, as though nothing had happened. Yet here, gashing across it and the land, for miles on either side, is this gully. The ragged walls are strange. Not black, which I thought when I was riding the whale, but greyish orange, like my bruises, or animal hide brushed the wrong way. And they're pitted, these walls, with reaching mouths and nostrils.

'What is this?' I ask, as Gertjie runs over.

'No, but I told you – erosion.'

'This? Never!'

'Miraculous, isn't it? Miraculous ugliness. It's grown even since I was a little *pikkie*. Pa can remember a bridge going across. The old people can remember the road with just a huge dip. Did it crack open one night?, I asked them. Did you wake to hear the earth splitting asunder? No, they said, gradually, softly it opened. Like a cunt, some told me as I grew older.' He laughs. 'Didn't you, my baby?' he asks, sprawling on the ground and slipping his hand over the edge of the gully. 'You opened softly, hey? But so dry. Too dry for Marius. C'mon, babes, *kom nou stukkie*, give us something wetter there.' He looks up at me, and blushes. 'Sorry. I had another quick line in the car. You the hell-in with me?'

'Have as many as you want.'

'No, I mean my driving.'

''S cool. We're still in one piece. But why aren't there signs? Warning the public?'

He laughs – trying not to, forefinger clamped over his lips.

'What gives?' I ask.

'Your words. So sweet. Let's warn the public, let's warn the public.'

'Well, why not?'

'Well, why not?' he mimics. 'Agh, Leon – what public? It's the old road, the dead road. Nobody uses it anymore.'

'But what if . . . ?'

'But what if?' he sings back at me, 'But what if?' Then, seeing my expression, he flinches (as though scared of me – for real), and quickly says, 'I'll go get you a line, hey?'

I watch him run back to the car. Despite his scrum-half's build, it's not a supple run; it's uncoordinated, feet falling anywhere. I close my eyes, and listen. No dry bushes creaking. No insects – it's too cold. There can't even be ghosts in this air. No voyeurs. Nothing. Not even my theme playing.

I listen to his footsteps return, and open my eyes.

He's carrying the gear, looking for somewhere to put it all.

'Perfect,' he says, kneeling at a thin, smooth rock, flat as a plate. There aren't many other rocks about. Nothing big or heavy enough for what I need. The scrappy vegetation looks dead: low spidery grass, greyish-white, fastening to my socks as I walk, pricking through. I kneel by Gertjie. He's busy cleaning the rock, examining the surface minutely, blowing here and there, in every dimple, anywhere the precious powder might lodge. Now he straightens his neck, checking whether the breeze is safe. Satisfied, he sits, unplugs the straw, and sets to work.

'*Ja*, sorry,' he says. 'Driving like that. Stupid, cruel. Making you suffer. Like they used to do when I was a kid. We'd come out here on our bicycles, and dare one another to drive at it full speed. I hated it.'

'Your dad showed me photos of you as a kid.'

'Photos,' he repeats listlessly. 'Beautiful baby, beautiful boy, look how beautiful. Doesn't matter if he doesn't *feel* beautiful. No, no, everybody just keeps staring. Why can't they stop? A friend who was with me in the army, up by the border, he had a leg amputated. He felt the same thing. *Make people stop staring!* But you can't. Pa's camera over the years, cold, black, aiming at me. Bang! That's you finished. Now you're just a lovely memory on a piece of paper. But how can a piece of paper be a memory? It can fool even the person himself. Do I remember that day, or do I remember the photo of that day? But Pa had this terrific *lus* for photos. Ignored my terror. Ignored Mommie's shame – kept taking photos as she got sicker; photos to save for his loneliness afterwards. He ignored everything. A silent man. Did you notice?'

'*Ja.*'

'But we mustn't pick them out, hey?'

'Who?'

'Our folks. Or anybody. We try to do our best.' He touches his forehead, then jerks away. '*O' liewe Here*, it burns me up, I'm on fire!' He snorts his line, hands over the rolled-up note, and lies back, stretching one arm towards the gully a few yards away. 'D'you think my baby's wet yet? Is she?'

'Dunno,' I mumble, quickly blowing my line away.

He suddenly goes very still (*did he see?*), then relaxes again, and asks, 'What were we saying?'

'Photos.'

'No, movies are better. They tells lies openly, so then we can too; we cry, we laugh, it's all play-play. Just the music doing it, hey?'

'Suppose so,' I say, listening to the silence around us.

'Like music in the army or at police college. Fokken *slim* tactic, hey? Everyone loves it – loves marching to it, 'cause it's being played just for you, a thousand guys on the parade ground, but it's being played just for you, inside you, in, in, in your veins. Doesn't fool me. The human voice is what I want inside me. Like that night, hearing him. Didn't need the music beforehand . . .'

He stops. I wait. He waits. Like his father, he's not scared by silence.

I clear my throat. 'Sorry – hearing who?'

He sits up and leans close to me. His eyes are full of red and yellow mess. 'Why are you so together?'

'What?'

'You remember everything we're saying. How so? My brain's in a hell-out hurry, just *sommer* going everywhere.'

'No, mine too,' I splutter. 'I promise. Just –'

'OK, shh, shh. A night. I'm stationed in Pretoria. This is now still army, still citizen force – before police college. Had a pass, Friday night, your Sabbath. Pretoria's a quiet city, dead at night, complete fokken ghost at the weekend. Bunch of us with fok-all to do. He's speaking, so we jawl along to hear him. Ready to scoff, and we do, and there's lots to scoff at – fat bus conductors pretending to be gangsters, guns in their belts, and the corny *sakkie-sakkie* music on the piano accordion. But then he comes in the hall. He's hardly opened his mouth and something goes through me, I dunno, a . . . a spiritual *dinges*, a sexual *dinges*, I dunno. Couldn't recognise the feeling – from my great experience

265

of the world, all seventeen years of it.' He drops his head, smiling bashfully, and suddenly here's Gertjie again, the one I knew in London.

'A man on a platform speaking. A voice coming into my veins. But not just from the man. From the centre of the earth. *Yirra*, till then I wasn't even aware what piece of the earth I came from. I came from home, Suurvlei, ordinary, everyday. But no, this voice told me that I came from a special piece of the earth, God's piece. And I could believe it. They seemed like one and the same – God, the earth, and this man. Within an hour, we became his, his people, closer than blood family. Within an hour! O K – now what else was possible?'

Gertjie studies my face. I've gone still. I quickly remember to sniff, lick my gums, fidget.

'*Ja.*' He smiles, and tips another portion out of the McDonald's straw. 'This stuff – or booze, sport, combat, patriotism – the times when a person can feel beauty *inside* himself. You understand, hey?'

'Some of that, *ja.*'

'*Ja*. It's what drew us together.'

We gaze at one another, both frowning slightly.

'Trouble is,' continues Gertjie, chopping on the stone, 'even as you're buzzing, hurtling, faster and faster, it's ending. But agh, if a person starts to think about it, he just wants to give up, isn't it so?'

He scrapes the stuff into two huge lines, the length of the stone, and offers me the rolled-up note, saying, 'You go first.' I hesitate. Maybe I should just refuse outright? I need to provoke him: I need to provoke *myself*; I need to get some more threads snapping. I stare at him, bringing my hands together nervously, again and again, the fingertips meeting with a bony click. (It's my skeleton – I can hear my skeleton!) Gertjie offers me the note again. I shake my head. He smiles oddly, then lifts the stone itself and passes it over to me. Oh shit, the stuff looks so tempting, so white, the chopped crystals sparkling in the sunlight. (Maybe this job would be easier with just *one* line in me?)

Suddenly Gertjie puts the stone aside and peers into the hollow where it was resting. There's a nest of insects, veld worms or grubs, many-legged, pink, dozily squirming, amazed to suddenly find themselves in the bright, cold winter air.

'Look,' he whispers. 'Levi's men.'

'What? Who?'

'Huh? No, we had this one tutor on the training course. This is when I was at police college – Special Section. A hand-picked few of us, but all shit-scared of this one tutor. Not scared of the sergeants and them-all – fok it, man, we've been on the border, we chant the army motto "I feel nothing"; we can handle it when the beasts are let out. But this bloke isn't a beast, he's a scientist. A psychiatrist. There to observe us – just observe, like a camera, waiting for you to show yourself, signs of weakness, signs of sentimentality.' Gertjie covers his face. 'Oh hell, *pa*, I wouldn't get past him now! He wasn't at my medical on Friday . . .' Gertjie stops, puffing deeply, privately, angry with himself. He takes his time, then asks, 'What was I saying?'

(Is this a trap? Should I pretend not to know? I can't think fast enough.)

'Levi . . . ?' I mutter. 'Levi's men?'

'*Ja*, this tutor, this psychiatrist, he gave us lectures, made us study the victim, read stuff like Primo Levi. His experiences in Auschwitz, the detail of humiliaton – Levi describes it so damned beautifully! Like you're dying of thirst, and there's a tap, but a sign says *This Water Is Poisonous*. What do you do? Or when he's first arrested, and it's done roughly – it gives him a helluva shock. How can a man hit another man, he asks, except in anger? And hair . . .' Gertjie points to the insects in the hollow. 'Strip a man not only of clothes, but hair, all hair, and you strip his identity. It's why all black people look the same to us. Their hair's too short. Cut a man's hair off, says Levi, and – *ga!* – the man changes to a worm. Naked, slow, ignoble, on the floor. Isn't that beautiful?'

'Beautiful?'

'Beautiful words. We are beautiful, miraculous creatures.' Gertjie puts the rolled-up note to his lips and blows softly on the insects. They shift in confusion. 'Here,' he says, handing me the note. I blow on the insects. 'No, no,' he laughs, and replaces the stone, lowering it exactly into place, careful not to crush

267

anything underneath. Now the rolled-up note in my hand is pointing at the lines of white powder.

Gertjie's watching me – waiting.

'Angela's disgusted with you,' I say. His brow thickens. 'Oh sure,' I add, 'she was disgusted that you'd been using this Levi man for your –'

'*Ja*, she's a good wife,' says Gertjie. 'She's disgusted on your behalf. *Ja*, the woman's a Christian Jew, *né?*, like she's a white kaffir.'

'Don't,' I shout. 'She loved you.'

Gertjie goes very still – for a long time. Then he touches his face, and in a hushed voice, says, 'Tell her I'm on fire. Tell her I'm sorry – *jammer engeltjie 'sblief*. Tell her I loved her too.'

I blink, fazed by his retreat.

'Tell her not to worry – on your behalf. It's OK, it's OK. *Of course* we'll get rid of the swastika, *of course* we need the Jews. If only I could get well again, *pa*, if only I could come completely right again, the way ahead is so clear. We must combine our might and our resolve with words that can match them, words that will stand up, words that people won't laugh at, beautiful words. And then, by Christ, we could really put the Party on the map! Or form a new one. So you must tell Angela not to worry on your behalf. We'd be fools to drive you away.' He smiles gently. 'It's your turn.'

'Huhn?'

He nods to the line on the stone. 'Your turn. To go first.'

Whimpering inside, I bow over the stone. The first blast cuts into my bruised nostrils. I back away, stifling my squeal, trying to staunch my streaming eyes. I steady myself and laugh. 'Went down the wrong way.'

'Try the other side,' he says, studying me attentively.

The other nostril, thank God, is less bruised, and takes the powder no prob at all, almost eagerly.

'It may be broken,' he says, stroking my nose. 'Doesn't always show at first, through the bruising. Mine didn't.'

'Ah-huhn?' I say, feeling the first gorgeous glob slipping down my throat. I swallow quickly, dismissing it. 'So . . . how did you break yours?'

He snorts his line and tosses his head back.

'Last year. We had this detainee in. Special detainee. Well, special for us. By where I work we don't get the famous ones, but this one, a black woman, she was quite famous, yet she'd come our way.' He pauses, and smiles at me. 'I shouldn't be telling you this. One is sworn to secrecy. Perhaps that's the trouble, hey? Whenever anyone tells you *Don't*, you want to. Isn't it so?' He twitches his face from side to side, sniffing hard, hastening the buzz. 'She was strictly out of bounds, this woman, strictly "red area", and I wasn't on the working party, but I had this, like ... sense of her, down there. Almost like when you fancy someone, and you know the person's in the building; can't think of anything else. Y'know?'

'Mm-hh,' I answer, feeling another gorgeous glob slipping into my throat.

'And it wasn't just me. We were all feeling it. At lunchtime, in the bar, everybody asking, How's it going? And they'd shake their heads, the ones busy with her, and say "*Nee jong, sy's so hard soos klip!*" You know what this means?'

'Hmn?'

'Like stone. And we're all thinking, No, no, it's not her, she's not the problem. You are. If *I* was down there, *I* could soften her – your stone.'

Gertjie starts scratching his hair, busily, harder and harder, until he must be grazing the scalp. 'Saturday afternoon. A group of us had been boozing all day in the station. I couldn't walk by 1600 hours. But into the shower and on, on, jawl on, a nice *kiff* evening ahead. This joint downtown where we go, swimming pool, saunas, rooms. Paragraph one, rule one – no wives! Girlfriends and *hoere* only! Except my dollie was in the middle of her blood-time. So I just stayed by the bar, through the night, boozing on, right through. Normally life runs smoothly, like film, sometimes like fast film, like now, Charlie Chaplin film, *gi-gi-gam-ti-ti-ta*! But by that fokken Sunday sunrise, life was dealing me cards, these fokken sharp-edged cards, so that even if you blink, your lids are full of crust, and you're stuck with sharp edges, life on paper, Pa's photos. No prob. I could walk, I could drive – along sharp edges – back to our station, down the stairs, down to this woman. "Red area", did I tell you th – ?'

'*Ja.*'

'*Ja*, you're so clear. She wasn't. She let me lead her to the room. We called it *Die Sentrale*, The Exchange, as in telephones, because of all the electri – agh, you have to make jokes, or you go mad, ask any doctor or undertaker. Human nature. But even so, none of us liked going into The Exchange. Even after the cleaners had been through, there was still something in the walls, in the corners, like, I dunno, a Third World slum, and no natural light, no natural air, so far indoors, so far underground . . .'

'Like babies,' I say, suddenly leaning forward, and meeting his messy, yellowy gaze.

'Huh?'

'Babies. So far underground.'

Gertjie looks at me, then laughs. 'You're firing up, man, you're going, going! *Ja*, so, anyhow, she was on the bed –'

'A bed?'

'Wire bed. No mattress.'

'Hey! I had a dream this morning –'

'No, shh, shh, not a dream. She was there. A schoolteacher, mid-thirties. Like my mother, or your wife. A schoolteacher – black – but even so, why didn't she just reprimand me? Or call in someone to stop me? She could, I kept thinking, yet somehow she can't. Incredible. They said she was like stone. No, no – skin. Easy to break. Like rules. Paragraph one, rule one: you can waste electricity and water, you can waste muscle and bone – but don't waste blood. Waste blood and you waste the person. They'll endure a hang of a lot as long as it's invisible. They'll keep thinking they're going to pull through. But when they see their blood running out, then they see their spirit running also. And then they lose hope. And then you might lose them.' Gertjie stops, jerking his head as though struck, then says, 'I shouldn't be telling you this.'

'Then don't.'

He laughs. 'Oh *ja*? *Jou fokken liegbek*, you're dying to know. Everybody always is. What's it like, what's it like? – people want to know – what is something else like?' He touches his forehead.

270

'Is the weather hot, we ask, or have I got a temperature? Is it me, or is it the world? So all right, what's it like in the police force? To be the law of the land? Laws turned into people, paper into people, the police force, the –'

'May the Force be with you!' I cry, feeling the line pulsing in my veins, my lines. 'Yaaaay!'

He laughs. 'You're going, you're going, up, up, up!'

'Up, up and away!'

'*Ja*. People do when we tell our secrets. You shouldn't. We only tell when we're safe. And we're always safe. You should warn the public, Leon.' He grins and mimics my voice, 'Warn the public, warn the public.'

'Don't,' I say.

'Leon, shh, shh, and just –'

'Don't keep telling me to shush!'

'Why not?' he replies instantly. 'You've got fok-all to say, all your life, fok-all to say. So that's OK, that's cool – so long as you shush, so long as you don't waste oxygen, *boetie*.'

(Threads are suddenly snapping again, everywhere. My brain feels like a chunk of earth, spilling out roots and dust.)

'But . . .' I splutter, 'I have got something to say.'

Gertjie smiles.

'Maybe, OK, fair enough, not before. But I do – now. Thanks to you. You've given me things to say. I can run through the streets saying them. Warning the public. About you.'

He smiles again.

'How d'you know I won't?' I ask. (I'm not fooled by his smiles – he's going to blow, any sec, if I just keep pushing.) 'Hey? How d'you know I won't?'

'I don't,' he replies calmly.

'So what're you going to do about it?'

'Whatever you want me to do. I'll be whatever you want. Whatever anybody wants. Lover, son, dumb blond hairy-back, freedom-fighting student. You name it, I'll do it. So long as the other person keeps doing the *wanting*. Me – I feel nothing.'

I stare at him, suddenly ashamed – an odd, terrible shame.

He gazes back sympathetically – I suppose I'm blushing – then says, 'I'm sorry. I just haven't slept. Make us another line, hey? Please.'

Unbelievably, I obey him. Unbelievably, I pick up his ID card and start chopping another two lines.

(Can't help it. Such a teasing taste. Just one more and that's it. *Then* I'll do it.)

He watches me work, for about fifteen seconds, then says, ''s OK!', nudges me aside, and without splitting the stuff into lines, snorts some, the rolled-up note darting around like the snout of an ant-eater.

Without hesitation, I follow. *Oogh! oogh!* – I hear as it shoots up into my head, and then a silence, a numbness, as it settles, settles into the membranes – soothing at first, before it starts to excite and spread its mischief, and this weird new feeling: half-shame, half-excitement.

He sits back, forward, back again. 'I was telling you something. What was it?'

'A Sunday morning. A black woman on a bed –'

'No, no, I was telling you how I broke my nose, how . . . What did you say? The woman? Huh-uhn, there's nothing more to tell about her. I failed. She *was* a rock. Not her body, no, no, but something in her was. I had tried everything, way beyond the rule books, those dead, dead books, so I gave in and helped her up from the bed –'

'I remember this! When I woke this morning –'

'No, no, last year. A woman. I helped her up. You'd be amazed how miraculous we are. How someone can climb to their feet, watch some of themselves fall to the floor, climb over it and keep on walking. So bright, so alive, the colours inside us. The colour of fat – it's so yellow, glowing with the miracle of light, of life, of being. Of strength! No, she won my admiration, that woman, no, no, she definitely won that round.'

'And you?'

'Monday morning troubles! The excesses of the weekend. They often have to pull us up on a Monday morning and show us the rule book. But this was more serious. The woman was a write-off, which I hadn't intended, but they wouldn't listen, would-not-listen! I was suspended from duty – indefinitely. They threw the book at me, the whole, dead book. And so . . . my nose broke.'

'They broke your nose with a book?'

'No, no. Alone. In the shower later, back at home. I was feeling too depressed. Time had slowed down, down to a standstill. Nothing happening in your veins, everything such an effort – to get undressed, to get into the shower. It's depressing . . . undressing. Undress, dress, press, dess, pess, ess, sssss . . .'

Gertjie has unzipped his anorak, and now starts unbuttoning his shirt. I gaze at the hard, tanned skin of his chest coming into view – tanned by that long-ago London summer. We watch one another, both going sniff-sniff.

'Good stuff, hey?' Gertjie says, undoing another button, 'Charlotte's finest, pure, the stuff her customers never even see.'

'Ah-huhn? How is Charlotte, by the way?'

'No, fine, the usual, y'know, busy killing herself.' He undoes another button.

'Ah-huhn. You must give her my best.'

'Can't. We're bad friends, had a fight – I harmed her.' Another button. 'She'd probably forgive me if I say sorry. People do – even when I've harmed them. If I whisper I'm sorry, they believe me, they trust me again.'

'I won't,' I say.

'No, no. You will.' Another button. 'People do. Even detainees. They're looking at a boy, not one of the thugs, but a boy, a schoolteacher's son, well-spoken, well-read, a beautiful smile, tears flowing – if that's what they need to see. No, no, I'm good at my job, my duty – so how could anyone suspend me from it? Indefinitely.'

He's unbuttoned to his navel. He knows how I love the next bit; each cross-stitch of dark hair. He undoes another button slowly, one finger touching the hair, tracing it downwards.

'Don't,' I say quietly.

'Why not?'

'It's cold.' I swallow. Another gorgeous glob slips down. 'You'll catch cold.'

He stops unbuttoning. 'Whatever you want, *pa*, this boy will do.' He sighs. 'So anyhow, then I got into the shower, that Monday morning. Suspended from duty, so I showered instead. And showered. And I then I realised I couldn't get out of the shower. Smells had never bothered me before. Smell my cuff, we'd say in the bar, *sê vir my soos wat ruik dit*? Laughing. You have to. But suddenly I couldn't get out of the shower. Just because of the smell, a bright yellow smell – the woman's fat – on my fingers. More and more water, and tears, real tears . . . No! sentimental tears – because, me, I feel nothing. So I hit myself. Very hard. *Slaat hom*! – I could hear, like someone else was speaking – *slaat hom*! I didn't know you could hit yourself so hard.'

Despite the chill, he's pouring with sweat. He collects some, stroking his neck. 'Some people think I look more beautiful now,' he says, fingers moving up to his nose. 'Do you? From seeing my Pa's photos?'

'Yes,' I say, without lying.

He suddenly bashes his face. Full force. I gasp and blink. He takes his fist away. The imprint of his knuckles is left, like the marks on dice. 'And now?' he asks in a dull voice. 'Even more beautiful?'

'Gertjie . . .'

'And – !' He does it again. 'And now?'

'Gertjie!'

'No, no, it's OK, it's OK, I feel nothing – it's OK, *boetie*, you like it in the movies, don't you? Cops, cowboys, *skop, skiet en donder*, Dracula, exorcism. Everybody likes it in the movies. And in some of the UK newspapers. Man, I was damned shocked when I was there. Every morning – people pinned out on the kitchen table. And Alphons saying, "Ho, ho, bit of a laugh." Remember Alphons? She was black. With the right to vote. Hey, *wag 'n bietjie*, remember that the blacks are good! All of them. Shame, hey, how they've suffered! Like the Jews. They've suffered, so they're all good – except for the Israelis. They're bad. Like the Afrikaners. They're bad – except for the ones who betray their own people: they're good. Good traitors – like good bombs and good violence – good, decent, bloody violence that'll make the world a better place!'

He stops, and leans on all fours, panting. Then without warning, he lunges. (The bastard – he got in first.) I fight like anything, screaming and thrashing. He keeps attacking with his face, his mouth – to bite? to suck blood? – and it takes several more of these mad seconds before I realise he's trying to *kiss* me. Amazed, I settle, wait till he does too, and then I draw back, muttering, 'My bruises. You're hurting my –'

'Sorry,' he says, rising abruptly, unbuttoning the rest of his shirt, and then his flies. Jeans and undies come off in one, down to his boots, where they lodge. He turns and waddles to the edge of the gully, and stands there, his back to me.

This is it.

I spring to my feet and charge at him, picking up speed, sharp grass piercing my socks.

He half-turns.

'Uh . . . !' I say, coming to a stumbling stop. He looks at me, eyebrows raised. 'Uh . . .' I say again, 'Uh . . . how deep is it?' I gesture to the gully. The opposite wall, greyish orange when we arrived, has fallen into shadow – the winter sunlight is moving fast, weirdly fast. 'Hey?' I ask again, 'how deep d'you think?'

'Dunno,' he says, rubbing himself. 'I remember a goat fell in once. We brought it here on our bikes. We could hear it down there, quite far down, but clearly, a kind of echo, terrible noises – I think there are sharp rocks along the way. Hell, I *smaak* this. Being naked out here. *Kaalgat*! And talking about other things while I'm *kaalgat*, pulling my wire. What do the Coloureds say? *Skommel*, hey? Shake that milk, till you make that milkshake! Keep talking, keep talking. Ask me about the goat.'

'The goat?' My heart's up to such speed now, it's churning, missing beats, back-tracking, whirling round this strange fear, strangely nice. 'What goat?'

'Terrible noises, like a cat; like when they're on heat, *verskriklik jags*! Weird things, hey, cats – cat's eyes, hey?'

'Like baby's eyes – before they're born!'

'Huh? Eyes. Mine are closed. I'm going to wait a bit and then look. Are you naked yet?'

'Not y –'

'No? Good, save it, make it last. My *piel* isn't stiff yet. Are you looking?'

'Yes.'

'At my face or at my *piel*?'

'Your face.'

'What do you see?'

'Beauty. Eyes closed. Sunlight.'

'D'you want to look at my *piel* now? If you looked now – don't! – you'd see it still isn't stiff. But *I* am, the rest of me, inside. OK – and – let's look!'

With a long, calm, half-pitched moan, he opens his eyes and looks down – at his hand working his dick, his goosepimpled legs, his jeans round his boots, and the black, steep shadow of the gully. '*O' Jissus man,*' he whispers, jigging on the spot.

Some dust and a single pebble falls.

'Gertjie!' I say.

'Marius. You try!' He demonstrates with a little jump. Now a small piece of the gully edge breaks off, with a sort'f flop, a dry *WHUSH*, and a reddish cloud.

I leap back. 'Marius!'

'Try. For me. Try it. Don't worry, nothing can happen. It takes years for her to open wider. She's a slow sick dry cunt who's just going to have to get used to what Marius is now.' He jumps again, harder each time. 'Try it. Don't just read about it in your kitchen. Try it. Don't just watch it in the dark. Try it.'

I back off from the gully, well back.

'OK,' Gertjie says, abruptly turning, and waddling back to our stone, 'must trek homewards.' He tips out the last of the powder, snorts it direct, nose to stone, then sits back, with a kind of relief, sighing, sucking the residue off his finger, grinning at me. A kid at the end of a long, good game, with sherbet on the end of his finger. Despite his nakedness, the grown-up hair on his body; despite the coke pulsing through his face – yellow eyes, streaming nose – and despite his stories, all of them – the different Gertjies I've known; despite these things, he still looks so bloody innocent, so bloody beautiful.

'No,' I cry, stamping on the veld. 'No!'

'It's OK,' he says, rising and pulling up his jeans, 'we'll go home now.'

'No!'

'Yes, they'll be waiting on us.'

'No!'

276

'Your dad, my dad, and Angela.'

'No...!'

What was that thump? My hand goes to my chest. Is the terrible thing happening at last – the explosion or puncture? I pat myself all over. Nothing hurts. Then I notice that Gertjie is also poised, as though he felt it as well.

How dare he look so frightened!

I stamp again.

Something shifting. A soundless crack.

Puzzled, I turn to face the gully. The fast-moving winter sunlight has shifted the shadow again, showing that an entire piece is missing under the opposite bank. It must've dried and fallen away, leaving just a thin surface above. If that's what it's like over there, what about where we're standing? Next to the car; the big heavy car which Gertjie stopped here like he was ramming home a missile.

A low noise now; angry, but drowsy. A growl – or drums? My music!

'*Kom*,' says Gertjie, '*kom, hardloop – hardloop.*'

I smile. He's suggesting I run. 'Sorry,' I reply, 'don't speak the lingo.'

He reaches for me.

'Thank you,' I say, taking his hand.

Now our piece of the veld breaks – but doesn't fall – not yet. An outline just suddenly shows, clearly, all the way round, as though God marks the section that's going, and then pauses – giving us one last chance to reach safety.

Gertjie tries to pull away, but my grip is tight. And here we are again. *Yaaay!* The Tom and Jerry cartoon is over, and now it's the adventure serial. Two blokes struggling on a clifftop, with no way out for either of them, the goodie or the baddie – serious peril! – and the music swells, taking you to the edge of your seat, and your newly swapped comics fall from your lap, and – *ai!* – you fear it'll suddenly end, like it has before, making you wait another whole week to find out what happens next. And sure enough, hell's bells, thrills and sadness, any sec now. Any sec.

acknowledgements

When I wrote my first book, I remember being surprised that my editor didn't get a printed credit in the finished work. This omission, although customary in book-publishing, struck me as odd – rather like opening a theatre programme to find no mention of the director. For me, a good editor is similar to a good director: overseeing the whole creative process, guiding the tempo of the storytelling and the definition of the characters, suggesting changes, cuts, improvements. In the case of *The Indoor Boy*, Jonathan Burnham has done all of these things, and I'm immensely grateful to him. I'm also indebted to Mic Cheetham, my literary agent, whose encouragement has been inspiring. And special thanks to Susan Powell, who has been the most excellent research assistant.

In addition, my thanks to: Alfred Bradley, Riccardo Branca, Maretha Butler, Leon Coetzee, Greg Doran, 'Bokkie' Duvenhage, Jim Hooper, Norman Isaacson, Fritz Joubert, Hüseyin Karagöz, Kenneth Lester, Tom P., Rafael Scarf, Alan Slater, Chaim Tannenbaum, Yesim Turan; also the Kaplan Centre at the University of Cape Town, the Safmarine Corporation, and my family in South Africa.